THE NAYA'S CROSSING

The Naya's Crossing

PRERNA ASHOK

For those who walk their own path.

CONTENT WARNING

This story explores life and love as well as loss and grief. There are discussions of death in different forms. This book contains potentially triggering subject matter, including past trauma, death of a parent, mental health issues, and exploration of fertility issues and reflections on this subject. It also contains explicit sexual content and depictions of violence.
Please read with care.

LENEIRA

Gothborg
Portal
SKANDOR
Bluestone
Quarry
Portal
Portal
SAILON
LaHong
TERRALEA
Erindell
Delphos
ISLES OF
MINOS

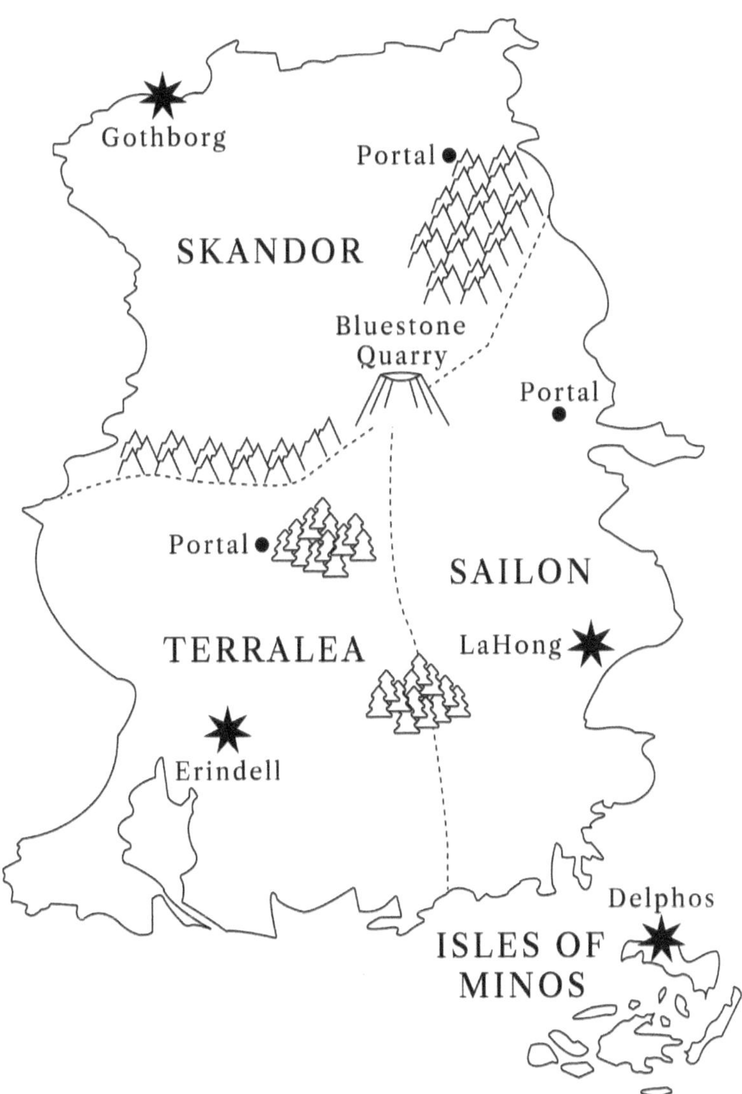

PROLOGUE

After a hundred years of living life in the shadows, it was time for Henry Graham to leave everything he had ever known behind. It was the end of September. Soon, England would go back to being rainy and perpetually covered in a thick gray blanket of clouds while the sun set in the middle of the afternoon. He thought he might as well move to sunnier climes and clement weather—Antigua, perhaps? Or Fiji?

It was well past the hour the inhabitants of the village went to bed when Henry stumbled through the doors of his countryside manor. He raked his hands through thick dark hair that was damp with rain and sweat as he walked down the hall to the living room. After switching on a light that bathed the opulent room in a soft, warm glow, he made his way to the bar cart by the fire, poured himself a healthy dose of whiskey, and took a large gulp.

Henry paced in front of the fireplace, rubbing his face for the umpteenth time. It wasn't how he wanted to leave, but his latest job had been a shambles. He had discovered, too late, that his grifting partner turned out to be an undercover police officer. It was only a matter of hours before the police would be knocking on Henry's door with a long list of charges.

Henry cursed himself for being so careless, for trusting another person in such a high-stakes job. His greed and pride had been his downfall. It wasn't just that his reputation had been shattered; the consequences of the authorities investigating his past could have resulted in him being incarcerated in a medical testing lab. Deep down, Henry knew that the smallest DNA sample he provided would cause alarm and curiosity.

His distinctive, gold-flecked blue eyes swept around the manor that had been his home for the past seventy years. The sleepy village of Sway in Hampshire was perfect for the life of a ghost. Henry had been forced to go to great lengths to navigate a world where there was no explanation for the fact that he had stopped aging in his thirties while friends and acquaintances grew old and ultimately found eternal peace. Records of his existence and evidence of his crimes were destroyed in mysterious fires or misplaced in paperwork.

Henry gazed at the Rembrandt painting hanging above the carved marble fireplace. It had been stolen from a Boston gallery thirty years earlier and was his most thrilling heist. While the Gardner Museum Theft had made headlines around the world, word of the missing Rembrandt being stolen yet again from the original thief was making the rounds in grifting circles. Never had a thief stolen from another in such a manner. Henry rubbed his chin, ruefully thinking about how he wouldn't be able to enjoy the spoils of the last successful heist.

"It would seem we're both wanted men," a voice rasped from the shadows, making Henry jump.

Without hesitating, he grabbed a wrought iron poker from the fireplace and whirled around, searching for the source.

A vaguely familiar man in a ragged black cloak lounged in the wingback Chesterfield chair tucked away in a dark corner.

Henry inched closer to the man who hadn't reacted to being threatened with the poker. His oily black hair slicked back from a pale, long face. Heavy, dark brows sat low over pale gray eyes, and his hooked nose jutted out prominently.

"Who are you? How did you get in here?" Henry asked roughly, clenching his fist around the handle.

"It's only been six months since my visit, Henry," the man drawled. "Am I that forgettable?"

The memory of a man delivering a letter and package in the spring flashed through Henry's mind.

"Who are you?" he repeated with slight trepidation.

"My name is Raz." The man stood up and strolled around the room. He examined the valuable pieces and artifacts in the room. Each had its own nefarious story of how it came to be in Henry's possession. Raz's gaze shifted to a black-and-white photograph in a silver frame on the mantelpiece. It was a portrait of a woman with a heart-shaped face, doll-like eyes framed by long, spidery lashes, bow-shaped lips, and dark hair styled into finger waves.

"Who sent you? Are you with the police?"

Raz chuckled darkly.

"I don't have time for this," Henry said when he offered no response. "Either explain yourself or leave."

"Do you still have the package I delivered?" Raz asked, stepping away from the fireplace and eyeing him critically.

Henry bit his lip, wondering if he could trust the man.

"You don't have much time," Raz reminded him. "And neither do I."

Henry lowered the poker and crossed the room to an elegantly carved antique wooden writing table. Glancing furtively over his shoulder, he slid his hand under the desk and pressed a hidden button. A small compartment popped out from the wooden panel. Reaching in, he pulled out an envelope made of thick parchment. It had been torn at the top, leaving the red wax seal intact. A piece of folded parchment poked out from the ripped edge. He also pulled out a dark velvet box and walked back to where Raz stood. Without taking his eyes off the man, Henry placed both items on the table.

Raz swooped down on the letter, reading it with a furrowed brow.

"Well?" Henry asked impatiently.

"They'll recognize Lord Zanthus's handwriting," Raz muttered to himself. His pale eyes scanned the letter closely, inspecting the lines between the ink. He held the parchment up to the light, illuminating the letter further. Raz squinted and appeared to be satisfied when he brought the piece of paper down.

"You know Zanthus?" Henry asked, taken aback by the use of the title.

Raz gave him a brief nod.

"Why isn't he here?" Henry asked impatiently. "I was waiting for him to explain."

"You'd be waiting a long time," Raz said ominously. "Lord Zanthus is dead."

Henry paused, taken aback. Another memory hit him like a thunderbolt, as vivid as the day before and not some ninety years prior.

The gloomy, rainy morning in October was a fitting backdrop for Rose Graham's funeral. Only the priest, a ten-year-old Henry in an ill-fitting secondhand suit, and a strange man were present to say a final farewell to her.

"You can call me Uncle Zanthus," the man said, placing a large hand on Henry's bony shoulder and squeezing it reassuringly.

Henry recalled the tall, imposing man with the same blue-gold eyes as his own. He also had the same emblem inked into his left wrist that Henry had apparently been born with, according to Rose. It was a curious symbol depicting a circle divided into quadrants, a different element in each. It was all the proof the naive boy needed to feel a kinship with the man.

"Tell me about yourself, Henry," Zanthus requested. They sat on a bench in a nearby park. Zanthus had bought them both ham and cheese sandwiches, chocolate bars, and bottles of lemonade, all of which Henry ate and drank greedily. The orphanage he had been placed in following Rose's death served the children meager portions of bland oatmeal and dry bread.

Henry merely shrugged and turned away.

Zanthus slipped a gold ring off his index finger and held it out with a thoughtful expression.

"Keep this with you at all times, my boy," he told Henry, who examined the ring curiously. "It's a family heirloom."

Henry twirled the ring around his own index finger—the only tell that gave away his nerves—as he remembered his first encounter with the man who had been the closest thing to family for almost a century.

The ring had a strange emblem engraved into it. Zanthus's only instruction was for Henry to keep it on his person at all times. He did not provide any explanation about the eye chiseled into the gold face. Henry's sporadic research about the symbol inevitably led to religious texts that referenced the Eye of Providence, the Evil Eye or the Divine Eye in various forms.

From that day, Zanthus checked in on Henry every year, always knowing where to find him. They would spend a few hours together as Zanthus regaled a young Henry with fairy tales of people who could command the elements; stories of kings, queens, wars; a land imbued with magic and watched over by Divine entities with powers great and terrible. Henry waited eagerly for Zanthus's annual visits. Those hours where he could escape his grim existence were bliss. The stories fueled his imagination, and Henry dreamed of flying horses and living in a palace where every wish was fulfilled.

As Henry grew older, the stories were replaced with strategies for his next confidence job. Times were still tough after two world wars, and Henry had resorted to pickpocketing and petty crime to survive. Under Zanthus's guidance, he learned the art of the long con, adopting different personas, and using his good looks and charm to coax even the stingiest of marks out of bigger sums of money than he had ever dreamed possible.

Raz made an impatient noise, dragging Henry back to the present.

"Go pack," he ordered. "You'll need clothes that a gentleman would wear."

Henry stared in disbelief.

"Didn't Lord Zanthus tell you about Leneira?" Raz asked. "Terralea? Erindell? Elementals, Empaths, Shifters ..."

As Raz listed off the words that had enraptured Henry as a young boy, his anger grew. How dare that man toy with him and entertain the idea that Henry still believed those fairy tales.

"Get out!" he hissed.

Raz stopped.

"You have trespassed long enough, and I have to leave now."

"You and I both need to leave," Raz said calmly. "I'm offering you a way out."

"You're mad." Henry stared. "How the hell do you plan on going to this ... fairy-tale land?"

"It's not a fairy tale, it's real." Raz snorted. "Didn't you read the letter I gave you? It explains everything."

The antique grandfather clock chimed in the corner, signaling the late hour. The rain continued to pour outside as Henry contemplated his options.

"So I'm really the heir to the throne?" he asked slowly, uncertainly. The thoughts and doubts swirled through his mind. *Is this my way out of a wretched, lonely, unending life? Or am I being conned and will find myself cheated out of house and money?* The possibility that Henry could ever rule a fantasy realm was too far-fetched, even after the things he had witnessed over the past century.

Raz's thin lips twisted. "It's not that straightforward."

Henry glared.

Raz sighed and held out the letter. "With Lord Zanthus's death, things are different now. We need to proceed with caution and make a foolproof plan."

"It sounds like you've made one already," Henry said drily, placing his empty glass on the coffee table.

Raz looked at him sharply.

"What do you need me for?"

"To play a part," Raz replied. "Get rid of the woman who threatens my existence."

Henry crossed his arms. "That's a little dramatic, don't you think? I'm not a murderer."

Raz merely appraised him.

"Why can't you get rid of her yourself?"

"I've tried." Raz grimaced. "Several times. But she's always surrounded by guards or with the royal family."

"Why do you need her out of the picture?" Henry asked, his curiosity piqued.

"She knows who I am, what I do, and what I look like," Raz replied. "They've circulated detailed descriptions of me throughout Leneira, which makes it difficult for me to move around. Between the desert storms and the guards from all three countries on the lookout for me, I've had a few near misses already. I need her gone so I can continue to operate the way I do and avoid being captured by the soldiers and guards."

Henry wondered if the stranger had spiked his whiskey. It was the most fantastic story he had ever heard.

"This is all real, Henry," Raz assured him as though reading his mind. He pointed to the photograph of the woman. "You were born just after your mother was in Terralea. You have a claim to the throne, and I can help you get there."

Visions of himself ruling a magical land slowly overtook the panic that had been growing about the police imminently knocking on his door.

"Go pack," Raz repeated the order, interrupting Henry's daydream. "The last train leaves in less than an hour."

"Where are we going?" Henry asked.

"To Gatwick Airport, then Istanbul." Raz grinned, revealing cracked yellow teeth.

Henry decided that was a good enough plan given his current circumstances. Before he left the room, he threw a glance over his shoulder and saw that Raz was seated on the couch and had pulled out a blank piece of parchment and a small bottle of ink. He set down both items on the coffee table and was twirling a short stick between his fingers.

"The police are probably leaving the station now," Raz remarked without looking up.

That was enough incentive for Henry to hasten to his room, where he pulled out a small suitcase already packed in the event he had to leave at a moment's notice. He had filled it with bespoke suits he'd had made by various Savile Row tailors. Polished brogues, leather belts, quiet cravats, pocket squares, and a small bottle of cologne were neatly tucked into their assigned pockets and holders. At the last moment, he added a small platinum case concealing a pocketknife. The case had cost Henry more than he cared to admit, but it was worth it to be able to carry his trusty pocketknife and other contraband through airport security undetected.

Satisfied with the items in the carry-on, he changed into a comfortable suit. Henry strapped on a luxury watch to complete the image—he was a high-level executive on a business trip. As he went through the motions, his breathing slowed down, and he entered the meditative state that helped him prepare for the final stages of his heists and cons. He formulated backup plans for all points of the journey, should Raz betray him, running through scenarios and escape routes if required.

When Henry returned to the living room, suitcase in hand, Raz was stuffing the torn envelope with his newly drafted letter. The parchment Zanthus had written on lay on the coffee table until Raz pulled out a lighter and held Zanthus's letter to the small flame, watching the corners blacken and furl before catching ablaze. He tossed it into the fireplace, where it burned to ashes in moments.

Raz noticed Henry standing in the doorway, gaping, and explained, "Leave no trace."

Henry pursed his lips together and strode to the fireplace. He pulled the photograph down from the mantelpiece. He took in the features he shared with her, which were admittedly few and far between. The dark hair, the dimpled chin, and the wide-set eyes. Rose Graham was beautiful. There was no doubt about that.

"Nice touch," Raz said approvingly as Henry shoved the photograph into his suitcase. "You'll need this too." He held out the velvet box to Henry, who took it hesitantly.

The ornate talisman that had been delivered along with the letter was a heavy gold chain with a large gem pendant of rainbow-hued swirls of color under the pearlescent sheen. It was beautiful but ostentatious. Zanthus's letter informed Henry that the talisman had protective properties.

Henry tucked the letter that Raz drafted and the box with the talisman away into an inner pocket of his coat, along with his passport and birth certificate.

"Now, listen carefully," Raz said, beckoning Henry closer. "Here's what you need to do ..."

The journey to Istanbul was uneventful. Henry had his doubts when Raz said they'd be traveling separately, but Raz assured him he'd follow and meet him in Terralea.

"Make an excuse to visit the market square in Erindell alone," Raz instructed Henry. "I'll meet you there."

With those parting words echoing in Henry's mind, he arrived in Istanbul on schedule just after the sun had set. He hailed a cab outside the airport and instructed the driver to take him to the area around Sultanahmet Park, where he could while away the evening in a coffee shop. The peak-hour traffic was heavy, but the skilled driver wove in and out of the lines of cars, dropping Henry off at the end of a bridge where the entrance to the old town was located. He paid the driver in cash, adding a generous tip, and the cab zoomed off, leaving him to walk leisurely into the heart of Istanbul. Henry found himself walking down a familiar street lined with coffee shops and restaurants. The city was too old and established to have changed much in the years since his last visit. Most of the development and modernization were in progress in the outer suburbs and extended city borders.

The late-summer night was thick and heavy. The scent of petrichor lingered in the air, indicating a storm threatening to break soon. The narrow streets heaved with locals and tourists with no intention of slowing down any time soon. Henry chose a coffee shop that was relatively quiet and settled into a seat. The owner of the shop gave him a sharp nod when Henry raised a pointed finger. Within minutes, a small cup of thick, richly scented coffee and a glass of water were placed in front of him, and Henry settled back in his seat to watch the hustle and bustle of nighttime activity.

Street vendors haggled with tourists, men working in *dondurma* ice cream trucks teased and taunted children who laughed and shouted at the theatrics. Cats prowled the streets scavenging morsels of food that diners tucked into at restaurants, and locals leaned back in chairs sipping cups of tea and puffing on *shisha* pipes. The air was thick with sweet-smelling smoke and chatter, punctuated every so often by the call to prayer from one of the many mosques in the city. Henry let it all wash over him, content to wait until it was quiet enough for him to make his way to the spot instructed in the letter.

***

A few hours later, the crowds began to thin. Weary travelers dragged their feet back to their hotels, groups of men wished each other good night and clapped each other on the back before parting ways, and even the lounging stray cats thinned out as they went about their nightly business. When the shopkeepers switched off the lights and dragged down the metal doors, Henry stood and walked toward Gülhane Park, one of Istanbul's oldest and largest parks on the edge of the Topkapi Palace. There was no one in the vicinity to see him walk through the unlit park and make his way to a large tree that stood, silent and serene, in the middle of the night.

Henry placed his suitcase on the ground and assessed the tree. A warm breeze rustled through the park, carrying the scent of grilled meat from the main road. He glanced around furtively before bending down to open the case and pull out his trusty pocketknife.

He held up the blade and hesitated for a moment. According to the letter, his blood would open a portal to the mysterious land of Leneira. Under the cover of darkness, and with no one to witness his absurd actions, Henry felt he had nothing to lose. Still, it was with a hammering heart and a silent prayer on his lips that he dragged the knife across the palm of his hand. Drops of blood immediately pooled on the surface of his skin, and he rubbed his bleeding hand over the tree bark.

Exhaling a long-held breath, Henry stepped back. The night had gone still, and there was not a sound to be heard. Just when he was about to turn on his heel, the tree branches creaked, and the leaves rustled softly despite the still air. He gaped at the sight of a fracture growing in the tree trunk that evolved into a yawning rent. It was large enough for two grown men to walk through.

Henry put a hand out tentatively, but it was swallowed by the blackness. He felt a pull toward the opening, and his heart pounded with excitement. Snatching up his suitcase, Henry stepped into the hole and peered into the darkness as the entrance closed behind him. At first, nothing happened. It was as though he were standing in a dark room. Then a small light appeared in front of him and grew brighter and larger until he found himself staring at a vast desert under a clear, starlit night.

Henry took in a deep breath and stepped out of the tree trunk, which shuddered and creaked as the hole he had stepped through grew smaller and smaller until the bark hid all evidence of the portal. The air was cool and crisp, and although it was dark, the waning moon flooded the area with enough light that he could make out the soft sand before him. He stepped away from the tree, standing at the edge of a forest.

A flickering light through the dense trees caught Henry's attention, and he carefully navigated his way through the dark. The sand gave way to soft grass, and he was careful to tread lightly lest the crunching of twigs and branches underfoot give away his presence.

Sounds of laughter and music reached his ears, and he moved eagerly toward the revelry. As he approached a small clearing, the light grew brighter. The scent of pine and smoke from a bonfire filled his nostrils. The air thrummed with electricity as he crept through the bushes and squinted at the sight that greeted him.

A group of men and women dressed in blood-red tunics, dark pants, and boots sat around the bonfire, laughing and teasing each other. Two men sat opposite each other, staring intently at the tips of the flames. Henry followed their gazes, and his jaw dropped at the sight of two swords suspended mid-air fighting each other, as though invisible people were dueling above the bonfire.

The audience cheered and called out to the men, who stared unblinkingly at the swords, the clashing metal echoed around the forest.

Too late, a whisper of fabric and the crunch of footsteps approached.

"You there!" a loud, angry male voice called out from behind him. "Who are you? Where did you come from?"

Henry dropped his suitcase and instinctively raised his hands in surrender. The crowd around the bonfire didn't hear the commotion, and the merriment continued.

"Who are you?" the voice repeated. Something sharp pressed against his neck, and he looked down to see the tip of a sword shining in the dark. Henry felt the warmth of his interrogator's body against his back, along with a trickle of sweat that collected at the nape of his neck and slowly inched down his spine.

"My name is Henry Graham," he replied calmly, his voice not betraying his nerves and misgivings.

"And how did you get through the portal, Henry Graham?"

Instinct told Henry that he needed to be on his guard.

"I'm here to meet my father," he said, evading the question.

"Is that right?" the voice asked coolly. "And who is your father?"

A flame flickered to life next to Henry's face, and he blinked several times to make sure he wasn't dreaming. He slowly turned his head so his interrogator—still behind him, holding the sword to his throat—wouldn't accidentally slice his head off. A woman with tawny skin and dark hair pulled back from her face was holding a small ball of flames in the palm of her bare hand. At that distance, Henry could make out a gold crest embroidered over her heart. A dagger was sheathed at her waist, and a quiver of arrows and a bow strapped to her back. From the stories that Zanthus had told him, he guessed that he was dealing with royal guards

She stepped closer to Henry to examine him; he flinched at the heat of the flames against his face. Her dark eyes widened with surprise as she took him in. The man holding his sword against his neck didn't falter as the female guard examined Henry from top to bottom, taking in the expensive suit jacket and patent brogues. A bead of sweat rolled down Henry's temple as the guard paused on the sigil peeking above the cuff of his left sleeve.

"Well?" the man prompted, pressing the blade harder against his neck.

"Tarrick," Henry blurted out. "My father is Tarrick."

~ 2 ~

Sweat rolled down Elena's back as the early morning sun beat down on the training ring. Her breathing was heavy, but she refused to stop. Zahra had increased the intensity of training over the past week, and she was feeling the effects every day in her sore muscles. After that fateful night when she killed Zanthus by pure luck, Elena swore she would never be that defenseless again. She would train like the Terralean guards and learn how to defend herself. Properly.

Clashing metal rang through her ears as she deflected the guard's advance. Elena thrust her sword, but Zahra anticipated the move, stepping nimbly to the side. The whistle of the guard's blade through the air was Elena's only warning that she was being attacked again. She leaped back, the edge of the blade narrowly missing her nose, and let out a hiss of relief and frustration.

Though she relished the satisfaction and rush of endorphins that came with the high-intensity workouts, too often, Elena found herself wishing she had Elemental powers. Aside from the advantage it would have given her when training with Terralea's elite royal guards, rebuilding Erindell had been a longer, slower process than anticipated. Zanthus's guards had distributed enough toxin to suppress the Elemental abilities in the town's water sources to keep the people's powers at bay for almost six months.

However, within a day of the carnage, wagons loaded with enough supplies to last the summer made their way to Erindell. Elena would forever be grateful to Queen Lin of Sailon and King

Halder of Skandor for putting aside their differences and helping Tarrick in his time of need.

She was still haunted by the memories of the late King Arran and Erik being roasted on the spot by a traitor guard. Her nightmares were filled with memories of Erik and Arran leaping in front of Adina and Amaya. In a cruel twist, her subconscious mind slowed down the flames licking up their bodies. Their screams reverberated in her ears, and the scent of charred flesh lingered in her nose when she woke up gasping, covered in a sheen of sweat.

To keep her mind from dwelling on the horrors of that night, Elena worked with the people of Erindell to assist in any way she could. She made sure to keep busy from dawn to dusk, distributing supplies and assisting those who struggled without their Elemental powers. Elena even looked after children when the school day ended while their parents worked tirelessly to purify the waters.

Elena was brought back to the present when Zahra attacked with a series of blindingly fast lunges. Gripping the hilt with both hands, she pivoted and retreated the way the guard had taught her. The guard hadn't even broken a sweat despite training for almost an hour, but that was to be expected from the head of the elite guards.

Zahra had been promoted in a unanimous vote. Elena was grateful that, despite the additional responsibilities that came with the position, she still trained her. They had become close friends as a result of spending every morning together working on Elena's hand-to-hand combat, sword fighting, and archery. It also helped that Zahra was one of the few people in the palace who treated Elena no differently after she had been officially welcomed into the Terralean royal household. While other palace staff and members of Tarrick's council treated her with cool courtesy and politeness, Zahra and Leon still jibed and teased her.

Adina, who she considered her best friend in Leneira, was withdrawn and still grieving the losses of her father and lover. Elena tried to give the princess space to work through her grief, understanding only too well after losing her own parents that the process could be lengthy. But she missed the days of wandering through the streets of Erindell with Adina, sneaking around the palace's hidden passageways and spending long afternoons relaxing in the palace bathhouse.

Elena jumped back and raised her sword, attempting to gain some ground and switch to offense. She huffed and grunted as Zahra blocked her attacks with minute movements of her own sword. They continued dueling until Elena finally stepped back, holding up her arms in surrender. She wheezed as she doubled over, cursing for not pacing herself during the exercise.

"Getting better." Zahra grinned, pulling back. "Let's leave it there for today."

Elena nodded, panting as she threw down the sword. It hit the dusty ground, the loud *clang* echoing around the space. Her training in those days was a far cry from the self-defense classes and marathon training she had done back home.

She took in deep lungfuls of cool morning air, trying to remember the last time her muscles hadn't ached and protested from all the physical activity. Fall was close to its end, though the summer heat had lingered longer than expected. For the first time in a long time—in her life and since arriving in Leneira—Elena was optimistic about change in the air. They made their way to the water station by the training rings, where Zahra poured them both glasses of water. They sipped slowly, watching the sky lighten and *lyrabirds* swoop through the air, calling out to each other.

"How is His Majesty feeling?" Zahra asked quietly.

"I don't know," Elena replied. She was being honest in her uncertainty about how Tarrick was coping with being king of Terralea and the responsibilities the role entailed. He was still attentive, loving, and respectful of Elena, but both of them struggled to spend more than an hour at the start and end of every day together without him being called away by Leon, attending to political matters with nobles, or meeting with Erindellians who visited the palace with updates on the town's recovery progress.

"Today is the first official meeting of the Council of Nobles." The guard cocked her head to the side. "He must be nervous."

Elena had been introduced to Terralea's Council of Nobles at Arran's funeral. It was made up of twelve Terraleans—men and women—who advised on all internal political, economic, and social matters. With the end of the Peace Summit and Tarrick becoming the king of Terralea, it was time to turn their attention to ensuring the ongoing peace and security of the country.

"Is it an official meeting if some nobles aren't present?" Elena asked.

"The desert storms have been bad this year." Zahra tilted her head toward the sky. "The worst in centuries, according to my mother. Lord Darius was lucky to have missed them on his way here. The other nobles who are unable to be here because of them may further delay issues being approved and actioned until they can travel again. These council meetings should have started weeks ago, but with everything that's happened ..."

Elena frowned. "I've heard people talking about how the desert storms don't usually last this long. And that they are manageable if Terraleans can control the winds."

"The portal guards' roster has been affected." A crease formed between Zahra's brows. "They operate on a six-week rotation, but that's now turned into twelve-week stints because of how difficult it is to travel. The princess is worried it'll deter Terraleans from signing up to our defense force. It's also unfortunate we lost that last shipment from Skandor."

"Will this affect trade?" Worry crept into Elena's voice.

Zahra shrugged. "I'm not sure. King Halder and His Majesty can work out alternate routes if the storms persist, but the ones they've been using over the summer are the quickest way between Gothborg and Erindell."

Elena chewed her lower lip, trying not to let panic consume her. *It's just an annual seasonal thing,* she told herself. *It happens every year. Tarrick and Halder will still be able to honor the agreements from the Peace Summit. Terraleans will still sign up to join the royal guards. Everything will be fine.*

Elena sighed. "Tarrick won't say it out loud, but he's getting frustrated by the number of nobles resigning," she told Zahra. "And the ones who haven't decided if they want to continue serving him. I hope Lord Darius has answers for this."

"It's very odd." The crease between Zahra's brows deepened. "I've never known nobles to resign *en masse*."

"Quee—" Elena stopped to correct herself. "*Lady* Amaya said that she would speak directly with them if this isn't resolved by the time she's back."

"We need a full council," Zahra agreed. "The king cannot take action without the support of one."

Elena shook her head, frustrated. "I don't understand why they would decline to stay on. It's an honor to serve on the king's council, right?" From her understanding of Leneiran politics and the Terralean hierarchy, she could think of no higher honor than being asked to fill such an important and influential position. Aside from council positions being invitation-only, those who filled the roles were also offered suites at the palace and had access to the same luxuries and privileges as the royal family.

"It is." Zahra hesitated. "The position comes with influence and a say in making decisions for Terralea."

"Then what's the problem?" Elena sighed. "I mean, I get that the older members might want to retire."

"I have a feeling we might be stuck with Lord Malik," Zahra said.

Elena groaned. "No! There's a reason Arran didn't ask him to be present at the Peace Summit."

"He's the only one who's still keen on the job," Zahra pointed out.

"Yeah, and not being subtle about it," Elena grumbled. "He, Lady Sofia, and Rhea have pretty much made the palace their home now."

Zahra chuckled.

"I need to shower before meeting Darius." Elena gulped down the last of her water.

She made her way back to the palace while Zahra went to the barracks to clean up before her shift. The palace was a hive of activity with staff scurrying about the halls, guards patrolling inside and out, and nobles ambling about the grounds in pairs or with their families.

The air was a pleasant mixture of cooking smells emanating from the kitchens, the rich aroma of freshly brewed coffee being enjoyed on terraces and balconies, and the gentle floral scents from the garden.

The increase in the number of people who resided at the palace meant that a hum of conversation, whispers, and giggles was everywhere. Elena felt more at home with every day that passed, and would forever be grateful for that second chance at life.

There were moments when she caught sight of Tarrick staring at her with an odd expression on his face when he thought she wasn't looking. She wondered if it had anything to do with the price he'd paid to bring her back from the brink of death—something he was still reluctant to share with her in explicit detail. Their relationship was still too new, too exciting for her to push for details. But in those moments, Elena's heart would race, and she'd check on the Leneirans she had come to regard as her new family. After ensuring Amaya, Adina, Leon, Jet, and the royal guards who'd fought alongside her against Zanthus were all well, she would relax and continue as though the moment of panic never happened.

Elena waved at a woman and a young girl strolling past. The woman had smooth, pale skin that had the appearance of marble. Her striking copper hair was up in an elaborate chignon with braids and shimmering gold thread woven through her tresses, while wavy tendrils framed a heart-shaped face. The emerald silk dress that flowed down her tall, willowy body matched deep-set eyes filled with judgment.

"Good morning, Lady Sofia, Lady Rhea," Elena called out cheerfully.

Sofia merely inclined her head in greeting, wrinkling a delicate nose that was dotted with light freckles. Her daughter, Rhea, who was also dressed as though she were attending a feast in a pale pink silk dress with gold embroidery at the cuffs and hem, gave Elena a small smile before her mother tugged her away. Rhea was a younger, softer version of her mother, but she didn't look at Elena with the same disdain.

Elena grimaced as she watched the pair walk away, the fabric of their dresses rustling softly in their wake. She was not surprised, for it had been like that since Tarrick's coronation. Lady Sofia wasn't the only one who viewed Elena as an interloper in their world; a number of members of the Council of Nobles held the same belief.

***

"How was training?" Tarrick smiled when Elena entered their room. She crossed the large suite to where he stood at his desk. A sense of calm and peace settled on her when she raised herself on tiptoes and wrapped her arms around his neck. A light breeze floated in through the large window, carrying the faint sounds of gravel crunching from outside. The sound of rustling leaves mingled with soft voices from the garden. She exhaled a sigh.

"Brutal." Elena grimaced, rotating her shoulder and feeling a twinge of pain. "Just as I get the hang of something, Zahra switches it up and makes it more intense."

Tarrick laughed. He was already dressed for the day, and Elena pulled back to allow herself a moment to appreciate the man standing before her. He wore his usual attire—a simple yet regal tunic that did little to hide the muscular body underneath, fitted black pants, and polished boots. His dark hair was swept back from his tanned, clean-shaven face. Elena cupped his strong jawline and traced her thumb along his cheekbone while his amber eyes glittered hungrily. He bent down to brush his lips against hers, and her stomach immediately exploded with butterflies, even after months of living with him.

He pulled away from her reluctantly. "Darius will be here soon," he reminded her.

"Then you should let me shower in peace," Elena teased.

"I believe *you're* the one who keeps interrupting me every time you hear the water running." He grinned at her.

"It was one time, Tarrick." She rolled her eyes and pushed him back. "And I've regretted it ever since," she added in a playful voice.

"Liar." He flicked her nose, and she bared her teeth at him. "Go on. I swear I'll control myself today."

If they had a little more time, Elena could have easily persuaded Tarrick to join her in the shower, but even she was eager to learn what Darius had to say about the nobles. She stepped into the large bathroom and sent a prayer of thanks to Tarrick's great-great-grandfather for introducing the realm to modern plumbing. Anticipating the luxury of standing under the hot spray of water was what got her through training every morning.

"Is Lord Malik meeting you too?" Elena asked when she emerged from the bathroom. A cloud of steam billowed behind her. She clutched at the large, fluffy white towel wrapped around her as she padded barefoot to the expansive wardrobe. Opening the door, her heart sank as it did every morning at the sight of so many dresses in every color, fabric, and style hung up neatly.

It was an arduous task, picking out clothes for the day when she had no idea what awaited her. She normally took her cues from Adina—the princess had a knack for making even the simplest tunic and pants appear regal. Elena felt like an imposter even in the most exquisite dress. She longed for someone to tell her what to wear. Leon only saw her at breakfast, and if he didn't laugh at her attempts to dress "casual-royal" as she labeled it, Elena took it as a sign she had made an appropriate choice.

"No," Tarrick replied from his seat at the desk. He frowned as he read a document. "I want to hear what Darius says first."

Elena ran her hand through the array of satin, silk, and cotton as she pondered her choices.

"Do you plan to spend all day staring at your clothes?" Tarrick asked, amused.

Elena looked over her shoulder at him, but he was still engrossed in whatever he was reading.

"Is there a ball or feast today that I don't know about?" Elena asked.

"No, why?" Tarrick replied, head still bent over the document.

Deciding on an embroidered navy dress that was elegant enough without being over the top, Elena pulled it out and dropped the towel.

"I saw Lady Sofia this morning," she said, stepping into the garment and wriggling her hips as she tugged the soft fabric over her curves. She peeked up at Tarrick to see if he was enjoying the show, but he was still reading. "She's been here, what, a month now? I don't think she's worn the same dress twice. And those ladies are all so ..." Elena paused, trying to find a diplomatic word for *judgmental.*

"She likes to keep up appearances," Tarrick explained absent-mindedly. "She and Malik are responsible for one of the most prosperous regions of Terralea."

"Of course they are," Elena muttered. "We're making friendship bracelets today with all the jewels she's brought with her."

"Mm-hmm."

Elena smoothed the soft fabric over her body and turned to him. Still, he didn't notice her. She was slightly miffed that she had literally been naked in front of him and he hadn't noticed.

"In fact, I thought about hosting a tea party where we could discuss our embroidery and the benefits of a ten-step beauty regime," Elena continued as she made her way to the gorgeous carved timber vanity that Tarrick had commissioned to be added to his room the day after Elena agreed to stay in Terralea. She took a seat and picked up her hairbrush.

"That's a great idea," Tarrick mumbled, absorbed in the document.

"And while we're at it, we're planning a girls' trip to Skandor where we have orgies with Shifters and dance naked around bonfires."

"Sounds like fun."

"Tarrick!"

He snapped his head up. "What?"

Elena glared and pointed her hairbrush at him. "You haven't listened to a word I've been saying."

"I have," he sighed and tossed the document onto the desk. "I think you *should* get to know the ladies here."

Elena snorted and glared at her reflection in the mirror as she brushed out her wet hair. Tarrick moved so silently she didn't register him until his reflection appeared behind her in the mirror.

He placed his hands on her shoulders and kissed the top of her head. Elena's limp, wet strands transformed instantly into glossy, dark waves that fluffed up and cascaded around her shoulders. Tarrick grinned at her reflection.

"I'm serious, El," he said softly, running his hands lightly up and down her arms. "You've been spending so much time in Erindell. The nobles hardly know you."

"I've been helping," Elena argued.

"I know," Tarrick responded. "And you've done a tremendous job. The people are so grateful for your help. *I'm* so grateful for everything you've done."

Elena narrowed her eyes. "But ...?"

Tarrick sighed. "It's time to think about your role here at the palace. Erindell's waters are back to normal, and you're not required to spend every single day there."

Elena remained silent, unwilling to admit that she'd been avoiding her responsibilities in the palace.

"I know you've been struggling with adjusting to life here," he continued gently. "I don't need to be an Empath to see that. And I'm trying to give you the space and time you need to adapt."

"You're not using Jet to read me, are you?" Elena accused him.

"Of course not!" He looked offended at the idea. "I want us to be open and honest with each other."

"I want that too," Elena mumbled. She flushed, slightly ashamed that she'd think Tarrick would go to such lengths.

"Well, let me be honest with you now. I'd like you by my side at meetings and events," Tarrick implored. "As queen, you have re-sponsibilities here. You might as well start getting used to being at the palace and working here instead. Get to know the people you'll be dealing with."

"I know," Elena said, brushing the ends of her hair.

Her stomach clenched at the thought of being queen. Tarrick, Leon, and Adina had agreed that Elena wouldn't be pushed into the role until she had finished her lessons on Leneira. Its history, politics, and understanding of the governments were overwhelming. She felt wholly unprepared for the role and her new life.

Elena had to process the fact that she had almost died at the hands of Zanthus, but it was something she pushed away every time it cropped up. It was too soon to go over those events and her encounter with the Divine Beings. *Intimidating* was an understatement for the three all-powerful deities. Their eerie violet eyes, otherworldly beauty, and cryptic advice made the hair on the back of Elena's neck stand on end every time she thought about them.

"Talk to me, El," Tarrick coaxed. "What's worrying you?"

Elena sighed and met his concerned gaze. She tightened her hold on the hairbrush.

"I'm scared," she whispered. "I'm scared of messing up. Lady Sofia already hates me."

"She doesn't hate you," Tarrick said with a little laugh. "She just doesn't know you."

Elena turned away, unable to explain why her instincts were telling her that she was right.

"I know it's a huge adjustment, being surrounded by people all the time." Tarrick sighed. "The week of the Peace Summit was quiet in comparison."

Elena winced, still unable to suppress the haunting images in her mind every time someone mentioned anything related to that week. Aside from the memories of Erik and Arran, Zanthus's twisted, angry face looming over her also made her stomach churn. Serkin torturing her by restricting the airflow and choking her to death featured heavily in her dreams.

"I didn't realize your councilors would be spending so much time here," she admitted.

"Get used to it," Tarrick said with a crooked smile. "I barely get a minute to myself these days."

"I'm sorry." Elena peeked up at him, but Tarrick wasn't upset.

"Don't be." He shook his head. "This is normal for me, although I'm still getting used to delegating and assigning tasks. Any time Father asked for something to be done, I'd do it myself if no one else volunteered."

Elena huffed. "Of course you did."

"And now I'm delegating you with the task of getting to know Lady Sofia," he said firmly, pulling Elena to her feet. "You're not going to mess this up, El. I know you won't. I need you by my side."

"Yes, Your Majesty," Elena muttered, placing the hairbrush back on the vanity and adjusting her dress.

Tarrick leaned in, and his intoxicatingly spicy scent shrouded Elena. "Call me that tonight and *you* can delegate tasks to me," he whispered.

Elena shivered at the way his warm breath tickled her ear, and her core coiled in anticipation. She turned her head to reply, but his lips found hers, and she moaned into his mouth. Tarrick's tongue traced the seam of her lips, and she parted them willingly. Elena relished the rumble in his chest as she wound her hands around his neck and pulled him against her. His hard muscles pressed into her soft curves, and his hands tightened around her waist.

Elena ran her hands up and down the planes of his torso, eliciting a growl from him as she traced the grooves of corded muscles under the thin fabric. His hands moved lower, slowly pulling up the fabric of the skirt of her dress, exposing her bare thighs. She gasped against his mouth when a hand slipped under the dress, and his fingers trailed up her thighs.

"Divine Beings," Tarrick cursed when his fingers skimmed the wet fabric of her underwear.

"Tarrick," she moaned, arching her hips, wanting to feel more.

A loud banging on the door interrupted them, and Tarrick pulled back with a groan.

"Tarrick! Darius is waiting in your office," Leon shouted from the other side of the door. "Your hair is fine. Stop preening and get out here."

"My brother has impeccable timing," Tarrick muttered as Leon continued hammering the door.

Elena giggled and stepped away, straightening her dress and running her fingers through her hair. Her cheeks were flushed, and her eyes sparkled at the sight of Tarrick readjusting himself, cursing his younger brother.

When he nodded at her, she opened the door before Leon could break it down.

"Good morning, Your Majesty," he greeted her with a kiss on the cheek and a grin. "If I was interrupting, it was intentional, and I won't apologize for it."

"I don't think you've ever done anything unintentionally, and you've never apologized for anything," Elena groused. "And I'm not queen."

"But you will be," Leon said airily. He peered around the doorframe and waved at his brother. "Hurry up, Tarrick. You're going to want to hear what Darius has to say."

"He's told you already?" Tarrick strode toward the door.

Leon's smile disappeared. "It's not good news."

~ 3 ~

They walked in silence to Tarrick's office. Elena's heart was pounding as they neared, her mind conjuring all kinds of possibilities at Leon's declaration. Tarrick pushed open the door to reveal Adina and Darius standing by the window.

At the sound of the heavy wooden door creaking open, Darius swung around with a broad grin. Elena had met him briefly at Tarrick's coronation. He had been the friendliest of nobles in attendance, and as the son of Lord Rokeby—who had also died by Zanthus's hand—thanked her for everything she did for the realm. Darius was the same age as Leon and had wavy brown hair, sparkling brown eyes, and a handsome, chiseled face. His slightly crooked nose hinted at misspent youth. Darius had greeted her as though she were an old friend, and Tarrick had spoken warmly about him, cementing Elena's belief that the young lord could be trusted. He was unlike the other nobles, who were more formal and conservative in their manner.

"Your Majesty." Darius inclined his head toward Tarrick, who gave him a grin and clapped his shoulder.

"Darius," he greeted his friend. "Welcome back to Erindell."

"I'm glad to be back." Darius bounced on the balls of his feet. "I've missed the city!"

"You remember Elena?" Tarrick pulled her forward.

"Of course, my Lady." Darius reached out for her hand and brushed his lips over her knuckles.

"Please, call me Elena, Lord Darius," she told him.

"Only if you call me Darius." He winked at her.

She grinned. "Deal."

"Tarrick mentioned you frequently in his missives while I was away. I'm looking forward to getting to know you better now that I'll be here for a while."

"Translation: Tarrick wouldn't—and still won't—shut up about you," Leon snickered, earning himself a glare from his brother and a bark of laughter from Darius.

"Leon, he's your king." Darius chuckled. "Show some respect," he added playfully.

"He's still my insufferable brother," Leon shot back with a grin.

"Terralea's royal advisor, ladies and gentlemen," Adina grumbled while Tarrick pinched the bridge of his nose, uttering a prayer for strength.

"Welcome back to Erindell, Darius," Elena said, fighting back the laughter. "As you can see, not a lot has changed in the weeks you were gone."

"Not a lot has changed in the last hundred years between these two." Darius grinned, his gaze bouncing between Leon and Tarrick.

Tarrick cleared his throat. "Perhaps you should catch us up before we meet with the other nobles?"

"A good idea," Leon said, motioning for Darius to take a seat before Tarrick's desk. "Adina, why don't you keep Elena company this morning?"

Adina opened her mouth to object, but closed it when Tarrick gave her a stern look.

Elena shifted uncomfortably at the veiled request to babysit her. She was perfectly happy visiting Erindell with Zahra, as usual.

"Of course," Adina murmured.

"You don't have to if you're busy," Elena mumbled.

The princess had been distant of late, in part because of her new responsibilities as head of Terralea's defense force and a member of Tarrick's royal council. Adina was also still grieving. Gone was the tinkling laughter that announced her before she entered the room, and her easy, bright smile. The purple shadows under her eyes from lack of sleep were a permanent feature on her pale face that saw less of the sun than usual. She could usually be found in her office, hunched over papers, pushing back strands of unruly curls. Her dull brown eyes were noticeably bloodshot after she slipped away by herself to visit Arran and Erik's graves. Elena had spotted her a few times when she herself visited the site to place fresh flowers and pay her respects. Aside from keeping her distance and giving Adina space that she seemed to want, Elena wished there was more she could do to help her friend.

Adina reached out and squeezed Elena's hand reassuringly. "We'll have fun."

"I believe the ladies are having tea on the terrace this morning," Tarrick said in a light voice. "I might have suggested it to Lady Sofia yesterday. I believe she needs some help making bracelets, and I told her that you were an expert on the matter." His lips twitched while the others looked between the couple, bemused.

Elena squinted at him, wondering how Tarrick had already conspired to set it up before her sarcastic comments that morning.

"I won't approve any trips to Skandor, especially ones that involve orgies or dancing around bonfires," he continued while the corner of Elena's lips curled up. "But if there's anything else you need..."

"We might have to wean you off the water pipes, brother," Leon muttered, thoroughly confused by the out-of-context conversation.

"Let's go." Adina tugged on Elena's arm and led her out the door.

"I'll brief you on everything later," Tarrick said softly before Leon closed the door.

Elena followed Adina down the corridor, who gave her a sidelong look as they walked.

"What's wrong?" Adina asked.

"Nothing," Elena replied.

The princess snorted.

"Leon said Darius had bad news," she sighed. "I don't suppose he told you what it was?"

Adina shook her head. "No. I saw him in Tarrick's office just before you arrived and stopped to say hello."

"I wanted to hear what he had to say," Elena admitted.

"Tarrick will let us know," Adina assured her. "If it was really bad, Darius would have told us immediately."

There was a pause in conversation, and Elena stared at her friend intently.

"What?" Adina asked.

"If you want to talk about Arran or Erik—" Elena began.

"I don't!" the princess snapped, suddenly out of character. "Especially with you."

"What do you mean?" she asked, taken aback by the last part.

"Nothing," Adina mumbled, looking down at her toes.

"I just meant that I know what it's like to lose loved ones," Elena tried again, softening her tone further. "I know the pain, the grief, the loss ..."

Tears filled Adina's eyes. "It's not the same," she argued.

"I know they died under different circumstances," Elena said, ignoring the voice at the back of her head advising her to stop talking. "But it's still a loss that I also feel. Arran reminded me of my own dad, and Erik was my friend too."

"Just drop it, Elena," Adina said in a harsh voice. "You didn't know Father or Erik. You're not my mother or my sister. You don't understand what I'm going through."

Elena's temper rose at Adina's outburst, and she opened her mouth to retort, but they rounded a corner and were greeted by laughter and feminine voices from the terrace ahead. A group of women dressed in fine silks and brightly colored dresses draped themselves over comfortable lounge chairs and settees. Their hair and makeup were immaculate, not a strand moved out of place as they sipped cups of tea. They all spoke in affected voices, emphasizing the vowels and dragging out some of the words to make their inconsequential points.

Plates of dainty pastries and sandwiches floated around the group. Elena still marveled at the way the Elemental abilities made even the simplest of tasks—like helping oneself to food—so magical. Some women piled their plates high with the treats on offer while others glared at the array of food balefully as though the presence of such delights would affect their waistlines.

Multi-hued spots of light danced around the terrace pillars and floors, the sunlight catching the jewels glittering at earlobes, throats, and fingers. It had shocked Elena to see people dressed so extravagantly when she first attended a tea party hosted by Amaya, but she soon came to realize that it was the norm in the royal palace. It was one of the reasons Elena preferred to spend time with the Erindellians in town; she was more comfortable in simple tunics and pants, working with her hands, and being part of the easy conversations around her about the practical issues and day-to-day life in Terralea.

Everything done at the palace was carefully considered, scrutinized, and judged by the nobles present. Amaya and Adina had given Elena a crash course in royal etiquette and insisted she learn by doing. However, no matter how perfectly she carried herself, held conversations, and dressed, the other ladies had already formed an opinion about her—and it was not a flattering one. She caught them staring at her at mealtimes with odd expressions on their faces, giggling about her clothes and hair when they thought she couldn't hear them, and some didn't even bother being subtle about snubbing her or brushing her off when she offered to accompany them to the town.

"Your Highness!" Sofia called out in delight. "We are honored to have you join us."

Adina politely greeted the woman who had taken the lead at the affair, judging by her seat in the middle of the group. She and Elena crossed the threshold, past the carved sandstone pillars that framed the marble-floored terrace that overlooked the manicured gardens where the lush foliage was starting to turn fiery shades of orange, red, and yellow. The space was covered so people could enjoy the views year-round. It was one of Elena's favorite reading spots.

Sofia motioned for Adina to sit beside her, ignoring Elena. Zahra stood guard in a corner, alert as she watched over the scene. Elena locked eyes with the guard and forced a smile. The corner of Zahra's lip quirked up ever so slightly, noting Elena's discomfort at being there.

"May I?" Elena asked Rhea politely. The young girl was seated at the edge of the group on a settee, hunched over as though trying to make herself invisible.

Rhea nodded but didn't say a word as Elena perched on the edge of the seat. A cup of tea and saucer floated down to her. Elena wondered if it was Adina's way of apologizing for her earlier outburst. Everyone's attention was on the princess, and Sofia stirred sugar into Adina's cup as she droned on about Amaya's visit to her family.

"It will be *so* nice to have Amaya back again," Sofia gushed, holding out the cup and saucer to the princess. "Any news from your mother, my dear?"

"Yes," Adina replied, accepting the cup of tea that Sofia held out to her. "She's having a wonderful time in Karsh."

"A beautiful part of Leneira." Sofia sighed. "It's been decades since Malik and I visited."

"She'll be back soon," Adina said, sipping on the tea.

"And I'll be sure to tell her you've been doing a wonderful job in her absence, managing the palace and your brothers," Sofia said with a tinkling laugh.

It took every effort on Elena's part not to snort out loud. She glanced up at Zahra, who pursed her lips, having heard every word Sofia's carrying voice said.

"And how are you enjoying Terralea, Lady Elena?" a curvy woman with raven hair and cornflower-blue eyes asked kindly. "We've hardly seen you since we arrived."

Mari had been the kindest of the group to her, but they never did more than exchange pleasantries and small talk.

"I love it here, Lady Mari," Elena replied sincerely. "I've been helping the people in Erindell. It started with distributing supplies and necessities during the first few weeks, but then it became a much bigger—"

"How very charitable of you," Mari exclaimed, cutting her off. "I'm sure they have been equally fascinated by you."

Elena chose to take a sip of her tea instead of reacting to the woman's interruption and patronizing comments.

"Mari, that was rude," the older woman beside Mari scolded her. "Lady Elena was still speaking."

"Were you?" Mari's eyes widened. "Oh, I do apologize, my dear. I didn't realize."

"That's okay," Elena mumbled. It was the most anyone had spoken to her directly without a snide comment or backhanded compliment being thrown in.

Mari beamed at her before turning to the older woman. The two of them were soon engrossed in a conversation about gardens and plants.

"I heard about your project, Lady Elena," Rhea said in a soft voice.

Elena gave the shy young woman a smile. "When we worked together, the Erindellians told me that Zanthus's attempts to take over brought back memories of the uprising. So many of them wanted to leave, fearing another large-scale attack."

"You convinced them to stay?"

Elena shrugged. "I can't say for sure. I listened to them, let them voice their concerns for the possibilities of what could happen. Their fear over the consequences of losing their powers. Luckily, I was able to assure them of their safety since I witnessed everything firsthand." She spoke the words casually, trying to quell the panic that bubbled up every time she thought about that week.

"You just ... listened to them?" Rhea asked, not following.

"Acknowledging your fears and that they exist is a step toward conquering them," Elena replied. "More people came forward with their stories, and everyone bonded over their shared experiences. We created a space for group support, I guess? It's now a regular event at the school."

Rhea simply stared at her.

Elena cleared her throat and changed the subject. "Are you enjoying Erindell, Lady Rhea?"

Rhea glanced at her mother, who was still talking to Adina, before replying. "Yes, my Lady."

"Please, call me Elena. Tell me more about where you're from," Elena asked, determined to have a civil conversation with at least one person that morning.

"There's not much to tell," Rhea said, slightly terrified and ignoring Elena's request. "I live with my mother and father on our estate and spend my days helping Father's advisor manage the accounts."

"You're an accountant?" Elena asked with interest.

Rhea darted a glance at her mother again before giving a sharp nod.

She must be nervous around people, Elena thought to herself.

"That's impressive." Elena smiled, hoping she conveyed enough warmth to keep Rhea talking.

"I like numbers," she mumbled, eyes dropping to her empty teacup.

Elena waited expectantly, but the young girl didn't offer any more information.

A cool breeze swept through the terrace, carrying the scent of roses, temporarily distracting Elena and offering a welcome reprieve from the heavy air that hung over the terrace. She breathed in the crisp air, relishing its refreshing caress on her face until it suddenly became warm and cloying. A thin woman with a mass of blonde hair piled high on her head sat on the settee beside the one Elena sat on. The woman shivered in her satin gown but stopped the moment the warm air reached her, and Elena sighed quietly.

"Would you like more tea?" Rhea's soft voice filtered through.

Elena glanced down at her empty teacup. "Thank you."

Rhea passed her the teapot, but when Elena tilted it over her cup, it was empty.

"Apologies." Rhea blushed and stared at the teapot.

It immediately weighed heavier in Elena's hand, and piping hot pale liquid poured out of the spout.

"Maybe it should brew a bit," Rhea mumbled.

"Thank you." Elena passed back the teapot. She felt like she should be the one apologizing for being unable to refill the teapot without trekking all the way down to the kitchens for hot water.

"Once His Majesty establishes his council, Malik and I were thinking about finding a place in Erindell," Sofia continued, dominating the conversation. Adina listened politely, interjecting the odd comment and suggestion every so often.

Elena watched the two of them enviously. Despite the fact that Adina was dressed in a tunic, pants, and boots—clearly intending to work with the guards and in her office, which did not require elaborate dresses—she fit in seamlessly with the group. All of the noblewomen treated her with respect and listened when she spoke. Their husbands showed her the same level of courtesy as they did Amaya.

To be fair, Adina showed a greater—and genuine—interest in the mundane topics the women favored. Elena struggled to keep up with conversations about Terralea's influential families and the social politics. From what Tarrick had told her, social activities of the nobles filtered into the country's politics, so Elena made an effort to keep up with the gossip and listen to what the women talked about.

"Did you know Lord Lazar is thinking of retiring his family?" Mari said.

Elena's ears pricked up.

"What do you mean?" Mari's companion asked. Elena racked her mind to try to remember the woman's name—she had arrived the day before with her husband, who was on the Council of Nobles and was required to attend the fortnightly meetings.

"He wants to retire from the council, and his son isn't interested in taking his place," Mari continued.

"But then the king would have to assign the title to someone else," the woman exclaimed.

Elena continued to sip her tea and feign interest in Sofia and Adina's conversation so Mari wouldn't catch her eavesdropping.

"Eli and I were also talking about retirement." Mari sighed. "He served Arran for over 200 years, and we were thinking about buying a villa by the sea. There are some beautiful ones on the southern coast."

"What will he do there, Mari?" her companion asked. "Lord Eli doesn't strike me as the kind of man who is content to sit on a beach all day. He loves politics and palace life."

"He does," Mari agreed.

Elena continued to stare at the garden and pretend to daydream.

Mari lowered her voice and continued, "But if I'm being honest, Helene, he's not comfortable with some of the, ah, recent arrivals at the palace. It's making him uneasy about what's to come."

"You mean the Empath?" Helene asked, lowering her voice.

"Among others," Mari said and sipped her tea.

Elena tried to keep her face void of expression, but she was fuming.

"Lady Elena?"

Zahra peered down at her with concern.

"You promised to help my mother today," the guard said.

Elena blinked in confusion.

"She asked if you could stop by this morning," Zahra said pointedly.

Elena took the hint and rose to her feet.

"Thank you for the tea," she murmured to Rhea as she placed her cup and saucer on the table.

After hasty thanks and goodbyes to the group that barely acknowledged her departure, she followed Zahra down the corridor. They didn't speak until they were confident that no one could hear them so far from the terrace.

"You lasted a lot longer than I was expecting this time." Zahra grinned.

Elena flushed and rubbed her arm nervously. "You think they're onto us?"

"Probably." Zahra shrugged. "But it was painful to watch your fake smile. You need to work on your *I'm-interested-in-what-you're-saying-and-giving-you-my-full-attention* face."

"Thanks," Elena grumbled. "I'll remember that next time I'm in front of a mirror."

"Mother doesn't need to see you, but we can still go if you want," Zahra offered.

"Will you get into trouble?" Elena raised a brow.

Zahra's role as head of the elite guards meant that she was required to follow a strict code of conduct and set an example for the younger guards. That included sticking to her roster and assigned position.

"The rest of the guards are on duty, and we're only going to Erindell." She shrugged. "His Majesty would consider you going to town by yourself a bigger risk than one guard going off schedule."

Elena rolled her eyes. "He's way too overprotective."

"He loves you," Zahra said gently.

Elena couldn't argue with that. They continued walking toward the entrance, passing the council chamber along the way. Raised voices behind the closed doors made Elena pause. The corridor was empty, save for herself and Zahra, so she quietly moved to the door and pressed her ear against it.

"—Your Majesty, we understand Lady Elena has done a lot for Terralea these past few months," a deep voice rumbled.

A sense of foreboding took over Elena. She strained her ears, trying to catch what was being said, but all that followed were indistinguishable mumblings.

"—but the bottom line is she has no Elemental powers, is a human, and does not understand our ways," the deep voice said.

"She is not a suitable candidate for the council."

"We do not support your petition to marry her."

"She *cannot* be queen."

Elena backed away slowly and turned to Zahra, who looked at her with sympathy.

"Terralea's rulers have traditionally come from noble families and wielded powerful abilities, reassuring people of being able to protect and defend our lands." Lazar threw out his arms and addressed the gathered council members seated at the large oak table in the middle of the room.

Tarrick sighed internally, mentally preparing for another long-winded speech from the elderly Terralean.

His white hair contrasted against weathered brown skin. Brown eyes flashed around the room searching for approval and support from the other council members gathered. The elderly Terralean had served Tarrick's grandfather and father. He had been talking about retiring years ago, so his resignation didn't surprise Tarrick. However, the king did take issue with the fact that Lazar was bringing Elena into his reasoning.

The meeting of the Council of Nobles had been a disaster. Tarrick had expected to face resistance and opposition to many of his ideas for the future of Terralea. So far, only a handful of the gathered nobles—which included Netta—were open to his suggestions.

Admittedly, the nobles had not been present during the Peace Summit to witness Zanthus's betrayal and Elena's heroic actions. To them, she was merely a human woman who had captured Tarrick's heart. Netta was the only councilor who advised Tarrick and his family on international and internal matters who could vouch for Elena.

"Who will you name as your successor, Lord Lazar?" Leon asked in a frustrated voice. He, too, was tired of Elena's name cropping up in every argument against Tarrick's proposals. The king had already warned him of his suspicions that her name would be used in the conservative nobles' arguments against his ideas. Leon had reacted as his brother expected, ranting and raving about the slow rate of progress until he finally calmed down. They agreed that they would steer the conversation away from her as much as possible.

"I'm afraid I cannot name one." Lazar shook his head regretfully. He stroked his full white beard, addressing Tarrick when he spoke. "My son is not interested in politics and wants to set up a private business in which I will invest."

Tarrick's gaze swept around the table at the Council of Nobles as it currently stood, all of whom stared at him with unreadable expressions on their faces. There were a few missing from the outer regions where the desert storms prevented them from traveling to Erindell, but Darius had gleaned information on his way to the palace that most of them were of the same mindset as Lazar.

"What about your daughter?" Tarrick asked.

Heads swiveled in Lazar's direction.

Tarrick had watched his father skilfully navigate challenging council meetings thousands of times, allowing the nobles to say their piece and argue with each other before stepping in at the end and making a final decision. It was the tactic Tarrick had chosen to adopt for the meeting, knowing full well that the nobles would test him to see if he would live up to Arran's legacy.

"What about her?" Lazar asked after a pause.

"Is she interested in taking your place on the Council?"

Lazar blustered and flushed a blotchy red. "Well, ah, no, I don't think—"

"I remember Adriana was interested in international relations and economic policies at school," Leon interrupted with a smirk.

"I will gladly send her an invitation myself to join the council," Tarrick continued coolly. "In fact, I would like her to attend this year's Harvest Feast so we may discuss the possibility in person."

There was more silence as Lazar weighed his options.

"I cannot do that, Your Majesty," he finally sighed. "If I am to speak openly—"

"*Finally,*" Leon growled.

"I was here when Rose infiltrated the palace and nearly destroyed our realm," Lazar said.

Tarrick flexed his hand, trying to maintain his composure and not let the beast starting to rouse inside take over. He had been afraid of that cropping up. The nobles who had been in the palace during Rose's stay agreed to never speak of her again. Tarrick, however, would never be able to escape that youthful mistake.

Darius frowned, but he was one of the minority who didn't understand what Lazar was referring to. Others turned away and coughed awkwardly.

"That was different," Tarrick said roughly. "Elena is not interested in ... acquiring Elemental abilities. And the uprising would have happened regardless of Rose's presence. It's been a century since that happened, and we have all learned from our mistakes."

Netta and Darius nodded in solidarity while others muttered under their breath and shook their heads.

"If I may get some context ...?" a man with a boyish face and chestnut hair raised his hand.

"It's a past incident that has no bearing on the current circumstances, Aiden," Leon snapped at the lord, who shrank back in his seat.

"Leon," Tarrick reprimanded his brother. He didn't want him turning the few nobles who were on his side against him. Aiden had joined the council only a few years prior, inheriting the role and title when his father died. "I can tell you the facts later, Lord Aiden, but I assure you the past is in the past, and there are others present who can vouch for Elena's character," he said to the young lord.

But Lazar was shaking his head. "You are as besotted now as you were then, Your Majesty. You forget I was there, along with many others," he gestured around the room again. "We witnessed everything."

"Not *everything*, surely," Leon muttered, glaring at the nobles who wore stony faces.

"The fact that we know nothing about this young woman also doesn't help," Lazar continued as though Leon hadn't spoken. "We would like to take a cautious approach to the future of the country to maintain the peace and stability your father worked so hard to establish."

Darius cleared his throat. "Is it true that you have Empaths in the palace now, Your Majesty?" he asked.

"We have one Empath ambassador," Leon corrected him.

"Jet has been helping us find traitors within the palace," Tarrick replied. "An invaluable service and a way to strengthen ties with Sailon."

"And have there been any more traitors?" Lazar asked skeptically.

"He found some of the palace staff who assisted Zanthus and his guards," Leon responded. "They have been dealt with, and we have not found any more traitors in our midst. But Jet has agreed to stay on as a precaution. When our army begins training with Sailon and Skandor, he will also be the point of contact for the Sailonese soldiers."

Tarrick made a mental note to tease Leon about his justification for Jet's indefinite stay at the palace once those tedious talks were over and they had a moment alone. It would be payback for all of Leon's insufferable ribbing about his relationship with Elena.

"Then I am comfortable with the security and safety here," Darius said, sitting back in his chair and grinning at Tarrick and Leon.

Tarrick's heart lifted slightly at the lord's support,not that he had any reason to doubt Darius, having known the man since they were in school together. Aiden's expression cleared and his shoulders dropped in relief—further confirmation of Tarrick's suspicions that only the older council members were prone to caution.

"If you would like us to add Shifters to our rotation of guards as an added security measure, I'm sure King Halder would be thrilled to send us a few of his people," Leon said sarcastically to Lazar and the other lords, who still wore skeptical expressions.

"You do spoil us, Your Highness," Darius murmured.

"But it doesn't resolve the problem of Elena," Lazar argued. A few nobles rumbled in agreement.

"Lord Lazar." Netta glared at him. "Do you have a problem with Lady Elena, or *women?*"

Lazar gasped in outrage.

"You won't allow Adriana to have a say in whether she wants to take your place," Netta continued. "You won't take my word that Lady Elena is a good person and worthy of being queen of Terralea one day. I understand you've even questioned some of Princess Adina's changes to the guards' training and roster."

Silence fell over the room. Lazar looked nervously at his fellow councilors, seeking support, but no one spoke in his defense.

"She is simply not well-versed in Terralean and Leneiran politics to join the council, which is a position automatically granted to the king and queen," Lazar finally said.

Tarrick clenched his fists beneath the table and forced himself to remain calm.

Leon noticed his brother's reaction and jumped in swiftly. "There is no problem where Lady Elena is concerned," he announced. "She will understand the politics in time. From what I've heard, she's making great strides in learning our history. After all, none of *us* were born knowing what we know now. Besides, the people of Erindell don't view Elena as a threat. They love her."

Lazar scoffed while Darius raised an eyebrow.

"She distributed water, food, and necessities to the people earlier this summer and took on new initiatives to help the people of Erindell," Leon continued eagerly. "She's been teaching the children at the school in Erindell to read and write, and she even worked at the tea stalls during the last Full Moon Festival."

Several nobles sat up in surprise. Tarrick let his brother speak while he carefully assessed those who sat around the table. It was becoming clear who was in opposition, and it occurred to him that it might be an opportunity in disguise.

"It's true." Netta nodded vehemently. "I already have a petition from the Erindellians for funding to set up a community center based on Lady Elena's suggestion."

"A what?" Lazar blustered.

"Community center," Netta repeated. "We've already identified an unused building near the market square that can be used, but it does need some renovations and sprucing up."

The councilors stared at her, bemused.

"It may come as a surprise to many of you that Erindell is Terralea's largest city with a constant influx of people around the country," she said drily. "This space is where Erindellians can connect in meaningful ways. Several locals have already volunteered to run programs to help initiate newcomers to the city, help those who want to strengthen their powers, activities for children, a place for widows to partake in recreational activities ..."

"She didn't mention the community center," Leon murmured to Tarrick. "Did you know about that?"

Tarrick nodded his head a fraction in confirmation. Pride swelled within him as Netta listed everything Elena had done. It had been difficult to ask her to focus her attention toward palace matters that morning. But the attitudes of the councilors was exactly why he needed her to be present and show them that she deserved their respect and support. His words would only go so far in convincing them.

"Well, I'll be," Leon said admiringly.

"This is nonsense!" Lazar shook his head vigorously. "You support this venture, Lady Netta?"

"I do," she replied firmly. "Lady Elena had my wholehearted support for this project as soon as she put forward the proposal."

"It sounds like the perfect place to start a rebellion," Lazar groused.

"Well, it's a good thing we have an Empath who can alert us to such things." Leon sniffed, earning himself a glare from the irate lord.

"Why can't these people meet in a coffee shop?" Lazar demanded.

"I don't think there's a coffee shop in Erindell that can accommodate hundreds of people at once," Netta replied coolly.

"Hundreds—?"

"Yes, hundreds," Netta snapped, showing the first signs of irritation. "Say what you will about Lady Elena, but this is your future queen—someone who listens to our people and isn't afraid of hard work when it comes to making life a little bit better for them."

"Thank you, Leon, Netta," Tarrick spoke up. "I think it's clear that there are several members of this council who are ready to … retire. And I understand if your families have other priorities."

Netta stared pointedly at Lazar, who glared back at her.

"I thank you for your services to our family," Tarrick continued, ignoring the animosity and daggers his council members were shooting at each other. They had already silently picked sides, and there was no point in delaying the inevitable. "Many of you have done so for centuries, so it's only fair you get a chance to enjoy time with your own families."

At Tarrick's words, the cold expressions relaxed, and shoulders dropped. A few men exhaled soft sighs now that the fear of severe repercussions for their choices had been quashed.

"We will need to recruit new councilors and assign titles." Tarrick's eyes flicked over to Leon, who bent his head over his notebook to scribble down notes. "I propose that if entire families are retiring, perhaps it is time to change how we recruit councilors."

Leon snapped his head up. "What do you mean?"

Even Aiden and Darius held their breath as Tarrick looked warily at the sullen faces around the table.

"Perhaps now is when we start recruiting councilors based on merit and character instead of lineage and status," he announced.

A few gasps echoed around the room.

An older man with dark, wavy hair streaked with silver leaned forward with a concerned expression on his handsome, bearded face.

"Your Majesty," he spoke up.

Tarrick turned to the noble. "Yes, Lord Malik?"

Malik propped his elbows on the table and steepled his fingers. His brown eyes were devoid of warmth as he assessed the king. "There are those who would argue that if we recruit members for the Council of Nobles based on merit, we should be holding elections for rulers as well. Or is the royal family above this law?" His gaze held a hint of challenge.

Malik and his family had been staying at the palace ever since Arran's funeral. The man was adept at the art of diplomacy and soothing ruffled feathers during heated arguments and debates, but both Tarrick and Leon were wary of his underlying intentions. It was no secret that Malik was a conservative man. He had been in the royal guard during Tarrick's grandfather's reign, then joined Arran's Council of Nobles after he saved Arran's life during a vicious campaign against the Skandorians. Despite their differences over Arran's progressive ideas, the two of them had remained close friends until the late king's death.

Malik had not opposed anything Tarrick proposed during the meeting, which had unnerved the king. In fact, it was the first time the man spoke up during the entire meeting.

"If this is your decision, you are effectively stepping down as king and giving the current council thirty days to nominate and decide on a new king," Malik advised.

Darius frowned at him. Leon glanced nervously at Tarrick, who frantically tried to think of a way out of the hole he had dug in a fit of rage.

It was Netta who swooped in with a solution. "It would appear there are a lot of conflicting opinions and ideas at the moment, not helped by the fact that we have missing councilors who are unable to advise on this matter, and many who are retiring after this meeting."

The men in the room gaped at her, but the pressure in Tarrick's chest eased at her words and her attempt to salvage the consequences of his thoughtless comment.

"Without a full council to vote on internal or external matters, we are essentially at a standstill," Netta continued calmly.

"What do you suggest, Lady Netta?" Tarrick asked, mirroring her steady voice. "I agree with everything you're saying, and I would rather spend a little longer finding the right people for our council than simply filling spots for the sake of it."

"A year," Leon suddenly piped up beside him.

"What?" Tarrick drew his brows together.

"Let's give it a year for things to ... settle." He gave Tarrick a beseeching look, trying to convey a silent message. "Let's focus on filling the empty positions on the council with the right people. Then we can circle back to your request to marry Elena next year."

Tarrick took in deep breaths to stop himself from throttling Leon on the spot. He didn't want to wait an entire year to marry

Elena. Anything could happen in that timeframe, but it appeared that he had little choice in the matter.

"That sounds reasonable," Malik said thoughtfully. "After all, it took almost a year for Rose to show her true colors."

Tarrick glared at his brother, who turned red.

"We will focus on filling the empty council positions first, based on His Majesty's criteria to recruit based on merit. And Lady Elena will have a year to prove she is worthy of being queen and sitting on the council," Malik declared as though the matter had been settled. "If the Council of Nobles is still divided on the matter and cannot find a compromise that appeases the majority, we will vote on a new family to rule Terralea."

~ 5 ~

"Yet!" Elena winced at the loud, croaky voice. "You don't know how to rule *yet*."

The woman who sat across from her had dark eyes that glittered as she spoke. Her silver hair was woven into intricate, tiny braids swept back in a large knot at the top of her head just like Zahra's. She waved a silver-handled ebony walking stick that was carved with ancient symbols along the shaft in the air to emphasize her point.

Ninaz was a formidable woman whose presence commanded both fear and respect. But Zahra's mother was one of the oldest living Terreleans intimately acquainted with the inner workings of the palace. Having served Tarrick's grandmother as a companion, she had helped Elena navigate the complexities of royal life over the summer, teaching her about palace protocol and unspoken rules about hierarchy.

Elena and Zahra visited her almost daily at her opulent townhouse in an affluent neighborhood in Erindell. It had started as a delivery stop at the start of the summer when Ninaz decided to move back to Erindell to be closer to her only surviving child. Elena delighted in Ninaz's stories and pearls of wisdom, even when they were unsolicited.

"And having preternatural powers as a prerequisite to rule was a reasonable argument when this land was fractured, and we relied on brute strength and magic to lay claim to territories." Ninaz pierced Elena with a stare, waving her walking stick as she spoke. "But we are long past that. We need people with wits and brains to make decisions now that our countries and politics have been established for millenia. I should like to see *some* progress. Tarrick is the third king to take the throne in my lifetime. I have high hopes for him and you, Lady Elena, with both your education and backgrounds—despite the Leneirans' suspicions of humans, the social progress in their realm is something to aspire to."

Elena mumbled incoherently in response.

"No pressure, Mother," Zahra muttered from her seat beside Elena.

"It doesn't matter what you or I think." Elena stared into the cup of tea in her hands. "The Terraleans who make the decisions don't think I'm capable of being queen or being part of the council. Especially after everything with Rose."

Ninaz snorted. "The Terraleans who make the decisions at the highest level beg to differ." Her eyes bored into Elena's. "Have you asked Amaya and Tarrick for help? Have you shown you are brave enough to ask the councilors directly what it is they expect from their future queen?"

"Amaya and Tarrick have already done everything they can to help me." Elena flushed. "The others ... They don't talk to me."

Ninaz sighed and asked gently, "Do you always have trouble asking for help?"

Elena bit her lower lip. She had heard that question a number of times over the years. How could she explain that it became more and more difficult to ask others for help when people inevitably let her down? Friends canceled catch-ups when other priorities in life took over; her old manager claimed to "have her back," but only when he needed her to work weekends and outside regular hours; even her therapist failed to give her the advice and comfort she needed. In the end, it was always easier to do things herself and deal with problems directly.

"Have you attended a council meeting yet?" Ninaz asked.

Elena shook her head, fully aware that she was in for a berating.

"Am I not one of your subjects?" Ninaz asked sharply. "My opinion is one of thousands of Terraleans. It is your job as the future queen to decide who you will listen to—a bunch of old sycophants who don't understand the world we live in now or your people. There is absolutely nothing stopping you from marching into that council chamber and asking those skeptics what you can do to prove them wrong." She paused before adding, "Tell them exactly what I and hundreds of other Erindellians have told you—we have the utmost faith in your ability to rule and become one of Terralea's greatest queens."

Ninaz, who spent most of her time alone, enjoyed Elena's company and the daily check-ins from her daughter. She had taken one look at Elena's face when they arrived and instructed Zahra to make them all tea straight away.

Ninaz eyed Elena thoughtfully. "Queen Samara was the daughter of a farmer, and she didn't let the naysayers stand in her way."

Elena stared at her. "Who?"

She sighed. "Queen Samara, the first and last queen of Leneira. Have you not come across the song '*The Naya's Crossing*'?"

Elena would have been offended if anyone else had said that, but Ninaz's assessment was the only honest one she could count on.

"Queen of ... *Leneira*? The entire realm?"

Ninaz cleared her throat and took a deep breath. "Before the present-day countries were formed, Leneira was occupied by many tribes and factions. Just as they did in the human realm, everyone fought over land and resources. Unlike humans, we had extraordinary abilities. As you can imagine, this caused conflict on a much greater level, and in times of constant war and battles, people aligned themselves based on the tribe's magical needs rather than their common powers to protect themselves."

Elena and Zahra both ignored their tea growing cold, enraptured by Ninaz's storytelling. Like Amaya's family, Ninaz came from a nomadic tribe before marrying Zahra's father and settling in Erindell to raise her family. She, too, knew the songs of the realm, and her words cast a spell over Elena every time she treated her to a history lesson.

"These were dark times. Leneirans could never put aside their differences and stubbornness. Samara was a Seer born in Delphos, one of the Isles of Minos. She was attuned to the land, the seasons, the way Nature dictated our lives, and she lived in harmony with the realm. One day a creature unlike any other approached her. A water horse—a *naya.*

"The *naya* was a powerful creature who could cross the land faster than you could blink. Its water form meant that blades and arrows were useless against it. It could put out flames with a sweep of its tail and dissolve into the earth only to rise again. Word spread of Samara and her *naya.* Elementals, Shifters, and even Seers more powerful than her tried to steal it, but the water horse protected the girl as if it were her own foal."

"I wouldn't mind having a *naya,*" Elena murmured.

Zahra grinned at her. "This story is so ancient it's basically a myth."

Ninaz gave her an incredulous look before continuing. "Petty fights exploded into full-blown battles within clans. The lands were covered in blood. Despite the precautions the people of the Isles took to prevent war, death, and tragedy, they eventually spread. The prophecies and visions did nothing to help those who received them or prevent their inevitable deaths. When she was but a few years shy of adulthood, Samara's village was destroyed and her family killed by raiders. She was the sole survivor, and realized that her Seer powers hadn't changed the outcome—it was all out of her control. After witnessing such horror, Samara vowed that she would bring peace to the land. It was the one thing she couldn't See for certain, but her own actions were the only thing she could control."

Elena's gaze drifted to the floral pattern painted onto the pale blue walls of Ninaz's sitting room. The space had beautiful dark timber furniture carved with decorative emblems. A plush pile rug covered most of the floor. Terralean throws and silk cushions with delicate embroidery added color and luxurious touches. The light curtains framing the large window that overlooked the street below fluttered in the breeze. Snatches of voices floated through as people walked past. It was a soothing space, and Elena allowed herself to be drawn into Ninaz's story as she relaxed into the comfortable couch.

"Samara gathered supporters—those who had lost family to invaders like herself—and led them across the land. She used her words to convince tribe leaders to put away their weapons and find common ground with each other. Her actions reflected those of one who held the unwavering belief that peace and unity was possible. This conviction was what helped Samara's own vision manifest. Not one she received from the higher powers or anyone else, but her own faith that she could unite this land."

"That was all it took? Self-belief?" Zahra asked. She, too, was under Ninaz's spell and felt the emotion behind her words.

"She had a *naya*," Ninaz replied, raising her brow. "And Seer powers, which may have helped sway a few people."

Elena stifled a laugh.

"Samara never wanted to be the one who killed unnecessarily," Ninaz continued. "She became a beacon of peace and hope with her ability to avoid bloodshed and calm even the fiercest warrior with her words and understanding. Her reputation preceded her. By the time she and her supporters reached the other side of the realm, Leneirans greeted her with joy and happiness. Our people were finally united under the banner she carried and named her queen of Leneira.

"Under Queen Samara, Leneira experienced an exponential growth in industry and progress. When she died a natural, peaceful death in her village, her *naya* dissolved into the earth where she was buried. She never married and never had children who could inherit the title and rule when she passed on. The people of the realm waited for the *naya* to rise again, to choose another worthy Leneiran to rule the realm, but it was never seen. When signs of unrest rose, the four most powerful tribal leaders of the time, with the assistance of the Divine Beings, divided the land amongst themselves to maintain the peace," Ninaz continued with a far-away look in her eyes. "When the borders of the realm were established, people with similar abilities banded together, although many argued for an equal division of magic. In time, the Elementals came together to create Terralea, the Empaths Sailon, Shifters created their hamlets in Skandor, and the Seers settled in the Isles of Minos."

Elena lifted her cup to her lips, thinking about how much she had yet to learn when Ninaz remarked, "You need to be like Queen Samara, my dear, and have more faith in yourself. You can absolutely be queen and sit on the council beside Tarrick. There are those who need you. You have proven yourself to the people of Erindell. They will support you."

"If I had Seer powers, I could convince the councilors that my rule is inevitable," Elena said half-jokingly. "Or a *naya* to choose me as a worthy queen." She laughed. "Do you know where I can find one of those?"

Zahra snorted into her tea.

"You don't need a *naya*," Ninaz retorted. "You're fighting a battle of wits and intelligence, aren't you?"

"I guess," Elena muttered, thinking back to the tedious superficial conversations that she didn't consider witty or intelligent.

"Those fossils on the council will try to block you every chance they can get," Ninaz sniffed disdainfully.

Elena grinned at the exaggeration. Given that some of the nobles were around 500 years old, they were only middle-aged by Leneiran standards.

"I'm still learning about Leneira's history and politics." Elena sighed. "Tarrick won't marry me until I'm ready, and that's the only way I can sit on the council. Besides, I guess I'd be a queen consort more than an active ruler," she said slowly, using the term she had come across in her history lessons. "I would be by his side for official events, but I don't think I would get a say in making decisions or be as involved as Lady Amaya was when King Arran ruled."

"Is that really what you want?" the older woman demanded. "To stand silently beside him? A pretty ornament hanging off his arm to be paraded around at his will?"

"No." She flushed and took a sip of tea to soothe the swirling pit of anxiety within her.

"Mother," Zahra chastised. "Don't get involved in Lady Elena and His Majesty's relationship."

"I wasn't." Ninaz huffed. "I just happen to have opinions."

"Which you're entitled to," her daughter sighed, "but you don't need to inflict them on everyone. Especially your future queen."

"Her actions today will affect our future too," Ninaz argued. Her face softened when she spoke to Elena. "My dear, let me be frank."

Elena sat up, wondering how much more frank the old woman could be, and braced herself for whatever Ninaz was planning to say next. She lifted her cup to her lips, trying to exude a calm she didn't feel.

"The king is in love," Ninaz told her. "Nothing against you, but he's thinking of you as his lover, not as his future queen." She lifted her cane once more, pointing it at Elena. "You need to learn the inner workings of the council *now*, by his side while everyone is still finding their place at the start of his reign. Earn their trust and faith in you before you have children."

Elena choked and spluttered on her tea.

Zahra thumped her on the back as she looked up with watery eyes.

"Our history has shown that you and Tarrick will not have a child with Elemental powers, given your different backgrounds," Ninaz said gently.

"So?" Elena asked incredulously. "Tarrick would still love our child even if they couldn't control the elements."

Elena used the word *if*, but the probability of their child inheriting Tarrick's powers were slim to none. The king had already explained how the non-magical Leneirans came to be when humans were brought to the realm eons before and served those with preternatural abilities. Their eventual coupling resulted in a hybrid generation that had the long lifespan of their Leneiran parent without inheriting their magical ability.

"I don't doubt that." Ninaz sipped her tea. "But you say there are those on the council who don't want you to be queen because you lack Elemental abilities?"

Elena nodded, feeling her stomach hollow as she recalled the words she had overheard behind the council chamber doors.

"Is that how you want your child to be treated?"

Elena froze.

"You have the opportunity to create a world where he or she will be accepted based on their character and intelligence," Ninaz advised. "Not their Elemental powers. Or lack thereof."

Elena sat in silence, her mind spinning from the barrage of information and Ninaz's bombshell. She barely registered Zahra berating her mother.

"Lady Elena!"

Elena blinked. The guard was waving her hands to get her attention.

"We should go," Zahra glanced out the window at the late-afternoon sun. She stood and collected the empty cups and saucers. Elena downed the last of her tea and helped her friend wash up.

"Thank you, Ninaz," Elena said to the woman, who stayed sitting in her seat, watching Elena thoughtfully and tapping on the table. "For the history lesson and songs."

"I'll visit again soon, Mother." Zahra bent down to kiss her mother's cheek. Ninaz patted her affectionately.

"Thank you, my dears, for letting this old woman rant and rave." Her eyes twinkled. "I look forward to your next visit," Ninaz said, hinting heavily that she wanted to hear Elena's update.

Elena vowed to speak with Tarrick that night about their future and her role in it.

The young women left and slowly made their way through the narrow, cobbled streets of Erindell back to the palace. When they reached the stretch of flagstones on the edge of the city, an idea flashed across Elena's mind, and she tugged on Zahra's arm.

"Do we have time to visit the Temple of the Divine Beings? Is it still open to visitors?"

Zahra grinned. "Didn't you get enough of a workout this morning?" She pointed up to the temple that sat atop the hill adjacent to the one where the palace was located. "See the stairs?"

Elena's gaze followed Zahra's outstretched arm, and her stomach dropped at the narrow stone stairs cut into the steep, rocky path.

"Didn't think so." The guard laughed.

"Is that the only way up?"

Zahra nodded. "Anyone can go at any time. *If* they're willing to climb those stairs."

Elena hesitated for a moment, but her curiosity won over. "Fine," she said determinedly. "Let's go."

Zahra raised her brows but said nothing as she led the way to the bottom of the path. Elena took a deep breath and slowly started the climb.

$$\sim 6 \sim$$

Tarrick was once again seated at the table in his bedroom, this time with his hand curled around a glass of whiskey he had been nursing for the past hour. He took another sip, relishing the burn that eased into a sweet honey flavor that coated his tongue.

A fresh pile of documents that required his attention perched precariously on his desk, however, he couldn't concentrate. It was almost time for dinner, and Elena hadn't returned. She had an inexplicably soothing presence and always calmed him down. He just wanted to be with her and forget about his shitty day with uncooperative nobles, if only for an hour. Tarrick was beginning to fear that he couldn't give her everything he wanted to with the number of obstacles before them.

"There you are!" His eyes lit up when Elena entered the room. "How was your day?"

Elena crossed the room and wrapped her arms around his neck. She planted a kiss on his cheek as he pulled her onto his lap, burying his face in her neck and kissing the sensitive spot beneath her ear. He smiled against her neck when she shuddered.

"I thought I told you no work in our bedroom," she reproached him, scowling at the documents spread out over the desk and the growing pile in the corner. She peered at the top of the pile, trying to decipher Leon's scrawl.

"I'm sorry," Tarrick murmured, not sounding sorry at all as he continued to trail soft kisses down her neck. He wound his arms around Elena, pinning her against him. She relaxed into his hold, and he squeezed her warm, soft body.

"I'm going to get rid of this desk," Elena grumbled.

"Okay," he agreed, grinning as she moaned when he nipped at her skin.

"How was the rest of your day?"

Tarrick paused. He knew he should tell her about the meeting and the men who opposed their relationship, the deadline, the possibility that he may only rule for a year, but it didn't feel right. Tarrick pulled back to meet her soft brown eyes and genuine curiosity to learn about his day.

"Not great," he finally admitted.

Elena reached out for the glass he had been holding moments before. She took a sip of the amber liquid and wrinkled her nose as it slid down her throat.

"Ditto," she said, making a face. "At least it wasn't just me. Was it the council meeting?"

"A few of the older council members want to resign," Tarrick said, careful to omit the reasons for their resignation.

To his surprise, Elena didn't react.

"I suppose it wouldn't hurt to have some fresh blood on the council," she said thoughtfully, tapping her finger against the glass.

Some of the tension Tarrick had been feeling dissipated, and his shoulders sagged with relief. He had already been thinking that when Lazar spouted his nonsense, but Elena saying it out loud was comforting.

"Have you thought about who you'd like to have on the council?" she asked.

"I have," Tarrick replied. "Leon is sending out invitations this week."

"How many want to resign?"

He paused.

"Tarrick?"

"Half."

Elena sucked in a breath. "That many?" she asked softly.

"Hey, it'll be okay." Tarrick tightened his hold on her, saying the words to convince himself as much as Elena.

"I didn't mean to make things difficult for you," she said, setting the glass down on the table with a sigh.

Tarrick furrowed his brow. "What are you talking about?"

Elena hesitated. "I know at least one of the lords doesn't think I can be queen." She held his gaze.

Tarrick's stomach dropped.

"How—?" he started to ask.

"I was walking past the council chambers this morning," she explained. "Whoever it is was talking loudly."

"What exactly did you hear?" Tarrick asked, his heart beating faster.

"Just that they don't think I can rule because I wasn't born here and I don't have Elemental powers," Elena shrugged, turning to the window to watch the sunset.

The golden light illuminated her tanned skin. Tarrick noted the light freckles that dotted her delicate nose and cheeks from working in the sun all summer. He brushed back her hair, catching the faint scent of the lavender shampoo she had used that morning. Her forehead creased with worry.

"Not all of them believe that," Tarrick said softly. "And I know you will make a great queen one day."

"My presence here is getting in the way of you ruling properly and causing division amongst your councilors," Elena said sadly. "My first thought was to leave."

"Elena, no!" Tarrick said, holding her tightly.

"Don't worry," Elena assured him with a small smile. "I visited Ninaz today, and she gave me some tough love and got me thinking about the kind of queen I'd like to be."

Tarrick made a mental note to personally thank the woman.

"...and then I went to the Temple of Divine Beings."

Tarrick tilted his head to the side. "Did it hurt?"

Elena grimaced. "I'll probably feel it tomorrow."

He let out a low chuckle. "How was it?"

Elena thought for a moment. "Enlightening. Inspiring."

"Oh?"

"Ninaz told me about *The Naya's Crossing*, and I wanted to learn more about Queen Samara," she told him.

"I remember learning about her in school," Tarrick said.

"She managed to unite the entire realm without magic." Elena sighed. "I feel like having a *naya* would help me out, but Ninaz was right."

Tarrick remained quiet and let Elena finish that thought. He rubbed soothing circles across her stomach with his thumb.

"I feel like I have a second chance at life here," Elena said slowly. "I messed up in the human realm."

"How?" Tarrick asked, not following.

"I let myself get caught up in a dream that wasn't my own," she admitted. "I wanted the corporate job in the big city, work my way up to the top, make my parents proud." She shook her head regretfully. "Along the way, I lost myself. I didn't realize it. I just thought I was burned out and put pressure on myself to keep up with everyone else until I lost sight of what was really important."

"What was that?" he asked gently.

"Family, community, being true to oneself," she replied. "After my parents died, I was forced to face the fact that I was lonely and had no purpose."

"I'm sure that wasn't true," Tarrick murmured, placing a soft kiss on her shoulder. "You had just gone through a horrific time and were processing."

"Perhaps." Elena shrugged. "I was lonely, and life was meaningless without them. But now, here with you and your family, I feel different. These past few weeks, as difficult as it's been for everyone, have given me purpose. I know what I want to do, and I want to make the most of this second chance at life." Elena took a deep breath and spoke words she had rehearsed. "I want to be a member of the council. I don't want to wait until we're married. That could be ages away, anyway, since we need the full council's permission. I don't want to be sitting around, doing nothing while we wait for the rest of the council to get here. There's no sign of the desert storms easing up, and there are issues that need to be resolved right now. Peace Summit agreements to uphold, alliances to strengthen ..."

"El—" Tarrick began, but she cut him off.

"I know you said we'll talk about getting married and me joining the council when I've learned more about Terralea and feel ready, but I want to join now," she told him. "While it's new and we're all learning together. I want to be by your side and help make decisions for the good of Terralea from the start, not in a hundred years"—Tarrick squeezed her lightly at the thought that they would have centuries together since they were bound to each other—"when Lord Malik and Lady Sofia and whoever else thinks I'm qualified to be a queen. Consider this a trial or internship," she said hopefully. "It makes sense anyway, doesn't it?"

A crease formed between Tarrick's brows as he considered her words. His heart beat faster at the thought of having her by his side, supporting him, challenging him when required, and working together to bring their vision for the country to life.

"When you think about it, you don't use your abilities in council meetings and in making decisions for the good of the country," she continued. "Elemental powers will not help me in the council chambers."

Tarrick studied her for a moment.

"Why?" he asked finally. "Why do you want to join the Council of Nobles of Terralea?"

"I want to help our people," Elena replied steadily. "I want every Terralean to feel valued and heard, to know they play a part in helping us flourish and live in a peaceful, safe country where they can thrive. I want to earn their trust and respect, and show them how I will serve them as their queen. "

Her eyes sparkled and cheeks flushed as she spoke. Tarrick realized with a jolt that it had been a long time since she was that passionate. They still had the chemistry and sparks when they made love, but outside the bedroom, he had only ever seen her that way a handful of times. Like when she had staggered back to the palace after spending all day in town and announced they were close to hitting another milestone in Erindell's recovery plan.

"My father and mother joined the police force, and I didn't understand how they willingly put their lives on the line every day." She broke Tarrick's gaze.

The sky was darkening, and torches were flaring to life in the garden below. "But Dad told me that every time he helped a person, no matter how small the job, it was fulfilling to know he and his team made one person's life better that day. It was all part of protecting and serving the community."

"I wish I could have met him," Tarrick murmured.

"I wanted to be just like them. They were my heroes, my world," Elena said sadly. "But I got caught up in the rat race and only ever thought about myself. I want to change that. I want to represent the people of Terralea. The real people, like Yas, Bri, and Ninaz, who deserve to have a voice at your table."

She held her breath, waiting for his response.

"We'll have to think of a way to ease you into it so everyone has time to adjust to the idea." Tarrick rubbed his chin thoughtfully. "But, speaking as your king, I'm interested in your ideas, and I like your passion."

Elena let out a long breath.

"Does that mean you'll have me on the council?" she whispered.

"I'd like that." The corner of Tarrick's lip tugged up. The hope shining in Elena's eyes was reflected in his heart. But she didn't know about the deadline—the cost if Tarrick failed to fill the remaining council seats with people who would be suitable for the roles and vote to keep his family in power after a year. His priority was to find three Terraleans who had a good grasp of politics and would be willing to be part of the Council of Nobles as soon as possible without deterring those who were still undecided.

By the end of the meeting, he'd had the unwavering support of Netta, Darius, Aiden, Leon, and Adina. Two other nobles—Rami and Eli—were undecided, but Leon and Darius had formulated a plan after the official meeting to persuade them to stay on. The lords had inclinations toward the conservative side, but they needed a balanced council of conservative and progressive nobles. That would be his brother and Darius's argument when they spoke with the lords—along with a few discreet perks and benefits, including permanent suites at the palace for their families and access to the royal estates around the country to seal the deal. Tarrick hoped that would be enough to convince Rami and Eli's wives to influence their husbands.

Malik had agreed to stay on the council, but his motives were still unclear. Leon and Darius suggested using Jet to find out what they could about the inscrutable lord, but Tarrick was hesitant to use such underhanded methods at the start of his reign. Besides, Malik was a powerful Elemental capable of shielding his thoughts from the Empath, highly influential, and experienced in politics. He would be a valuable asset, but could be an equally strong threat. Malik had also been a close friend of Arran's, and the last thing Tarrick wanted to do was dishonor his father's memory by playing the lord.

As he contemplated his options, happiness filled Tarrick as Elena spoke more animatedly about who she could persuade to support her petition to join the council and be an ally. His future queen barely noticed he hadn't been paying attention as she voiced strategies and outlined key points to support her arguments.

"El?"

"Yes?" She paused expectantly.

"Let's keep this plan to get you on the council between us"—Tarrick hesitated—"just for now, okay?"

Her smile waned slightly, but she nodded understandingly. "Sure."

Tarrick dropped a kiss onto her shoulder, and because he couldn't help himself, he moved a hand to the nape of Elena's neck and fused their mouths together in an all-consuming kiss. She parted her lips for him, and Tarrick could taste the lingering whiskey on her tongue as he slowly pulled up the hem of her dress, tantalizing her. His fingers trailed up her thighs, and he shoved her panties to the side, marveling that his future queen could truly be so amazing and that he had the privilege of giving her that pleasure.

Elena writhed against him when he teased her wet, aching pussy, the sound of her whimpers sending a bolt of lust straight to his cock. He slid a finger inside her, relishing the moan that she released into his mouth as her walls clamped around him. His thumb moved in slow circles around her clit, and she ground against his hand, desperate to feel more friction.

Tarrick plunged another finger into her and stroked that elusive sweet spot that made Elena throw her head back and cry out his name. His cock twitched in response to her breathless voice and the sensation of her fingers digging into the hard muscles of his shoulders.

"That's it, baby," Tarrick growled, thrusting his fingers in and out, feeling her pleasure build as he continued to rub her clit with his thumb. He might not have been able to marry her as soon as he would have liked, but he could give her that for the moment. "Come for me!"

Elena clawed at his back, her breaths coming out in quick, shallow puffs before she shuddered and shook for what felt like a blissful eternity before she relaxed against him. Tarrick held her limp body up as the last waves of her orgasm coursed through her. She wore a sated smile on her glowing face as he gently withdrew his fingers, kissing her softly, sweetly.

"I love you," he murmured.

"I love you too," she whispered, resting her forehead against his.

His heartbeat accelerated the way it always did when she said those words out loud to him.

~ 7 ~

"Have you drafted the invitations?" Tarrick murmured to Leon, sitting beside him at the end of the long table.

Elena leaned forward to hear the prince's reply. She sat on Tarrick's right, across the table from Leon. Laughter and amiable conversation echoed around the dining chamber. Elena had enjoyed the feasts and banquets during the Peace Summit when she was included in conversations with the Empaths and Tarrick's family, but dinners with all of the nobles and their families present every night were overwhelming. She longed for a quiet meal in their private dining chamber. Not to mention the opportunity to be an active participant in the discussions.

"Yes," Leon replied in a low voice.

The nobles continued talking and laughing with each other, not paying attention to the group at the end of the table. "You just need to sign them after dinner."

Everyone except for Tarrick, Leon, and Adina had forgotten about politics and were enjoying the lavish feast before them. The scent of spiced rice, grilled meats, hearty casseroles, and mounds of roasted vegetables filled the air while the drinks flowed freely. Kitchen staff ducked in and out of the room, clearing empty dishes, refilling water decanters in the blink of an eye, and catering to the whims of the nobles.

Further down the table, Malik and Lazar swirled their brandy snifters, enjoying their third round. They toasted to Lazar and the others who had resigned from the council that day. It was the outgoing nobles' final night at the palace; the dinner was, in part, a farewell extravaganza, and everyone indulged in food and drink.

Darius sat on Elena's right, but he was engrossed in conversation with Mari, who had abandoned the green salad that had been prepared especially for her. She sipped from her glass of white wine, her cheeks flushed, and raised a hand frequently, directing small puffs of air to cool her face.

Jet—the Empath from Sailon who had agreed to remain in Terralea as an ambassador—sat next to Leon. He ate serenely, savoring every bite, and was caught off guard when the prince placed a sudden kiss on his cheek. Elena smiled to herself; Adina had been right about Leon and Jet. The attraction had been there from the start of the Peace Summit, and she was glad it had blossomed during Jet's appointment in Terralea. She caught the stolen glances between him and the prince when she wasn't distracted by her own prince—now king.

"Did you include details about the titles and estates they would be awarded after accepting?" Tarrick continued questioning Leon, still donning his king persona in the company of his councilors.

"Yes."

"What about the allowances?"

"Increased by twenty percent like you said, with the promise of yearly bonuses."

"Good." Tarrick sat back, satisfied. "Hopefully, that's enough to entice them."

"Hopefully, we're done with this interrogation," Adina muttered, slicing a carrot and spearing it with her fork. She sat next to Jet and rarely contributed to the conversations at meal times anymore, choosing to eat quietly and leave as soon as the meal ended.

"You worry too much," Leon scoffed. "Mother has already said she would remain on both councils and continue to advise."

"I miss her," Elena said softly.

Adina gave her a crooked smile. "Me too. She'll be back soon."

"Who are you inviting?" Elena asked Tarrick.

"A few prominent Terraleans, lawyers, analysts, business experts," he replied, sipping his wine. "Lazar and the others who resigned have retired their entire families. Normally, when a noble resigns from the council, their son or daughter, whom they have trained and prepared for the position, takes over the role to minimize the disruption and make the change easier. Without legacies, we need to recruit Terraleans who have a good grasp of politics and can learn the job quickly."

A pregnant pause followed as Leon and Tarrick exchanged a silent conversation.

Elena frowned—they were keeping something from her. "And these people understand politics?" she asked.

Leon replied, "Better than most. The ones we're planning to contact are experienced in economics, managing private estates, and have had some dealings with Skandor and Sailon."

The tightness in Elena's chest eased, knowing that Tarrick had options for new councilors.

"I mentioned the deadline too, Tarrick," Leon added.

"Deadline?" Elena furrowed her brow.

"We will not rush anyone into making a decision." Tarrick glared at Leon. "Nor will we resort to underhanded means that influence their future choices."

"Noted." Leon flushed slightly and busied himself with cutting the meat on his plate.

Elena stared at the brothers. It was obvious the pair of them were keeping something from her. Tarrick reached for her hand and gave it a squeeze.

"So, how was your day, El?" Leon asked brightly, throwing her off guard with the abrupt change in subject. "Did you enjoy the ladies' luncheon? Was there any juicy gossip from the tea party?" He gave her a grin.

"It was fine," Elena replied, not wanting to admit she had only stayed for a short time.

When the last dinner plate was cleared, silver trays floated above the table and settled down gently. They carried tulip-shaped glasses filled with steaming mint tea and crystal bowls of sweets—the customary end to every meal at the palace. A few kitchen staff also returned, carrying plates with silver cloches. They placed the dishes gingerly along the table while people whispered to each other at the unexpected addition.

"What's this?" Leon raised a brow.

The cloches levitated and floated toward the staff, who had stepped back. They plucked the cloches from the air with disgruntled expressions on their faces.

"I arranged a treat for us tonight," Sofia announced, beaming at everyone. She sat in the middle of the table next to her husband, Malik, Rhea on her other side.

Darius leaned forward to inspect the pie that sat before him. "It's a bit early for pumpkins, isn't it?"

The deep orange custard filling peeked out between clouds of airy whipped cream piped onto the surface.

"It is, but I persuaded the cooks to speed up the ripening process so we could enjoy it tonight," Sofia said proudly, as though she had accomplished the feat herself.

"Is that even possible?" Jet asked Darius.

The lord nodded. "The cooks and gardeners would have spent a lot of time and energy expending their Elemental abilities to manipulate the soil and water levels to achieve in a few days what normally takes weeks."

"That's impressive," Jet said, helping himself to a slice.

Elena turned to Tarrick, but the king had a faraway look on his face. He wore a slight frown that indicated he was worried about something as he played with the cup of tea in front of him absent-mindedly. To appease the kitchen staff who had worked overtime, Elena accepted a slice of pie even though she was full to bursting.

"It's my family's recipe," Sofia continued to boast to anyone who would listen. "Marcel, the palace head chef, was *most* gratified when I gave it to him. He said my chef had told him about it."

"Probably because her chef complained about how much time it took to make in the middle of summer," Darius muttered.

Jet grinned at Elena while popping a forkful of pie in his mouth. She took a bite of the dessert.

"Oh, my god," Elena moaned softly before she could stop herself.

It was one of the most delicious desserts she'd ever tasted. The rich filling was sweet and laced with delicate spices that brought out the pumpkin flavor. In contrast, the crust was buttery, crunchy, and decadent.

The sound she emitted shook Tarrick out of his reverie. He nudged her with his foot and wore a roguish grin on his face as he watched her eat. Blushing, she lowered her head, trying to take small, delicate bites to show a sense of decorum by not having a foodgasm in public.

"How are you enjoying Terralea, Jet?" Darius asked the Empath.

"It has been interesting," he replied. "I have learned so much about Elemental abilities and life in your country."

"I imagine there's much for us to learn about Sailon." Darius chuckled. "I'm glad our international alliances are taking a step forward with action. It's always been contained to contracts and agreements on paper until now."

"I agree," Jet assented enthusiastically. "There's nothing like immersing yourself in a new culture to truly understand its people and way of life."

Elena paused mid-bite and studied Jet—she wondered if he had been able to immerse himself more than she had as a Leneiran and a native to the realm. As hard as she tried to fit it, the task felt impossible. The nobles, and even some Erindellians, still viewed her as an outsider despite the Terralean royal family's support.

"I have never been to Sailon, but it's a place I would love to visit," Darius admitted. "I must have read every book about your country by now."

"Are you hinting at an ambassador position in Sailon, Darius?" Leon teased.

"I'm always open to new experiences." The lord grinned.

"I won't lie, my Lord," Jet said, his smile fading slightly, "this job has its challenges."

Leon placed his hand over Jet's hand and squeezed in silent apology.

"Jet has faced some hostility," Leon explained. "People are nervous around him, but I'm grateful that he's staying and helping to protect us despite everything."

"We all are," Elena agreed.

"It all boils down to ignorance." Darius shook his head sadly. "After all this time, people still don't understand the nuances of our magic. They value it so highly they forget that a person's character is also important. My father faced opposition and challenges. He was not the most powerful Elemental. He only ever used his abilities for daily tasks, and people called him weak. But he was the smartest man I knew. He could weigh up the risks and probable outcomes of any scenario so accurately. He was on the late king's royal council, and King Arran trusted him implicitly."

"Lord Rokeby was a good man," Elena murmured. "It was an honor to have known him."

Darius gave her a sad smile.

The conversation made Elena feel guilty for only thinking about herself. Jet was always so cheerful and talkative, exclaiming over Terralea's quirks, that she assumed he adjusted quite easily. She considered the Empath one of her few friends in the palace, given his natural inclination to connect with everyone and their shared experiences. But Elena had been too wrapped up in her own troubles to consider that he was also facing hostility.

"Lord Darius," Sofia called out. "Did you enjoy the pie?"

"I did, Lady Sofia," Darius replied. "My compliments to both your chef and the palace for doing your region's most prized dish justice."

Leon snorted into his cup of tea.

"I have promised my daughter I will give her the recipe when she marries," Sofia said with a conspiratorial wink at the lord.

Darius stared at the noblewoman, lost for words.

Elena sucked in a sharp breath at the unorthodox hint of a proposal. Rhea's cheeks became blotchy red spots, and she looked like she wished a giant hole would appear in the ground and swallow her up. Elena looked back at Lady Sofia, unsure if she should step in and take the spotlight off Darius and Rhea.

Across from Elena, Leon's shoulders shook as he tried to hold in his laughter.

"How lucky for Lady Rhea's future husband," Darius stammered.

Sofia, oblivious to everyone's reaction, said to Rhea, "Why don't you go for a walk around the gardens with Lord Darius tomorrow morning, darling?"

Rhea mumbled something incoherently. Elena nudged Darius, and he shrugged helplessly.

"We're all going to be living here together for the foreseeable future." Sofia beamed. "We should get to know each other better. We're practically family now!"

It was Elena's turn to snort. That wasn't the attitude Sofia had taken when they were first introduced.

Tarrick stood, indicating the end of the meal.

"Let's go to my office and sign those papers, Leon," he said to his brother. "You can send them first thing tomorrow."

Leon stood and brushed the crumbs off his tunic.

"I'll come with you," Adina told her brothers. "I need Tarrick's signature on letters to the portal guards."

Tarrick gave Elena a soft smile. "I won't be long."

She returned the smile, albeit a little half-heartedly. Elena wished she could be part of the conversations with them. She hoped that would change once he announced that she would be joining the council. He leaned down to kiss her lightly before bidding the rest of his guests good night.

The nobles murmured their thanks to the king. Leon and Adina followed him out of the room. The shuffling of chairs being pulled out and the rustle of people standing up and stretching filled the space as others decided to turn in for the night.

"Shall I walk you to your room, Lady Elena?" Jet offered.

"Thank you, Jet," she replied gratefully.

"I'll walk you both out," Darius said hastily with a furtive glance down the table. Sofia was still seated, arguing quietly with her husband while Rhea played with the pieces of pie on her plate. Her face was still stained a bright pink from her earlier embarrassment.

Darius hustled Elena and Jet out of the room amidst their teasing him about his possible upcoming nuptials to Lady Rhea.

"Would you like me to talk to Tarrick about expediting your request to move to Sailon?" Elena chuckled, glad for the opportunity to speak to Darius and get to know him as a friend.

"What happened to being open to new experiences, my Lord?" Jet asked with a teasing lilt to his voice. "Surely marrying an eligible young lady such as Lady Rhea would count?"

"Lady Rhea is fine, but her mother is a nightmare," Darius muttered. He threw cautious looks over his shoulder every few steps as they walked down the torchlit corridors. "She was all over Leon a few years ago before he told her that he wasn't interested in anyone's daughter."

He hushed them as their laughter floated down the corridor. Elena continued teasing him mercilessly.

"Think of all the pumpkin pies you could have," she said with a wicked grin.

Darius gave her a withering look. "Tarrick would have to double my salary if I had to hire extra staff to ripen them in the off-season."

"Would be worth it if it meant marrying Lady Rhea," Jet said softly with a wink.

At that, Darius blushed. They reached the end of the hallway, where they parted ways. Elena and Jet made their way to the wing where the royal family's private apartments were located, and Darius headed toward the guest rooms.

"I'm so sorry, Jet," Elena said as they walked together. She tucked her hand in the crook of his arm. "I had no idea you were struggling here."

"It's alright, Lady Elena," he assured her. "I've faced worse hostilities in my own home country. It's an occupational hazard of having Empath abilities."

"It's still not fair to you." Elena sighed. "You've done nothing wrong. You're helping to protect us."

"His Majesty and Leon have done everything in their power to make me feel welcome and ensure my safety," Jet told her. "They check in with me every day to make sure the people I interact with cooperate."

"And do they cooperate?"

"For the most part." Jet shrugged. "Some more willingly than others, but it's actually been a good challenge for me."

He lowered his voice even though they were alone.

"It's allowed me to practice reading people without touching them." He leaned in closer to Elena. "I'm getting better at it, and can read emotions just by standing next to someone now. I don't need to touch them the way other Empaths do."

"That's amazing!" Elena exclaimed quietly.

Jet beamed. "Only our queen is capable of reading people on sight, and even she has to be standing quite close to them."

"She'll be so proud of you," Elena said, genuinely happy for him. "And your sister will be pleased that your abilities are becoming stronger now."

"Mika will be jealous." Jet smirked. "But it only works when people are open with me, and if the individual isn't hesitant or closed off to the reading. Like you, for example."

Elena tilted her head to the side, frowning slightly.

"You aren't afraid of me reading you," he explained, "so I can read your emotions and thoughts easily."

"I don't love the idea that you can read me," Elena admitted after a pause. "But in the six months I've known you, you haven't told anyone what I'm thinking. Leon told me about your strict code of honor."

Jet inclined his head. "You have my word. I won't reveal what you're thinking and feeling. But the nobles and some of the palace staff are on their guard, careful with their thoughts. Some of the nobles are also quite skilled at shielding, which I didn't realize, like Lord Malik."

"Does that put Tarrick at risk?" Elena asked in concern. "If someone who can shield their thoughts is plotting against him, would you know?"

"I'm confident that no one currently in the palace is plotting against His Majesty or the royal family," Jet replied.

Elena released a sigh of relief, but he continued.

"There are those His Majesty needs to watch, and I have alerted him to that."

Elena looked alarmed.

Jet patted her arm reassuringly. "Don't worry, His Highness is safe. I promise."

"That's all I can ask for, I suppose," she sighed.

They walked in silence.

"I don't suppose you know anything about the deadline Tarrick and Leon mentioned at dinner?" she asked slyly.

"Ah, Lady Elena." Jet sighed. "You just called me an honorable man. Besides, if there's something you want to know, you should probably ask His Majesty directly."

"I know," Elena grumbled, realizing she really needed to work on her issues about asking Tarrick for help. It had been a big step, voicing her desire to join the council before she was crowned queen, but Elena needed to follow through with setting up a clear plan to make it happen. "I suppose I should thank you. For everything you're doing for us."

"It's my pleasure." Jet's dark eyes twinkled. "And for the record, I don't know anything about the deadline."

~ 8 ~

Leon and Adina stood in silence before the king's desk as he signed the letters. Like his father, Tarrick was neat and methodical, with labeled piles of documents and missives stacked on the dark mahogany desk.

"Any updates about the assassin, Adina?" Tarrick asked as his stylus scratched the parchment. "We have a name and detailed description of his appearance, thanks to Elena."

"We're still searching," she replied. "I've alerted Lin and Halder and sent them the brief. He could be hiding along the borders."

"Agreed," Tarrick said. "Ask them to circulate the profile amongst their guards."

"Yes, Your Majesty," Adina said tentatively.

Tarrick noticed her hesitation and raised a brow.

"It's such a generic description," she said. "Are you sure Elena didn't miss any details? A birthmark, scar on his face ... Something that's more helpful and conclusive than what we've got? I've received reports of sightings, but every time our guards get close enough to the man, he either disappears, or it's someone who resembles him. We've released suspects as soon as they've proven they have Elemental powers, but it's hard to identify that on sight."

"He was holding a knife to her throat and threatening to kill her in Zanthus's office," Leon said drily. "Anyone else wouldn't have even registered the spots on his hands. El gave us a thorough description and report, if you ask me. Probably something she learned from her parents."

Awkward silence settled over the room as the king continued signing.

"Out with it, Leon." Tarrick signed the final letter with a flourish. "You've been fidgeting and shuffling your feet the entire time."

The prince hesitated before saying, "You should tell El about the meeting today, and the deadline."

Adina frowned at her brothers. "What deadline?"

"Leon has suggested we give it a year for El to prove to the council that she is qualified to be queen and sit at the table." Tarrick sighed, throwing down his stylus and rubbing his hands over tired eyes. "It bought us some time. We need to prioritize filling the empty seats. But if the new council doesn't approve of my marrying her, we're stuck. They also have a right to vote in a new family to rule the country because we are now recruiting council members based on merit and not inducting legacy family offspring like we've always done."

"What?" Adina exclaimed. "Is that even allowed?"

"I researched it after today's meeting to confirm," Leon said somberly. "It's how our family came into power. The king from the previous dynasty was a tyrant, and his entire council resigned. He threatened to kill anyone who opposed him, and the people fought back. After he was defeated in battle, the Terraleans voted in our great-great-great-grandfather to rule."

Adina stared at Tarrick, stunned. "But you're not a tyrant."

"Thanks. That's the nicest thing you've ever said to me."

"You need to tell Elena, Tarrick," Leon repeated. "She's part of the family now and deserves to know."

"She already knows some of it," he said heavily.

"She does?" Leon's eyes widened.

"She overheard Lazar this morning," the king explained. "At least, she heard the part where he said she was incapable of ruling and didn't approve of my marrying her."

Adina snorted. "It's a good thing he resigned, then."

Leon and Tarrick exchanged a look.

"What?" Adina demanded.

They filled her in on the reason Lazar and the other nobles resigned. By the end of the recap, Adina was spitting rage.

"Those pompous, arrogant—" she seethed.

"Settle down, little sis," Leon consoled her. "Tarrick and I have already made a plan to fill those empty seats."

Adina was unconvinced.

"El said this was a chance to get some fresh blood on the council," Tarrick said slowly.

"She's not wrong," Adina remarked. "Some of those men served our *grandfather*."

"She wants to join the council too," Tarrick told them.

"Yeah, that's a given." Leon waved a hand impatiently. "When she's queen, she'll be on both councils."

"No, she wants to join *now*," he clarified. "The council opposes our marriage because that would mean she joins the council by default. She thinks if she earns their trust as a councilor, they will support it."

Tarrick was met with silence.

"Is she ... ready?" Adina asked hesitantly.

"I believe so. She's more than proven herself over the last few months." Tarrick leaned forward and steepled his fingers in front of him. "Her joining now would technically qualify as the 'recruiting based on merit and character' angle I've been pushing for."

There was a pause as Leon and Adina considered his proposal.

"That could work," the prince said finally, "if someone other than the man who's sleeping with her seconded the vote."

Tarrick glared at his brother.

"What?" Leon held his hands up. "I'm just pointing out that it's a conflict of interest if you were to vote in favor of her joining. All of us" —he swept his hand out to indicate the three of them—

"would be considered biased for fairly obvious reasons. We need an impartial councilor to support her petition to join."

"I've told her to keep it between us while we try to recruit new council members and figure out where Rami and Eli stand," Tarrick explained.

"She's not stupid, Tarrick." Adina's frown deepened. "She'll work it out."

"What are you talking about?" Leon swiveled his head toward his sister.

"You're not going to tell the others about her joining now, are you?" Adina continued glaring at Tarrick. "At least, not until you've convinced Rami and Eli to stay and your other preferred candidates to join. You're keeping her as a last-minute stand-in because you know even Darius and Aiden will question her suitability for the role right now. You're trying to keep everyone happy. Leon may buy your story"—she jabbed her thumb in the prince's direction, who protested indignantly—"but I don't. And Elena will figure out that you're playing everyone to keep the peace. Will you actually take her advice if it goes against what your council decides? Will you get *her* to cast the deciding vote on things when there is an even split in opinions? And now that our family's legacy as Terralea's ruling family is also under threat, how are you going to handle the council's inevitable ultimatum?"

Tarrick squeezed his eyes shut. His sister was far too perceptive. Everything she said was true.

"It may work in the short term," Adina said, moving forward and gathering up the letters Tarrick had signed for her. "But at some point, you're going to have to make a choice between Elena and your duty to your country. And if you're not honest with her now, she'll leave. I know I would."

Adina strode out of the room and shut the door loudly as she left.

"Fuck," Leon swore.

"She's right," Tarrick groaned.

Leon chewed his lower lip. Tarrick massaged his temples, trying to think of a solution to the ever-growing list of problems he faced.

"What are you going to do?"

"I don't know. I was optimistic at the thought of having a new council."

"But?" Leon prompted.

"What if the potential councilors we contact decline because they see Elena as a threat too? Or, as Adina said, make me choose between being king or our entire family having to step aside because I want to marry Elena? I really thought those who knew about Rose would be able to move past it. They promised Father that what happened would have no impact when I took his place."

"The Terraleans we're contacting now don't know about Rose, and neither do the newer councilors," Leon pointed out. "Unless someone tells them. But the only people who know about her are the old hats who are leaving anyway."

Tarrick sighed. "I guess so. We need to have a balanced council to rule fairly," he said more to himself. "Otherwise, the people will accuse us of being biased and turn against us. Remember how Nasim could be an ass when he wanted to?"

"Yeah, I remember." Leon rubbed his face wearily. "But he's one of the few who's dealt directly with Skandorians through his import-export business and has a good head for numbers."

"Lidia is decent, though. Knows the law inside out."

"You're overthinking this," Leon said, shaking his head. "And you're putting too much faith in those around you and not enough in yourself."

"What do you mean?"

"You're the *king*, Tarrick," Leon said, massaging his temples with his fingers. "*You* rule the country. The council exists to keep you in check and stop you from becoming a dictator. You've watched Father rule your entire life. Even he had to set up a new council after the uprising, which he did successfully. Sure, he faced some opposition, but that comes with the job."

"You're right." Tarrick scrubbed a hand over his face.

"You do realize you can order Nasim and the others to join the council, don't you?" Leon smirked.

"I'm not about to force people into a job they don't want," Tarrick said firmly.

"They won't say 'no' outright, but they'll probably show some resistance when you need their support with marrying El, so that won't work," Leon said thoughtfully. "But it would be improper to refuse their king. You'll need to pander to their egos, flatter them, bestow them with favors before they agree."

"It's stupid," Tarrick muttered.

"It's how things are." Leon shrugged. "Why don't I invite them to the Harvest Feast? Your powers of persuasion are better in person. Although your dwindling charm needs work."

Tarrick glared at his brother. "Fine," he agreed. "But that doesn't solve the problem of keeping Elena away from this until we fill at least the majority of the empty seats."

"You should still tell her everything," the prince said gently.

"She considered leaving, Leon," Tarrick said, his voice breaking. His heart warred with his head, especially after their conversation that morning about being open and honest with each other. "She actually considered leaving because she thought her presence was causing conflict and division."

Leon sank into the chair in front of Tarrick's desk, rubbing his chin with a troubled expression. "But she's staying, right?"

Tarrick nodded. "Ninaz talked her out of it."

"Zahra's mother?"

"Yeah. Send her an invitation to the Harvest Feast too. I want to thank her in person."

"Of course," Leon said automatically.

"Apparently, Ninaz told her the story of *The Naya's Crossing*," Tarrick said. "And that convinced El to stay." He exhaled a shaky sigh at that. "I can't lose her, Leon."

"I understand," Leon said tightly. "But someone will let it slip. You know how those women talk. El will find out the whole truth one way or another. It will be better if it comes from you, even if it hurts."

"No," Tarrick said decidedly. "I'm taking her away for a few days. Just until we know where the potential candidates stand and their response to our invitation. Mother will be back by then, too, and we can all work on a plan together."

"But—" Leon started to object.

"Send this to Lin by the fastest messenger," Tarrick said, pulling a fresh sheet of paper toward him and picking up his stylus. "I'll take El to Sailon to get away from the palace politics and gossip."

"Is that the best idea, Tarrick?" Leon sighed. "Are you sure you want to leave at a time like this?"

"As Netta pointed out, we're at a standstill." Tarrick glanced up at Leon. "She, Darius, and Aiden are staying, so I'm not worried about them. You and Adina can use the time to find out where the others' heads are at and Malik's agenda. I have a feeling he's biding his time and going to drive a hard bargain later on."

"I didn't sign up to be your spy," Leon grumbled, but took the letter that Tarrick wrote to Lin, requesting he and Elena visit Sailon as soon as possible. "I'll send this now."

"Thank you." Tarrick leaned back in his chair and exhaled loudly.

"Don't worry, brother," the prince said softly as he moved to leave the room. "It'll all work out."

***

Elena's face broke into a sleepy smile when Tarrick entered their bedroom. She had kicked off her shoes and climbed into the large bed, still fully dressed and nestled against the fluffy pillows with a large tome. Her eyes had begun to shut of their own accord only a few chapters in, and she jolted awake several times. The torches and candles in the sconces dotted around the room were still brightly lit and danced merrily in the breeze.

"You said you wouldn't be long," Elena accused, snapping the book closed and hefting it to the side. She crawled over to the end of the bed and straightened to wrap her arms around Tarrick's neck.

"Sorry," he apologized, sliding his hands around her waist and kissing her. "It took longer than I expected."

"That's okay. You're here now," Elena said, stroking his cheekbone with her thumb. "You look exhausted."

"I feel exhausted," Tarrick said, resting his forehead against hers. "I need a break."

"A holiday would be nice," she agreed. "I'm thinking a beach, cocktails, massages ..."

Tarrick lifted his head. "What do you think about visiting Sailon?"

"Sure. When were you thinking? In a few months?" Elena cocked her head to the side.

"I've already written to Lin," he said, smiling at her. "I'm hoping we can go in a few days."

She straightened her head slowly with a worried expression.

"You're not excited," Tarrick said, running his fingers through her hair.

"Is now the best time to leave Terralea?" Elena asked. "You need to fill council seats, and with your mother away—"

"Something will always come up," Tarrick interrupted her. "And the council is at a standstill until those we've invited to fill those seats respond, and the desert storms calm down enough for the remaining councilors to travel. Leon and Adina can take care of anything that comes up, and we'll only be gone a few days."

Elena chewed on her bottom lip.

"Hey." Tarrick placed a finger under her chin and tilted it up. "What's wrong?"

"You're sure your absence won't compromise anything with the council?"

"Positive."

"I guess a few days away won't hurt," Elena said slowly.

Tarrick broke into a grin. "The hot springs are perfect this time of year. And I'm sure Lin would love to take you on a tour of the countryside on a *pihasi*."

Elena didn't need any more convincing. "Can we go now?"

"As soon as she replies." Tarrick laughed. He stepped back and started for the washroom. "I sent her a letter tonight. She should get it by tomorrow."

Elena bounced on the bed in excitement, sending the heavy book she had cast aside flying.

"What are you reading?" Tarrick asked, bending down to pick up the book.

"I'm trying to learn as much about Terralea as possible," Elena said, jumping onto the plush carpet and taking the book from him. "This is the shortest history book in the library since the country was first established."

She ambled to the desk by the window and placed it carefully amongst the piles of documents that covered the dark wood. The whiskey decanter on the desk reminded her of their earlier conversation.

"I forgot to tell you," she said, glancing over her shoulder. Tarrick had stripped off his tunic and was rummaging through his wardrobe for a clean shirt. "I read your father's song at the temple when I was there. It's right in front of the Sacred Pool."

He went still at Elena's words. The muscles along his back tensed. Although he wore a mask of indifference when people brought up Arran, Tarrick missed his father deeply, and hadn't allowed himself to grieve his death properly. He had thrown himself into the role of king the day after Arran's funeral and hadn't paused since.

She walked over to where he stood and slipped her arms around his waist. He relaxed slightly at her touch, but the tension in his shoulders lingered as she rested her cheek against his back.

"You should visit. It's beautiful."

"He and Mother composed it a few years ago when they talked about handing over the reins," Tarrick told her in a bland voice.

Elena didn't say anything. She held him tighter and planted a kiss on the taut skin between his shoulder blades. Tarrick placed a hand over hers, and he relaxed fully.

"Father used to take Leon and me to the temple before the Full Moon Festival every month," he said softly. "It was one of his favorite places in Terralea. He said it was where he felt most connected to the land and the people."

"I understand that," Elena murmured. "There were songs about ordinary people, not just kings and queens. And it was so peaceful. We can go together tomorrow if you want?"

"You'd take the stairs again?" She heard the smile in his voice.

"For you? I would."

Tarrick prised her hands apart and wriggled out of her hold. She stepped back, confused and slightly hurt.

"We'll see," he said gruffly and entered the washroom.

~ 9 ~

The morning sun pierced through the trees as Elena strolled along the back of the palace with a book in hand to find a quiet spot in the garden. As she walked past the kitchen service entrance, the door flew open, and she nearly collided with Rhea, who held several documents and looked happier than Elena had ever seen her.

"Lady Elena!" Rhea gasped in surprise. "My apologies."

"That's alright," Elena brushed away the apology. "What are you doing here, Lady Rhea?"

"Oh, I, uh ..." Rhea stammered, turning a bright red.

Elena eyed her curiously. Rhea normally trailed behind her mother and the gaggle of ladies.

"I came to apologize to the chef," she finally managed to say. A guilty expression took over her pretty face. "Mother doesn't really understand how much time it takes to ripen pumpkins for her pie when they're not in season. But Marcel was good about it."

Elena peered at the papers Rhea clutched in her hands.

"I, uh, offered to help him with the kitchen inventory and accounts to make up for the inconvenience." Rhea flushed a deeper red.

Elena studied the girl for a moment, noting the way she shifted on her feet and how her eyes darted nervously around the garden.

"I'm sure there's an empty office in the palace you can use," Elena offered. "For privacy."

Rhea stared at Elena in surprise. "Thank you," she blurted out.

"Why don't we take a walk?" Elena suggested. "Unless your mother needs you?"

"Oh, no." Rhea shook her head. "Mother is in the bathhouse with Lady Mari and Lady Helene. She won't miss me."

"Great!" Elena led the way down winding paths lined with full bushes and flowering beds. *Lyrabirds* swooped overhead, scattering bright feathers over the garden before disappearing into the trees. A few bright pink heads and rainbow hued feathers peeked out from shady nests as they walked past. Elena tilted her head up to the sky and savored the warmth of the sunshine kissing her face. She soaked in the trilling and chirping of *lyrabirds* calling to each other before continuing down the pebbled path.

"Do you like it here, Lady Elena?" Rhea asked softly.

"I love it," Elena said sincerely. "It feels like home in a way the human realm never did after I lost my parents. The Erindellians have been so welcoming, and open to teaching me about the history of the realm and sharing their stories with me. Obviously, Elemental powers still blow my mind," she added with a sheepish grin.

"Is it true the Divine Beings marked you?" Rhea asked, nodding down at Elena's wrist.

She held up her hand and twisted her wrist so the young lady could see the tattoo of a *lyrabird* inked in fine lines. "Yes," she replied. "After Tarrick took me to the temple and asked them to ... heal me."

Rhea examined the tattoo closely. "My grandmother used to say that those marked by the Divine Beings heralded change," she told Elena. "That they were the chosen ones."

Elena winced at the last part. "I'm not sure about being *chosen*. But change can be a good thing," she added cautiously, knowing that many Leneirans feared progress.

"Perhaps," Rhea said contemplatively. "We haven't had much luck in recent years."

Elena wondered if the girl spoke broadly or about something more personal. "Disruption in routine, good or bad, always requires adjusting and getting used to."

"There are a lot of disruptions happening at the moment," Rhea said with a faraway expression. "Yet, everything feels the same."

"Are there things you'd like to change?" Elena asked gently.

Rhea hesitated, then shook her head. "I'm a lucky girl. I have parents who love me and only want the best for me. I shouldn't complain."

"You can want things for yourself too," Elena pointed out. She paused in the middle of the path and turned to the girl. "What is it you really want?"

"Nothing." Rhea blushed. "I was speaking generally."

"Hypothetically, what would you change?" Elena asked, determined to keep the lady talking now that she had opened up a little.

Rhea gave her a long look before replying softly, "More freedom. More say in how we live our lives. More ... options."

Elena reached out and squeezed Rhea's free hand, surprising the young woman.

Rhea smiled shyly at her.

"I don't know if you know this," Elena told her, "but I'm pretty good friends with the king of Terralea." Rhea giggled. "If there's anything I can do to help you adjust to life at the palace, please let me know."

Rhea's smile widened, revealing dimples in her pale cheeks that Elena had never noticed before. Perhaps because Rhea had never smiled like that in her presence. "Thank you, Lady Elena. That's very kind of you."

They continued walking in comfortable silence. When they approached the palace training grounds, Elena had to blink several times to make sure she wasn't hallucinating. Rhea blushed and stared determinedly at the small pebbles that lined the path to the ring. Instead of guards training and the usual good-natured jockeying that filled the air during sparring sessions, Tarrick and Leon were fighting each other in hand-to-hand combat. Without their shirts on.

Of course, Elena had seen Tarrick without clothes on, but Leon was always impeccably dressed and put together, not a hair out of place. Sweat glistened on their tanned skin as they twisted, dodged, threw punches, and moved fluidly. They were faster than any of the guards. It was like watching a violent dance. Both brothers were nimble on their feet. Tarrick prowled around Leon, his muscles rippling as he held up his fists in a defensive pose, but his brother had a competitive edge, and struck out with sharp, precise punches that had Elena gasping.

She and Rhea moved to the edge of the training ring where Jet, Adina, Darius, and Zahra leaned on the rope encircling the space. They, too, were watching the scene intently.

"You're drooling," Darius teased when Elena and Rhea came up to them.

Rhea's face went bright red again, and she looked around desperately for something that wasn't a half-dressed member of the royal family. She mumbled greetings and curtsied before Adina, who welcomed her graciously.

"So is Jet," Elena retorted.

The Empath barely acknowledged the jibe. He was too engrossed in the fight, and Elena couldn't blame him. Leon had always been the cheerful, cheeky sibling who was busy scribbling in his notebooks and shuffling sheafs of papers and documents in his arms. She had assumed that he preferred books to physical activities, but in the training ring, he was a honed, lethal weapon.

They watched the brothers exchange blows and grapple with each other. Rhea peeked up every so often, alternating between reluctantly watching the royals and sneaking looks at Darius.

"Ten gold marks Tarrick wins." Darius grinned without taking his eyes off the king.

"No way," Zahra exclaimed, momentarily forgetting that she spoke to a noble. "Prince Leon's got an edge."

"You're on." Darius held his hand out to Zahra to shake on their wager. Adina snorted when Zahra eagerly shook on their deal.

Elena couldn't make a call on who she thought might win. Tarrick was bigger and stronger, but Leon was more cunning. Her breath caught several times when he feinted and nearly handed the king his ass. However, Tarrick dodged Leon's blows at the last second.

"You're slowing down in your old age, Tarrick!" the prince called out with a laugh.

"And you're as predictable as ever," the king scoffed.

At that retort, Leon dropped to the ground unexpectedly. He kicked out his leg and swiveled around sharply, tripping Tarrick, who landed on his back on the dusty ground.

Leon stood up and grinned down at his brother.

"How's that for predictable?" he announced, holding out a hand to him.

"You got lucky," Tarrick grumbled, clasping Leon's outstretched hand and pulling himself up.

They clapped each other on the back and headed to the audience at the side of the ring.

"You owe me ten gold marks, Lord Darius." Zahra smirked.

Darius groaned and cursed under his breath.

"You bet on us?" Leon asked when he and Tarrick drew near the group. "Rude."

"You were asking for it," Darius teased. "Showing off as usual."

"As usual?" Elena inquired. "This is the first time I've seen Leon fight."

The prince wiped a bead of sweat off his forehead smugly with the back of his arm. "You're welcome." He grinned at her before winking at Jet. The Empath blushed.

"You should have seen him in school." Darius shook his head. "He'd whip off his shirt at every opportunity and show off in front of the students. And teachers. As if he needed any more attention," he added with a snicker.

It was Tarrick and Adina's turn to roll their eyes.

"Enjoy the show?" Tarrick asked Elena in a low voice.

Her lips curled up. "Very much. I'd like Leon to teach me how to kick your ass."

Unfortunately, Darius and Leon heard her response and burst out laughing while Zahra bit back a smile. Adina chuckled quietly, watching the guards, who had emerged from the barracks near the ring and started going through their warm-up exercises.

Tarrick leaned forward in Elena's direction and picked up his tunic. "Been thinking about my ass?" he murmured. Elena swallowed hard as she inhaled his intoxicatingly masculine scent. Her lower abdomen contracted as he brushed against her, and it took every ounce of her being not to jump on him then and there.

"The element of surprise," Leon said loudly, interrupting Elena's fantasies.

"What?" She whipped her head around to him.

"You need the element of surprise when it comes to my brother." He grinned, pulling on his own tunic. Jet looked slightly disappointed when Leon's head popped through the collar. "Tarrick here does everything by the book."

Tarrick made a disgruntled sound but didn't disagree.

"And we've fought together enough times to know each other's strengths and weaknesses," Leon continued. "The real challenge is reading your opponent's tells and predicting their next move while dodging their blows."

Elena stared at Leon.

"Seriously, can I train with you?" she asked. "Sorry, Zahra," she added quickly to the guard, who gave her a reassuring smile.

Leon looked to Tarrick, who nodded brusquely.

"May I join these sessions, Your Highness?" Zahra asked with the appropriate level of deference, but Elena caught a wicked gleam in her eye.

"Sure." Leon's lips curled up. "It gets boring being the only one who beats Tarrick in combat."

Darius sniggered, and the king glared at his brother.

"I'm sure I can find you more accounts to audit and tax reports to check, if you're bored," he growled, and Leon held his hands up in surrender.

"Not bored at all, Your Majesty," Leon said, shaking his head. He ducked under the rope and started walking back to the palace. "See you tomorrow morning, El. At dawn!" he called back over his shoulder.

"Did he say dawn?" Elena groaned.

"Yep." Adina popped her mouth on the *p*. "Careful what you wish for. Leon can be ruthless when he trains."

"What have I signed up for?" she asked with a nervous laugh.

Grunts and heavy breathing filled the air as the royal guards moved through various training sequences. Elena was familiar with them, but Rhea stared open-mouthed at the display.

"I better go back and do some work," Tarrick sighed, copying his brother and ducking under the rope. "Jet, any updates?"

"No, Your Majesty." Jet shook his head. "But I should expect to hear back tomorrow, the day after at the latest."

"Tarrick, why don't you get Lady Rhea to work on the palace accounts?" Elena asked.

Rhea's head snapped around at the sound of her name, and Tarrick raised his brows.

"She's helping Marcel with the kitchen inventory," Elena explained. "And she's good with numbers."

"Is this something you'd be interested in, Lady Rhea?" Tarrick asked.

Elena was surprised when Rhea maintained eye contact. "If it would help, Your Majesty, I'd enjoy that very much. I used to do Father's accounts back home."

"Very well," Tarrick told her. "Come by my office in an hour and I'll show you what needs to be done."

He pulled on the tunic and pressed a chaste kiss to Elena's cheek. "I'll see you at dinner."

Elena admired the way his tunic and pants clung to his body as he walked away.

"Thank you, Lady Elena," Rhea said fervently.

"My pleasure." Elena smiled. "I hope this makes your stay here a bit more enjoyable."

"You'll be doing us a huge favor," Adina added. "Leon hates doing the accounts and puts it off for as long as he can."

"Not many people enjoy working with numbers," Rhea told her. "But I love it."

"Don't look too happy about it when he's around." Adina smirked. "He'll pile on more work for you to do."

~ 10 ~

Elena shivered in the thin fabric that made up her pants and shirt as she made her way to the training ring, squinting in the darkness. By the time she crossed the silent palace grounds, it had lightened enough that she could make out Zahra, Leon, and Jet's silhouettes in the middle of the largest ring. The air was still, but she could feel the energy radiating off Zahra as she neared the group.

"Good morning!" Leon greeted her cheerfully.

Thankfully, everyone was dressed in dark training gear, so she wouldn't be distracted by chiseled abs and muscles. "Nice to see you fully clothed for a change," Elena grumbled by way of greeting.

"Someone got up on the wrong side of the bed." His voice shook with laughter.

Elena threw her fist out, trying to catch him off guard, but he stopped her easily.

He wrapped his large hand around her balled up hand and held firm. "First rule: never strike in anger."

"I was told I could hit you without consequence," Elena said sarcastically. "As payback for making me leave my bed at this ungodly hour."

"You can try," Leon said, amused. "Let's warm up."

He put Elena and Jet through their paces with the standard warm-up routine that Elena was used to when training with Zahra. Once again, Zahra barely broke into a sweat as she jogged silently ahead of them.

"How did he bribe you to be here so early?" she asked Jet as they finished sprinting their final lap around the ring, each stride pushing their legs to the edge of exhaustion. Elena shook her head, remembering the way Jet had ogled his lover the previous day. "You know what? Never mind."

Sweat dripped from every pore as the group transitioned into brutal calisthenics—burpees that left their chests heaving, push-ups performed on knuckles that scraped the rough ground, and lunges so deep they felt the stretch tearing through their thigh muscles.

Elena had witnessed Jet fight against Zanthus's men. He was one of Lin's best warriors. The fact that he was breathing heavily meant that Leon was putting them all through an intense training routine.

"Let's move it," Leon called out from the center of the ring. "Time to do some real work." He rubbed his hands together glee-fully. The pale light of dawn had grown brighter, and they could observe his footwork and movements.

He started off by demonstrating basic punches and jabs with Zahra, who executed the correct techniques. He made them practice over and over again, standing next to Elena and guiding her arms so she could feel the way her arms and torso moved. Unlike Zahra, who stood at a respectful distance during their training sessions and corrected Elena's posture verbally, Leon placed his hands on Elena and Jet's waists and guided their movements slowly until he was satisfied with their technique.

"Alright, El," he beckoned her forward. "Let's see it in action."

They started sparring slowly while Jet and Zahra paired up and did the same. Just as she did with Elena, the guard patiently showed Jet the correct way of moving and preparing to attack his opponent.

Elena could already feel the difference in how her body reacted to Leon's attacks. The only problem was trying to remember his instructions, which, even at his slowed down pace, were faster than she was used to. Elena focused on keeping her core tight, her feet apart for balance, exhaling with the right movement, hands in front of her face—not so high that she couldn't see him move—bouncing on her toes so she was always ready for his attacks. All while trying to block any incoming strikes.

"Oof!" Elena stumbled back as his fist caught her square in the diaphragm. "That hurt!" She glared, rubbing the spot between her ribs and stomach. There would definitely be a bruise.

"Did you notice the way I led with my left foot?" he asked, demonstrating the strike again, but much slower.

"I was a bit distracted by your fists," she replied drily.

"Keep your eyes moving," Leon instructed. "You know my fist is coming, so watch my feet and hips to anticipate which arm I'll be using, then step in the opposite direction." Elena observed his left foot, placed slightly forward and his hips angled to the right. She should have moved to her left to avoid his punch.

They practiced the sequence several times, Elena's eyes roving to note his movements. After a few more attacks, she finally managed to dodge a blow.

"Great!" Leon smiled. "Now try with Jet."

Elena and Jet were cautious with each other at first, but with Leon encouraging and instructing from the side, their steps quickened. Soon, they were both dancing around the ring and attacking each other, managing to avoid the other's punches and strikes.

Leon showed them how to take advantage of their opponent's momentary distraction to strike them where it hurt the most. The sun had risen fully, and Elena wiped away the sweat rolling down her face with the back of her hand as she copied Leon's moves. Her favorite move of the morning was when he showed them how to feint to create a distraction and throw their opponent off balance. She watched him carefully spin and swivel at the last minute, marveling at the way he seamlessly changed direction. He knocked Zahra down before she could dodge his outstretched leg.

"That's amazing!" Elena exclaimed.

Leon grinned as he helped Zahra back up. "It's come in handy plenty of times."

"We need to practice that one," Jet said eagerly to Elena.

"We'll train again tomorrow morning," Leon assured them, leading the way to the water station. "We should head back to the palace. Otherwise, Tarrick will make me go through the accounts," he said, wrinkling his nose.

***

The small room was quiet as Elena raised her head from the tome in front of her. Rhea's stylus scratched the parchment as she worked methodically through the accounts that Tarrick had assigned her. Occasionally, the young woman hummed a little tune to break the silence. Her dimples made more frequent appearances that morning.

The women had transformed the empty room into their own workspace. It was a few doors down the hall from Tarrick, Adina, and Leon's offices. The majority of the space was taken up by a wooden table that was long enough for Rhea to spread out her papers and Elena to sit across from her and read.

A tea service laden with sandwiches and pastries sat on the small table under the open window. The teapot emitted a steady flow of steam, Rhea glancing at it every so often to keep the water warm. Elena stretched her aching legs under the table, wishing she could muster up the will to drag herself to the window and make herself a cup of tea. An old couch was pushed against the back wall—it was tempting to sink into and take a nap on after Leon's grueling training session that morning.

Sunlight filtered through the windows, casting a glow around Rhea's copper strands and giving the illusion of a halo around her head. Her curls bobbed every time she cross-checked figures on the documents laid out before her and consulted her notes. Elena's heart was lighter as she watched Rhea work—it felt good to help someone find their purpose. She knew the feeling of being aimless and lost all too well.

Rhea wrote down figures and notes in her neat, flowery script in a ledger. She occasionally referred to a book that lay open next to her and scribbled down calculations on a scrap piece of paper. Elena had flipped through the book when Rhea brought it in, and her head immediately hurt from the numbers, symbols, and formulas littering the pages—something that hadn't changed since her high school math class.

Elena sighed and clutched her hair as she pored over the heavy text. "I can't get my head around how Leneirans got their powers."

Rhea raised her head, revealing the dimples once more. "History was my worst subject," she said, the smile turning into a grimace as she caught sight of the book Elena had been reading. "I can't believe you read half that book in three days." She shook her head in disbelief. "It took us nearly five years to get through it at school."

"It's not big enough," Elena grumbled.

"Would you like me to tell you Leneira's creation story?" The corner of the young lady's lip quirked up.

"Yes!"

Rhea tapped her chin with her stylus. "There are many theories about how the first Leneirans came to be in the realm."

"Did they come with powers?"

"No one knows," Rhea said thoughtfully. "I believe there are philosophers on the Isles of Minos who have dedicated their lives to researching our origins, referencing philosophy, songs, and written records."

"Well, why do some Leneirans have extra powers, like Tarrick and Adina?" Elena frowned at the tiny letters in the book.

"That's also a mystery." Rhea shrugged. "We accept that they are blessed with extra powers because the Divine Beings have foreseen their future and how they will shape the realm. That's why they are elected to rule the country."

"Is Tarrick considered a Shifter?" Elena sifted through the pages. "Do other Leneirans have crossover powers?"

"There are two schools of thought about the instance of Leneirans with different abilities mating. One theory is that they will produce offspring with hybrid powers. The other is that their offspring will have no powers at all." Rhea furrowed her brow. "I've never heard of a Leneiran with dual powers. I suppose people are too afraid of the latter. Technically, I suppose His Majesty would be considered a Shifter, but the Skandorians would never claim him as one of theirs as they only Shift into wolves."

"Because he Shifts into a jaguar?"

Rhea nodded. "And not a common jaguar—his impenetrable skin and metal claws are otherworldly."

"I see," Elena said, rustling through the pages. "I'm trying to learn as much about Terralea as possible," she explained, "so that when Tarrick's council is established, I know what I'm talking about."

"There is a lot to get through," Rhea said sympathetically. "But are you expected to know about our origins?"

"Not really," Elena replied. "I find all your powers fascinating. Well, they're more interesting than all your battles and wars."

Rhea let out a laugh. "What part are you up to?" she asked, leaning over to squint at the book.

"After the battle between King Hamid and the people of Terralea that ended his reign of tyranny, Kilam, one of the heads of a prominent Terralean tribe who fought in the campaign against Hamid, gathered all citizens in the market square of Erindell and announced that they would

hold a vote. The people rejoiced, for after centuries of being oppressed and subjected to King Hamid's rule, they were finally free." Elena looked up from the passage she read aloud.

"Kilam was my ancestor," Rhea said absent-mindedly. "Our families have had close ties to the Terralean kings and queens ever since that battle."

Elena continued reading, slightly in awe of Rhea's lineage and the powerful Terralean she was a descendant of. "*The vote took place thirty days after the battle ended, with the majority of votes in favor of Cassius, a powerful Elemental who was blessed with the additional ability to cast a shield around himself and those in the vicinity. It was his shielding abilities and Kilam's strategy that led the people to victory.*"

"That was a turning point in our history." Rhea twirled the stylus between her fingers as she spoke. "It was the first time the people of Terralea were able to vote and experience democracy in action, and they embraced the concept. It was a relief to be able to voice their opinions and choose a leader after such tyranny."

"But not true democracy," Elena corrected her. "Because King Cassius was Tarricks's ancestor, right?" she asked, flipping ahead a few pages. "The title was passed down through generations. When Cassius was elected king, it was the only time the people of Terralea voted."

Rhea's copper curls bobbed. "All of Cassius's descendents have been blessed with extra abilities. His Majesty's family has ruled the longest because they are the most powerful Elementals." She paused before adding, "According to Father, we are the second most powerful family in Terralea, although we don't have the additional powers like His Majesty and Princess Adina."

"Making half this book about both your families," Elena said, noting the names that cropped up as she continued turning the pages. "There's not much about King Arran in here," she said, slowing down her perusal toward the end of the hefty book.

"The next volume will probably cover his reign," Rhea noted. "Although, it wouldn't surprise me if they wrote a separate book about him. He was the first king who maintained peace in Terralea for as long as he did."

"He was a great man."

"His Majesty must feel immense pressure following in the late king's footsteps," Rhea said softly. "I hope he stays in power. The people respect him, and he will be a good king."

"Why wouldn't he stay in power?" Elena's head snapped up, brows drawn together.

"Because the council is changing the way they recruit new members, and the king is held to the same law," Rhea said, slightly confused at Elena's reaction. "The council can't make any decisions or action any policies without all members of the Council of Nobles voting. Since many legacy families are retiring, His Majesty has suggested recruiting civilians based on their experience and suitability to fill the roles. Once that's done, the council then has the opportunity to vote on whether they want the current ruling family to stay in power or elect a new one."

Elena's chest constricted as she tried to recall the conversation she'd had with Tarrick about the council.

"Didn't he tell you?" Rhea asked, shifting uncomfortably.

Elena shook her head dumbly.

"I believe Prince Leon suggested giving it a year, given the desert storms and, um, other factors delaying the usual process," Rhea said warily.

The blood drained from Elena's face as she stood on shaking legs and picked up the history book. She realized *that* must have been the deadline Leon mentioned at dinner the other night.

I need to see Tarrick. Elena stumbled across the room and fumbled with the door handle.

~ 11 ~

Tarrick leaned back in his chair and released a sigh of relief. Finally, something was going his way. There was a knock on the door. Before he could say anything, it flew open, and Elena marched in.

"Lin has replied," Tarrick said, waving the letter he had been reading in the air. "We can leave for Sailon tomorrow!"

He paused as he took in Elena's blazing eyes when she stood in the middle of his office. She had a white-knuckled grip on the heavy history book that she'd had her nose buried in for the past few days.

He rose to his feet alarmed. "What's wro—?"

"Why didn't you tell me about the new recruitment process for councilors?" she demanded. "And the fact that your council has the right to vote you off the throne?"

Before Tarrick could respond, the door opened again, and Leon's voice cut through the room.

"Your Majesties," he said as he strolled in and stood next to Elena, assessing her. "I came to see if El was still able to walk after this morning." He winked at her, oblivious to the tension in the room.

"Leon," Tarrick growled.

"What did I do?" His brother wore an alarmed expression.

"Did you tell Elena about the deadline and conditions?"

"No!" Leon exclaimed, swiveling toward Elena.

The anger radiated off her in waves.

"You knew?" she choked out.

"I'm the royal advisor," Leon said, slightly bemused. "It's my business to know."

"Let me rephrase." Elena narrowed her eyes. "You knew *and didn't tell me?*"

The door opened yet again, and Adina's head poked in. She wore an irate expression. "What's going on here? I'm trying to work."

Tarrick rubbed his face with his hands and let out a frustrated snarl.

"Elena found out about the new council recruitment process and … consequences," Leon explained with a wince.

Adina stepped into the office, shutting the door carefully behind her.

"How did you find out?" she asked in a gentle tone.

"You knew too?" Elena's expression went from anger to hurt.

The princess's cheeks flushed, and she hung her head.

I thought we were friends. Elena breathed heavily, blinking back tears.

"Leon, Adina, I'd like to speak to Elena in private," Tarrick said, massaging his temples.

"Apparently, a democratic voting process was how your family came to rule Terralea in the first place," Elena said, shoving the book into Leon's chest. He let out a soft grunt when the tome made impact, but Elena ignored him as she moved around the carved wooden desk. She clenched her fists. "Rhea told me your new council recruitment process extends to the king and his family."

"I wondered where this book went," Leon muttered, flipping through the pages.

Adina grabbed his arm and dragged him out of the room. She shot Tarrick a sympathetic look before closing the door. He had a feeling they wouldn't go far.

"El, I can explain—" he began.

"Explain what, Tarrick?" Elena choked out, fighting back the tears that threatened to spill over. "Explain why you don't tell me what's really going on? Why you downplay a significant moment in your life? Why the council legacy members are *really* retiring? It's because of me, isn't it? You're not going down this path because you want to. You have no choice but to recruit civilians and, in turn, risk your throne *and* your family's legacy."

Tarrick moved around the desk and reached for Elena, but she shrugged him off and stepped back, putting more distance between them.

"I'm so sorry," the king whispered, wishing he could hold her.

"If you don't respect me enough to tell me the truth and what's really going on, how can I earn the nobles' respect? Their trust?" she asked, fisting her hands by her side, shaking her head sadly.

"I was trying to protect you," Tarrick admitted, running his fingers through his hair. "You don't deserve their harsh words and judgment."

"I don't care about popularity contests, Tarrick," Elena said. "I'm just asking for a chance to earn my place by your side. You promised we'd do this together, but every time we speak, it feels like you're keeping something from me. *You're* the one who said you wanted open and honest communication between us."

Tarrick bit his lower lip, berating himself for letting things go so far. He should have told Elena everything, but the fear that she would leave weighed on him. It was easier to tell himself he was protecting her by waiting for the right moment to soften the blow.

"You still haven't told me the price you paid the Divine Beings to bring me back," she continued.

Tarrick's lips flattened into a thin line, and his jaw tightened.

"I didn't want you to leave," he said after a pause, choosing to tell her half the truth. "When you told me you wanted to after what Lazar said ... it-it scared me. I couldn't bear the thought of that."

"I thought it would be better if I left so you didn't lose your councilors and turn everyone against you and your family." Elena sighed. "Not because I was hurt or upset by his words. I know there are still people out there who are afraid of humans. But I'm doing my best to change that perception—it's just taking longer than I expected. And now you're at risk of losing your position as king of Terralea while I do what I can to convince people I'm not like Rose or non-magical Leneirans."

"I know," Tarrick said, stepping closer to Elena. But she moved back.

"Lately, it feels like nothing I do is helping anyone," she said sadly. "The Erindellians are back to normal. The nobles' wives have their routine and know their place in this realm, and your councilors play their part to keep the country running. I honestly believed that when you said we would work together, you meant it," she told him.

Tarrick shifted uncomfortably, and his stomach hollowed as she held his gaze before spinning on her heel and walking toward the door.

"Where are you going?" he asked, reaching out to grab her. She dodged him and continued with her head held high. "Where are you going, El?" he repeated.

"To town, to find something special for Lin," she snapped.

The door closed with a loud bang.

Tarrick cursed as he walked back around his desk and sank into his chair. He pressed his face into his palms, thinking about how he could fix the mess with Elena.

For the fourth time that morning, there was a knock at his door.

"Enter!" he bit out, not in the mood for Leon or Adina's chastising.

"Your Majesty!" Malik entered, holding a sheaf of papers.

"Lord Malik." Tarrick straightened in his seat and greeted him stiffly. He gestured toward the chair in front of his desk.

Malik lowered himself into the chair and made himself comfortable, fussing with his heavy brocade tunic and stroking his graying beard. He voiced pleasantries and commented on the weather, all of which Tarrick tuned out as he waited for the lord to get to the point.

"I think this hiatus is a good opportunity for us to review potential candidates to fill the empty seats on the council," he said pompously. The heavy jeweled rings that adorned his fingers glinted as he rustled through the documents in his hands. "I understand you have already sent invitations to a few Terraleans, but I have compiled a list of peers who might be interested in the roles. I think you'll find that they are, ah, aligned with our views."

"And what are your views, Lord Malik?" Tarrick asked in a tired voice. "So far, you have not voiced your opinions like the others."

"Your Majesty," Malik exclaimed. "Am I not supporting you? Helping you maintain your rule?"

"You are." Tarrick kept his expression neutral.

"I will serve you as I served your father. To honor his memory and legacy," Malik continued. He dropped his notes on the table and leaned forward, resting his elbows on the surface and clasping his hands together. "You have the makings of a great king, and I am on your side."

Tarrick raised an eyebrow and drummed his fingers on the table. Despite his vacillating tendencies in the council chambers, Malik was sincere in his loyalty to Tarrick's family. "What if I told you that Lady Elena wishes to join the Council of Nobles? Before she is crowned queen?"

"Ah." Malik nodded. "Understandable that she would want to do so, Your Majesty. But might I suggest we approach her with caution?"

"She is not a wild animal who will attack," Tarrick said sharply. "You will show her the same respect you show me."

"Of course, Majesty," Malik murmured, turning a deep shade of red. "My apologies."

"She wants to join the council, which will happen when she becomes the queen." Tarrick steepled his fingers and watched the lord's reaction carefully as he spoke. "Why wait decades for the inevitable when there are positions to be filled now?"

"I admire her ambition," Malik said after a pause. "But, with all due respect, I don't think that's the best course of action."

Tarrick eyed the man, torn between relief that he was finally getting the truth out of him and despair that yet another noble was suspicious of Elena.

"I'm not saying get rid of her," Malik said, holding his gaze. Tarrick started at that, but the lord continued, "I'm just saying don't make her such a prominent part of your life. Your people need to know that their king values them over a single woman. Terraleans want a king who is connected to them, understands them, and shows an interest in them."

"Have I not been doing that?" Tarrick asked drily. "Has Elena not spent the past six months doing that?"

Malik flushed. "Of course you have, and so has she."

"But?"

"There are other ways of showing them your intentions," Malik said hesitantly.

"Such as?"

"Your Majesty." Malik sighed and stroked his graying beard. "If I may be frank, you won't win any favors with Lady Elena by your side. She has no ties to our realm, no roots, no real connection. Those who remember the events preceding the uprising are wary of her, and rightly so."

Tarrick felt his patience waning. "Lord Malik, you came here with a purpose. Please tell me what it is I need to do to show the people that I value them."

"Would Your Majesty consider courting Lord Hanan's daughter, Leila?"

Tarrick blinked several times, unsure he had heard Malik correctly.

"She is a bright woman, and very beautiful, I'm told," Malik said in a rush. "Lord Hanan is deeply respected in his region and would consider it the utmost honor if you were to convey your interest in his daughter."

"You're joking, right?" Tarrick prayed fervently that it was a prank. That Leon was behind it in some asinine attempt to cheer him up.

"Not at all!" Malik puffed up indignantly. "Lord Hanan would withdraw his resignation from the council in a heartbeat if you agreed to marry his daughter. His region supplies Terralea with wheat and grain. He is an essential member of the council, and you would have the council's support to marry her next week, if you so desired. We needn't wait a year for you to fill the current empty positions and plead your case to the new councilors. Your family's position as Terralea's ruling family will be secure."

"He *was* an essential member of the council," Tarrick said faintly, still trying to process Lord Malik's proposition. The line of thinking was absurd. The king wondered if it was Malik's own idea or if he was the spokesperson for the councilors plotting behind his back. "He can and will be replaced by another Terralean who can manage the lands and attend to council duties as he did."

"But—"

"Lord Malik," Tarrick interrupted loudly, shoving aside his swirling thoughts to stop the lord from saying something they both might regret. "I will not cast aside Elena, who I love very much, for an ex-councilman's daughter in an attempt to lure him back to a position he doesn't want."

"I'm not saying you should forsake Lady Elena." Malik waved an impatient hand. "Keep her as your mistress, if you want. Leila will be your wife and appear with you in public. What you do behind closed doors will be your business."

The frown on Tarrick's face deepened, and a muscle twitched in his jaw at the suggestion he keep Elena as his mistress. Tense silence filled the room, and Malik shifted in his seat warily. He must have realized that he had crossed a line because he offered an uneasy smile and cleared his throat to fill the silence.

"Lord Malik, for my father's sake, I will pretend you did not just say that," Tarrick finally said slowly through gritted teeth. "I will put this entire conversation down to a temporary lapse in judgment and forget it ever took place."

Malik's expression became one of regret, and he rubbed his beard awkwardly again, realizing too late that he had overstepped.

"If Elena wanted Elemental abilities, she would have sided with Zanthus." Tarrick glared at the noble in front of him. "I understand why you might question my judgment"—Malik started to protest, but Tarrick held up a hand to silence him as he continued—"but you are now questioning the judgment of my family, including my late father, who welcomed Elena with open arms once we established that she had no ill intent."

"Majesty, it is not I who you need to convince." Malik shook his head.

"No?"

"I trust you implicitly," Malik implored.

"Do you?"

"Of course! It is the others who—"

"Then why haven't you spent time getting to know Elena?" Tarrick fired back, tired of the charade and trying to remain diplomatic. The time for subtlety was over; he was going to have to call out Malik's behavior. "Lord Darius and Lord Aiden have made an effort with her. Lady Netta always speaks highly of her. The people of Erindell trust her. In time, the rest of Terralea will also come to love her."

Malik's face started to turn red with shame.

"You and your wife have made no attempts to be friendly with the woman who saved us all. Need I remind you, were it not for her, you would have been forced to serve Zanthus or killed by his hand?"

The lord mumbled incoherently under his breath.

"I will contact these Terraleans you have recommended," Tarrick said, pulling the documents with the list of names toward him and scanning it. "Your efforts in this matter are appreciated."

"Yes, Your Majesty." Malik smoothened his expression and plastered a benign smile on his face. "If there is anything else I can do to assis—"

"You're dismissed," Tarrick said curtly, holding up the pieces of paper, pretending to read them intently.

Malik rose to his feet and gave Tarrick a short bow before slinking to the door.

"It would serve you well to dance with Lady Elena at the Harvest Feast, Lord Malik," Tarrick said, glancing up at the noble. He hated that he had to resort to issuing commands to his councilors, but they hadn't responded to his collaborative approach. "Just some friendly advice," he added, trying to soften the directive.

Malik held the doorknob, hesitating for a moment before giving a sharp nod.

When the door closed once more, Tarrick flung the papers onto his desk and took several deep breaths. His rage fueled the urge to shift into his jaguar form. To tear into the next person who entered his office. The lethal claws beneath his knuckles fought to spring free. His body shuddered as he battled against his primal instinct to protect the woman he loved.

When the shuddering stopped and his breathing slowed, he scrubbed a hand over his face, ashamed of nearly losing control. It had been decades since that had happened. He called out to the empty room, "You can come out now, Adina. And Leon, if he's with you."

The fireplace behind Tarrick creaked and shifted before slowly swinging forward. Adina and Leon shuffled out from the hidden passage and stood in front of Tarrick with sheepish expressions on their faces.

Leon voiced what they were all thinking. "Well, fuck!"

~ 12 ~

Elena sat at a small wrought iron table opposite Ninaz in a shaded corner of Erindell's market square. It was home to Bri's tea cart, *Guiltea Pleasures*, and Yasmina's coffee shop, *Meant To Bean*. She sipped on a cup of herbal tea that refilled itself every time Bri, the owner of the popular tea cart, glided past. The walk into town had given Elena time to calm down and think things through. She understood Tarrick's desire to protect her from his council's suspicions and harsh words, but she wanted the chance to earn their respect on her own. From the outset, Elena knew she would face opposition—she just didn't want it to be for the wrong reasons.

"You did very well standing up for yourself," Ninaz said over the rim of her coffee cup. The older woman had come across Elena and joined her. Ninaz had used her Elemental abilities to coax the sapling climbing the wall beside their table into a shady canopy overhead to protect them from the sun. It had inspired others sitting around them to do the same, transforming the corner of the square into a whimsical scene.

The lush dark leaves attracted *lyrabirds* and more Erindellians to seek respite at *Meant To Bean*. Excited children giggled and squealed at the sight of colorful flowers blossoming in the greenery. They held up their small hands and wore expressions of concentration as they urged small, pale flowers to grow among the leaves with their parents' encouragement and guidance. Soon, the air was filled with the scent of jasmine that mingled with the freshly roasted coffee grounds from inside Yas's shop.

The vivid colors of the market square stalls and the scents of pastries, freshly baked bread, and the newly blossomed flowers helped Elena forget about the earlier argument and forced herself to pay attention to her surroundings. She let the buzz of chatter and laughter from the townspeople wash over her. As Elena exhaled, she focused on the warmth of the dappled sun filtering through the gaps in the leafy canopy on her bare arms and face. She reminded herself that she had survived all of her bad days thus far.

"You were right," Elena said, shaking her head. "Tarrick is acting out of love and not as a king should. If Lazar had spoken that way about any other councilor, the meeting would have gone very differently."

"It's not a bad thing," Ninaz said gently, leaning forward to grasp Elena's hand. A tray of tea and coffee cups whizzed past and settled on the table next to theirs. "You need to give Tarrick a little time and grace too. But he does have a point about you spending far too much time in town and not enough time at the palace."

"I thought you were on my side." Elena gave her a withering look.

"I'm on both your sides," Ninaz said pointedly. "You're a team. Arran was husband to Amaya before he became king. They had worked on their differences long before he took the throne. His Majesty is trying to be a good king and partner to you at the same time. There's bound to be some teething issues as everyone adjusts."

"Lady Elena?" A woman with bright blue eyes and curly brown hair that fell to her waist stood by their table with a hesitant smile. "I wanted to thank you for helping my husband at the school ..."

They had been interrupted every so often by Erindellians who stopped by their table to thank Elena for her help with rebuilding the town. She was equally pleased that the people she had come to know over the past few months had recovered their powers. Elena greeted everyone and listened patiently as they gave her updates on their lives and families.

"Thank you, Kaylee. It was my pleasure," she told her. "How is Chloe?"

A small girl with the same dark, curly hair peeked out from behind the woman's skirt. She gave Elena a shy smile, her warm brown eyes framed by long, thick, dark lashes.

"I'm good," she said in a high voice.

Kaylee nudged her forward. "Tell her what you told me, Chlo," she said in a staged whisper.

Chloe hesitated.

"I miss you," she blurted out before hiding her face in Kaylee's dress. The little girl squirmed in embarrassment and held up her small, chubby arms.

"We all miss you, Lady Elena," Kaylee said, bending down to pick up the girl.

"I miss you too, Chloe." A warm, fuzzy feeling came over Elena at the sight of the girl resting her head on the woman's shoulder. Her thoughts drifted to the other expectations people might have of her as their queen. One day, a small Terralean could be wrapping their arms around Elena's neck. Being a mother felt like a stronger possibility now that she was with Tarrick—an idea that made her heart skip a beat. "I promise I'll visit again soon. Would you like that?"

Chloe nodded vigorously.

"We're excited about the community center." Kaylee beamed at her.

"I'm so glad people are enjoying the space," Elena said, returning the smile.

The woman hesitated for a moment.

"What's wrong, Kaylee?" Elena asked, frowning slightly.

"It's just that there's not enough of us to manage it. It's that popular, we need more help," she answered, twisting her fingers and blushing as she spoke.

"Maybe I can come—" Elena started to say, but Ninaz chose that very moment to clear her throat loudly and glare at her over her cup of coffee.

Elena bit back the words that were about to spill out and turned to Kaylee, who looked at her hopefully. "Why don't I speak with the king about setting up a proper volunteer program for the center?" she said slowly, her mind whirling through the possibilities. "Perhaps there's a way we can compensate volunteers and sponsors financially or with incentives?"

"That sounds like something the Council of Nobles would be amiable to discuss," Ninaz said loudly. "An excellent idea, Lady Elena."

Kaylee stared at Elena, who gave her a tentative smile.

"I didn't even think of that," she said in wonder.

"Great!" Elena exclaimed. "I'll bring it up at the next, er, council meeting."

They chatted for a few more minutes before Kaylee and Chloe bid them farewell.

"That was handled in exactly the manner I would expect from a queen," Ninaz said, watching them walk away. "I have no doubt you will win over the nobles with that idea. What else are you going to do to show them you have the makings of a leader?"

Elena pierced Ninaz with a glare. "I don't know," she said, injecting as much sarcasm as she could. "What do you suggest?"

Ninaz leveled her with a gaze. "I'm trying to work *with* you, my dear, to maintain your relationship with the Terraleans and establish yourself in the council."

Elena's face fell as she realized she had been unfairly harsh on one of her few supporters.

"We've spoken about this," Ninaz continued severely. "You do not need to do everything yourself. You are allowed to ask for help."

"I know, I'm sorry," Elena mumbled.

She took in her surroundings with renewed appreciation for what she had in Terralea. The market square was a hive of activity, as usual. Vendors and stall owners shouted out their wares and prices. Locals jostled each other as they crowded around some of the stalls, trying to catch the attention of the servers. It was loud, colorful, and lifted Elena's spirit. She loved that so much life returned to her beloved city.

"Your doubts and fears are normal, but don't let them take over. Trust yourself." Ninaz sat back in her chair, looking at Elena thoughtfully. "It was good of you to help Lady Rhea. Divine Beings know that poor girl needs a friend like you. News will spread, and you'll have a band of supporters in no time."

"How did you know about that?" Elena asked, startled.

"My dear," Ninaz said, leaning forward. "Just because I don't live in the palace anymore doesn't mean I don't know what's happening."

"I don't know if that's supposed to reassure me or scare me." Elena laughed.

"Both." Ninaz winked. "Do not allow the council's eventual vote to stop you from what you're doing. You need to work on winning over as many nobles as you can, especially the younger ones who are more open-minded and progressive."

Bri walked over and placed a beautifully wrapped box on the table. "Here you are. My finest selection," she announced proudly. Elena had helped Bri while she had been short-staffed that summer, and the woman had promised her free tea for life, despite Elena's protests.

"Thank you so much, Bri," Elena exclaimed, examining the pretty bow and colorful wrapping paper that covered the box filled with a variety of tea flavors and infusions Bri made herself. "Queen Lin will love it."

"It's an honor." Bri's lips tilted up. "And thank you for introducing me to Loz. She's been helping me this past week."

"I'm glad you two clicked." Elena grinned. "I had a feeling you'd like her."

"Her powers with flames and knowledge of herbs are incredible," Bri said fervently. "I'll be able to sell my new range of tisanes at the next Full Moon Festival."

"I'll be the first to try them," Elena promised.

***

Back at the palace, Elena laid out her clothes and mentally ticked off everything she would need for their stay in Sailon—from what Jet had told her, it would be warm and humid. She had pulled out all the cotton and linen clothes she could find in her new wardrobe and assessed her options. The bedroom door opened, and she stiffened slightly, knowing only one person who would enter without knocking. She sensed Tarrick's presence, as she always did, as he made his way closer to where she stood by the bed.

"Hey," he whispered, standing behind Elena.

"Hey," she replied, placing the folded items one by one in her case. Her stubbornness had prevented her from seeking him out and forgiving him the moment she returned to the palace. Elena had spent the rest of the day in their bedroom to rethink her strategy in winning over the nobles. The sadness in his voice cracked her heart, and her anger started to melt.

"How was your afternoon?"

"Fine."

Elena slowed down packing her clothes to delay having to face him. She tapped her chin thoughtfully before spotting the gift-wrapped box of tea sitting next to a pile of books on the desk. When Elena nestled it carefully amongst the clothes in her case, there was nothing left to pack, and she reluctantly faced the king.

Tarrick stood in the middle of the expansive room, watching her with a heavy expression on his face. He hesitated, unsure of what to say next. They regarded each other for a moment before Elena broke the silence.

"You promised we would be in this together," she said in a low voice.

"I know." Regret laced his words. "I shouldn't have kept the details of the council meeting from you."

"Good to know my efforts to stop Zanthus boosted my popularity with Terralea's most influential nobles," Elena said sarcastically.

"I would prefer if they opposed me directly." Tarrick knitted his brows, anger seeping into his voice. "I knew I'd face some backlash and resistance, but using you as an excuse angered me more. You've done nothing wrong."

Elena sighed half-heartedly. "That doesn't help us right now. You need to do whatever it takes to set up a full council as soon as possible and keep your crown."

"I've invited several Terraleans to the Harvest Feast so they can meet you in person and see you have the makings of a queen," he told her. "But if I'm being completely honest, there's a chance they might decline with you and Jet here."

Elena paused for a moment, and her heart went out to Jet. He didn't deserve the discrimination from people who didn't understand his abilities. She tamped down the hurt at the latter part of Tarrick's statement.

"If they met you, they'd change their minds," the king continued, rubbing his chin the way he did when he was upset and anxious. "But I don't want to force them and cause even more animosity, even though Leon pointed out that, as king, I have the authority to do so."

"The vicious circle of life," Elena muttered, sinking heavily onto the bed and glaring at the rug. She tried to wrap her head around the fact that she had been able to win over the kings and queens of Leneira—even the Divine Beings—more easily than nobles. As easy as it would have been to ask Tarrick to use his authority over his councilors, Elena's stubbornness and pride wanted to show them herself that she was worthy of sitting at the table alongside them.

"This is not the vision I had for Terralea, even before you came along." He sat on the bed next to Elena. She inhaled his comforting scent, feeling the warmth of his body and wanting nothing more than to crawl into his lap and forget the day had happened. But she kept her arms glued to her sides and continued scowling at the rug. She forced herself not to spiral down the path of wondering how things had been between Tarrick and Rose, if she had experienced the same discrimination and had been regarded as an outsider.

"I had hoped that, when news of Zanthus's actions and everything that happened spread, people would realize that not all humans and non-magicals are out to get us," he said wistfully. "But they're holding onto old prejudices because they're scared."

Elena remained silent. When Tarrick could stand it no longer, he reached out to her, wrapping his arm around her shoulder. He pulled her toward him so she was pressed against his body.

"Jet was telling me about the hot springs in Sailon," he murmured, catching sight of a bathing suit in her suitcase. "And Lin has staff on hand who know these massage techniques that make you feel like jelly afterwards."

"That sounds nice."

"He said that a few days away will help us see things more clearly." Tarrick traced circles on Elena's shoulder with his thumb.

She dropped her shoulders and rolled her neck to ease the tightness and tension that had been building there since morning.

"I'm still not sure this is a good idea," she admitted, feeling guilty about leaving the dwindling council and issues that needed to be resolved. "But I want to ask Lin for her advice on how to deal with things."

Tarrick hesitated. "Is it just the nobles bothering you? Or is there something else?"

"Apparently, there's a superstition that those marked by the Divine Beings bring about change"—Elena indicated the tattoo on her inner wrist—"and not everyone thinks change is a good thing."

"I'm sorry," he whispered. "I thought my people were past those old wives' tales."

"It's not everyone." Her voice softened when she remembered the Erindellians she had spoken with that day. "I guess the nobles are still processing the shock of everything that's happened. They want proof of your commitment to protect them and the people of Terralea before more changes take place."

"That's not an excuse." Tarrick shook his head. "We don't know what's around the corner, and my council needs to learn to adapt and be flexible."

"You can't force change," Elena said.

"I know, I know." Tarrick leaned forward and rested his head on her shoulder.

"You're not that kind of person. You'd be no better than Zanthus and a terrible king if you did that," she continued.

Tarrick frowned into her shoulder. "But we cannot stay stagnant and stuck in the old ways if we are to make progress in this world. I've been racking my mind trying to come up with a way to keep them all happy."

"You're never going to make everyone happy, Tarrick," Elena told him gently. "Even if I weren't in the picture, you'd face opposition."

Elena reflected on how easy it was when it was just the two of them, talking and making plans for the future. When Tarrick had voiced his ideas, she jumped in with suggestions, and things made sense. Their vision seemed possible. As soon as other people had gotten involved, things became unbearably complicated.

"I really thought I could do this. Father taught me so much from day one," Tarrick confessed. "But I felt like I could contribute more when I was a prince."

"It's practically your first day." Elena huffed out a laugh. "Most jobs have a three-month probation period and training program. You need to take it slow and give yourself a break. There's only so much you can do, even as king."

"Probation?" Tarrick scrunched his face in confusion.

"A trial period," Elena explained.

"Father taught me everything about *being* king, not *becoming* king," he said sadly. "I have to remind myself that even he faced opposition and had to rebuild his council after the uprising."

Elena reached up to stroke his hair. "Darius, Aiden, and Netta are on board, Halder and Lin support you, and the majority of Terraleans favor you as their king. It's just a few naysayers. And you're taking things personally because they oppose *me*, not you."

Tarrick lifted his head. "Is that really how you see it?"

She shrugged. "Yeah."

He shot her a skeptical look.

"I've had a lot of time to think," Elena said, seeing the expression on his face. "I know I get emotional and reactive, but at the end of the day, I know I can't control the actions of a bunch of ignorant nobles. Your family and the Erindellians know I'm a decent person. That's all that matters to me right now. We can figure out how to win over the others together. We still have time."

"I don't know what I did to deserve you," Tarrick murmured, pressing his lips to her temples. "I love you."

"I love you too." Elena softened.

They sat in comfortable silence, Tarrick continuing to trace circles around Elena's arm.

"I should go pack." He sighed, standing up and making to leave.

"Tarrick." She reached out and grabbed his hand.

He paused.

"Please don't shut me out," she pleaded. "I want to be here for you, but I can only do that if you're honest with me."

Tarrick dipped his head. Elena dropped his hand and flopped back on the bed.

"El?"

"Yeah?" she murmured.

"There's something else I need to tell you," Tarrick said softly, stepping back to the bed and taking her hand. He rubbed slow circles in her palm with his thumb.

She tilted her head toward him. "Is it to do with the payment to the Divine Beings?"

His expression confirmed that it was.

Elena sat up and glared. "You swear that you haven't sacrificed your mother or Leon or Adina or any other family members?"

"I swear," Tarrick replied. "I already told you, I didn't part with anything I wasn't willing to give up."

Elena considered him for a moment before relaxing again.

"But just ..." He hesitated. "Just give me some time, okay? I promise I'll tell you. I need time to ... think things through."

She tamped down the anxiety bubbling in her stomach. At that moment, Elena wished she had Empath abilities.

"Okay," she whispered, taking slow, deep breaths.

~ 13 ~

Elena grumbled about the early start as she wrapped an embroidered shawl tightly around her shoulders to ward off the chilly dawn air nipping at her skin. Tarrick chuckled as he led her to the carriage waiting for them and reminded her of his promise of hot coffee and pastries at their first rest stop.

Leon, Jet, and Adina had woken early to see them off, promising Tarrick to send word the minute they had news from the Terraleans they had written to.

"We'll miss you at training." Leon hugged Elena extra hard, and she understood it was his way of apologizing for keeping her in the dark about the council and deadline.

"Try not to burn down the palace," she said, squeezing him back just as hard.

He chuckled and pulled away. "We'll do our best."

"Jet, watch him," she told the Empath sternly, who saluted in response, a grin spreading on his face at Leon's protest.

As the carriage trundled along, Elena pulled back the curtains every so often to admire the landscape. The streets of Erindell had been quiet when they left. The cobbled, narrow streets gave way to wider dusty roads lined with densely packed trees. As the sun rose higher in the sky, the greenery and foliage grew more vivid against the blue. *Lyrabirds* continued to flit in and out of the trees, their bright pink and rainbow plumes teasing Elena as she gazed out into the sea of green.

She shrugged off the shawl and peered between the thickets and woodlands they rode through. The greenery was broken up by villages and hamlets where the houses and shops along the main roads could have been out of a children's picture book. The thatched roofs with smoking chimneys, pretty flower boxes with pink, blue, and purple flowers frothing down the walls, well-kept front gardens, and shop fronts decorated with seasonal bunting all added to the charm of the Terralean countryside. The carriage driver slowed down in high-traffic areas, giving Elena the chance to observe rural Terraleans ambling past with baskets of produce, bags of clothes, calling out to each other, smiling and waving just as the Erindellians did.

Tarrick sat next to Elena in the carriage and read through contracts and reports from Lin in preparation for a semi-official meeting. Elena smiled to herself at the sight of him scrunching his nose as he read. Tarrick tapped a stylus against the pages he held in one hand and, every so often, scribbled notes in the margins or crossed out certain items.

Elena peered at the parchment he was reading, covered with his notes and amendments. "She's your ally. Give her some of the things she's requested."

"Yes, dear." Tarrick huffed a laugh and placed a quick kiss on her cheek. "What are you reading?"

Elena held up the book she had brought along for the journey.

"*Leneiran Anatomy and Function?*" He raised a brow in surprise.

She blushed and lowered her head. "I want to learn more about Leneiran biology."

"Whyyyy?" he dragged out the word.

"Zahra's mother told me that our child will not have Elemental abilities," Elena explained, picking up the book and attempting to understand a complicated explanation of Leneiran DNA. Tarrick wore a shuttered expression that concerned her.

"Are you okay?" she asked.

"I'm fine," he said, roughly shaking his head and shying away from her hand. "Why are you talking to Zahra's mother about our offspring?" He struggled to get the last word out.

"She brought it up." Elena shrugged, picking up her book again. "It was one of the reasons I wanted to join the council—to lay the foundation for Terralea being open to having non-Elementals, Shifters, and Empaths live in our country, like Sailon."

Tarrick gaped at her.

"*That's* why you wanted to join?" he finally asked.

"It was *one* of the reasons I wanted to join," she corrected him, flipping the page and continuing to read.

"I don't think we need to worry about children right now," Tarrick muttered, tightening his hold on his report. Elena missed the way his hand shook as he underlined a sentence.

"I'm not expecting to fall pregnant tomorrow." She rolled her eyes. "But it will happen one day, and I don't want my child shunned from society just because he or she isn't an Elemental."

Tarrick didn't answer and buried himself deeper in his own readings and notes. Elena watched him with a frown but decided not to say more on the topic. Instead, she gazed at the intense concentration on his face as he studied the documents he held, wondering for the first time if Tarrick even wanted children. It was a conversation she wanted to have with him when she had his full attention.

They stopped at a small coffee shop where Tarrick bought them coffees and pastries as promised. The owner, recognizing the royal crest painted in gold on the carriage's black-lacquered door, hurried out to greet them. They entered the small shop, where they were led to a small table at the back and welcomed by the owner's wife, who greeted Tarrick with the appropriate level of deference. Their order was placed within minutes, the owner's wife informing them the pastries were fresh out of the oven and still hot.

Elena brightened at the plate of fried pieces of dough drizzled with honey and sprinkled with salt flakes. The first bite had flakes of golden, crunchy pastry crumbling down her chin. The soft dough inside was soaked in rich honey that oozed onto her tongue, chunks of sea salt offsetting the sweetness. The strong, bitter coffee slid down Elena's throat, making her feel more awake. She hummed in appreciation as she alternated between bites of pastry and sips of the rich, sweet elixir.

Elena thanked the owners a little too enthusiastically when they left, the caffeine coursing through her veins and giving her the buzz she had craved after having to wake up at the crack of dawn two days in a row. The jolly old Terralean, who had known Arran and Amaya, appreciated her fervent praise and waved them off with a broad smile.

Back in the carriage, both of them relaxed into easy conversation.

"Do you miss the human realm?" Tarrick asked.

Elena shook her head without hesitation. "No, definitely not."

"Because if there was something you missed, I could make arrangements for you to go back through the portal, if you wanted," Tarrick pressed.

Elena leaned into him, touched by the offer. "It's easier to start a new life when you leave everything behind. Literally and metaphorically." She barely thought about her old life in the human realm. There was no one she missed, and it was unlikely anyone missed her.

Tarrick didn't look convinced. "Even your books?"

"Turns out, there are some great writers in Leneira." Elena smirked. "Madame Zorra's sister owns a bookshop in town. Did you know that?"

Tarrick knit his brows together. "What?"

"She has an excellent selection of romances," Elena replied in a low voice. "I ran into Madame Zorra there once, and she showed me the section she tells her staff to visit if their clients have, um, particular requests."

Elena had to hold back her laughter at the expression on Tarrick's face.

"Did you—" he croaked. "Did you ... buy any books?"

"Perhaps," she drew out the word with a sly grin. "You know that thing we did the other night when I was on top?"

Tarrick nodded slowly.

"That was from a book."

The carriage jolted at that moment when it rolled over a pothole, and Tarrick cleared his throat.

Elena smirked again when, out of the corner of her eye, she saw him adjusting his pants. "When was the last time you visited Sailon?" she asked, changing the subject.

The conversation moved onto more neutral ground, and by lunchtime, they were laughing and exchanging stories about their youth and escapades. Tarrick held out his hand to help her out when they stopped for lunch at a tavern, and Elena felt butterflies in her stomach as though it were a first date. She noticed that he was lighter and happier away from the palace. The tavern owner was awestruck at having the king of Terralea dine at his humble pub. He gave them a private booth next to a window that offered views of the little garden out the back.

Elena exclaimed over the kitschy decor and charm of the pub, unlike any pub or bar she'd ever been to. The owner—another welcoming man—introduced his wife, who blushed and curtsied when she was presented to Tarrick. They chatted while their food was being prepared, and Elena admired the way Tarrick made the owners feel comfortable in his presence by showing a genuine interest in their lives and making lighthearted conversation. Not once did he act like the politicians Elena had witnessed working the crowds and rallying their supporters with big words and empty promises.

As they ate, the tavern filled with locals and tourists. They slapped each other on the back and chatted happily. The owner and tavern staff made every patron feel welcome and at home, asking travelers where they were from, offering suggestions on what to see and do in the town. Every glass was filled with home-made sherbets and cordials at all times. Those who recognized the king as they walked by paused and curtsied, Tarrick acknowledging them with a smile.

He introduced Elena to everyone who stopped at their table, and she was given the same enthusiastic greeting and warm welcome to the realm. Tarrick had kept his promise to be open and transparent with the Terraleans. Word had spread of Zanthus's plans to seize the throne and the human woman who had saved them all, but only the Erindellians knew Elena in person.

Despite his self-doubts and moments of uncertainty, Tarrick enjoyed engaging with his people and connecting with them. It was evident in the way he listened to what they said and his honest replies to their questions.

Tarrick had ordered them a selection of regional specialties and insisted Elena try some of the lamb stew. He fed her from his spoon, and his eyes crinkled with delight when she gasped and moaned as the spices and flavors—savory meat, sweet dried fruits, hot chilli flakes, and cooling mint all at once—danced on her tongue. They swapped half their meals, flirting in between bites of food, and ended with sharing dessert.

"This is the most fun date I've been on in Terralea," Elena teased, licking the last of the custard off her spoon.

"I could say the same." Tarrick chuckled, reaching out to wipe a bit of sugar from the corner of Elena's lips. He winked at her, and she blushed.

"We should do this more often," she said, lowering her voice. "There are so many restaurants in Erindell I want to try."

"Deal," Tarrick said immediately.

When they finished eating and paid for the meal, they walked out of the tavern hand in hand. The size of the king's tip left the owner and his wife speechless.

Tarrick held the door open for Elena and helped her back into the carriage before climbing in himself and settling into the seat. He pulled her closer, and she leaned her head happily against his chest, holding the hand he had casually thrown around her shoulder.

There were moments when Elena opened her mouth to ask if Tarrick was ready to tell her everything about his bargain with the Divine Beings. Instead, she enjoyed the semblance of normalcy the flirty, easy-going afternoon brought. Elena closed her eyes, enjoying the gentle rocking of the carriage and the feel of Tarrick's body against her own. Before long, she fell asleep.

***

When she woke up from her nap, Tarrick had pulled back the curtains, revealing the sun lower in the sky. Elena sat up and rubbed her face with her hands. She smiled gratefully when Tarrick handed her a canteen of water to quench her thirst. At the concerned expression on his face, Elena sat up straight and leaned over to peer out the window.

The sight that greeted her was unexpected; after Jet described forests and greenery, Elena was not expecting such dry, barren land. Brown and grey scrub dotted the dull brown earth, hinting at the foliage that once thrived in those parts.

"Have we crossed the border yet?" she asked tentatively.

Tarrick nodded, a crease forming between his brows. "An hour or so ago. Sailon must have had an exceptionally intense summer. Usually, these parts are green and shady."

"Have other parts of Leneira experienced such extreme weather this season?" Elena wondered aloud.

"I'll ask Lin if she's heard from Halder," Tarrick told her. "He didn't mention anything in his last missive."

The landscape eventually turned into a curtain of bright green, and Tarrick relaxed back into his seat, allowing Elena to appreciate the Sailonese countryside. Lush trees with enormous flat leaves, dense bamboo forests, clusters of maple trees with spindly leaves of varying shades of yellow and light green created a hazy watercolor effect from a distance.

"We're almost there," Tarrick said with a smile on his face.

~ 14 ~

"Welcome to Sailon, Your Majesty, Lady Elena." Lin beamed at the couple when they stepped out of the carriage at the entrance to her palace in LaHong, Sailon's capital city. Her wife and second-in-command, Zen, stood by her side, smiling at the couple and waiting patiently for her queen to greet them first.

"Queen Lin," Tarrick greeted her with a broad smile. "Thank you for hosting us."

"Tarrick, I was so pleased when you wrote and said you wanted to visit." Lin stepped forward to embrace the young king.

"And Lady Elena." Lin welcomed her warmly, placing her hands on her shoulders and planting kisses on each cheek. "Are you well?"

Lin scrutinized Elena as she held onto her. Tarrick moved away from the pair to shake Zen's hand and greet a couple of Lin's council members who had just stepped out of the palace.

"I have a feeling you and I should have a talk?" she murmured.

"I need your help," Elena whispered.

"And you shall have it, my dear," the queen assured her. Lin took her hands off Elena and gestured toward the front doors. "Please, come in and make yourselves at home."

Tarrick and Zen walked ahead with the Sailonese councilors, talking intently about Sailon's defenses and border patrols.

"I noticed the countryside bore the brunt of your summer," Tarrick said lightly.

Lin gave him a sharp look before shifting her gaze to Zen, who wore a worried expression at his words. "It's worse than we thought," Lin murmured.

"I wondered if the blight extended to the borders," Zen told her, the frown on her face deepening.

"Blight?" Elena asked.

The queen and her wife exchanged a glance before Lin answered. "This is the first time in centuries our forests and jungles have been so affected by the heat. Mind you, it hasn't even been a particularly hot summer."

"I wonder if it's connected to the desert storms we've had this season in Terralea." Tarrick rubbed his chin. "They've been so intense that even our strongest Elemental soldiers have been unable to control them."

"We lost the last shipment of supplies from Skandor to a vicious storm," Elena added.

Zen's expression turned to one of alarm, but Lin looked at Tarrick thoughtfully. "Perhaps tomorrow you and I can discuss expediting bringing your guards to Sailon, and they could spend some time investigating the cause of our dying countryside?"

Tarrick was nodding before Lin even finished her request. "Of course. I was thinking the same thing. When we return to Terralea, Adina and I will put together the training force we were planning to send here following our Peace Summit agreement."

"Thank you, Your Majesty." A look of relief washed over Lin's face.

"Perhaps you could also send some Elementals who specialize in manipulating the earth," Elena suggested. "I'm sure there are a few botanists who would be interested in visiting Sailon and could add their expertise and recommendations."

Lin's eyes twinkled at Elena. "I see you're well on your way to becoming one of Terralea's illustrious leaders, Lady Elena."

Elena blushed and gave her a half-smile. "There are a few Erindellians I've spoken to who have expressed an interest in travel."

"You mean besides the princess?" Zen chuckled, recalling how Adina had told them how she felt stifled and wanted to explore more of the realm.

Tarrick laughed. "Perhaps I'll send her too. She's been working far too much lately."

They walked through the spacious yet simple palace—a square structure that was only two levels high. It was unlike the palace at Terralea with its grand rooms, sweeping hallways, and multiple stories. They entered a large open courtyard in the middle, where lush bamboo palm trees lined the borders of the space, which had a large pond in the middle.

Elena trailed behind the group, crossing a wooden bridge over the pond that connected one side of the quadrant to the opposite. She marveled at the neatly trimmed bushes and plants that poked out of the stone beds surrounding the pond. Colorful fish darted among the flowering lily pads that floated lazily on the surface, drawing her attention to the water that rippled in the evening breeze.

"The northern wing of the palace is where you'll find the throne hall, my office, and council chambers," Lin explained, pointing out the wing. "Bedrooms are along the second floor, kitchens and dining halls to the east, the guards' chambers to the west."

The palace was open and airy, with passages and corridors leading to the inner courtyard and out to the palace grounds from every wing. The sun was setting in the west, bathing the palace in a warm glow.

"We thought you might like to stay in one of the private guest houses since this is a holiday for you two," Lin offered, leading them out to the palace grounds through the southern wing. They walked down a stone path lined with manicured bushes and flower beds.

Lanterns hung from tree branches and torches embedded into the ground at regular intervals. The sound of cicadas and a tranquil hum of insects hiding in the shrubbery added to the peaceful ambience. Soft notes of someone playing a soothing tune on the flute somewhere on the palace grounds reached Elena's ears, and the tension in her shoulders eased.

She finally released a long exhale, not even realizing how on edge she'd been since seeing the dying Sailonese countryside. And thinking about the important conversation she was yet to have with Tarrick.

Lin veered off the main path down a smaller one that led to a bamboo villa. She opened the door and walked down the short entryway. Elena entered and gasped at the luxurious bed that took up most of the extravagant room. Zen grinned at her reaction and stepped to the side, allowing Elena to walk through.

A pot of steaming tea and two cups were already laid out on a tray on the black lacquer bench at the foot of the bed. The two small bedside tables held vases of fresh flowers that had spiky, vibrant fuchsia petals. A wooden divider wall past the bed revealed a large white bath with soft, fluffy towels draped over the edge and a long tray of soaps and oils.

"You might like this part." Zen winked at Elena and opened the door at the back of the villa.

"Zen," Elena exhaled, taking in the private little backyard. "This is stunning."

Her eyes fell on the raised stone pool in the corner. The water lapped at the deep edges and trickled over, rolling down on the grass that surrounded the pool. A set of steps was cut into the stone at the side to climb in.

"One of the palace's natural springs," Zen explained, walking over and reaching out to dip her hand in the water. "The water stays warm, even in winter."

Elena moved to the side of the pool and dipped her own hand in the warm water. She let out a happy sigh. "I don't think I want to leave. This is paradise."

Zen laughed. "We get that a lot from our guests."

They went back into the villa, where Lin and Tarrick were making plans to discuss official matters the following day.

"We'll have your belongings sent to your room," Lin said warmly to Elena. "Feel free to relax and explore if you wish. I'll send a guard to fetch you for dinner."

"Thank you, Lin," Tarrick said quietly. "For everything."

"A pleasure."

When Lin and Zen left the villa, Elena sat on the bed and took in the details of the room she hadn't first noticed—gold-framed paintings, decoratively carved moldings, and even a book she recognized from her new favorite bookshop back in Terralea.

"This is so nice." She leaned forward to admire the lighter wooden floral pattern inlaid into the dark base of the lacquer bench and traced the lines with her fingers.

"Tea?" Tarrick took a seat next to her and picked up the wrought iron teapot.

"Yes, please," Elena said eagerly.

He poured out two cups of fragrant, steaming tea, and Elena held her own to her nose, inhaling the unique scent of ginger and something floral. She sipped the hot liquid slowly, savoring the delicate taste, and hummed happily.

Tarrick took a sip of his own tea and watched her over the rim of his cup.

"El," he said hesitantly.

Elena looked at him inquiringly.

"While we're here in Sailon, can we just be Tarrick and Elena?" he asked softly. "Not king and future queen, council members or representatives of Terralea."

She knitted her brows in confusion.

"Just us," he said beseechingly. "Like we were this afternoon."

"We still need to have an important conversation," she said, placing her cup on the tray.

"We do," he agreed. "And we will. I will tell you the full story of what happened with the Divine Beings before we leave. Just for a few days, I want to put that and the responsibilities of Terralea to the side and enjoy being on holiday with you."

Elena hesitated, searching Tarrick's earnest amber eyes. She considered his request, her heart leaning toward his suggestion of taking a break and having a few days off. But her head told her that she had to stop putting off the conversation they should have had months before about his bargain with the Divine Beings.

Her heart won out in the end, and she assented. Tarrick reached out and squeezed Elena's hand with that smile that made her weak at the knees.

"Thank you," Tarrick whispered.

~ 15 ~

"The food is delicious, Lin." Elena dabbed her mouth with a napkin. It was just the four of them at dinner, and the atmosphere was as familiar and congenial as her dinners with the royal family in Terralea.

All of the dishes she had tried that evening were bursting with flavor. The skewered grilled meats were charred to perfection but still juicy, thanks to the citrus marinade. Elena had practically drunk the dipping sauce from the small bowl that accompanied the meat. The salads were refreshing and crunchy, with finely sliced vegetables brought to life with a tangy dressing and garnished with toasted nuts. There was fragrant, fluffy rice, chewy noodles, and crusty bread on the side to mop up the leftover sauces.

"I'm glad you're enjoying it." Lin beamed at her guest. "These are some of Sailon's signature dishes. Has anyone told you have a big appetite for such a small person?"

Tarrick chuckled. "That's what my father said the first time Elena joined us for a meal. I don't think we had sent such clean plates back to the kitchen before then."

"Quiet, you," Elena retorted, but her voice lacked the force or conviction to make anyone believe she was upset with him. It was so easy to talk to Tarrick, the man she fell in love with, and not the closed-off king of Terralea he had been forced to become too soon. She hadn't realized how strong his regal mask was until he dropped it and tore down the metaphorical walls he'd built around himself.

Zen snickered over her plate of noodles. "You should see Lin over a bowl of her favorite soup."

"It's true," the queen admitted. "I become an animal."

"What kind of soup?"

Lin described a complex broth with layers of flavor that took hours to make with native Sailonese herbs, spices, and aromatics added to create its unique savoriness. Hand-pulled noodles and thinly sliced meat were added to the piping hot broth before it was served with fresh herbs and pickled vegetables. Despite the amount of food she had just eaten, Elena drooled over Lin's description.

"It's something I indulge in during the cooler months," Lin explained. "It's still too hot for the kitchen to make it. But there are a number of regional specialities and delicacies that you will be able to sample at tomorrow night's Lantern Festival."

"Lantern Festival?" Elena asked eagerly.

"You timed your visit well." Lin nodded. "At the start of the harvest season, we hold a festival to honor our ancestors and thank them for a prosperous season. The people of Sailon light lanterns on the night of the festival and let them float into the sky, carrying our prayers and wishes. It's a beautiful sight."

Elena's eyes shone. "I'm so glad we'll be here for that."

"LaHong really comes to life during the festival," Zen said enthusiastically. "There are food carts and craft vendors along the canals. The children make paper boats and float them on the water with candles to light the way for the *naya's* crossing."

"You celebrate the *naya's* crossing here?"

Lin nodded. "Our people adore the story of Queen Samara."

"Battles and bloodshed aside, it's a journey I'd like to make someday." Elena grinned at Tarrick. "I want to see as much of the realm as possible."

"You've caught the travel bug." Lin laughed.

"Malina told me about the lights in the northern skies of Skandor," Elena said dreamily. "They sounded quite spectacular."

"Did she mention they are only visible during the coldest months?" Zen grunted.

"Oh," Elena frowned, not liking the sound of the cold.

"I'll keep you warm." Tarrick winked at her, wriggling his fingers.

"Tomorrow will be a late night," Lin told them. "And you must be tired after your journey."

Elena hadn't thought about being tired until Lin mentioned it, and the fatigue suddenly hit her. She tried to stifle a yawn, but Tarrick pushed back his chair. Lin and Zen did the same and rose to their feet.

"Thank you for a wonderful evening," Tarrick thanked their hosts.

Elene stood and thanked Lin and Zen, who brushed away the formalities with friendly waves of their hands.

"We're so glad to have you here." Lin smiled at them. "It's rare for us to be able to show visitors from other parts of the realm what our country has to offer."

The four of them walked out of the dining chamber and bid each other good night before parting ways. Lin and Zen took the stairs at the end of the hall up to their bedroom. Tarrick slipped his hand into Elena's and intertwined their fingers as they made their way to their villa.

"It's not that late." He leaned down and kissed her neck. "Do you want to check out the hot spring?"

Elena's eyes lit up. The night was cool and quiet with no one around to disturb them. They crossed the villa to the back door and made their way to the pool of spring water, where Elena stripped off her dress without hesitation. She ascended the steps cut into the thick stone wall of the pool and lowered herself into the warm water. Elena found a ledge that she could sit on and lowered herself onto it. A light haze of steam rose from the surface of the spring, and she smiled invitingly at Tarrick, who stood in the middle of the garden, still fully clothed and enjoying the sight of Elena in the pool.

He inhaled sharply and reached back with a hand to drag his shirt over his head, revealing taut, rippling abs. Elena sucked in a breath at the sight of the king undressing in front of her, and her pulse quickened. He took off his pants and climbed into the pool, lowering himself until he was submerged up to his torso. He waded over and stood in front of Elena, staring at her intently, a thin ring of amber circled his pupils. She bit her lower lip, swallowing hard when he drew close enough for her to feel the heat radiating from his chest above the surface of the water. Tarrick caged her in by placing an arm either side of her body, and Elena was reminded of the first time he did that in the pool in the gardens in Terralea.

"This looks familiar," he said in a low, teasing voice, dipping his head and brushing his lips against hers.

"Mmm," she agreed. She pulled back and said, "I vaguely remember this happening before."

"I think I gave you three orgasms that night," he said thoughtfully.

Elena's core tensed in anticipation. "Are you going to set a new record tonight?" she asked, leaning forward, nipping at his lip, and wrapping her arms around his neck.

"I can try." He huffed a laugh. "You don't ask for much, do you, my queen?"

"Not at all, Your Majesty," she breathed as he traced a hand down the side of her body, stopping at her hips and squeezing. She stretched out her legs and wrapped them around his waist, pulling him closer.

His hard length pressed against her stomach as he continued to tease her with his mouth, pressing soft kisses down her neck and biting the skin gently before soothing it over with his tongue. Elena peppered his jaw with kisses and ran her hands all over his back, feeling the muscles move under her touch as she traced the dips and curves. She reached down between them, squeezing and stroking his cock as he groaned against her mouth. He was vibrating with need as she continued running her hands up and down his shaft, circling the head of his cock and cupping his balls.

"Let's take this inside," he gasped when she squeezed gently. "I don't think I'll last much longer if you keep doing that."

Elena smirked and let go of him. She waded to the steps and climbed out as gracefully as possible. Before her feet touched the grass, the water sluicing down her body evaporated, and she looked over her shoulder at Tarrick, who was still in the pool.

He slicked back his hair with his hands, and her mouth watered when he climbed out of the pool and stood before her. His wet body gleamed in the moonlight, water running down his chiseled abs in rivulets. She blinked and he was dry, but before she could protest, his lips were on hers again and his tongue explored her mouth, tasting and teasing with deep strokes.

Tarrick lifted her up as if she weighed nothing, and she instinctively wrapped her legs around his waist and arms around his neck. He squeezed her ass and she emitted a squeak of surprise, jerking her hips forward as a laugh rumbled from his throat. Tarrick carried Elena to the villa and shut the door behind them before lowering her onto the bed and covering her body with his own. He moved faster, his hands exploring every inch of her writhing form. She lifted her hips and rubbed her center against his cock to feel the friction she so desired, coating him in her slickness.

Tarrick finally moved his fingers to Elena's slick folds, and she sighed with satisfaction as he inserted two fingers into her aching pussy and stroked the sensitive bundle of nerves.

"You like that?" he asked.

Elena hummed with pleasure as he increased his pace and pressure.

"Orgasm number one coming up," he whispered. Before she could say anything, waves of pleasure coursed through her body, and she curled her toes before calling out Tarrick's name as stars exploded behind her eyes.

She pulled him closer, wanting to feel every inch of his body on her as she panted and caught her breath in the aftermath of her orgasm.

"Fuck, I've missed seeing that look on your face," he murmured, kissing her softly. Elena's eyes fluttered open when he moved down her body to tease and taste her nipples.

"Tarrick," she whispered, shivering when he flicked his tongue over her hardened nipple. She whimpered and moaned when he squeezed her other breast hard and pinched her. Elena felt herself getting wet between her thighs again.

"Were you saying something?" Tarrick lifted his head and grinned at the sight of Elena watching him worship her body.

She shook her head, unable to speak.

"Good," he said, continuing to knead and massage. "The only word I want to hear from you tonight is my name as you come all over me."

"Okay," she whispered. He frowned and pinched her nipple harder, a jolt of pain shooting through her. She cried out.

"What did I say?" he demanded. "Just my name. No other words."

Elena's breath caught, too afraid to ask him for more in case he stopped.

"Good girl," he growled, moving both hands to her hips and kissing her stomach as he moved further down to the apex of her thighs. Her skin pebbled in the absence of his warmth, but when his mouth latched onto her clit and he began sucking and licking, she cried out again. Elena reached down and tangled her fingers through his hair, tugging and encouraging him to keep his talented tongue on her.

He obeyed the silent command, licking long and slow before thrusting his tongue into her pussy. Elena's hips writhed as she rode his face, the appreciative sounds from his throat vibrating through her center and making her shudder as the familiar, pleasurable waves took over her senses again.

"Tarrick, Tarrick, Tarrick," she moaned his name as though it were a prayer. She tightened her grip on his hair as he held his face against her pussy and she came.

He placed a kiss on her center and moved up. He stroked the hair from her face, wiping away the tear tracks shining down her cheeks.

"That was intense," she gasped. Her release shone on his stubbled chin.

"You taste exquisite." Tarrick licked his lips.

Elena pulled his face to hers and kissed him, a new wave of arousal filling her as she tasted herself on him.

"Ready for number three?" Tarrick grinned when he pulled away from her. Elena shook her head.

"I don't know if I can," she admitted. "I think I'm done tonight."

Tarrick's eyes glinted at the challenge, and he kissed her slowly, passionately. He caressed her body lightly with teasing movements, his tongue gliding over hers until she was once again squirming and moaning with need.

He positioned himself between her legs, Elena's knees falling apart despite her earlier protests, and thrust into her without warning.

Elena cried out when his hard cock entered her, but before she could adjust to his length, he started moving hard and fast. Tarrick lowered himself over her and propped himself up on his elbows as he moved relentlessly in and out of her. Their breaths mingled, and he rested his forehead against Elena's, kissing her lightly when their lips met between thrusts.

With every rough movement Tarrick made, Elena realized there was a lot of pent-up pain and frustration and need. She pulled him closer and angled her hips higher so he could enter her more deeply. He kissed her shoulder hard in gratitude, understanding that she gave him permission to release whatever emotions he suppressed. He continued his frantic thrusting and came with a roar, spilling himself inside Elena. Her walls shuddered around his cock, and she cried out as she came.

They held each other tightly until they both stopped shaking and breathing raggedly. Tarrick pulled out of Elena as gently as he could, but she still winced.

"El," he said softly, cupping her face with his hand and stroking her cheek with his thumb. "I'm so—"

She placed a finger over his lips and shook her head.

"No," she said. "Don't you dare apologize."

Tarrick kissed her finger and held her tightly while she breathed in and out slowly. Her hands sought his, intertwining their fingers. He lifted her hand to his mouth and kissed her knuckles.

"Are you okay?" he asked, worry creeping into his voice.

"I'm more than okay," she assured him. "But I definitely don't think we'll be breaking any records tonight."

"I don't care about that," he told her. "I just want to hold you and love you."

Elena huffed a laugh and rolled onto her side to face him. "You can do that any time."

They gazed at each other.

"I intend to do that all the time." The corner of Tarrick's lip tugged up.

He lifted the quilt and tucked them both in.

Elena snuggled into his chest and swung a leg over his hips. It wasn't long before she felt him relax into the bed and his breathing slow down. *It's the first time he has fallen asleep first*—a worrying thought that Elena pushed away before sleep claimed her too.

~ 16 ~

The next morning, Tarrick woke Elena with kisses on her bare shoulder. He had already showered and dressed for the day.

"Lin wants to tie up some loose ends from the Peace Summit," he told her, "and discuss our plans for the Elementals to investigate the forests."

Elena started to rise, but Tarrick gently pushed her back into bed.

"She told me to tell you to sleep in and rest." He smiled. "It's your holiday, remember?"

"Okay," Elena mumbled, burying her face back into the soft pillows and pulling the quilt around herself. She was disappointed she wouldn't be able to speak to Lin that morning. Despite promising Tarrick that they would put aside Terralea's politics and council issues, they still weighed heavily on Elena's mind, and she wanted Lin's advice on how to handle it all.

Tarrick laughed softly and brushed back a stray strand of hair from her face. He planted a soft kiss on the small bit of exposed skin. "I'll see you when we're done."

He closed the front door gently when he left, and she allowed herself to doze for a little while before dragging herself out of bed.

***

"Did you sleep well last night?" Zen asked Elena with a knowing smirk when she entered the dining room.

Elena blushed and examined the bowl of rice in a thick broth that Zen pushed her way. It wasn't really a question since Zen was one of Lin's strongest Empaths and could probably read everything that happened the night before on Elena's face. Nonetheless, she replied, if only to pretend they were two ordinary people having an ordinary conversation. "Yes."

She examined the array of unfamiliar condiments and ingredients lined up on the table. "Is this breakfast?"

"Lunch for me, breakfast for you." Zen grinned. "You add whatever you'd like to the rice and mix it together," she explained.

Elena helped herself to a little bit of everything. She added pickled vegetables, different colored sauces, and crunchy nuts to her bowl. Her mouth started watering at the savory smell that wafted up when she lifted a spoonful of the mixture to her lips. The rice porridge was rich and unctuous, and it tasted as good as it smelled.

Elena polished off everything in a matter of minutes, in part because of the appetite she had built up between dinner and the late breakfast, in part because it was so delicious. The flavors danced on her tongue, and she dabbed at her mouth to make sure she hadn't left traces of the savory sauces around her chin.

Zen moved her own empty bowl to the side. "I thought I'd show you around LaHong this morning."

"That sounds great," Elena said eagerly.

"Let's go." Zen pushed back her chair and stood.

Elena did the same, and they walked out of the palace together.

It was a cloudy, humid day. Tiny droplets of water clung to the tips of the spiky green leaves of bamboo plants and trees that lined the palace entrance. In the distance, a *pihasi* whinnied, and voices called out to each other.

"Do you have many guards at the palace?" Elena asked curiously. The night before, she had only seen one patrolling the grounds.

Zen shook her head. "Most of our guards are assigned to protect regional towns and villages, as well as the borders and bluestone quarry. We get by with just two or three at the palace."

"What if something happens?"

"Lin likes to handle conflict with words, not weapons." Zen sighed. "I've told her on a number of occasions we should have more, but she refuses."

"I kind of love that about her," Elena murmured.

"Me too." Zen gave her a crooked smile. "While it drives me insane sometimes, I trust that her abilities will protect us. She's also an incredibly skilled fighter."

"She's pretty badass," Elena agreed, recalling the way Lin had fought off Zanthus's guards and flown around the room, leaving a trail of bodies in her wake.

As they walked down the road that led to LaHong, Elena noticed that the inhabitants moved at a much slower pace than the Erindellians. People dragged carts of fresh vegetables and fruit, calling out their wares while others stood at their stalls grilling skewered meats, fanning the smoke and embers in a leisurely manner. Locals ambled along, stopping by shops, chatting to vendors and each other. The relaxing atmosphere of Lin's palace seeped out into the city.

"How are you settling into your new life?" Zen asked.

"That's a loaded question." Elena laughed nervously. "There's a lot to learn, that's for sure."

Zen nodded understandingly.

Elena bit her lower lip, forcing herself not to offload everything she was feeling. "How do you manage it?" she asked instead. "Being in a relationship is work, I know, but being in a relationship with a newly-crowned king is ..."

"A challenge?" Zen supplied with an amused smile. "A pain in the ass?"

Elena laughed again, glad the woman understood.

"I know what you're going through. Lin and I faced many challenges when she first took the throne, that's for sure," Zen said, leading the way down a quiet path. "You think you have it bad? Imagine trying to convince a country that hadn't had a queen rule in centuries that a ruler who was unlikely to produce an heir, given that she married another woman, would be a good idea!"

"Wow," Elena exclaimed.

Zen walked quickly and purposefully, giving Elena no time or breath to carry a conversation as she tried to keep up with the tall woman. Only when they reached the heart of the city did she slow her pace to give Elena time to take in the sights.

At the end of the street, the canal that Zen had mentioned the previous night came into view. The water rippled in the breeze that provided little relief from the heavy air, and people in long boats rowed past with parcels and baskets of purchases. A few were docked along the edges, some empty, others with a lone Sailonese lying on their back, enjoying the warm day and gentle rocking of the canal water.

Children laughed and played in the streets, women walked past with wicker baskets filled with vegetables and herbs, men sat on the edge of the canal with fishing rods that they flicked in the water every so often to tempt the fish with bait. The buildings on either side of the canal were painted bright colors—sunshine yellow, jade green, cerulean, dusty pink. Some with vines creeping up the walls, others with large leaf trees at the front.

As they meandered along the canal pathway, Zen pointed out various shops and restaurants. Sailon's unique architecture was evident in the buildings that had shuttered timber windows, decorative wrought iron balustrades on the balconies, and unique fish-scale tiles that curved outwards at the corners of the roofs.

They crossed a large, covered bridge with dark wooden beams that Zen explained was The Bridge of Peace, built after a highly destructive civil war some centuries past.

"It wasn't just the Terraleans and Skandorians who wanted to use Empaths in their battles against each other. Past Sailonese rulers—really powerful ones—have exploited their ability to manipulate and control the population through their emotions," Zen explained. "Some even used compulsion to force people into joining the army and fighting battles in the realm."

Elena's eyes widened in horror. She had believed from the outset that Empaths were the more compassionate of the Leneirans, but hadn't considered how emotional manipulation could be as destructive as physical violence.

Intricate symbols and calligraphy covered the beams that supported the bridge's roof. Tiny gold bells and strings of beads hung off the struts, chiming in the breeze. Although the bridge was crowded, people spoke in low, reverent voices.

Zen pointed to the three free-standing altars—one at either end and another in the middle. "The structure symbolizes the past, present, and future."

The altars were decorated with sprigs of fresh flowers, strings of colored wooden beads, and handfuls of incense sticks that burned slowly, emitting a beautiful scent that perfumed the air.

They were forced to slow down when they crossed The Bridge of Peace because, like Elena, crowds of people stopped every few feet to admire the tiles and art on the ceiling.

Elena paused to watch an old Sailonese woman standing at one of the altars, holding an incense stick between the palms of her hands, her head bowed reverently. She murmured prayers in a low voice before waving the incense stick and placing it amongst the cluster jutting out of the little sandbox placed on the altar. She shuffled away, and another woman took her place, performing the same ritual. It was then that Elena noticed a line of people holding incense sticks, garlands of flowers, and rolling strings of beads between their fingers, patiently waiting their turn to place their offerings on the altars and pray.

"That's beautiful," she said softly.

"Some people do this every day." Zen stepped aside to let a group of people walk past. "I've never known a day go by without the altars being decked in offerings."

"There's a real sense of tranquility here." Elena sighed.

"There is now," Zen agreed. "But we've had our fair share of war and conflict."

"I honestly cannot picture it." Elena shook her head.

"We've had a few internal wars and skirmishes since Lin took the throne almost a hundred years ago," Zen said, gazing at the line of people, but not really seeing them. "We also had to convince our people that we would rule in a fair and just manner."

"Why did they believe you'd rule in any other way?"

"Our people were afraid of Lin's extra ability to control shadows and the fact that she's one of the few Empaths who can read people on sight," Zen continued, staring into the distance. "They thought she would use it to spy on them. But in the days after the rebellion—the one that was part of the same uprising in Terralea and Skandor—Lin was able to show our people that she would be a fair and just ruler."

"How did she convince her council that she would make a good leader and create such a beautiful, peaceful place?" Elena asked, aware that she was being nosy, but desperate to learn how Lin overcame her own challenges.

"She and I had to show them through our actions. It took a long time, but she said from the outset that those who did not align themselves with our values would be refused asylum," Zen explained. "The influx of non-magical Terraleans and Skandorians naturally made the Sailonese nervous, especially when they told us such horrific stories about what they had experienced. Our people feared the rebellion would spread to Sailon."

Elena's heart went out all over again to the people who had lost so much in the uprising, and the difficult choices that had to be made.

"Naturally, most of the council—who, by the way, were all powerful Empaths—were opposed to taking in the displaced Leneirans." Zen started to lead them away from the bridge down another narrow street. She continued speaking as they wove their way through the throng of people who were unaffected by their queen's wife walking among them. "They believed *all* non-magicals were rebels who would take over as soon as they settled in." Zen shook her head. "Our council at the time was full of men with conventional views."

"This sounds vaguely familiar," Elena said drily.

Zen huffed a laugh.

"It surprises me." Elena frowned. "Even Empaths who could read people and find traitors were opposed to change?"

Zen nodded. "We set up a system where the council members who supported us read every non-magical person who sought our protection and wanted to make a home for themselves in Sailon. If there was even a hint of ill intention, they were denied entry in our country."

They continued walking, but Elena barely paid attention to where Zen was taking her. She reflected on how she was on more or less the same path as Lin on her journey to becoming queen of Terralea, and had the same ideas as the female leader she admired. It gave Elena a little hope that it would be possible, in time, to show the Terralean councilors that she was worthy of being a good leader, just as Lin had.

"I thought we'd take a little break," Zen suggested when they walked down a wider street crammed with shops and buildings on either side.

Elena followed her to a large, dark building where a gold plaque advertised the establishment as LaHong's oldest teahouse.

Although they had been walking at a leisurely pace, the humidity was draining, and the tightly packed streets of slow-moving people were beginning to feel claustrophobic. Tea and savories were a welcome relief.

Through the building windows, she caught sight of people sipping cups of tea and picking at small trays of food. They entered the teahouse, and Elena was immediately enveloped in the cozy atmosphere. The space was filled with the low hum of people talking quietly, and perfumed with fruity, floral, and herbal aromas.

A soft-spoken woman with a friendly face greeted them. "Good afternoon, Commander Zen. A table for two?"

"Good afternoon, Misha," Zen greeted her.

While Zen spoke to Misha, Elena stared in wonder at the number of dark lacquer tables of varying shapes and sizes.

While a large part of the room was occupied by groups of two or three people, there were also long rectangular tables along the edges of the space. Lone customers read books while sipping their tea or simply people watched from their seats on the cushioned benches.

The air was filled with steam emanating from pots and cups. Elena caught the scent of jasmine and roses along with stronger herbal citrus notes, deep woodsy aromas and bright fruity flavors. The staff weaved effortlessly among the tables, refilling empty pots and replenishing refreshments.

The young woman Zen had been speaking to motioned for them to follow her to a small table at the back of the teahouse. The two chairs were positioned so both Elena and Zen had a clear view of the shop but could also talk to each other without raising their voices.

Zen thanked Misha, who pulled out the chairs for them, and she and Elena made themselves comfortable.

"Our tea of the day is a blend of jasmine and green tea from the Nadang region," their host spoke in a gentle voice that matched the soft expression on her youthful face. She placed two menus on the table, lining them precisely in front of Zen and Elena's seats. "I'll give you a few moments to decide."

"Thank you."

"I don't know where to start." Elena ran her finger down the long list of teas.

"I've been coming here for decades, and there's always something new." Zen laughed softly.

They perused the menu in silence before Elena gave up.

"You choose for me." She sat back in her chair and eyed the people closest to them who were sharing a plate of colorful rice cakes. "I like the sound of everything."

"Alright." A crease formed between Zen's brows as she scanned the menu.

Misha glided back to the table.

"A large pot of your *çai bloum* tea and two cups, please," Zen placed the order.

"An excellent choice," Misha affirmed. "And a plate of snacks for you to share?"

Zen grinned at her. "Of course!"

Within minutes, Misha returned carrying a tray laden with their order, deftly placing everything on the table in the same precise manner she had placed the menus earlier. After pouring tea for both of them, she bowed and wished them an enjoyable experience.

Elena inhaled the comforting scent of jasmine and a woodsy herb she assumed was green tea.

"This is exactly what I need." Elena sighed as she sipped on the tea and ... almost gagged. The gentle aroma of the tea that had melted away her fears and worries masked a strong, bitter taste that lingered on her tongue. She dribbled out the mouthful of tea while holding the cup to her lips and pretending to drink deeply.

Fortunately, Zen was busy dividing the snacks between the two of them, and didn't notice Elena's reaction to the tea. "I have every faith that you and Tarrick will convince your own council to come around to your vision," Zen told her, pushing a plate of food in front of Elena. "If Lin and I did it, so can you."

Elena hung on Zen's every word as she listened to more stories of how Lin dealt with issues during the early years of her reign. Her tea grew cold, and her share of the snacks lay untouched.

"As you can imagine, there were very few people who entered our lands with traitorous thoughts when word spread about Lin's vision," Zen said, spearing a rice cake with her fork.

"But did that convince the council members who opposed Lin?"

"It was a difficult time," Zen admitted while taking a sip of tea. She relished the bitter aftertaste. "Many council members resigned and refused to be involved with the system we had set up. Lin was devastated—a few were her father's closest friends, and they abandoned her when she needed them most." Zen's voice took on a steely note. "Lin will not mind my telling you this. I think she wanted to tell you herself yesterday."

Elena's breath caught as the parallels between what Lin had experienced and what Tarrick was going through grew stronger.

"There were moments of doubt," Zen said quietly, "but we persevered with her plan and stayed true to our dream."

"And it worked?" Elena asked.

"In time, the people came to value the faith and trust we placed in them." Zen gestured to the patrons in the teahouse. "We have to also give them credit and acknowledge the Sailonese who welcomed those who sought asylum. Our people gave them jobs and opportunities to make an honest life for themselves and their families. The Leneirans who made an effort to live according to our principles also played a part in shaping Sailon."

Elena's heart lifted at the positive turn in the story.

"Have faith," Zen said, reaching out to squeeze Elena's arm. "Have faith in yourself, in your king, in your people."

"Thank you," she said, her voice wobbling with emotion. "I needed to hear that."

"You already have Lin's and my support," Zen reminded her. "But you also need to learn to ask for help, and not lose yourself in the process."

Elena looked at her in confusion.

"At what point were you going to tell me you didn't like the tea?" Zen's eyes twinkled in amusement. "Or were you going to pretend it was the tastiest beverage you've had in your life?"

Elena gave her a sheepish smile. "So, what you're saying is, I need to ask for help, tell Tarrick when I don't agree with what he and the council decide, and stand my ground?"

"You're a fast learner." Zen grinned. "Here, try this rice cake." She pointed to a small, lurid-pink cake on Elena's plate. "And tell me what you *really* think of it."

~ 17 ~

Tarrick pushed open the door to their villa, trying to work out how to tell Elena about the impending apocalypse. It wasn't an exaggeration or him being dramatic. He would prioritize Elena's safety above everything else, and he would send her back to the human realm if he had to. She wouldn't make it easy, he was confident of that, but Elena was the most important thing to him now. He didn't want to let her go—her

confession about wanting to leave because of Lazar still weighed on his mind despite her assurances that she was going to stay.

Tarrick wanted to confide in her, tell her everything. But he would break the news gently without making the situation and task sound impossible.

"Damn that Minotian prince," Tarrick muttered to himself as he walked through the room to the private backyard. He stopped short at the sight. Elena was lounging back in a chair, legs propped up on the sides of the pool, the hem of her dress gathered at her knees, revealing smooth, brown calves that tapered into slim

ankles. The water of the hot spring splashed over her bare feet as she turned the page of her book, humming softly to herself.

He tried to recall the last time Elena had been so relaxed, and realized with a pang that he couldn't. More often than not, he found her in quiet corners and hidden alcoves of the palace in Terralea. She normally had her knees drawn up to her chest, a crease between her brows as her eyes darted back and forth over the pages she read.

When she gave him an adoring smile, he had to force himself to hide the guilt over having to break the news about cutting their holiday short.

"Hey, you," she said lazily as he dragged a chair across and placed it opposite her.

Elena emitted a squeak when he wrapped his hands around her ankles and dropped them into his lap as he lowered himself into the chair. Before she could protest or wrench her feet out of his grip, Tarrick pressed his thumbs into the soles and began massaging them. She let out a sigh as he kneaded her arches and slowly made his way down to her heels.

"How was your day?" he asked. "Did Zen show you around LaHong?"

Elena happily recounted all that she had seen, oblivious to his grim mood as he continued to massage her feet.

"I was thinking we could visit the monasteries in the mountains tomorrow," Elena said eagerly. "But it takes half a day to get there, so we'll need to stay overnight. Zen told me the countryside in that part of Sailon has amazing views at the top of the mountains. We could go for a few days and walk the trails during the day? Oh, and she mentioned one of the elite training camps run by non-Empath soldiers further north. We could visit and ask the soldiers there to give us a few tips and show us some moves we could use on Leon? Zen said she'd put in a word for us with the master trainer there." She gave a wicked laugh. "Thank you so much for bringing us here. You were right. We really needed the break."

Tarrick's heart hammered in his chest as he gently lowered Elena's feet onto the soft grass. He leaned forward and placed his hands on her knees.

"El, I'm afraid we're going to have to go back to Terralea," he said gently.

Her face fell for a moment before her expression changed to concern.

"Did something happen to your mom? Leon? Adina?" she asked anxiously.

Tarrick shook his head. "No, they're all fine."

But the worry remained on her face.

"We had an unexpected visitor." Tarrick sighed, rubbing his chin. "Prince Killian, from the Isles of Minos, arrived in LaHong today and has requested our help."

Elena's brows shot up her forehead. "You know him?" she asked with interest.

"I do now," Tarrick replied in a disgruntled voice. The meeting had been tense from the moment the prince stated his request. Tarrick still wasn't sure he believed everything the Minotian prince told him.

"You sound as though it's a bad thing," Elena laughed. "What does he want?"

"Well, we now have an explanation for the strange weather in Terralea and Sailon," he told her, exhaling a long sigh. It had been a relief to learn there was a reason for the storms and deadened lands, but the reason behind them was far worse than he could have imagined.

Elena arched a brow. "This prince knows about the desert storms and dying forests?"

Tarrick confirmed. "He's asked us to help him find the Scepter of Ilona." The king tried to keep his voice light to hide the fear he felt at the thought of the devastating consequences if he had chosen to ignore Killian's request. "It's hidden in Terralea, and the strange weather is only going to get worse if we don't."

"What's the Sceptre of Ilona?"

"It was created by a mystic named Ilona who lived in the Isles," Tarrick told her. "I always thought it was a myth—that's how Father told us the story. But Killian confirmed that it's a real object."

"He wants us to cut short our vacation to go on a *treasure hunt*?" Elena crossed her arms and leveled him a look.

Tarrick winced. It sounded ridiculous without the full backstory and context.

Elena leaned forward, and her brown eyes locked onto his amber ones. "How about you tell me the truth, Tarrick? Aside from the strange weather, what else will happen if we don't find it?"

Tarrick stared at the grass as he spoke. "King Theo"—Elena recalled Lin mentioning his name during the Peace Summit—"has been having disturbing visions about the scepter." Tarrick rubbed his face wearily. "Killian's interpretation is that someone intends to find and use it."

"How dangerous is this scepter?"

Tarrick hesitated, but Elena was already gazing thoughtfully into the distance.

"If it's considered a myth, one of the palace archivists might know about it," Elena murmured. "Can we ask Celine when we get back?"

"That's a good starting point," Tarrick agreed, squeezing Elena's knees. "Killian insists on accompanying us back to Terralea to track it down."

Elena's face dropped at that piece of news.

"I know," Tarrick said at the expression on her face. "But Lin trusts him. He also knows more about the scepter than anyone else."

"You agreed to this already?" Elena's frown deepened.

"I had no choice," he replied, biting his lip. "When Killian outlined what was happening around the isles and his father's vision, well, I—"

"Perhaps *I* should speak directly to Prince Killian." Elena crossed her arms and glared at Tarrick. "I'd like all the details before agreeing to anything."

They were interrupted by a loud knocking on the door.

"This conversation isn't over." She gave him a final glare before flouncing off to the villa. "Zen said she'd come get us when everyone was ready to go to the Lantern Festival."

Tarrick stood reluctantly, regretting not biting the bullet and telling Elena everything. Perhaps it was better coming from Killian; there were parts of the story that even he had trouble understanding.

***

The sun had finally broken through the blanket of pearly clouds late in the day, and the deep red orb was setting on the horizon.

As they followed Zen through the palace, Elena mulled over what Tarrick had told her about Prince Killian and the Scepter of Ilona. Once again, she had the sinking feeling that the king was keeping vital details from her. The way he avoided giving her specific details, not looking her in the eye while he spoke, and his gentle tone suggested he didn't think she could handle the enormity of the situation. She clenched and unclenched her fists to work out some of her aggravation before meeting the others. If Zen noticed her mood, the Empath didn't comment.

Having never met the prince, Elena wasn't sure how she felt about him tagging along and poking about Terralea in search of this fabled object. She was protective of her new home and people. An ugly thought flashed across her mind. *If the scepter isn't found in time and lands in the wrong hands, it could end up being something else the council blames me for.* Zanthus had tried to blame the failing Elemental powers on her. Another disgruntled councilor—such as Lord Malik—could do the same again.

They approached the palace entrance where Lin waited for them. She beamed at Elena, who had calmed down enough to return the smile. Her attention shifted to the tall, handsome man standing beside the Empath queen.

His tanned skin indicated that he spent most of his time out-doors. He had sharp cheekbones and Elena could make out a chis-eled jawline under the well-groomed short beard. A lock of sandy brown hair fell across his forehead as he and Elena assessed each other. He was dressed in an ivory-colored tunic, dark pants, and shiny black boots. Despite the simplicity of his attire, Elena could tell the fabric was of the highest quality and tailored to fit his lean, muscular build. The man gave her and Tarrick a welcoming smile that reached his twinkling green eyes.

Tarrick dipped his head with pursed lips.

"Elena," Lin greeted her. "I'm so sorry I was unable to join you at the teahouse today."

"That's alright," Elena accepted the queen's apology. "Zen was a wonderful tour guide."

Lin threw her wife a grateful look.

"I'm sure Tarrick has told you about our guest," she said, ges-turing toward the man, who stepped forward and inclined his head. "Prince Killian, son of King Theo of the Isles of Minos."

Elena curtsied and offered her hand to shake his.

"Killian, this is Lady Elena of Terralea," Lin introduced her to the prince.

"Lady Elena," Killian said in a deep, slightly accented voice as he bowed and reached for her hand. She felt rough skin and calluses on his palm as he brushed his lips across her knuckles. "Tarrick and Lin have told me so much about you. I hope to get to know you better."

Elena caught sight of a gold chain around his neck that was partially visible under the tunic collar.

"Likewise, Your Highness," she said graciously. "Especially since you will be spending a lot of time in Terralea, from what Tarrick has told me."

Killian blushed and rubbed his chin remorsefully. "I have already apologized to Queen Lin for barging into her territory without invitation, and now I must apologize to you for interrupting your sojourn."

Elena glanced at Tarrick, who gave her a small smile. She assessed Killian, debating whether he would expect her to be formal and show him the same deference she would King Halder and Queen Lin. She tilted her head to the side and decided his friendly, open manner reminded her of Leon and Darius. "You are either very arrogant or very desperate, Your Highness, if you are requesting the assistance of strangers."

The guards standing by the main door shifted uncomfortably at the bold way she addressed Killian. However, Tarrick and Zen chuckled behind her while Lin smirked.

"The latter, I assure you." Killian sighed, running a hand over his face wearily. "Believe me, if the circumstances were not so dire, I would do everything in my power to avert the impending disaster myself."

Elena narrowed her eyes at Tarrick. "You really downplayed that part," she muttered.

He opened his mouth to speak, but closed it and turned to Killian instead. "Please tell Elena everything. I know I agreed to help you find it, but I would like her to hear the facts from you, and let her decide on the best course of action."

Elena raised her brows and dipped her head slightly, acknowledging the permission in Tarrick's words to lead the conversation. She looked back at Killian. "What happens after we help you find the scepter? Do you intend to return home and break off all contact with us?"

Killian shook his head emphatically. "I have already discussed this with my father and told him that we cannot, in good conscience, expect you to help us without reciprocating your kindness."

Elena remained silent, waiting for him to continue. She was softening toward the charming prince who seemed honest and had, so far, been saying all the right things. Still, she remained on her guard as he spoke.

"We would like to extend the hand of friendship to you and yours," Killian said with hope in his green eyes. "Starting with an open invitation for you and King Tarrick to visit our home at any time. And you, Queen Lin," he added, glancing at Lin, who had remained quiet throughout the entire exchange.

She dipped her head in response.

"As captain of the navy, I will be your personal guide around the isles," Killian continued. "You'll be in good company. I trust my crew to take care of you, if my wit and banter don't win you over," he said with a roguish grin.

Out of the corner of her eye, Elena saw Tarrick pull up the expression he reserved for dealing with the Council of Nobles. Her lips twitched at the reappearance of what she affectionately called his "default expression."

"But I assure you, the coves and lagoons around the islands will certainly captivate you. I've spent my entire life navigating the isles, and every time, the beauty of the crystal clear waters and our lands takes me by surprise," Killian continued, oblivious to Tarrick's reaction to his blatant flirting.

Elena started warming to the Minotian prince. A cruise around the Isles of Minos also sounded incredibly tempting.

"My brothers are also keen to restore ties with Terralea, Sailon, and Skandor, especially Orion, who is heir to the throne. We swear to be present at the next Peace Summit."

Elena considered his proposal before finally saying, "Well, it's a start."

Lin chuckled and said, "And I thought I drove a hard bargain! You have the makings of a fine queen, Lady Elena."

"You'll find your actions speak louder than your words, Your Highness," Elena said to Killian with a grin. "I'm holding you to your promises."

Zen smothered a snort of laughter.

"Please, call me Killian," he said, holding out his arm.

Elena moved closer to him and tucked her hand into the crook of his elbow.

"If you call me Elena," she said warmly.

"As you wish." He bowed his head. "I'll tell you everything you want to know about the scepter and my home."

Zen cleared her throat. "We should start heading into town," she advised the group. "We don't want to miss the festivities."

~ 18 ~

The group walked leisurely into the city of LaHong. Lin and Zen led the way, catching up on each other's day while Tarrick, Elena, and Killian followed.

"It's my dream to explore more of Leneira," Killian told Elena wistfully. "I know our islands like the back of my hand, and I could navigate the waters in the middle of the night. I'm sure you understand the need to discover new places, meet new people ..."

"What's stopping you?" Elena asked curiously.

He sighed. "My father. He and King Halder had a disagreement a long time ago, and Father has since refused to be part of mainland politics and activities. He only corresponded with the late King Arran and Queen Lin on an as-needed basis. But now, he has no choice. I suppose it's the silver lining in this situation. While he stays in Delphos to fortify our islands and protect our people, I would like to re-establish ties with Terralea and Sailon."

"Tarrick told me you need our help finding the Scepter of Ilona," Elena said, glancing at the king, who kept close to her side. "It sounded as though the consequences would be dire if we didn't. I'd be glad to help you if you could tell us more about it."

"That's very kind of you." Killian's eyes flitted to Tarrick. "Your future queen is every bit as kind and understanding as you said."

"She is," Tarrick said with pride.

Elena didn't react to his response, still feeling angry about his withholding information. Instead, she wore a pleasant expression and tilted her head to the side.

"I would be glad of your assistance, Elena," the prince said. "Tarrick told me you know Erindell like the back of your hand. I suspect the scepter is protected within the city. King Arran, bound as he was by the scepter's magic and oath to keep its whereabouts secret, would not have hidden it somewhere remote or difficult to access."

"I don't think I know *every* nook and cranny of the city." Elena laughed. "But a treasure hunt will be one way of discovering more of Erindell."

Killian's expression became serious. "A treasure hunt with a deadline."

"Deadline?" Elena raised her brows.

"The scepter should have been passed on some years ago." Worry tinged his voice. "I'm surprised King Arran didn't do so," he said to Tarrick, who looked as worried as Killian sounded.

"Did you say Father was bound by an oath?" Tarrick asked.

Killian explained, "It's part of the scepter's power. Only the ruler who is guarding it knows about its existence and location. Even if they tried to speak of it, its magic would prevent them from doing so."

Elena's head spun at the idea of such complex magic and an object so powerful.

Tarrick rubbed his chin thoughtfully. "That must be why he told me the story of the scepter as though it were a Leneiran myth."

Admiration crossed Killian's face. "That was clever of him. So you know about it and what it's capable of?"

"Very little," Tarrick admitted. "It was one of our bedtime stories, and no one on the council or in the years since has mentioned it."

Killian sighed. "Only the rulers would be aware of its existence. Lin was also unaware of it until today. Prior to Arran, her father hid it here in LaHong. He had been unable to tell her about it before his death too. I'm surprised Arran didn't feel its pull when it became restless."

"What do you mean by 'became restless'?" Elena frowned.

"It is a sentient object. When it gets restless, it becomes agitated."

"Agitated how?" Elena asked cautiously.

Killian thought for a moment before replying. "Think of it like a volcano. If you are attuned to the land, and know how to read the signs, you can tell when it's time to take precautions and evacuate the area."

Elena nodded.

"The desert storms in Terralea, the dying forests of Sailon, the unpredictable waters and change in the tides in Minos are the initial rumblings. I have a feeling that its effects are also felt in Skandor, but King Halder has not sent word of anything yet. It won't be long until the full effects of the scepter's need to be passed on are felt, but we still have time to take measures to avoid death and destruction."

Elena's stomach dropped. "That bad?" she whispered.

"Yes," Killian said hesitantly. "Father's vision has indicated that if it's not passed on, it will make its presence known to anyone in its vicinity. We're facing an imminent catastrophe if its powers are contained for much longer. They'll explode out of the scepter and could destroy the realm if it is not passed on to Halder soon."

Elena leveled a glare at Tarrick, who looked at her apologetically. A thought struck her, and she turned back to Killian. "If the rulers are bound to keep the scepter's existence a secret, how do you know about it and what's about to happen?"

"Just as Arran found a loophole, so did my father," Killian told her, the corner of his lip lifting. "He couldn't tell me outright about the scepter, but I managed to put the pieces together from what he shared with me from his vision. We are taught about ancient magic as part of our history lessons at school. What Tarrick would have learned as myth and legend, Minotians believe to be fact. So much of the realm's magic originated from the isles. It makes sense."

"Suddenly, our library feels inadequate," Elena grumbled. "There's still so much to learn."

Tarrick chuckled. "It's a good thing you have centuries to cover Leneira's entire history."

"Only if we find the scepter in time to prevent the realm from imploding."

"You're not wrong." Killian shuddered. "Father's vision was truly horrific."

"You could see your father's vision?" Elena's brows shot up her forehead.

Killian pulled out the chain around his neck and held up the rainbow-hued stone set into the pendant. "Father can share his visions with whoever wears this talisman," he explained, fingering the heavy gold chain nervously.

Elena leaned forward and squinted at the gem that shone softly in the dusky twilight. "That's incredible."

"There are a number of charms and amulets from our part of the realm that have different magical properties. There are some that can protect the wearer or nullify their magic."

Her eyes flicked up to his. "Bluestone?"

Killian nodded. "Bluestone gems that some Seers wear."

"Why?" Elena asked curiously.

"To avoid self-fulfilling prophecies." Killian shrugged. "Or they haven't been trained to control their abilities. It's a useful stone that helps prevent unexpected surges of power in children whose abilities are just starting to manifest."

"That's also why we *protect* the bluestone quarry instead of destroying it," Tarrick told her. "Father wore a bluestone ring when his lightning abilities first manifested. Otherwise, he would have destroyed half the town."

Elena furrowed her brow; her only experience with the unique material had been when she used a bluestone dagger to prevent Zanthus from using his Elemental powers on her. Until now, she hadn't stopped to think about how a Leneiran would use it in a conducive manner. "I guess I never really thought about how bluestone could be useful."

"Very few people do." Killian gave her another crooked smile. "The only reason our realm exists is because we work to maintain the balance. History has shown the dangers of too much power and abusing the abilities we have been blessed with."

"I think those who want to abuse power will find a way around any obstacle," Elena said drily, remembering Zanthus's toxic formula that nullified Leneiran magic.

"Of course," Killian agreed. "There are always those who threaten the peace, which is why it is imperative we find the scepter before it falls into the wrong hands. It's due to be transferred to King Halder, in any case."

"So moving the scepter is the only way to prevent the realm from imploding," Elena summarized, the gravity of the situation finally sinking in.

"It's an object that feeds off the land, so if it's exposed to different parts of the realm and can absorb the powers present, it remains neutral," Killian explained.

Elena mulled over the information, trying not to panic at the thought of the consequences of letting the scepter stay hidden.

They neared the main road of LaHong that was heaving with locals and visitors from around the country. Everyone stared in wonder at the number of colored lanterns that lined the streets and hung over doorframes and windows. They were lit from within by candles that softly illuminated the city through the fabric and paper of the lantern casings. The city was even more magical at night. As they walked through a lantern arch, Elena craned her neck to take in as much as possible.

"Elena," Killian murmured, drawing her attention away from the crowded streets. "I will gladly tell you the full story of the scepter, but if you don't mind, I wish to refrain from talking about it in such close proximity to the general public."

She nodded understandingly. "Of course. We will have plenty of time to discuss everything on the way back to Terralea."

Tarrick placed his hand on Elena's lower back as he stepped around to her other side, sandwiching her between himself and Killian. She tried to ignore the heat of his touch and the reassuring presence of his body as he shielded her from the crowds.

People gathered by the canal with paper boats to set them afloat in the water. Children darted about the streets wearing fine silk clothes cut in the traditional Sailonese style with high necks and long sleeves. Lin smiled at them fondly. They grinned back at her and waved, while their parents bowed respectfully and stepped to the side as their queen and her guests walked past.

Zen had brought a large stack of decorated envelopes, and a crowd of children gathered around her gleefully. She crouched down to their level and distributed the envelopes amongst them. When each child accepted the gift, they ran back to their parents, exclaiming in excitement.

"It's tradition to give the children and young people of Sailon gifts during the Lantern Festival," Lin explained as they watched the children tear open the envelopes and pull out the contents. Elena caught sight of a small square of paper inked with long, uninterrupted lines of text.

"Those are prayers in our ancient tongue." Lin gestured to a Sailonese man who lifted a small girl in front of an altar and helped her place the piece of paper in a small golden bowl that sat on top of the plinth. Elena's heart melted at the sight of the girl clasping her chubby little hands together and bowing her head, repeating the words her father whispered in her ear.

When both father and daughter finished saying their prayers, they bowed at the altar and stepped away. The girl jumped out of his arms and ran to her mother, who held out the ripped envelope. She grabbed it eagerly and pulled out a small sweet that she crammed into her mouth before running off to play with her friends nearby.

Zen rose to her feet after the children around her dispersed and made her way back to the group. "Here." She held out envelopes to Elena, Tarrick, and Killian and pointed them toward an altar tucked beside a tree.

Elena went first, opening the envelope and sliding out the prayer. She took a moment to admire the swirling lines of calligraphy and brushstrokes before placing the piece of paper in the bowl already filled with prayers and offerings.

Her mind went blank at how to start. In the end, she settled for bowing her head as the locals did and silently thanking the higher powers for a second chance at life with Tarrick's family and her new home. Visions of her own parents came to Elena's mind's eye, making her heart swell with emotion as she remembered their smiling faces when they had said their final goodbyes to her.

When they had all finished taking it in turns to perform the ritual, the group wandered deeper into the city filled with people milling around food carts along the footpaths. Elena held onto Killian's arm as they took in the sights of street performers who perched themselves on impossibly high unicycles. She pointed at a man juggling flaming torches as Killian marveled at a petite woman wriggling out of rope bindings. Several Sailonese walked amongst the melee on tall wooden stilts, waving and smiling at those on the ground. The restaurants were overflowing with patrons, and diners observed the street from tables set on the balconies.

Elena laughed at a stilt walker who made his way to a balcony and opened his mouth for the diners to feed him. An elegant

Sailonese woman blushed and giggled, but held out a fork with a morsel of food speared at the end. The stilt walker clamped his mouth around the utensil and briefly let go of one of his stilts to tip his hat to the woman, who giggled again.

Her dining companion—a man dressed in a formal Sailonese suit—clapped at the little show. He held out some money to the performer, who accepted it and thanked the couple as he tucked the notes into his breast pocket.

They continued walking around the canal and crossed lantern-lit bridges. Despite the long lines in front of the altars dotted around the city, everyone was good-humored and waited patiently to pray and make their offerings.

The people milling about the town bowed to Lin, who greeted them graciously. Elena noted the way they maintained a respectful distance from her but were not worried or fearful of their queen and her guests walking alongside them.

Lin led her visitors to a bend where the canal met LaHong's main river. She carefully descended a set of old wooden stairs that led onto the sandy shore. Elena sucked in a breath when she realized what they were going to do. Ahead was a small crowd gathered around a man selling paper lanterns as tall as Elena. A handful of lanterns already floated into the sky. They danced and circled each other as they rose higher and higher until they were specks of light in the distance.

As she watched the lanterns rising, the moment felt significant. Perhaps it was the combination of the festive atmosphere and the revelations of how much power and magic the realm held. Elena felt that anything was possible and, for some inexplicable reason, what she wished for would come true. "I don't know what to wish for," she said aloud in a panic.

The man selling lanterns recognized Lin and Zen, and his face split into a wide, toothy smile. He bowed deeply before his queen, then handed each of them a small triangle of folded paper that

Lin unfolded carefully. Everyone copied her, and soon, five paper lanterns stood upright, ready for launch. The man placed large wax candles in the holders inside the lanterns.

"Allow me," Tarrick said, stepping forward. He waved a hand, and the candles flickered to life.

Elena had been fiddling with the crepe paper and tightened her hold on the lantern to stop it from floating away before she made her wish. Her mind raced through all the things she wanted, scrambling to settle on the thing she wanted the most.

"Everyone ready?" Lin called out. She counted down slowly, and they let go of their lanterns. Elena was the last to release hers, hesitating as her lips moved silently, forming the words to her hopes and dreams. She swallowed a lump in her throat at the sight of five lanterns floating up, carrying their wishes into the night sky.

~ 19 ~

The lanterns rose gracefully into the night sky. The group fell silent, overcome by emotion and serenity of the moment.

When the lanterns were mere pinpricks of light, Elena dragged her attention back to the sandy riverbank on which they stood. More people had gathered to send off their own lanterns, and it was starting to get crowded. Their group headed back to the streets. Killian was the first to break the silence.

"Shall we get something to eat?" he suggested.

Everyone agreed enthusiastically, the smells emanating from the food carts making their mouths water. The brightly painted wooden carts on rickety wooden wheels advertised an array of traditional Sailonese food—sandwiches stuffed to bursting with grilled meats and salad, omelettes garnished with hot peppers and bright herbs, steamed shellfish, skewered meats, and vegetable chunks barbecued on grills.

Killian bought them all plates of food that they took to a quiet spot by the canal to eat. Several people offered Lin their tables and seats as the group walked past, but she declined and insisted they remain seated.

"She is unlike any leader I've met," Killian observed. "Mind you, I haven't met that many, so I suppose I can't really compare."

Elena agreed with him.

She held onto the sandwich Killian gave her, holding her breath. Elena still couldn't eat grilled meat after the spring. Tarrick's warm hand covered her cold, clammy one, and she looked down.

"Here," he murmured, switching their plates, "have my omelette instead."

Elena gratefully accepted his plate of food that didn't make her stomach churn. "Thank you," she whispered.

They sat on a raised edge and carefully balanced the plates on their laps as they watched LaHong grow more and more lively as the night went on. Music filled the air, but it was impossible to pinpoint the source of the festive notes and uplifting tunes.

"What did you wish for?" Tarrick asked as they ate.

"I can't tell you." Elena shook her head. "It won't come true."

Killian chuckled.

"Give me a clue," Tarrick teased, nudging her with his elbow.

"No," Elena insisted. "I'm allowed to have my secrets."

He held up his hands in surrender. "Alright, I'll stop asking."

"Tell us what *you* wished for, Tarrick," Killian asked with a wink.

The king appraised him before saying, "I didn't make a wish."

"Oh?"

"I sent up my gratitude for what I already have," he told Killian, but looked at Elena as he spoke.

Her expression softened, and she opened her mouth to apologize to Tarrick, but splashing and laughter nearby caught everyone's attention. A group of children at the edge of the canal were urging their half-sunken soggy paper boat forward. Suddenly, the boat straightened and glided gently around the canal, eliciting clapping and shouts of amazement.

Elena swung her gaze to Tarrick, who was watching the children with a grin on his face. His eyes followed the boat, which floated in figure-eight formations on the surface of the water. A crowd gathered to watch the display.

"Are you doing that?" Elena whispered.

His smile widened in confirmation.

She watched it sail back to the children, who lifted it out of the canal with squeals of delight. They flipped it over and examined the bottom of the sodden paper for signs of magic, but found none. They set it back on the water, and Tarrick sent it on its way along with the other paper boats that were floating serenely down the canal.

The water shifted and rose. The crowd whispered and exclaimed in excitement as the water shaped itself into a horse. They gasped and pointed as the water horse rose on its hind legs. It shook its mane, showering those standing at the edge with mist.

There were more squeals of delight as the horse pranced on the surface, throwing back its head and galloping gracefully along the canal.

"My mother commissioned statues of the *naya* on all of the isles," Killian said, watching the water horse with interest. "I like them because it keeps the memory of her alive. She was a beloved queen, just as Queen Samara had been."

Elena reached out to squeeze Killian's arm.

"I'm sure she was wonderful," she said quietly.

"We must have you all visit every year for the festival," Zen declared. Her voice was laced with wonder as she watched the water horse canter. "Our people will be talking about this for months to come, and will expect a show again next year."

By then, the older Sailonese who had gathered by the waterside had worked out who Tarrick was and what he was doing. They whispered to each other in awe, looking between him and the children, who were reaching out to pat the horse's watery nose.

"I would love to come again," Elena said sincerely. "This has been such a memorable night. I'm sure Adina and Leon would also enjoy the festival and gladly put on a show for your people."

Lin's eyes lit up at Elena's suggestion.

"We're going to hold you to that." Zen laughed. "I think my wife will be extending a formal invitation before you leave."

Tarrick's expression softened as he watched the children's small hands grabbing handfuls of the horse's flowing mane and tail. Giggles bubbled from them as the water trickled through their fingers. The benevolent smile on his face reminded Elena of the time Arran had watched his own children over breakfast only a few months before—a normal family sharing a rare unguarded moment that the former king treasured. Her lips curved up at that memory.

"What are you thinking about?" Tarrick asked.

"What a great dad you'll be one day," she replied without thinking.

A small crease appeared between his brows as he made the water horse canter to the middle of the canal. It reared back once more, then galloped down the waterway, ducking and weaving between the paper boats before disappearing out of sight.

Everyone clapped and cheered, including Lin, Zen, and Killian. But up close, the smile didn't quite meet Tarrick's eyes, and he held himself stiffly. Elena reached out for his hand and interlaced their fingers together. He squeezed her hand in response.

A whistling sound overhead drew everyone's attention to the sky. An explosion of colored lights and flames lit up the night.

Elena was taken back to her childhood when she and her parents would drive down to the lake for the Fourth of July fireworks display. They were just as magical as they had been when she was a child. Elena recalled the way she had been sandwiched between her parents on the lakeshore, the loud bangs and whistling drowning out the squeals of children. Tears gathered at the memory of Elena's mum wrapping her arms around her and hugging her tightly. Her dad would ruffle her hair and plant sloppy kisses on her mom's cheek, making her cry out in mock disgust and smack him gently on the arm.

Elena leaned into Tarrick's side, and he put an arm around her shoulder, pressing her to him.

***

The following morning, Elena and Tarrick made their way to the dining chamber. Lin and Zen sat at the table with their heads bent toward each other, talking in low, urgent voices. Elena's stomach dropped at the serious expressions on their faces.

"Your Majesty," Lin addressed Tarrick formally.

"What's happened?" Tarrick asked calmly, but quickened his steps.

"We've received messages from Terralea." Lin gestured to an open letter on the table, a sealed envelope next to it. "Councilor Jet is asking for his sister to travel back with you. He needs Mika's assistance with reading someone. "

"Have they found more traitors?" Elena asked, her breathing becoming shallow. "Why would he need Mika for help? He was starting to read emotions and intentions on sight."

Zen's forehead creased. She and Lin appeared to have a silent conversation.

"We were waiting for you to read Leon and Adina's letter, hoping it would provide more context." Zen slid the envelope over to Tarrick, and he opened it carefully. Elena waited quietly for an explanation, drumming her fingers against her thigh.

Tarrick clicked his tongue impatiently and held the letter out to her. "This is the vaguest letter I've ever received from my brother."

Elena took the letter and read it herself.

Tarrick, you need to return immediately. You need to see for yourself.

Mother has sent word that she will be back in the next day or so as well. You should be here to greet her.

— Leon & Adina

~ 20 ~

Elena had read enough of Leon's correspondence and notes to know he liked to include lengthy detail and embellishments—sometimes too much. It was also unusually serious for the humorous prince who liked to tease his brother no matter the method of communication.

Tarrick read Jet's letter, at Lin's insistence, and his frown deepened. He said to Lin and Zen, "I will let you know of Jet's safety the minute I see him. I can assure you, he has been afforded every security measure. My brother has spent a great deal of time with him. He would have said if something was wrong."

Lin waved away Tarrick's assurances.

"Jet is fine. He's one of my strongest people," she said, shaking her head. "I'm worried about why he's unable to read someone."

"Is there a chance he's consumed that poison again?" Zen asked worriedly.

Tarrick shook his head. "No one has reported any lapses in their abilities in over a month now. We check the water purity daily."

"Perhaps we should double the checks and include surrounding areas if some of that toxin passed through or came from another source we aren't aware of," Elena suggested, placing a hand on Tarrick's arm.

"Consider it done," he said immediately, his gaze sliding to her. "I understand if you are reluctant to send us another of your councilors ..." Tarrick met Lin and Zen's concerned expressions.

"We can spare Mika for a few days"—Zen glanced at Lin, who bobbed her head—"but we would like confirmation that all is well in your country."

"Of course." Tarrick bowed his head. "Once I get a full understanding of what has happened, I shall send word."

Killian entered the room with a smile that faded when he took in the serious atmosphere of the room.

"Is everything alright?" he inquired.

"We have been summoned back to Terralea as a matter of urgency," Tarrick explained. "Elena and I need to leave straight away."

Killian's face fell.

Tarrick hesitated. "I know we planned for you to accompany us to Terralea …"

"But the scepter needs to be found," Killian said urgently. "We cannot wait on this matter."

Elena glanced at Tarrick. "Is there a chance the scepter is starting to affect more than the weather? Is that what Leon and Adina have noticed?"

"If Leon bothered to include even a little information that would be of use," Tarrick growled, running a hand over his jaw.

"Why don't Killian and Mika travel back in your carriage?" Lin offered. "You and Elena can return on a couple of *pihasi* to save time and find out what's happened."

Tarrick's face cleared. "Good idea."

Killian agreed to the plan reluctantly, but insisted that he and Mika travel without lengthy breaks. After thanking Lin and Zen for their hospitality, he spun on his heel and headed back to his suite to pack.

"I'll see you tomorrow, Your Majesty, Lady Elena," he called over his shoulder.

Elena placed her hand on Tarrick's arm as he glared at Killian's retreating back. "If something has happened and it's because of the scepter, it's better if he comes sooner rather than later. We don't know what we're dealing with."

Tarrick sighed. "You're right. Let's go pack."

Lin and Zen inclined their heads as Tarrick swept past, pausing to murmur his thanks to them both.

"Meet us at the stables," Lin told them. "We'll prepare the *pihasi.*"

Elena hurried after him, her heart beating fast from the anxiety that had spiked since reading Leon's letter and trying to keep up with Tarrick's long strides.

"I'm so sorry about all of this," he apologized while throwing their belongings into the bags. "This wasn't the relaxing getaway I had planned at all."

"We can come back," Elena said, adding her clothes to the mix without bothering to fold them neatly. "It's not your fault all this stuff is happening."

They finished packing and Elena stepped out to the backyard, gazing wistfully at the private pool. She would have enjoyed another night luxuriating in the natural warm spring water and everything that came with it.

The air was still and humid, the sky a pearly white. The stomping of hooves and whinnying greeted them when the stables came into sight. Elena felt a jolt of excitement at the thought of riding a *pihasi* again. A stablehand guided two magnificent beasts out to the paddock, where Lin greeted him and reached out to pat the horses' noses. They stretched out their wings and shook their manes, eager to take to the skies.

"Ky and Az will get you back home by afternoon," she told Tarrick and Elena. "It'll be faster if you ride separately, since you're crossing half the realm."

"We really appreciate this, Lin," Tarrick thanked their host, reaching out for the reins on the larger steed. "I'm sorry our visit was cut short, but I think it's safe to say we'll be back soon."

Elena agreed, echoing Tarrick's sentiments.

"You are both welcome any time," Lin told them.

Elena moved to the smaller winged horse, and Lin helped her mount the beast. To Elena's relief, the *pihasi* stood still and waited for his rider to scramble onto his back and adjust herself in the saddle.

Lin quickly explained to Elena what to do and how riding the *pihasi* was different from an ordinary horse. Elena's palms grew sweaty as Lin's instructions tapered off—last time, she had ridden with Tarrick, who was more competent. This time, she was in full control of the animal, who was calm and docile under her.

"Thank you for a wonderful time," Elena said sincerely. "As Tarrick said, we will come back for another visit. We'll let you know about Jet as soon as we find out what's going on. And I'm looking forward to seeing Mika again."

"Any time, my dear." Lin smiled at her. "It has been a pleasure to show you our city, but there is still so much more for you to discover in Sailon."

"I'll definitely be back," Elena promised. "Please tell Zen I said the same to her."

"I'll let her know," Lin assured her. She observed Tarrick, who was checking his saddle and tightening the straps. "Tarrick loves you, Elena," she said quietly. "He's learning too. Remember that."

Elena was startled by Lin's cryptic parting message. Before she could reply or question her, the queen smacked Az's hindquarters lightly to send him on his way.

Elena clutched the reins tightly, forcing herself not to scream out loud at the speed at which the *pihasi* was galloping across the grounds before spreading his wings and launching into the sky. The air rushing past whistled in her ears. The world fell silent, and she was both terrified and exhilarated by the sensation.

When the horse leveled out, Elena wriggled and adjusted herself in the saddle, trying to get more comfortable and secure. She twisted the reins in her hands and held onto the pommel for good measure. The countryside below was a blur of green and brown that flew by at a dizzying speed.

The sound of beating wings grew louder next to her—Tarrick sat far more comfortably and was in control of his steed. He was focused on the horizon, bending low as he flew ahead.

They stopped at a tavern around midday to rest the *pihasi* and eat something themselves, having skipped breakfast that morning. Tarrick guided Ky toward the ground, and Az followed obediently. Elena's stomach lurched, and she closed her eyes to stop herself from being sick at the sight of the earth hurtling up to them. Her eyes flew open when she bounced on the *pihasi's* back and its hooves clopped against stone.

Elena and Tarrick didn't linger over lunch. They ordered meals that were the quickest to prepare. There was a tightness in Tarrick's jaw, and Elena let him ruminate while they waited for their food.

"Tarrick," she said hesitantly when she swallowed the last bite of her sandwich.

"Yes?"

She reached out to him across the table. His expression softened, and he took her hand in his.

"Promise me something," she said earnestly. The ride had given her time to reflect on what Zen and Ninaz had advised her about making her voice heard. She wanted to show Tarrick that she was capable of handling whatever came their way.

"Anything."

"Whatever is waiting for us," she told him, "no matter what's happened or what's going to happen, we face it together. I want to work with you this time. I don't want to be sitting on the sidelines, waiting for you to tell me what's going on."

"Of course," he replied.

But Elena shook her head. "No, Tarrick. I'm serious. No more keeping information from me to try to spare my feelings or making assumptions about how I'll react to things."

He opened his mouth to speak, but Elena continued. "I want to help you and be by your side for all of it," she said steadily. "Promise me that we will make decisions together and put our people above all else."

Tarrick's face relaxed. "I promise, El. We're in this together, for better or for worse."

She leaned over the table and kissed him.

When they finished eating and paid for their meals, Tarrick inspected the *pihasi* to make sure they were rested enough for the final stretch of their journey. The winged horses responded readily to his touch and nuzzled the palm of his hand. He helped Elena mount Az, who complied with Tarrick's gentle hands and soothing, murmured words. Elena made herself as comfortable as she could in the saddle.

Az followed Ky into the sky without needing a smack on his hindquarters. They glided over the land, Elena focusing on the views of Leneira to distract herself from the burn and tightness in her thigh muscles that indicated she would be sore the next day.

A few hours later, Elena spotted the familiar sight of the Temple of Divine Beings shining like a beacon in the late-afternoon sun. This time, she was prepared for the landing, and braced herself when Az dipped forward and descended, landing with a gentle bump on the palace grounds.

Adina and Leon were already waiting for them at the stables. Tarrick didn't wait for Ky to stop completely before he jumped off and landed lightly on his feet. Az trotted to the group and stopped in front of Adina, whose grim expression disappeared for a moment when she gazed at the animal with delight.

"Tell me everything," Tarrick demanded, reaching up to help Elena dismount. She gave the winged horse a pat on his nose, and he nuzzled against her hand in affection. A guard stepped out from the stables and led the *pihasi* to the training rings for a thorough cool down and grooming after their journey across half the realm.

"No Mika?" Leon peered around.

"She'll be here tomorrow. Your letters were vague enough that I didn't want to risk bringing another of Lin's people into a potentially dangerous situation," Tarrick retorted.

Leon huffed and said to Adina, "I *told* you we should have given them more details."

"No," the princess countered in a steely voice that she had never used. "Until we confirm that Henry is not a threat, this stays inside the palace walls."

Tarrick snapped his head to his sister.

"It's bad enough the council is circling rumors about Elena, if word gets out about him …" Adina trailed off, glancing at Elena. The princess bit her lip and spun on her heel, striding toward the palace.

"Adina, stop being dramatic and tell us what's happened," Tarrick said through gritted teeth, keeping pace with his sister. "What rumors about Elena? Who is Henry?"

Elena and Leon scurried behind them, trying to keep up while Tarrick continued bombarding his sister with questions. He grew increasingly angry with her silence as they stalked through the corridors, somehow managing to avoid the nobles who had taken up residence in the palace.

"Adina, enough with the mystery." He folded his arms across his chest.

They had reached his shut office door, Zahra standing guard. She gave Tarrick a sharp bow and continued staring straight ahead.

Elena eyed the door in trepidation, not sure if she was ready to confront whatever threat lay behind.

"It's difficult to explain," Leon said slowly. "There are still a number of questions that need to be answered and details we need to verify."

Adina reached for the doorknob and paused. "It may be a bit of a shock," she said, twisting the knob and slowly swinging the door open. "I know it was for Leon and me."

A strange man was standing by the window, peeping out into the garden. He turned around when they entered. Full lips curled up in an arrogant smirk that tinged his otherwise handsome and distinguished features.

Tarrick's face crumpled at the sight of the man.

~ 21 ~

Tarrick paled.

The man held his stare, unfazed.

Tarrick's gaze roved over every inch of the stranger's face, honing in on the familiar chiseled jaw, sharp cheekbones, and distinctive eyes. They were exactly like his mother and Leon's, from the kaleidoscope of blues in his irises down to the gold flecks that shimmered like spots of sunlight dancing on the ocean.

"Hello, I'm Henry," the man said with a tentative smile, and held out his hand to Tarrick. "I believe I am your son."

Elena gasped beside him.

Tarrick's stomach dropped. He glanced down to see her cover her mouth with a hand. Elena wore an expression of shock as she took in the sight of the man who bore a striking resemblance to Tarrick, with a few deliberate differences. The chin, small forehead, and deep-set eyes were from Rose.

Henry moved smoothly to the center of the room with his hands hanging loosely by his side. He looked to be only a few years older than Elena. His short, black hair was parted at the side and combed back from his clean-shaven face.

He wore a crisp white button-down shirt under a navy suit jacket cut to his frame. The dark pants that covered his long legs met leather brogues, polished to a high shine. The gold signet ring on his left index finger was the only visible jewelry, adding to the image of an aristocrat.

Henry stood at ease, unperturbed by the fact that he had a number of people marking his every move. He scanned the group, and when he paused on Elena, the sunlight streaming through the window intensified his gold-flecked blue eyes. Tarrick was torn between wanting to inspect Henry up close and stand in front of Elena to protect her from his intense gaze.

She held his stare and lowered her hand. The expression of shock gave way to suspicion in the way Elena took him in from head to toe.

Leon coughed in the corner, alerting Tarrick to the fact that no one had said a word since Henry spoke.

Elena and Henry paid no attention to Leon. They were still locked in their silent duel. A crease formed between Henry's brows, and his stance stiffened as he tilted his head in challenge. Elena crossed her arms and jut her chin out defiantly. The tension in the air thickened rapidly.

"Please, take a seat," Tarrick said, collecting himself. He moved toward the fireplace, where two wingback chairs faced each other. It took every effort to smooth his features into a neutral expression, to hide the tremor in his voice and stop his hands from shaking.

Henry sat in the chair that Tarrick indicated. Adina and Leon stood on either side of their brother's seat while Elena took up a discreet position by the bookshelf. Her pale face mirrored the shock Tarrick felt, but she remained silent as he led the exchange.

"I'm sure you've been questioned by my brother and sister already," Tarrick said, glancing at his siblings, who nodded in confirmation. "But I would like to hear your story for myself."

"Of course," Henry said smoothly, as though he had been expecting to repeat himself. He summarized his childhood—living in a seedy part of town in the same townhouse as their landlord and five other women, sharing a room with Rose; living on ration coupons; having to walk to and from school by himself by the age of six because Rose worked long hours to make ends meet.

When he reached the part about being raised in a grim orphan-age after his mother passed away when he was ten years old, Tar-rick had to tamp down the rising guilt. He steepled his fingers and listened intently as Henry tried to compose himself. Had he known, if there were even an inkling that he had a son, he would have done what he could to save Henry from such a tragic childhood.

"They did their best," Henry told him, referring to the nuns who ran the orphanage, "but times were tough after the war."

Tarrick shook his head regretfully. "I'm sorry for your loss. If I had known …"

"I tried to find out about you," Henry said with a wry smile. "But the only records were Mama's stories. I had no living relatives or clues, except for this mark that Mama said I was born with." He hitched up the left sleeve of his jacket and shirt slightly to display the Terralean crest, inked on his wrist. Tarrick closed his eyes—even if there was some small chance that Henry wasn't his son, he was still a Terralean. With proof of his heritage, he could have been safe and protected in Terralea.

Elena leaned forward and sucked in a breath at the sight of the mark.

Henry paused and took in Tarrick's features, drinking in the king's face like a man in the desert, starved of water.

Tarrick rubbed his chin and sighed. "Please, continue."

"I worked odd jobs, secretarial and clerk work," Henry narrated. "When my friends and long-term acquaintances started to show signs of aging while I still looked like a young man, I knew something was … different about me."

He paused again, and his expression shifted.

"Go on," Tarrick encouraged, eager to learn how Henry had survived the human realm.

"I never feared for my life until my withered and wrinkled friends started whispering and pointing fingers at me," Henry sighed. "There was no logical explanation for the way I had stopped aging, and when they started spewing nonsense about selling my soul to the devil, I had to get away. Make a fresh start far away."

He hesitated again.

"I'm not proud of some of the things I did," he admitted in a low voice, shame creeping into his tone. "But, life on the run was difficult. Being orphaned at such a young age after a world war meant that identities and records could easily be forged and erased." His hands tightened their grip on his knees, and he peeked up at Tarrick. "I managed to move around unnoticed, unseen, and, for the most part, unknown. I stole identities and created aliases. I traveled far and wide, where I could lie low for a few years without drawing attention to myself.

"All the while, I tried researching my parentage and biology. DNA and genetic testing back then were non-existent. There were stories about how human subjects in testing labs were mistreated in those days."

Behind Tarrick, Elena made a sympathetic sound, the first sign of softening toward the stranger. He was going to have to have a very difficult conversation with her once they were done with Henry. His conscience wouldn't let him keep the truth from her any longer. Not after that bombshell. It was going to hurt, but it had to be done, and he would be there for her in whatever capacity she needed.

"I fell into a routine, staying in one place for a few years, taking up jobs where I could go about unnoticed, then moving on before people discovered my secret." Henry glanced over at Adina and Leon, who were watching him closely.

Adina wore the impassive expression to mask how she truly felt. Tarrick's sister was still haunted by the events that had occurred with Zanthus, and he was worried for her. Elena had confided in him that Adina had pulled away from their friendship and chose to spend more time by herself. It worried Tarrick, but his own experience of losing loved ones made him hold his tongue and not push. Adina would talk about her feelings in time. He trusted that she would confide in Elena or Amaya when she was ready.

"A few months ago, a stranger came to my home." Henry's eyes snapped to Tarrick, pulling him back to the present. "He gave me a letter and a talisman and told me about another realm where my father lived."

Adina stepped forward, pulling out a folded piece of paper and a heavy gold chain with a large gem from the pocket of her vest. She placed both items on the small table between the chairs, and Tarrick leaned forward to read the letter. His brow furrowed.

"I've already made inquiries with our scribes and the archivists," Adina reported. "No one recognizes the handwriting."

The scrawling words were brief and to the point. It told Henry about his parentage and provided instructions on how to enter Leneira through a hidden portal in a tree in Istanbul. It was almost clinical in its tone, as though it were a medical report that stated facts. Tarrick also didn't recognize the writing, but that didn't mean anything. Anyone could have dictated the letter to a scribe to avoid being caught.

"Can you describe the person who visited you?" Tarrick eyed Henry closely.

He shook his head. "Unfortunately, my descriptions are quite generic, and he had one of those faces you'd forget the minute he disappeared."

Adina spoke up. "Already investigating." She gave the king a knowing look, indicating that she, too, suspected the assassin was involved. But how would he know the pertinent details of Tarrick's past and who Henry was?

"I tried to find out more about the talisman over the summer," Henry explained. "Over the years, I've developed an affinity for antiques and valuables. I have a number of contacts who specialize in heirloom pieces."

"I take it you found no information?" Tarrick asked drily, placing the letter on the table and sitting back in his chair. "Leneira is a well-guarded secret. If any information about our realm finds its way through the portal, that record is destroyed by the portal guards and security teams."

All eyes rested on Henry once more. Despite the tense atmosphere, he remained calm and composed. Granted, no one was accusing Henry of ill intent or implying that he had an ulterior motive for being in Terralea. The information he had provided was … perfect. Perfect in its delivery, perfect in the level of detail he provided, and perfect in the things he didn't know. Tarrick could feel the suspicion and scepticism rolling off Elena and Leon as they watched the exchange.

"So you decided, after months of fruitless searching, to follow the instructions in the letter?" Tarrick raised a brow, his curiosity about the young man growing.

"Yes," Henry said steadily.

They stared at each other.

Elena shifted uncomfortably in the corner.

Henry's story was innocent enough—sad, even, given that he had lived most of his life alone and afraid of not knowing what he was—but there was something off about him that Tarrick couldn't put his finger on. He tried to push aside the maelstrom of emotion and assess Henry objectively. However, the nagging feeling persisted. Henry was well-dressed, well-groomed, and well-spoken. A little too smooth for Tarrick's liking, but perhaps the aristocratic gentlemanly veneer was his way of hiding nerves and wanting to make a good first impression.

"I need to confer with my family, Henry," Tarrick finally said, rising to his feet.

Henry rose to his feet and smiled easily. "Of course. I understand."

"Zahra will show you back to your room." Adina motioned for Henry to walk ahead.

He walked to the door with her a few paces behind him. Then, he hesitated and turned back to Tarrick, who was still watching him with a neutral expression on his face.

"I wasn't sure what to expect when I entered the portal," Henry said softly. "I have only been here a few days, but I can already tell that your family and people admire you. It brings me a great deal of comfort knowing that my father is a respectable and honorable man."

Elena huffed quietly but refrained from speaking. Adina ushered Henry out. When she stepped back into Tarrick's office and closed the door firmly, Leon let out a low whistle and flopped into the chair Henry had vacated.

"Well, what do you think?" He looked between Tarrick and Elena.

Tarrick rubbed his face with a hand and let out a heavy sigh. "What the fuck, Leon?"

Elena laughed out loud at the uncharacteristic reaction. Leon also grinned at his brother.

"Here's his birth certificate," Adina said, moving to Tarrick's desk and picking up a piece of paper. "I've had it authenticated and double-checked with both sides of the portal. It's legitimate. Henry arrived in Terralea a few weeks ago, but because of the desert storms"—Tarrick's stomach lurched at the reminder that he had to fill in his siblings about the scepter and Killian—"the guards were delayed in bringing him here. But their accounts state that Henry was obliging, patient, and polite the entire time he was with them."

Tarrick held out a hand for the document. Elena strode over to examine it for herself. She put a hand on his shoulder, and Tarrick pulled her into his lap. Her weight and warmth comforted him as they read it together.

"Tarrick Smith?" Elena raised a brow at the name recorded as Henry's father. "Really?"

"Try being Leon Smith for three years," Leon grumbled. "I wanted to be part of the peerage with a double-barreled name, but Father insisted we blend in."

"You don't like him, Adina." It was a statement rather than a question. With the growing evidence that Henry was, indeed, Tarrick's biological son, the king was still in disbelief at the thought that he had been blessed with the impossible.

"I don't trust him," Adina said abruptly.

"Why not?" he asked, almost defensively. But of course, Adina was unaware of the deal he had made with the Divine Beings. She didn't know he had accepted that he and Elena would never have children.

She shrugged. "Call it intuition."

Tarrick frowned at her before scrutinizing the certificate.

"He has a sad story, and there are parts that I would question," Elena said, looking at Adina in solidarity. But the princess didn't even turn her head. "He's a smooth-talker and basically admitted to conning people for most of his life."

"You don't trust him either?" Tarrick's eyes flew to Elena.

She bit her lower lip and spoke slowly. "I think we should be cautious. We don't know for sure if he's your son."

"I'm sorry this has all been sprung on you like this." Tarrick shook his head. "It isn't out of the realm of possibility that he could be mine." He blushed. "I took the tonic and Rose took ... precautions ..."

He squirmed slightly.

"Nothing is foolproof, especially the options available to women back then," she said brusquely. "But until we have solid proof of his identity—"

Leon coughed awkwardly. "He's got our eyes, El. At least, from Mother's side. And he had a bit of Tarrick in his features. The crest on his wrist is proof that he is, at least, Terralean. The portals only recognize Leneiran blood. It would have been impossible for him to enter by himself otherwise."

"I take it he met Jet?" Tarrick asked Adina, who gave a curt nod.

"That's why we wanted you to bring back Mika," she said. "Jet couldn't read him. We introduced him as an ambassador without revealing his origins and abilities."

"They shook hands for over a minute," Leon added. "I thought Jet was going to shake it right off."

No one laughed.

Tarrick's brows knitted in concern. "What do you mean he couldn't read him?"

"Jet said it was as though Henry had a mental shield up—the way we do when we're around Empaths," Adina explained. "But that's impossible if he's never learned how. It's a skill that we've practiced over decades, not something you can just do."

Tarrick leaned forward and held up the necklace. "This is of Minotian origins. It could have been protecting him from Jet's reading."

Elena leaned forward to inspect the necklace glinting in the setting sun. The gem was rainbow-hued with swirls of color under the pearlescent sheen. It was beautiful but ostentatious.

"How do you know?" Leon asked.

"The bail is engraved with an eye—a motif of the Seers from the Isles of Minos," Tarrick explained. Leon moved closer until the tip of his nose brushed against the gem as he squinted at the tiny engraving.

"How did it end up with Henry?" Adina demanded. "Was it a Minotian who contacted him?"

"Most of the creators of magical objects lived in the Isles because they connected strongly with nature and the elements there—the islands were largely untouched and pristine before Leneirans moved in and built villages and towns. The objects they created were not for the exclusive use of Seers or Minotians." Tarrick shrugged. "There are magical objects scattered throughout Leneira that were created by these mystics, but they have been in Skandor, Terralea, and Sailon for so long that it is assumed they have origins in the country in which they are held. Anyone could have found this necklace and sent it to him."

The crease between Elena's brows deepened. "There's a physical resemblance to Tarrick," she acknowledged. "But until we have solid proof of his identity and origins, Adina is right to be wary."

"We will never get that." Leon shook his head.

"Why not?" Elena demanded. "We could go to the human realm and get DNA tests done. These are extenuating circumstances, and we need to be certain."

"You've read the biology books, El," Tarrick said gently. "You know our bodies and makeup are completely different from humans. We couldn't get tests done without raising questions and risking the exposure of our realm."

She crossed her arms and jutted out her chin. "I don't like the idea of a stranger making such claims and taking advantage of you."

Adina nodded.

"What are you saying, El?" Tarrick asked roughly. Logic dictated that he should be heavily scrutinizing everything before accepting it, but the arguments and excuses for Henry being an imposter were growing weaker. The idea that he had a son when Tarrick had accepted the fact that he and Elena would never have children had planted a kernel of hope in his heart.

"I don't want you hurt," she said in a soothing voice. Elena's eyes flicked over to Leon and again to Adina. "Any of you."

"Leon," Tarrick addressed his brother. "Send Lin a message to let her know there's no danger, and Mika and Jet will be safe here for the time being. Tell her that we are dealing with a personal issue, that there are ... complications. We'll give her the full story once we are confident that Henry is who he says he is."

"On it." Leon stood and straightened his tunic. On his way to the door, he paused at Tarrick's table and grabbed a few pieces of parchment with Terralea's crest at the top that Tarrick had pre-signed.

"Adina, I want a full report on Henry from the moment he left his house in England to when I walked into this room."

She nodded and strode to the door.

When the lock clicked behind her, Tarrick wrapped his arms around Elena's waist and buried his face in her neck with a groan. "I leave for a few days with you, and all this happens."

She let out a quiet laugh and combed her fingers through his hair. "This is a plot twist I didn't see coming," she murmured.

Tarrick lifted his head. "You're not upset I had a son with Rose?"

She stiffened and hesitated before replying. "I am upset. Well, maybe not upset. Surprised? Shocked? Confused? But I want to know why now. Why, after almost a hundred years, he's here? Who sent him that note and talisman? We also don't know for sure he's your son."

"I took the tonic every day." Tarrick shook his head. "Even if Rose wasn't careful, Leneirans have been taking the tonic for millennia."

"Should I be taking it?" Elena wrinkled her nose. "I mean, if we don't want to start a family while we're still figuring things out with the council and running the country. Don't forget, there's a scepter that's waiting to be found before it destroys the realm," she added sarcastically.

"No, you don't have to worry about that," Tarrick mumbled.

Elena looked at him in disbelief. "I think we should all be worried about the scepter."

"I wasn't talking about the scepter," Tarrick said heavily. "I meant starting a family."

"But we've been sleeping together *a lot*," Elena blushed. "And I don't have any protection from the human realm. It's not a good time to have children, Tarrick."

Tarrick faltered. It was the moment to tell Elena everything. He pulled her closer to him so she was pressed against his chest. It wouldn't stop her from backing away when he finally told her the truth, but he wanted the moment to hold Elena and comfort her before he shattered her world.

"We're not going to have children, El," Tarrick said in a low voice.

"What do you mean?" she asked impatiently, her voice slightly muffled in his chest. "At the rate we've been going at it, it's inevitable. I've lost track of my cycle. I think I'm due soon, but I can't be sure."

"You won't fall pregnant," he said, the anger slipping through his voice. Anger at himself, at the Divine Beings, at the situation.

"Now you're an expert on my fertility?" she asked sarcastically.

"Yes," he snapped. "I know for a fact that you and I will not *ever* have a child."

Elena stared at him. "You don't know that," she said finally. "Leneirans have mated with humans before. It's how the non-magicals were created."

"It's not about compatibility," he said between gritted teeth, trying and failing to stop the words escaping so harshly. "It's about what I sacrificed to save you."

Elena leaned back, confusion and fear written on her face. "Wha—?"

"The Divine Beings saw a possible future in which we conceived a child." His voice was thick with emotion. "That was the blood they wanted in exchange for bringing you back to life. I sacrificed our child to save you. They were very clear—giving up the one child they saw us have in exchange for bringing you back from the brink of death means that future is no longer a possibility for us."

If Elena were pale before, she had turned a ghostly white now. "Are you sure?" she whispered in a hoarse voice.

"Yes, El," Tarrick said, the break in his voice betraying his own emotions. "We can never have children."

~ 22 ~

The blood pounded in Elena's ears as she processed Tarrick's revelation.

He ran his fingers through his hair, face full of regret and sorrow. "El, I'm sorry. I shouldn't have told you like that."

"You've kept this from me this entire time?" she whispered in disbelief. "You gave up our child—the one child we would have had—and kept it from me?"

"El." He shuddered. "I didn't have a choice in that moment. You were on the brink of death. Freya said you were heading toward the light—"

"You had no right," Elena interrupted, shaking with anger as she pushed him back and shoved to her feet. She didn't want him to touch her. To be reminded of all the nights they had spent together that could have been when they started a family. All that time, they couldn't, and he hadn't told her. Tarrick didn't make a move to stop her, as if he had anticipated her reaction and knew there was nothing he could do to stop it. He finally lifted his head sadly.

"It's *my* body." Elena's voice trembled. "You had no right, no claim over *my* body to make that decision." Hot, angry tears splashed down her cheeks. "And you kept it from me even when I asked you outright what the Divine Beings asked for in return for bringing me back."

"I know." Tarrick shook his head. "I messed up."

"No," Elena countered, clenching her fist and speaking through her teeth. "*Messing up* implies you can fix it. There's no fixing or undoing this."

"I'm looking into it," he said. "I've researched ways we can still have a child together."

"You never even asked me if I wanted children and what I wanted for our future." She wiped away her tears roughly. "I've been going along with everything you asked. I thought I was doing what was required of me as your ... whatever this is"—she gestured between the two of them—"and this whole time, you knew I wouldn't be able to fulfill the one thing that's expected of a queen."

"It's not the only thing that's expected of a queen," Tarrick argued.

"Your councilors already hate me because I'm human! Even if, in a few centuries, they come around to the idea that I'm not here to steal magic or harm anyone, how will they react when they find out the royal line ends with you? What then, Tarrick?" she shouted. "They will turn against your entire family for going along with this farce."

"It doesn't have to be that way," he said, standing up and shaking with anger.

"Oh, yes, how could I forget your long-lost son," Elena said sarcastically. "The answer to everyone's problems now."

"He's not," Tarrick bit back. "He's also human, without Elemental powers—like you. He will face the same prejudices as you when the people find out."

"But he's Leneiran. Something I will never be," Elena pointed out. "And if he is your son, he's a legitimate heir to the throne."

He stepped forward, reaching for her. "El—"

"No." She shook her head. "I can't believe you kept such a significant thing from me for this long. When were you planning on telling me if Henry hadn't shown up?"

Elena didn't wait for Tarrick to answer, fleeing from the room, ignoring his pleas to return. Her vision blurred as she flew past the guards and patrols in the gardens. Elena's legs carried her through the groves until she came to a small, secluded part of the garden.

She collapsed on a stone bench and let the tears flow freely. Elena sobbed for what felt like hours. Visions of herself playing with her and Tarrick's son or daughter in the garden flashed through her mind like a film reel. More scenes of them together as family dancing hand-in-hand at the Full Moon Festival. Tarrick throwing a little girl in the air, slowing her descent with his Elemental powers. A young boy sitting beside him on the throne, a shiny gold circlet peeking through dark curls.

Elena screamed out loud at the loss of a child she never knew and a future she would never have, not caring if anyone heard her. A shaky future that suddenly held more questions than answers. The trust between her and Tarrick had been broken the minute he started keeping secrets from her. She clutched her stomach, cursing her body and sinking into the dark depths of her mind, where the voices whispered about her worthlessness as a woman. How she was incapable of fulfilling the role that nature had bestowed upon her. She was futile as a queen. An anomaly in both the human world and Leneira, unable to conform to either realm.

Eventually, Elena ran out of tears. All she could do was take in deep, shuddering breaths. She sniffled, wiping her streaming nose with the back of her hand. Her throat was raw from screaming. She registered a stinging sensation on her cheeks and realized she must have been sunburned from spending all day on the *pihasi* with the sun blazing overhead.

A strong, warm hand slipped into her own, and she leaned into the familiar lean, muscular chest, inhaling Leon's bright, citrusy scent. It was so different from his brother's spicy, seductive cologne. He wrapped his other arm around Elena's shoulder and squeezed her tightly.

Jet's soft body brushed against her other side, and he let out a sigh as he sat down. He was careful to not make contact with her skin—respectful of everyone's personal space and privacy, only ever showing intimacy with Leon. But his presence was enough to let Elena know that he was there to listen and comfort her.

"Do you want to talk about it?" Leon asked gently when Elena simply stared into space with burning eyes.

The soft twilight air was hazy, and torches flickered to life around the gardens. *Lyrabirds* swooped in and out of trees, calling out to each other, flying to their nests and settling in for the night.

"Tarrick sacrificed the life of the child we would have had together to bring me back," she said dully. "And now we can never have children."

Jet sucked in a sharp breath. "Are you sure?"

"It was the price the Divine Beings demanded for ..." Elena trailed off, her chest constricting at the thought of the alternative.

Leon squeezed Elena's shoulder in a tighter half-hug. "Well, fuck," he cursed. "If the Divine Beings are involved, there's no way around it."

"I'm useless," she whispered more to herself than Leon and Jet. "I'm totally useless now."

"No, you're not," Leon said fiercely. "This changes nothing about you as a person. Although, it explains why Tarrick had me researching succession laws this summer."

Jet glared at Leon.

Elena lifted her head. "You knew?"

"No, no," Leon replied hastily. "I swear, I didn't, El. He just asked me to research how different families came into power in Terralea since the formation of the countries."

"Not making it better," Jet muttered.

"It doesn't matter," Elena sighed. Her shoulders slumped, and she rubbed her face. "I didn't even care if our child ended up ruling Terralea. I would have loved them no matter what."

"I'm so sorry, El," Leon said, sounding troubled. "Tarrick should have told you sooner."

"If he had you looking into succession laws, he must have been hoping to find a way around it before he told me," she said. "It wouldn't have softened things or made it easier. It would having fucking hurt, even if I found out years from now, but he would have found a solution to keep your family in power, at least."

The prince hesitated. "I also understand Tarrick's point of view," he said carefully.

Jet shot him an alarmed look that Leon ignored.

"My brother hasn't felt this way about anyone in the time I've known him," Leon explained. "When he left the palace with your body after you killed Zanthus, there was a chance you would've walked back in by yourself. I wouldn't have been at all surprised if he sacrificed himself to save you."

Elena's brows flew up.

Leon smiled sadly. "So imagine our relief when *both* of you returned. Especially after Father and Erik ..." He bit his lip.

Elena squeezed his hand, still interlaced in hers.

"It was the best outcome for everyone." Leon shook himself out of the haunting memories. "And I understand why he thought that giving up a child he had never met was the better option. It doesn't mean it was the right choice," he added hastily at the expression on Elena's face. "And I think he was afraid you'd leave if he told you. That's probably why he was putting it off. If you really want a child, you can still have one with someone else—"

Leon faltered under Elena's glare.

"There was never going to be an easy outcome, Lady Elena," Jet said softly. He insisted on using her title even though she had asked him a number of times to call her by her name. But he never said it in a way that made her feel elitist or above his own station—it was simply what he called her, the same way Leon and Tarrick called her El.

"The Divine Beings are not what you'd call compassionate or benevolent." Leon made a face. "They wouldn't have cared that we'd already lost Father, Erik, a few Skandorians …"

"They are all-powerful beings for a reason," Jet told her. "They have their own laws, and assess a person's worth using their own logic. "

Elena shuddered at the memory of the three imposing entities.

Jet sighed. "His Majesty waited until the very last moment to make his choice," he told her. "Freya was adamant he was going to lose you."

Elena bit her lower lip and recalled that brief period of time when she was so close to being reunited with her parents. She re-membered the tugging around her stomach while she had been debating whether she should cross the barrier to be with them or return to Leneira and Tarrick. She suddenly realized that the tugging must have been Tarrick urging her back and binding her to his life.

"How do you know this?" Leon whirled around at the Empath.

Jet blushed. "His Majesty forgot to keep his shields up in the aftermath of … everything that occurred."

Under different circumstances, Elena would have been livid that Jet never told her. But she was exhausted—the day had taken its toll. Between crossing half the realm on the back of a flying horse, finding out Tarrick had a son by Rose, and being slapped in the face with yet another revelation that she added to the list of her own shortcomings, the rollercoaster of emotions that had hit her in succession without a break in between left her feeling drained and numb.

"My parents appeared while I was in limbo, and we were so close to being a family again," Elena said listlessly. "They told me I had a choice to make, and honestly? I guess I couldn't tell you what I would've chosen at that moment."

Leon's lips thinned, and his brows knitted together as the implications of her words settled on him.

"What's done is done," Jet said wisely. "There's no point in speculating on what could have been and wallowing in the past. I think I speak for everyone when I say that we're all so glad that you're with us here and now, regardless of how and who made it happen. Nor does it serve us any good worrying about what is to come or possibilities."

"I wish you had told me, Jet," Elena said sadly. "I thought we were friends."

He hesitated. "I did tell His Majesty that I knew everything."

"You did?" Leon exclaimed.

Jet nodded. "Every time I met with him, I advised him to tell you," he told Elena. "He assured me he would. I believe he was planning to tell you in Sailon. He wanted you to have Queen Lin and Commander Zen for support if things went ... badly."

Sailon felt like a distant memory. Those few days were the first time in a while that Elena hadn't thought about the past or worried about the future. "Sailon was amazing. Zen gave me some advice that put things in perspective."

"I'm glad you enjoyed it, brief as your visit was." There was a wistful note to Jet's voice, and Leon's eyes flicked to him. "When this business with Henry and the council has settled, I should like to visit my family and tie up a few loose ends. And show Leon my home," he added with a laugh when the prince's face dropped at the mention of his leaving.

Leon brightened at the idea of traveling to Sailon with Jet.

"I could use another lantern right about now." Elena gave a little laugh. "Or a bunch of lanterns to make a few wishes."

"What did you wish for in the end?" Leon asked Elena.

She hesitated before looking at Jet. "Am I allowed to say?"

"Of course," Jet replied. "You've already sent it up to your ancestors. Saying it out loud won't change anything."

"I actually made wishes for all of you," Elena admitted. "I wished for Adina to find love and laugh again. I wished for Leon to be known as the best royal advisor in Terralea's history. And I wished for the people of Terralea to heal and continue to know the peace they have now."

"And for yourself?" Jet asked.

"Nothing." Elena shrugged. "I never thought I'd have so much after my parents died—now I have Tarrick, you guys, and a new home."

"Oh, El." Leon's voice was filled with emotion.

"It's probably for the best that I made wishes that could actually come true," she mumbled. "I imagine it would be a waste of a lantern, wishing to be able to have children, now that I know it's not possible."

"Keep the faith, Lady Elena," Jet said gently, reaching out and pressing his hand on hers. "None of us can predict the future."

He let go of her quickly, blushing slightly.

She glared at him. "Did you just read me? After withholding vital information?"

"Apologies, my Lady," Jet murmured. He had the grace to look embarrassed. "I was testing my abilities."

Leon snorted with laughter, and Elena swatted him on the arm.

"And were you able to read me?" she asked Jet, who confirmed with a look of relief mingled with guilt.

"That's why I sent for my sister," he told her. "So that we could verify that it's not me. There's something strange about Henry."

Elena's face cleared, feeling validated at Jet's assessment of the man. "I thought that too. But Tarrick said Henry was carrying a Minotian object that could have been shielding him against all Leneiran powers."

Jet tapped his chin with a finger thoughtfully. "That's a possibility."

"Try reading him again at dinner," Elena suggested. "I think Tarrick is holding on to the necklace now."

"I know you're a little emotional," Leon said hesitantly, "but we need to be careful not to put him offside. It won't go down well if Henry is, in fact, Tarrick's son, and you two have already made an enemy of him."

Elena and Jet both glared at Leon, who held his hands up in surrender.

"Just had to put it out there." He shook his head. "We need to keep our cool and stay objective."

"And if he's a fraud?" Elena challenged. "A rebel posing as Tarrick's long-lost son and taking advantage of us?"

"Then you have every right to go postal." He smiled slightly. "But we need solid proof of his intentions. For now, he's our guest, not our prisoner."

"Yet," Elena muttered, cracking her knuckles. She asked Leon worriedly, "What if we do find evidence that Henry is a fraud, but Tarrick is too blinded by the fact that he has a son? Especially since I ..."

"I will speak with him," the prince said determinedly. "I know he doesn't have the best track record with Rose and Zanthus, but we've all learned our lesson. That doesn't mean you should go *looking* for evidence that doesn't exist. We need to be careful with how we approach things."

"You all trusted Zanthus," Elena pointed out gently. Leon still felt guilty about not recognizing his uncle's true colors earlier, especially since he had spent the most amount of time with the traitor as his personal scribe and assistant. "He was family, and you'd known him since birth. He kept his plans to kill all of you"—Leon winced—"under wraps, and he was clever at covering up his involvement with the uprising. Even the other council members didn't suspect a thing."

"I guess," the prince said, unconvinced.

"Have you made any headway in convincing Eli and Rami to stay on?"

Leon shook his head. "Darius and I came up with a plan to talk to them individually, but then Henry showed up."

"How did the others react when they found out?" Elena asked curiously.

"They were surprised to see a stranger being escorted into the palace by the portal guards," Leon replied. "But Adina was quick. She escorted him to a private guest room away from the others before sending for me and Jet."

"The princess was aggressive in her interrogations," Jet admitted.

"She's really changed in the last six months," Elena said moodily, kicking at the pebbles on the ground.

Leon hesitated. "I don't want to speak for my sister or make assumptions about her feelings."

"Such a diplomat." Elena shook her head in frustration. "Is no one on my side anymore?"

Leon looked hurt. "That's not true, El. Of course I support you and will do anything for you."

"You don't need to be an Empath to understand that she lost two men very dear to her at the hands of her uncle," Jet said. "It will take her time to recover from that and learn to trust others again. And herself."

"She doesn't trust me?" Elena whispered.

Jet glanced at Leon before replying. "I have witnessed people grieve in different ways, Lady Elena. The princess is upset that you got a second chance at life when her father and lover didn't."

"Did you reveal my sister's thoughts?" Leon glared at Jet. "What happened to that sense of honor?"

Jet glared back at him. "She *told* me this herself when I found her crying in the garden."

"This day just keeps getting better," Elena groaned. "I didn't ask—"

"We know," Leon said quickly, preventing her thoughts from spiraling to dark places. "Let me speak with Adina. The way she's treating you is unfair and downright rude. She's allowed to be upset and take her time grieving over Father and Erik, but it has to be in a better way."

"I wish she would talk to me," Elena murmured. "At least this explains why she can't look at me without glaring or scowling." She missed hanging out with her friend, and hated that Adina had become a ghost of the vivacious and exuberant woman she once was. Adina's presence used to light up the room, but now, she skulked in the corners and avoided everyone except for Amaya and Tarrick. She contributed more in council meetings with defensive strategies and reports, and still cared deeply about Terraleans, but she had built up a wall that not even Tarrick could break through.

"We should go back," Leon sighed, tilting his head up to the darkening sky.

"Are the other nobles joining us?" Elena asked, hoping for a quiet night.

Leon nodded. "Adina wants to keep everything under wraps," he said in a low voice. "So we've told them Henry is a distant relative who's visiting, and kept him away from everyone as much as possible."

"Great, more secrets," Elena said dully. "Do I need to point out the consequences of keeping Henry's past a secret? This won't help your council trust you, Leon."

"I know." He bit his lip. "But now that Tarrick's back, how to handle the situation is his call."

"We're still in shock, Lady Elena," Jet explained gently. "And there are too many questions that need to be answered before we start broadcasting the news."

"You need to tell the Council of Nobles," Elena advised. "Especially the ones who have already pledged their support to you. Whatever happens with Henry, they need to be involved from the start—it will show they are trusted members of your circle."

"You're right," Leon agreed. "I'll tell Tarrick, and we'll talk to Darius and Aiden tomorrow."

"When does your mother get back?"

"Tomorrow, hopefully." Leon stretched and rolled his shoulders.

"Let's go to dinner," Elena sighed, standing up and brushing down her rumpled clothes. "I want to get this over with so I can go to sleep and forget this day ever happened."

~ 23 ~

Dinner was a tense affair. The nobles and their families who remained at the palace shot Henry covert looks in between bites as he ate steadily. Henry wore an embroidered tunic and pants, sitting straight-backed in his seat next to Tarrick. He carried himself like a Terralean noble with his chin raised and mirroring the king's movements. No one commented on the strong similarities between the two men, but looks were exchanged all around.

The sounds of cutlery against plates and slurping echoed around the room. Elena opened her mouth a few times to attempt polite conversation with Henry, but gave up when her mind went blank on topics they could discuss that included everyone at the table.

"Do you follow soccer, Henry?" she finally asked, attempting to show a semblance of welcoming and friendliness.

He gave her a long look before replying, "It's called 'football'. And no, it's difficult to follow sports when you're constantly on the move."

Elena scowled at the derision in his voice, deciding not to engage with him further. He clearly had a low opinion of her, although it was a little early to be brushing her off in such a manner.

Mari and Eli sat at the far end of the table, murmuring in low voices and casting furtive glances at Tarrick and Henry. Sofia, Malik, and Rhea took their usual seats in the middle, Sofia and Malik giving Elena polite smiles when she caught them staring at her. Rhea stared at her plate and kept to herself, as was customary.

Darius and Aiden's sharp eyes darted around the table every so often, ears pricking up when the other lords spoke in low voices.

Henry wasn't affected by the strained atmosphere at all, but he watched closely as the staff moved silently around the table and used Elemental powers to clear away empty dishes, refill water glasses, and adjust the torch lights. He ate every bite of food on his plate, dabbed his mouth with his napkin between courses, and sipped his wine slowly.

"The food is delicious," he said to Tarrick. "And everyone here is so … interesting." He cast his gaze around the table, staring intently at the women.

Sofia cleared her throat. "How are you enjoying your stay here, Henry?"

"I'm enjoying it immensely," he replied with a quirk of his lip. "I was just saying how I find everyone here so striking. It feels like you all have compelling stories to share."

"We've seen so little of you since you arrived," she purred. "You must join us for tea on the terrace tomorrow. I'm sure I speak for everyone when I say we would like to get to know you better."

Before Henry could reply, Leon jumped in. "All in due course, Lady Sofia." He flashed her a smile. "Henry has traveled a long way and is unaccustomed to our, er, ways."

Sofia didn't seem convinced.

"I would love to join you for tea, Lady Sofia," Henry said smoothly, "but His Highness is right"—he inclined his head toward Leon—"I have traveled a long way and am yet to get my bearings."

"Perhaps Lady Elena can show you around the palace tomorrow?" Tarrick spoke for the first time. "While you become, er, acquainted with each other."

Elena snapped her head toward him. He gazed at her pleadingly.

"Sure," she finally bit out after a pause. "We can meet at the library after breakfast," Elena said to Henry with a forced smile.

"How long have you lived here, Lady Elena?" Henry asked, sipping his wine.

"A few months," she replied.

His brow creased as he studied her over the rim of his glass. "I was under the impression you'd been here a lot longer."

"My story is a little complicated," she mumbled.

"I see." Henry didn't press her to elaborate, nor did he ask her more questions.

Adina ate quietly, assessing and analyzing everyone's movements. Under normal circumstances, Elena would have called the princess out on her cynicism and poked fun at one of her brothers to draw a smile from her.

"I should fill you in on everything else that happened while you were away." Leon finally broke the awkward silence and addressed his brother.

"First thing tomorrow," Tarrick said authoritatively. "I need to speak to Elena." He pushed back and rose to his feet, holding a hand out to her. "Shall we?" he asked tentatively.

Elena stood, placing her hand lightly in his.

"Good night," she murmured to Leon and Jet.

The other nobles rumbled their farewells, but Tarrick barely acknowledged them as he pulled Elena out of the room. They walked through the corridors in silence to his office. He held the door open and ushered her in.

"El, I'm so sorry for the way I spoke earlier," Tarrick apologized. He wrapped his arms around her, pressing her back to his chest.

Elena stiffened at first, still feeling raw from earlier, but she leaned back and let out a sigh. Her shoulders dropped, and some of the tension she had been holding all evening melted away. This was where she felt safe and loved.

"I wish you had told me sooner," she murmured.

"I know," Tarrick replied, burying his nose in her hair. "I was so afraid of losing you."

"It hurts, Tarrick," she said quietly. "I understand why you agreed to that bargain, and I am grateful to be here and have this second chance with you, but that also included a future where we started a family. You let me fantasize about it for months without saying a word, and it's not something I can forgive easily."

Tarrick held her tighter in response.

"The timing of it was also cruel," Elena continued, willing herself to stay strong. "It'll take me some time to be able to talk about it."

"I understand," Tarrick told her. "I'm angry with myself for how I blurted something like that out without thinking. It was never my intention to hurt you. I spent the entire summer trying to find the right words, the right moment, to prepare you."

He loosened his hold, and she turned to face him.

Elena leaned her forehead against his chest, trying to simmer the storm of emotions swirling within her.

"I know it will take you some time to be able to talk about ... our child," he said quietly, stroking her hair. "Take as long as you need, and I'll be here for you when you're ready. You should also know that I made that bargain knowing you and I would find a solution together. If you want children, we will find a way to make that happen. I-I would do anything for you, El."

Fresh tears threatened to spill over, and Elena buried her face deeper into Tarrick's tunic.

It was a few minutes—or it could have been hours—before the king cleared his throat.

"Is it alright if we talk about Henry?" his voice vibrated under her cheek.

Elena stiffened.

"I don't want to make any more decisions without your input," he explained when she didn't respond.

Elena jerked back. "I didn't appreciate you volunteering my services like that at dinner."

"I know," Tarrick said quickly, "but I had to say something to keep him away from Sofia and the others. If you don't want to do it, I can ask Leon or Adina. "

Elena considered his request. "Do you trust him?" she asked finally.

"I don't know." Tarrick rubbed his chin thoughtfully. "You can read the report." He inclined his head toward his desk, littered with documents and parchment.

Elena moved closer to the desk and picked up the document at the top. Her jaw tightened, and she tried to school her features into a neutral expression as she scanned the report on Henry.

"These are a lot of aliases for one man," she said carefully.

Tarrick bit his lower lip. "He is a hundred years old."

"William MacGregor, George Blofeld, Edward Gordon, John Parker, Frederick Ward," she recited, glancing back at the document. "Investors, stockbrokers, poker players, and entrepreneurs who disappeared without a trace."

"He's had a difficult life," Tarrick said reluctantly. "Everyone deserves a second chance."

"Even con artists? He hasn't held a single honest job." Elena raised a brow. "Your people have been incredibly thorough. I assume this has all been verified?"

"Henry volunteered all of this information himself," Tarrick said, going slightly red. "Which is why I think he wants a fresh start."

Elena gave him a skeptical look.

"Why tell us all the sordid details of his past?" he argued.

"I don't know." She frowned at the document again. "Why would he choose to con people out of money when he could have done anything else?"

"You don't know that, El." Tarrick's face softened. "It can't have been easy growing up alone, virtually abandoned. Rose wasn't even present when she was alive."

"I know," Elena said, feeling slightly guilty. "But people do have a choice, Tarrick."

At that, the king flushed.

"He could have chosen to work legitimate jobs," she explained. "No one *made* him cheat and lie to earn a living."

Tarrick exhaled and ran his fingers through his hair. "So you don't trust him?"

"Do you?"

"All evidence points to him being my son."

"That doesn't answer my question," Elena said pointedly. "Do you trust him?"

Tarrick didn't reply.

She stared at him. "You *say* you want to include me in decisions, but you've already decided about Henry, haven't you?"

He lowered his eyes.

"Tarrick!" Elena groaned.

"What would you do in my position, El?" he asked defensively.

"Are you doing this because you feel guilty?" she asked shrewdly. "Because no one would think badly of you. There's no way you could have known about Henry if Rose didn't tell you."

"He deserved better. No child deserves to go through what he did." Tarrick's face was stony. "I can't change the past, but I can help him now."

"How?" Elena demanded.

"By welcoming him into our family. By giving him a chance to live an honest life," he replied.

Elena hesitated.

"Please," Tarrick said softly, taking her hand in his. "I don't want to repeat the mistakes of my past. I let love blind me in both instances, and I missed the signs leading to everything that happened with them. I want to be more present with Henry and help him turn his life around. Make sure he stays true to his word about living an honest life here."

"Are you sure you're not letting your wish to be a father blind you now? Or is this a convenient solution to the succession issue?" Elena pointed out. "Henry is a grown man who knew what he was doing when he played out those cons and long games. I understand why you want to help him, but I think we should be cautious. You have a lot on your plate at the moment."

"Never a dull moment." Tarrick exhaled slowly. "It comes with the role, unfortunately."

"A role you might not have for much longer." Elena sighed. "We also have the issue of finding this scepter. Killian and Mika arrive tomorrow. How do you plan on explaining their presence here?"

"I'll tell Leon and Adina about it first thing tomorrow," Tarrick promised. "If I can," he added as an afterthought. "I don't have the scepter yet, so I don't think I'm bound by the oath to keep it a secret?"

"Get Killian to tell them, then," Elena suggested. "He was able to tell us. In fact, it might be better coming from him."

"I'll tell the council he's here to mend Minotian–Terralean relations," Tarrick said thoughtfully. "That part is true."

Elena frowned. "You shouldn't lie to your council. But in this instance, if Killian insists on the need for secrecy, I guess you'll have to."

Tarrick stared at her.

"I told Leon you need to be upfront with them, especially Darius and Aiden, and show that you trust them." Elena sighed. "I'll show Henry around while you sort out the mess with your nobles."

"You're the best thing that's happened to me," Tarrick murmured, brushing his lips against hers.

"I haven't forgiven you yet," Elena warned him.

"I'll do whatever it takes to earn it," he said determinedly.

She gave him a sad smile. "Right now, I'd like time and space." She rolled her shoulders and tilted her neck from side to side, wincing at the cracking sound.

Tarrick's expression softened as he brushed back a lock of her hair. "Go soak in a hot bath. I'll be up soon."

Elena stepped toward the door while Tarrick rounded his desk and picked up the dossiers.

She paused with her hand on the doorknob. "Why did you do it?"

Tarrick held her gaze. "I couldn't lose you," he said, knowing immediately what she referred to. "I don't regret my choice, but I am sorry for not telling you sooner, and for the way it came out this afternoon."

She left, shutting the door quietly behind her. The hot bath was a welcome treat after spending most of the day on the back of a *pihasi*. Elena groaned as she sank deeper into the tub and rested her head against the edge. As she soaped her limbs, Elena mulled over the events of the day and the ridiculous number of revelations. She thought wistfully of her original plans for the day to explore LaHong with Tarrick, ending at one of the restaurants Zen had recommended. She sadly wondered if she'd ever visit the beautiful country again. It suddenly felt so unlikely with everything that had happened and the uncertainties ahead.

Elena tried to practice breathing exercises and clearing her mind of thoughts and feelings. The water grew cold as she managed a few rounds of deep, slow breathing. After each exhale, her thoughts bounced erratically between Henry, Adina's behavior, and Leon's advice to be pleasant and diplomatic. Although she had calmed down a little, Elena gave up on achieving that inner peace and stillness she craved.

A familiar cramping sensation in her stomach was a cruel reminder of her inability to have children. If she chose to stay with Tarrick, her body would only ever expel, never create. Roughly wiping away a few residual tears that had crept down her cheeks, she toweled off quickly and pulled on her comfortable pajamas. Elena crawled between the cool sheets of their enormous bed, exhaustion finally catching up to her as she fell into a restless sleep. She didn't hear Tarrick slipping into the room, nor did she feel him slide into bed and curl his warm, muscular body around her.

~ 24 ~

Elena jolted awake. The fading stars and dark blue sky prepared for the approaching dawn. It took a few seconds for her mind to catch up to the events of the previous day. Knowing she'd be unable to go back to sleep, Elena slid out of bed as quietly as possible, trying not to wake Tarrick sleeping beside her.

After pulling on her training clothes, she jogged down the empty palace hallways and corridors to get her blood pumping. Elena followed the path to the training ring, the morning air cool and not a soul about. She used to love running at that time of the morning in the human realm. It was as though Elena were the only person in the world, and she relished the quiet hour to herself.

A few laps around the ring helped process her grief and work off some of her anxiety about the scepter, council, and her and Tarrick's future. The repetitive pumping of her legs helped to dispel the lingering frustrations. Elena got lost in the movements and was enjoying the state of flow she was in when a low chuckle cut through the still air.

Skidding to a stop and whirling around, she squinted in the darkness for the source of laughter, annoyed at whoever had interrupted her running session.

"Couldn't sleep either?" Leon asked, his silhouette growing larger as he moved closer.

"No," she replied.

He raised his fists and motioned for Elena to attack. "Let's go."

They moved in silence, dancing, striking, and dodging. The only sounds that punctuated the still morning were the occasional thumps when Elena's fists found their mark, and Leon huffing out breaths in response. The sky grew lighter, a pearly blanket of cloud diffusing the light across Terralea.

When sweat dripped into Elena's eyes, she requested a pause to wipe her face with the hem of her shirt.

"You good?" Leon appraised her.

She merely looked at him.

"You're a dark horse, El." He grinned, raising his hands and sending a gust of wind her way to cool her down. "You nearly had me there a few times. Where'd you learn those moves?"

She shrugged. "Guess all those self-defense classes with Mom and Dad are coming back."

"Nah, it's not just that." He shook his head. "You have an edge."

"Zahra's training," Elena said.

She took up a fighting stance again, but before Leon could attack, there was a cough at the side of the ring. An audience had gathered, watching them spar. Adina leaned on the rope barriers with an irritated expression on her face.

"Morning, sis," Leon called out cheerfully. "I'm afraid this is a ticketed show."

Elena snorted.

"You're delaying the guards' training, Leon," Adina said in irritation.

Elena turned back to him. "Let's do this again tomorrow."

"You got it." Leon winked at her and ambled to the edge of the ring, nudging Adina with his shoulder as he walked past her. She wrinkled her nose and punched him in return.

Elena greeted the guards who had arrived for the morning training session. Among them was Zahra, who had caught the last bit of Elena and Leon's sparring.

"Your form and technique have improved, Lady Elena," she said in her deep voice.

"Thanks to you, Zahra." Elena smiled at the guard.

However, the moment was fleeting. Tarrick came into view, Henry beside him. The young man was dressed in khaki slacks and a crisp white button-down shirt. Elena and Leon watched apprehensively as the two men approached the ring.

"I came to find you," Tarrick told her. "Did you sleep alright?"

"Yes," Elena replied tightly. She glanced at Henry, who looked back at her coolly. Elena wondered if his choice to wear his own clothes was a deliberate statement.

"Good morning, Your Highnesses," he addressed Leon and Adina. "Elena." He inclined his head at her. Henry sauntered toward the ring, where he leaned on the rope and watched the guards intently.

Zahra adopted the same stony expression she had worn the previous day outside Tarrick's office. Adina watched Henry with narrowed eyes. For a change, Leon
remained silent.

"I ran into Henry on the way down," Tarrick explained, filling the awkward silence. "He was curious about the guards' training."

When nobody said anything, Leon jumped in, tugging Elena's sleeve. "Let's go clean up."

Henry moved around the ring, inching closer to the guards who had started exercises using their Elemental powers.

As Elena followed Leon back toward the palace, Zahra leaned closer to her. "Be on your guard around Henry," she whispered. "The princess and Jet don't trust him, and nor do I."

***

Elena pushed the doors open and breathed in the familiar scent of books and parchment. A feeling of calm washed over her in the serene space.

"Magnificent!" Henry exclaimed as he took in the room.

Celine, the head archivist of the Royal Library, glided over. "Lady Elena, back so soon from Sailon?"

"I'm afraid so." Elena sighed wistfully. "But nice to be back in the library, Celine."

"And who is this?" The archivist turned to Henry, who was drinking in the sight of thousands upon thousands of books that lined the walls.

"This is Henry," Elena introduced. "He's a guest."

A slight crease formed between Celine's brows when his blue eyes snapped to hers. "I see."

Henry extended a hand. "A pleasure."

Celine shook it firmly. "Is there something with which I can assist you, my Lady?"

"I'm giving Henry a tour of the palace"—Elena waved a hand toward him—"but I also wondered if you had any information about ancient magical artifacts from the Isles of Minos? And myths and legends about the realm?"

"I believe there are references to powerful objects in some of the religious texts, and possibly in the geography section with all the other guides to the Isles of Minos," Celine said thoughtfully. "I shall set those aside for you."

"Thank you." Elena smiled gratefully.

"And for yourself, Henry?" Celine asked.

"Nothing specific at the moment," he said with his usual charm. "But am I able to come back tomorrow and browse through your collection?"

"Of course," she replied. "Any time you like. If I am not around, one of the archivists or scribes will be able to help you."

"Thank you. That's very kind."

Celine inclined her head and wished them a good day as Elena led them further into the library.

"Ancient artifacts?" Henry asked curiously.

"Oh, just something I find interesting," Elena replied lightly.

She pointed out the sections that contained books about Leneira's history and lore. Henry's eyes were wide as saucers as he took in the wealth of information housed within the space. It heartened Elena to see the awe on his face as they walked deeper into the library, and she showed him the alcoves with desks and chairs.

"I learned so much from reading the books here," Elena said enthusiastically. "But nothing beats talking to people. The Erindellians shared some incredible stories with me. I used to visit them every day over the summer."

Henry looked bemused. "Every day? I didn't think royalty involved themselves like that with the townsfolk."

Elena frowned.

"Oh, but you're not really royal, are you?" he said, slipping his hands into his pockets and looking around. "Not like my father or aunt and uncle."

Elena glared at him. "I spent the summer helping our people rebuild after Zan—it doesn't matter. But even when I'm queen, I don't intend to distance myself from the people of Terralea," she told him.

Henry studied her with an unreadable expression. "Forgive me, but you are unlike any royal I've ever known."

"I didn't realize you were so well-versed in royal protocol," Elena said, injecting as much sarcasm into her voice as possible.

"I am," Henry replied simply. "I worked in the palace when King George, and then his daughter, the late queen, ruled."

Elena's lips parted. She had missed that detail in the report, being too distracted by the aliases and long cons in his illustrious career.

"Their education was a little different," Henry said in a snide tone.

Elena bit back a retort, instantly riled up by the slight.

"It wasn't considered dignified or proper for the king and queen to be working alongside the, er, people," Henry continued, leaning forward to examine the spines of the books on the shelves. "They didn't hold onto power or rule such a vast empire by literally getting their hands dirty."

"Yes, well, aren't they losing popularity and relevance now?" Elena asked, wishing she didn't sound so defensive. "And being told they're out of touch with reality?"

"They were an important symbol during times of war and political upheaval," Henry said, unfazed. "That was what kept our soldiers fighting—that symbol of hope for a better future, and leaders who showed strength while the world was burning. The royal family, in whichever country or realm you're in, represents stability and continuity, which is what people need."

"Well, fortunately, we have peace in Leneira, and Tarrick is already working to make life even better for the people of Terralea," Elena said proudly.

"Of course." Henry waved a hand dismissively. "He was born into the role. He has the strength and power of a family legacy to back him. I'm sure his people have every faith in *him* as their king." He straightened and looked at Elena directly. "You, on the other hand, are a stranger. From what I understand, you're not even Leneiran. I'm sure you're aware of the retaliation interlopers in our own world faced when they tried to get involved with the upper echelons of society. I imagine it's the same here."

"You know a lot about me," Elena said evenly, not rising to Henry's bait. "And Leneira, considering you've only been here a couple of days."

"Servants gossip regardless of which realm they're in." He gave her a knowing smirk. "I've had a few days to listen and learn while you were away. They say you're just like my mother—a human woman captivated by a powerful man and the wonders of this realm."

Elena opened her mouth to retort, insulted by the comparison. She was not a scheming, manipulative, greedy woman. But Henry plucked a book off the shelf and wandered over to the nearest arm-chair. He lowered himself gracefully into the well-worn leather, where he made himself comfortable and carefully opened the book.

"I trust you know what you're doing, *Lady* Elena," he said, peeling apart the pages. "Learn from my mother's mistakes. It would be a shame if you were banished the way she was."

At that, Elena snapped. "First of all, I'm *nothing* like your mother," she said sharply, clenching her hands by her side. "I love Tarrick for the man he is, not the power he has as king or an Elemental."

Henry merely raised a brow.

"And second, things are done differently here. You'll learn that soon enough. This tour is over." Elena spun on her heel and marched out of the library, jaw clenched, reeling from the exchange.

$$\sim 25 \sim$$

Tarrick rounded a corner and immediately collided with a small body that emitted a gasp and stumbled back. Grinning, he reached down to steady Elena by the shoulders, hoping that she had worked off at least some of her anger and frustration in the training ring. It had been a relief to find her there with Leon after he had woken up to an empty bed. His first heart-stopping thought had been that she had left him during the night.

"I know it's only been a few hours since we last saw each other, but is that any way to greet your king?" he teased. His smile faltered when he caught sight of her flushed cheeks and brown eyes flashing with anger. "What's wrong?" Concern replaced the humor in his voice.

Elena opened her mouth to reply, but shook her head.

"El," he said gently.

"Nothing," she said loudly. "Nothing. I'm just ..."

Tarrick stepped back and knit his brows together before dropping his hands and holding out his arms. Elena sighed and stepped into his embrace, wrapping her arms around his torso and burying her face in his chest.

"Don't shut me out, El," he said, stroking her hair and taking in the scent of her lavender shampoo. "Please, let me help you."

"It's nothing," she mumbled into his tunic. "I'm just overreacting, I think."

"Overreacting?" Tarrick wrinkled his brow again. "What do you mean?"

"What are you doing?" Elena asked, lifting her head. "I thought you'd be in meetings."

"I'm about to go to a meet and greet now," he replied, noting the way she avoided his question. "Would you like to join me?"

"Did the nobles you invited to join the council agree?" she asked hopefully.

Tarrick shook his head. "They haven't sent word yet. Killian and Mika have just arrived."

He led them down the corridor to the palace entrance, linking their fingers together as they walked side by side.

"Where's Henry?" he asked, swiveling his head around.

"In the library," she replied in a stiff voice. "He found a book, so I left him there."

"How was the tour?"

Elena merely shrugged in response and quickened her pace at the sight of the entrance doors.

"Did Henry say some—?" Tarrick began to ask before she yanked her hand out of his hold and hurried down the steps, grinning at the arrivals.

Jet was helping Mika and Killian out of the carriage while Leon and Adina instructed the guards carrying suitcases and travel bags. The luggage included the pieces Tarrick and Elena had left behind in their hurry to return to Terralea.

Both Mika and Killian were alert and well-rested as they examined the grounds with interest. Mika wore a simple forest-green tunic with the traditional Sailonese high collar over cream pants and boots. Killian brushed down his embroidered Minotian overcoat and broke into a wide smile at the sight of his hosts.

"Mika, Killian," Tarrick called out to the new arrivals. "You got here in record time!"

"Queen Lin felt it prudent to send you reinforcements as soon as possible, Your Majesty." Mika grinned at Tarrick and Elena. "And

Prince Killian assured her that he would protect me on the journey."

Elena grinned at Killian, who beamed back at her, pleased at a familiar face. He bowed to Tarrick, squinting at the decorative tiles and ornaments on the palace walls with interest.

"You're both very welcome." Tarrick smiled broadly at the two of them. For a moment, he wished he could have been back in Sailon, away from the politics and family drama that had unfolded in the past twenty-four hours.

"This is my brother and Terralea's royal advisor, Prince Leon," Tarrick introduced his brother, who stepped forward to shake Killian's hand.

"A pleasure to meet a representative from the Isles of Minos, at last." Leon grinned.

"Likewise," Killian said sincerely. "I look forward to learning more about Terralea while I'm here."

"My sister, Adina." Tarrick gestured toward her.

She stepped forward and held out a hand that Killian bent over to brush his lips against. He stepped back, but continued to hold her hand, tracing circles over her skin with his thumb. A blush crept over Adina's cheeks, and she gave him a shy smile before dropping her gaze to the ground. She peeked up at Tarrick with a sheepish grin—a rare occurrence since the spring.

"The pleasure is mine, Your Highness," he said in a low voice. His green eyes twinkled as they swept over Adina.

Tarrick glanced at Elena, who was grinning at the pair. She, too, had picked up on the spark between the two of them.

"My brother has filled me in on your request." Predictably, Leon interrupted the couple, oblivious to the moment they had shared. "If there's anything I can do to assist, please let me know."

"I will." Killian bowed his head.

"It's nice to have you back, Mika," Leon addressed Jet's sister, who inclined her head toward him and Elena. She did not attempt to make physical contact with either of them.

"I'm happy to be back in Erindell, Your Highness," she said. "Although, I wasn't expecting to return so soon. My brother's note was suitably intriguing, and I'm pleased to see you all are well."

"Let us go inside," Tarrick said, motioning for everyone to follow him into the palace. "Leon and Jet will show you to your rooms. I'll have refreshments sent up while you settle in."

"With all due respect, Your Majesty," Killian said hesitantly, "I would like to start my search without delay."

"I agree," Elena spoke up. "Who knows how long it will take?"

Adina furrowed her brow, and her gaze bounced between the two of them.

"I have requested that our head archivist curate some books about Leneira's ancient artifacts," Elena continued, speaking to Killian, who nodded approvingly. "But I know a better resource who might have more information in town."

"I'm up for that," Killian said agreeably.

Tarrick frowned. Elena had recovered far too quickly from her earlier anger for his liking, and still hadn't told him what had upset her. Of course, she had every right to keep information from him given that he had done the same, but he was desperate to work out their issues and move past them together. He wondered if he should ask her to stay back and tell him what was going on. After briefing Leon and Adina on everything that had happened in Sailon, and them filling him in on council updates, he reluctantly decided he had to prioritize his duties.

Elena looked back at him innocently, and he sighed. "Fine, but take a guard with you."

Her eyes slid to Jet. "Jet, perhaps you would like to introduce Mika to our guest? He's in the library."

Jet dipped his head, immediately understanding the message Elena was conveying.

"It's almost as if you planned all of this," Leon muttered.

She bit back a smile and tucked her arm into the crook of Killian's elbow. "Let's go, Your Highness. We'll see you all later," she called out to Tarrick over her shoulder.

Killian followed her willingly, albeit with an expression of confusion.

Leon, Jet, and Mika waved them off and walked up the stairs into the palace, Jet immediately launching into a detailed explanation of the anomaly in his abilities. Leon reached out for Jet's hand and squeezed it.

Tarrick and Adina remained where they stood. He swung his head back toward the path that led to Erindell, watching Elena and Killian disappear down the hill.

"What was that about?" Adina asked, her eyes glued on the prince's back.

"I think something happened with Henry," Tarrick said, rubbing his chin. "I ran into her just now. Literally. She was upset but wouldn't tell me why."

Adina let out a scoff. "It would be easier to list the reasons why she wouldn't be upset with you," she said with a touch of her old humor.

"Hilarious," Tarrick bit out.

As they stared into the distance, the king mulled over the possibilities. "Do you think Henry is who he says he is?"

"I don't know," Adina said hesitantly. "He's told us everything, as far as we know. The reports match up to his story. He has nothing to gain by lying."

"Then why do I get the feeling something isn't quite right?" Tarrick sighed.

"You feel it too?"

They stared at each other.

"Are you okay, Adina?" the king asked gently. "Is there anything I can do? *Anything* at all?"

Adina turned back toward the direction in which Elena and Killian disappeared. "I'm not okay," she admitted, "but I will be."

Tarrick felt lighter at the hope and optimism that finally sparked in his sister.

"Want to come to the library with me?" He offered her the crook of his arm.

"Save that line for your next date with Elena," Adina teased, but she linked her arm through his, and they walked up the stairs.

***

Tarrick cursed internally at the sight of Sofia and Mari, who had pulled up chairs either side of Henry in the library. Sofia's carrying voice echoed around the space as she leaned into Henry's space as though they were old friends. Beside Tarrick, Adina released a resigned sigh.

"Your Majesty, Your Highness." Sofia stood to her feet and curtsied when they approached.

Mari did the same while Henry gave the siblings a sharp bow of his head when he stood.

"Ladies," Tarrick acknowledged. "Do you mind giving us a moment with Henry?"

"Of course," Mari said breathlessly, glancing at Henry, who winked at her.

Tarrick waited until the women departed before taking one of the vacated chairs, motioning for him to sit back down. Adina settled into the chair Mari had been sitting in, and Henry sat back in the leather armchair, glancing between the siblings.

"How are you settling in, Henry?" Tarrick asked, crossing a leg over one knee and clasping his hands together.

"Everyone I've met so far has been incredibly hospitable," Henry smiled politely. "Your staff have been most accommodating, and the nobles I've met have made me feel welcome."

"How was your tour with Elena?"

Henry hesitated, dropping his gaze to the floor. "It was fine."

Tarrick leaned forward. "Did ... something happen?"

"No." He shook his head, but the guilt was painted all over his face.

"Please, tell me if something is wrong," Tarrick pressed.

Adina watched Henry closely.

"She's a lovely girl," he said finally. "She reminds me of Mama in many ways."

Adina's brows shot up her forehead.

"How so?" Tarrick asked after a moment of stunned silence. He had never compared Elena to Rose before—or any other woman.

"She's ambitious, passionate, and has dreams," Henry said. Tarrick's shoulders relaxed slightly. "I can see why you're in love with her. She's charming. Captivating."

Tarrick held his breath, waiting for the "but".

Sure enough, Henry continued. "But I remember how, when she was alive, Mama fixated over things she wanted. She would stop at nothing to get them. No matter the cost." He looked between Tarrick and Adina nervously.

"What do you mean?" the princess demanded.

Henry flushed. "I found out about Mama's obsession with Elemental powers."

Tarrick inhaled sharply. "How?"

"Gossip from the servants," Henry said, waving a hand vaguely.

"You've been talking to the staff?" Adina raised a brow. "They are normally professional and discreet in front of guests."

Henry flushed. "I lost my way and stumbled upon the staff quarters by accident. I overheard them talking."

Tarrick noted the way Henry twisted the signet ring he wore on his finger. He made a mental note to have a word with the staff about maintaining discretion, and to also verify with someone that Henry did, in fact, lose his way. The staff quarters were in a completely separate wing of the palace. "What does this have to do with Elena?" He steered the conversation back to the main issue.

Henry paused for a moment, choosing his words carefully when he spoke. "When I entered this realm, I wanted a fresh start and a chance to live an honest life. Connect with family." His eyes lingered on Tarrick before shifting to Adina. "I'm not proud of the life I led in the human realm, but I did what I had to do to survive."

Adina fidgeted in her seat.

"I told you everything. I was honest from the very beginning," Henry said. "I want to earn your trust and respect. Show you that I will do whatever it takes to be part of your family. But I don't want to come between any of you or create animosity."

"Henry, please, tell us what's on your mind." Tarrick drummed his fingers on the armrest.

"In my line of work, I became very good at reading people. I learned to recognize other grifters, con artists, thieves," Henry said in a steady voice. "I-I know you're in love with her. That much is obvious to everyone. But you should know, Elena has some of those traits, along with the same ambitions as Mama. In my experience, that makes her dangerous."

Silence followed Henry's statement. He looked anxiously between Tarrick and Adina as they processed what he had said.

The princess finally snorted, breaking the silence.

Henry turned to Tarrick with a beseeching expression on his face.

The king shook his head. "Henry, with all due respect, you're wrong. Elena is a good, honest person who, I agree, is ambitious and passionate, but in the best way possible."

Henry's face fell. "I suppose I see things differently," he murmured. "She reminds me so much of the visitors to King George's palace who gave their unsolicited opinion on everything before declaring their ways superior."

"I appreciate you have a different view, given your upbringing and experiences," Tarrick said carefully, keeping his growing temper in check, "but throwing around unfounded accusations about Elena is unacceptable."

He started to rise, somewhat relieved that it was a simple misunderstanding on Henry's part. Elena could forgive that.

Adina stood, brushing down her pants and straightening her tunic.

"You never found the assassin, did you? The one who attempted to kill you in Istanbul."

They both paused and stared at Henry, who stared back, gold-flecked blue eyes filled with apprehension.

"You've heard an extraordinary amount of gossip in just two days," Adina said drily.

"Elena told me, actually," Henry explained. "She told me about her plans to get the people of Terralea on her side."

Tarrick and Adina exchanged a glance before sitting back in their chairs.

"I asked her how a human woman with no powers such as herself would be able to become queen," he admitted.

Tarrick stiffened. Henry had unwittingly hit a nerve as the king recalled Lazar's words about Elena not being fit to rule Terralea.

"She told you about Zanthus?" Adina asked slowly.

A strange expression crossed Henry's face.

"What does the assassin have to do with Elena?" Tarrick demanded, massaging his temples, trying to breathe through the irritation creeping up on him.

"They could be working together," Henry suggested with a shrug. "I find it difficult to believe that someone could disappear into thin air with the level of security you have in place," he said to Adina.

"That's enough. Henry, you're out of line." Tarrick shook his head. "We ran thorough checks on her. We know everything about her. Elena saved our lives. More than that, she helped rebuild the city after a catastrophic event in the spring. She's gone above and beyond what anyone expected of her."

Henry shrugged again. "Just feels like an odd coincidence that she was there that night and knew the exact moment to jump in and save you." He gave them a knowing look. "I've worked plenty of elaborate cons, and this feels like one to me. I would hate for you to be taken advantage of."

Tarrick schooled his face into a neutral expression as he stood. His head was spinning at Henry's words that echoed the very ones Elena had said to him. But Henry also pointed out that Tarrick was in love with her. *Could I be repeating past mistakes again because I'm too in love to see what is really going on?*

Adina and Henry rose from their chairs as well.

"Henry, I think you've lived a certain way for a long time that's skewed your view of the world," Tarrick said firmly. "I suggest you take some time to readjust your way of thinking and treat Elena with the respect she deserves."

Henry hesitated before saying, "Yes, Father. My apologies. I will apologize to Elena too."

Tarrick gave him a short nod and strode toward the library doors, ignoring the twinge in his chest at being called "Father".

Adina hurried after him, leaving Henry by himself in the nook. When they left the library, Tarrick slowed down, sweeping the corridor for guards and staff who could overhear them.

"Do you believe him?" he asked Adina in a low voice.

She stared at him as though he had grown a second head. "Are you crazy?"

"I had to ask." Tarrick shook his head. "But why would El tell him about Zanthus?"

"She wouldn't have," Adina replied. "Unless it slipped out accidentally."

Tarrick caught the note of doubt.

"Besides, Lin, Jet, and Mika would have mentioned if Elena was conspiring against us," Adina said with more confidence.

Tarrick's face cleared. "You're right." He checked the corridor once more. "Listen, why don't you spend the afternoon with Henry? Maybe try and understand why he would feel hostile about El."

Adina hesitated for a moment, then nodded, a determined look in her eyes.

They walked the rest of the way to their offices in silence. Once seated behind his desk, Tarrick propped his elbows on the mahogany wood and rested his face in the palms of his hands, hating what he was about to do. Henry and Elena were telling him the same things, to the point that the language and words they used were verbatim. One of them was hiding something and lying. Tarrick had to remove emotion from this task and put aside his personal relationship with both of them to go through the facts methodically. He had promised himself that he would never endanger his family again the way he had with Rose. What he was about to do was for their protection and the safety of Terralea.

After reassuring himself that it was just a precautionary measure, he opened the top drawer and pulled out a small metal key. Finding no other reason to stall, he reached down, unlocked the drawer at the very bottom, and pulled out a folder labeled "Elena Marie Russo".

Taking a deep breath, he opened Elena's file and read through every single document the Terralean guards and security team had gathered on her months before.

~ 26 ~

Elena and Killian walked through the Royal Quarter just as Zahra stepped around the corner. The guard had finished training and was heading toward the palace for her shift when Elena called out to her. "Zahra!"

She changed course and made her way to the pair.

"This is Prince Killian from the Isles of Minos," Elena introduced.

Zahra immediately curtsied. "A pleasure to meet you, Your Highness."

"And you, Zahra." Killian dipped his head.

"You're just the person I was hoping to catch," Elena said excitedly. "We're going to visit your mother. Will you accompany us? Tarrick insisted we have a guard."

Killian looked between Elena and Zahra in surprise.

"Trust me," Elena assured the prince.

Zahra spotted Illyas and hailed him over. The two of them quickly made arrangements to swap shifts.

"You owe me," Illyas added with a grin.

Zahra huffed in response. "Fine. I promise to go easy on you at training tomorrow."

Illyas's bark of laughter followed them as they walked through the Royal Quarter.

Elena filled in Zahra on Killian's request after promising the prince that she could be trusted.

"I have a feeling if anyone knows about the scepter, it will be Ninaz, Zahra's mother," Elena said.

"She's never mentioned it," Zahra said with a frown. "Mother would have told Erik and me about it."

"Only the rulers know about the scepter," Killian reminded Elena. "It's unlikely Zahra's mother knows anything about it. The only reason I'm able to tell you is because I came to the conclusion based on Father's vision. It may not be fact or the whole story, but the signs are there. In any case, the scepter needs to be passed on to King Halder."

Elena's face fell at the reminder. She had taken it for granted that Ninaz would know everything about the scepter and be able to help them.

"But Mother has moved in all the political circles and lived during three Terralean kings' reigns," Zahra said slowly. "She might have learned something in passing, or at least be able to tell us the last time Queen Lin's father visited Terralea to give King Arran the scepter."

"Yes," Killian said, stroking his beard thoughtfully. "We'll have to gather what information we can, and read between the lines."

"At least they fulfilled their promise to protect it at all costs," Elena said wryly. "I wonder if Amaya knows? Maybe we can ask her when she returns."

When they neared the outskirts of Erindell, they stopped talking about the scepter for fear of being overheard. When they reached the market square, Elena pointed out *Guiltea Pleasures* and *Meant To Bean* to Killian. He took it all in and admired the city in the same way Elena had when Adina had first shown her around.

Pausing at her favorite florist who made the bulbs bloom when the customer bought them, Elena asked, "Tell me more about Seer powers. Do they all have the same level of ability?"

"There are subtle differences and nuances, just as there are with Elementals and Empaths," Killian replied, watching the petals unfurl to reveal a burst of vibrant shades in the arrangement.

"So how do your Seeing powers differ from your father's? What about your brother's abilities?"

Killian gave a light laugh and continued walking. "Mine are less frequent and focus on mundane things like the weather and which island I'll be traveling to."

Elena tilted her head to the side, confused by his vague response. She wanted to ask more questions, but a tray filled with teacups brimming with hot liquid came flying through the air. She called out to Killian to duck instead.

The frequent stops made the trip to Ninaz's house twice as long, but Elena was content to let the prince absorb the heady sights and sounds of Erindell's spice market. She greeted the friendly locals she recognized along the way.

"You're practically a native," Killian complimented her on her knowledge of the town and its history. "And you know so many people."

"You probably know everyone in the Isles, don't you?" Elena laughed.

The prince shook his head. "I spend most of my time aboard my ship, sailing between islands and acting as a courier for my father. My dealings with the locals don't extend beyond economic or political matters with the island nobles. My brother, Orion, is heir to the throne and rarely leaves Delphos. But even he relies on courtiers to pass on information about our people."

"Lady Elena has spent weeks in town getting to know everyone and helping them in whatever way she can," Zahra said loyally.

Elena threw the guard a grateful smile.

They reached Ninaz's house, and Zahra knocked on the door to announce their arrival. She opened it and called out to her mother.

Ninaz limped into the living room, cane in hand. "Well, well! This is a nice surprise." Her eyes gleamed at the sight of Elena and Killian. She gestured for them to take a seat while Zahra busied herself in the kitchen preparing tea and coffee.

"Ninaz, this is Prince Killian of the Isles of Minos," Elena introduced.

"It is an honor to have a Minotian in my home, Your Highness. The last time I met your father was over a century ago." Ninaz bowed her head.

"He rarely speaks of his visits to the mainland, Lady Ninaz," Killian said apologetically. "This is my first time in Terralea. I'm grateful to Lady Elena and King Tarrick for welcoming me so warmly."

"And are you here seeking an alliance, Your Highness?" Ninaz arched her brow. "From what I understand, King Theo only fathered sons."

"Are you propositioning me, Lady Ninaz?" Killian asked mischievously.

Ninaz cackled with delight. "Oh, if I were a few centuries younger ..."

Elena snorted with laughter while Zahra groaned in horror, having entered the room in time to catch the last part of the conversation.

"Mother, he's still a prince," she pleaded as she set down the tray. "My apologies, Your Highness."

Killian waved away the apology.

"So, to what do I owe this pleasure?" Ninaz beamed around the room when everyone had a hot beverage and had made themselves comfortable.

Killian hesitated. Elena gave him an encouraging smile and sipped her tea, allowing the prince to tell Ninaz about his story and search for the scepter. Ninaz listened to the tale in its entirety without interrupting.

"We wondered if perhaps you knew anything about the Scepter of Ilona's current whereabouts, Mother," Zahra said when Killian finished narrating the story. "Because of your connections and knowledge of such matters."

"You mean because I'm an old hag?" Ninaz asked drily.

Zahra rolled her eyes. Killian laughed nervously.

"Don't forget a busybody too," Elena added.

Killian choked on his tea, but Ninaz only chuckled at Elena's impudence.

"I don't know about the Scepter of Ilona," Ninaz told them. "From what you've told me, the magic binding the rulers to secrecy is powerful, ancient magic. Only those directly involved with the object"—she inclined her head toward Killian—"would know. I'm surprised you're able to tell us about it. But then again, that could be for a number of reasons."

The prince's face fell, but Elena leaned forward eagerly. "Such as?"

"It could be a fabricated story," Ninaz said bluntly.

Killian stared at her in horror. "Lady Ninaz! I would never—"

She raised her cane and pointed the end at his face, silencing him. "I said *could*. But I don't think you're the type to go to such elaborate lengths for ... whatever purpose you may have."

Killian looked slightly put out, but relieved that Ninaz wasn't accusing him of lying.

"The scepter's diminishing power may mean that the magic keeping it a secret is also fading, thus enabling those who know about it to talk about it. If it is a sentient object, as you say, it could also take matters into its own hands."

"How do you mean?" Elena frowned, not following.

"It could reveal itself to someone in the vicinity." Ninaz shrugged. "That would also explain King Theo's vision of an unknown person wielding it. Such objects don't follow the usual rules of magic."

Elena and Killian exchanged nervous glances.

"The late king of Sailon could have visited in secret without the pomp and ceremony to fulfill the obligation of passing on the scepter to King Arran," Ninaz added.

"That's probably what happened," Zahra agreed.

"So we assume it's still somewhere in Terralea, hidden," Elena said, tapping her chin thoughtfully.

"I can make some discreet inquiries," Ninaz suggested. "There are people in Erindell who worked at the palace once upon a time and might know something."

"That would be greatly appreciated," Killian said gratefully. "But we need to move quickly. Father's vision was a warning from the scepter." He shuddered. "It showed us the consequences of neglecting it. Ash raining from the sky, forests of green ablaze in orange, the ground cracking and shaking, lightning striking cities and levelling them to the ground, waves bigger than I've ever seen washing away islands, cries of children echoing all around. It was a truly horrific sight—things I would rather not remember and wouldn't wish upon my worst enemy."

Elena went cold at the picture he painted. Ninaz's hands paused, the teacup she was holding shaking slightly. Even Zahra paled at his words.

"We'll continue our research in the library," Elena said, itching to get moving. "I'll ask Tarrick if Arran kept any journals or diaries. He may have written about the scepter or left a clue."

"Well, we have a plan." Ninaz rubbed her hands together.

"Thank you, Lady Ninaz," Killian said, rising to his feet. "We won't take up any more of your time."

"Thank you, Mother," Zahra said, swiftly clearing the empty cups and saucers.

Elena hesitated. "Why don't you two go ahead?" she suggested to Zahra and Killian, who raised a brow. "I'll wash up."

Ninaz picked up on the subtle message. "I'll see you out while Lady Elena washes up," she said firmly, lifting her cane and using the side of it to guide Killian to the door.

Elena stifled a laugh at the sight of the old lady chivvying the prince out the door in such a familiar manner. She moved with ease around Ninaz's kitchen, having helped the old woman with chores and daily tasks for months.

"So," Ninaz said in her crisp voice.

Elena paused, scrubbing the cups and saucers in the sink. She took a deep breath and quickly summarized Henry's arrival. Elena tried to remain objective, not wanting to sway Ninaz's opinion of a man she had never met, just in case she was wrong about him.

"It sounds so childish to say I don't like someone without articulating my reasons, but I have none," Elena finished with a sigh, rinsing a plate and placing it on the drying rack.

"Nonsense," Ninaz said briskly. "Your intuition is the most powerful tool. Those who dismiss it have nearly always been led astray for not listening to it. You were right about Zanthus. Why shouldn't you be right about this Henry?"

"Because I'm the only one saying it out loud," Elena grumbled. "Zahra doesn't trust him because Adina doesn't trust him. Adina doesn't trust him because she's still investigating his claims about being orphaned as a young boy and having no clear history."

"All as valid as you saying your intuition is telling you something's not quite right about him. I thought you were more confident and trusted yourself. You don't need me to validate your feelings, child," Ninaz scolded.

"No," Elena admitted. "But I do need your help finding out if he is genuine. Or if I'm blowing things out of proportion."

"Very well. I'll see what I can find out," Ninaz agreed. "But you need to speak to Tarrick and tell him your feelings."

"I can tell he's already taken with the idea that he has a son," Elena said, staring into the empty sink. She debated telling Ninaz the full story about Tarrick's bargain with the Divine Beings, but decided against it for the time being. She was still feeling fragile, and wasn't prepared for the woman's forthright views on the matter.

Ninaz hummed skeptically but didn't push her to explain further.

"I should go," Elena said, wiping her hands on a tea towel. "Thank you for hearing me out."

Ninaz walked her out. "I'll send word to the palace when I find out more about the scepter and Henry."

"Thank you."

She walked out to the front, where Zahra and Killian were waiting for her in the sunshine.

"Everything okay?" Zahra asked.

Elena nodded. "Let's head back."

They meandered through the crowded streets of Erindell. Brooding over the scepter and Henry, Elena barely noticed the people around her.

"Is that the princess with Henry?" Zahra interrupted her thoughts.

Elena and Killian followed Zahra's hand, pointing to a small crowd across the square. Sure enough, Adina and Henry were standing by a stall selling rugs and carpets, admiring the wares. Adina smiled at the vendor, which was nothing out of the ordinary. But what did make Elena stop and stare was when the princess laughed at something Henry had said. It was as though they were old friends. A crease formed between Zahra's brows as she, too, noticed the change in the princess's demeanor.

"Do they know each other?" Killian observed.

Zahra shook her head minutely, silently warning Elena not to reveal Henry's identity.

"Let's keep going," Elena decided. "Tarrick can explain everything." She hoped.

They increased their pace, walking back to the palace briskly. Killian glanced at Elena curiously but was polite enough not to probe with questions. When they arrived at the palace, they were greeted by a beaming Leon.

"Ah, you're back." The prince gave them his customary cheeky grin. "Prince Killian, I trust you've had a good morning with Elena?"

"I have, Your Highness," Killian acquiesced. "I think I would like to be shown to my room now."

"Of course."

"Is Tarrick in his office?" Elena asked.

"He's in meetings with the nobles until dinner," Leon replied.

Elena's shoulders slumped in disappointment.

"One would think after all this time you'd be able to stay apart for more than a few hours." Leon chuckled. "Don't worry. I'm sure he's just as keen to see you."

Elena forced a smile instead of showing him her middle finger.

"I guess I'll see you at dinner," she said with a wave to the two princes before making her way into the gardens.

~ 27 ~

Elena wandered through the gardens, running her hands through the soft ferns and foliage as she walked down the paths without a clear destination in mind. Zahra had left her to her own devices now that she was back in the safety of the palace grounds.

Laughter and familiar voices caught her attention, and Elena made her way toward the source eagerly. Pausing at the entrance to a clearing, she glimpsed Rhea and Darius sitting side by side on a stone bench, their thighs pressed together, leaning into each other. Elena smiled at the sight and called out to them.

"Lady Elena!" Rhea waved. "It's so good to have you back."

"I'm sorry I didn't get a chance to speak with you yesterday," Elena apologized, nearing the couple.

"We're glad you're back," Darius said warmly, standing and giving her a short bow.

Rhea scooted to the side of the bench to make room for Elena. The women sandwiched Darius, who didn't seem to mind.

"How was Sailon?" Rhea asked eagerly.

"It was amazing." Elena sighed. "I wish we could have stayed there longer."

"A lot has happened in your absence." Darius gave her a sympathetic smile. "Have you caught up on everything yet?"

"I think so," Elena said slowly.

"What do you make of Henry?" he asked quietly.

She paused, trying to think of the most diplomatic way of expressing herself. "He's unlike anyone I've ever met before."

Rhea wrinkled her nose. "What does that mean?"

"Speaking words without them meaning anything." Darius chuckled. "You've been taking lessons in diplomacy."

"That obvious, huh?"

"Mother and Father think he might be the solution to His Majesty's problem with the council," Rhea said in a low voice.

Elena raised her brows.

"What do you mean?" Darius frowned at the young woman. "Lord Malik hasn't said anything to me."

"I heard them speaking last night," Rhea whispered. Her eyes darted around the area as though expecting her parents to pop up between the bushes. "Father believes that if His Majesty acknowledges Henry as his son and heir to the Terralean throne, then the other lords will feel better about the continuity of the family's leadership. They'll be more likely to stay on the council."

"Henry is only half-Leneiran though," Elena pointed out. "He doesn't have Elemental powers."

Rhea shrugged. "His Majesty is the most powerful Terralean and still young. The future of the kingdom is secure for at least another couple of centuries. Lord Eli is going to propose that the council open talks with Skandor and put Henry forward to marry Princess Malina. We will have a stronger alliance with the Shifters, and our people won't fear attacks or threats from enemies with them by our side."

"Hypocrites," Elena muttered as Darius's eyes bulged comically.

"*That's* what Eli and your father are planning?" he sputtered.

"We *already* have an alliance with Skandor," Elena fumed. "No one needs to marry Malina to secure their support. I doubt she'd even agree to this plan."

Rhea shrugged again.

"This is bullshit." Elena's eyes flashed. "They oppose me because I don't have Elemental powers, but they're okay with Henry because, what? He's a man?"

Rhea shifted uncomfortably. "I'm sorry," she muttered, going bright red. "I shouldn't have said anything."

"I'm not angry with you, Rhea," Elena said wearily. "I just don't understand how these men think. No offense," she added quickly to Darius, but he waved off her apology.

"No, you're right," Rhea said. "They shouldn't treat you and Henry differently when you're both from the human realm."

Instead of explaining that even in the human realm, women are treated differently to men, Elena turned to Darius, who was staring into the distance with a contemplative expression. "What do you think?" she asked him.

"It doesn't make sense." He drummed his fingers on his thigh. "I'll speak to Tarrick myself. First of all, nothing has been decided or voted on yet. Second of all, none of us know Henry beyond the brief introductions last night. We cannot be planning alliances with Skandor or anyone else when Tarrick's priority is to fill those council seats."

Elena leaned into the palms of her hands. "Why can't we deal with just one problem at a time?" She groaned.

Rhea and Darius laughed.

"Do your problems include an elusive prince from the Isles of Minos?" Darius asked.

Elena's head snapped up. "How do you know about him?"

"You didn't see the line of noses pressed up against the palace windows this morning when he arrived?"

Rhea giggled.

"But in all seriousness, why is he here?" Darius asked with concern.

Elena hesitated, unsure of how much to tell the young lord. She was saved from answering when Mari and Helene entered the clearing.

Their faces glowed in the late afternoon sun, their relaxed expressions indicating they had spent a few hours in the royal bathhouse, indulging in massages.

"If we leave, I will miss these bathhouse sessions," Mari was saying before she caught sight of the trio on the bench. She clamped her mouth shut while Helene gave them polite smiles.

"Ladies." Darius stood and bowed in greeting. "I trust you are well?"

"Lord Darius," they murmured, gliding closer.

"Lady Elena, how nice to have you back," Helene said.

Elena offered her a smile in response.

"It's a beautiful day today," Mari said, blushing slightly at the realization they would have heard her talking. "The palace gardens are magnificent."

"They are," Elena agreed, hoping the small talk would not be drawn out.

"I miss my garden at home," Mari said wistfully, taking in the vivid colors of the flowers and changing leaves. "It's nice to be able to work on it every day."

Elena looked at her with interest. "Would you like me to speak to the gardeners about helping them here?"

Mari flushed. "Oh, no, dear! That's alright. I wouldn't want to intrude. Besides, they already do an excellent job. There isn't much for me to do."

"How about taking on a new project?" Elena offered.

Rhea and Darius snapped their heads to her. Helene raised a perfectly plucked brow.

"Whatever do you mean?" Mari wrinkled her forehead. "What kind of project?"

"Some of the buildings in Erindell are a little bare," Elena explained. "Maybe you could set up some rooftop gardens to brighten the space. I'm sure the people who live in those apartments would love gardens to relax in."

Everyone stared at her.

"They do this in big cities in the human realm." Elena shrugged. "But if you don't think it would work …"

"That's an idea," Rhea chimed in.

"The canopy above that little tea shop in the market square is utterly charming," Mari said, excitement slipping into her voice. "Maybe that's something I could create in these roof gardens."

Elena smiled. "Absolutely! I know the man who owns one of the buildings I'm thinking of. I'd be happy to introduce you."

"How do you know him?" Darius asked.

"I tutored his daughter during the summer," Elena explained. "Amos was one of the Erindellians who helped purify the water. He and the others who worked late at the river were unable to pick up their children after school, so I read to them or helped them with homework."

It was the first time Mari and Helene looked at Elena with respect and admiration since meeting her.

"Lady Mari is very good with children." Rhea nudged Elena. "Perhaps you could talk to the school about having her teach them how to set up their own vegetable gardens or something."

"Oh, my dear Rhea," Mari squeaked, clutching a hand to her chest. "You're too kind!"

"I'll see what I can do," Elena promised. "Lady Helene." She turned to Mari's companion, who remained silent. "Do you have any secret talents or a burning desire to do something that we can assist with?"

Helene hesitated, and Darius gave her an encouraging smile.

"I keep bees," she blurted.

Elena grinned. "That's perfect! You and Lady Mari can work together."

The women stared at her for a moment.

"You're serious?" Helene asked in a hushed voice.

"Why not?" Elena shrugged. "You could sell the honey in the market square or to local shops and cafés."

"That sounds ..." Mari trailed off in wonder at the possibilities.

"Only if you want to," Elena added hastily, worried she'd just loaded extra work onto the women.

Helene shook her head, smiling. "That sounds like just the thing for me."

Elena glanced at Darius, who gave her a wink.

"Why don't you both put together proposals for your ideas, and I'll draft those letters of introduction tonight," Elena suggested, relieved her idea was welcomed.

Mari and Helene beamed at her and walked off arm in arm, chattering excitedly about the possibilities for their joint venture.

"Nicely done," Darius remarked, giving Elena an impish grin.

Elena shrugged. "I figured if they had something worth staying for, they could convince their husbands to remain on the council."

"If your plan works, His Majesty might only have to fill three more spots," Rhea said in awe.

"Good suggestion, by the way," Elena told her. "I'll talk to the principal at the school and see if she's willing to have Mari and Helene onboard. Actually, I have a job for you, Rhea," she said, recalling her promise to Kaylee about compensating volunteers at the community center. "I need you to run some numbers for me."

Rhea's face lit up, but before Elena could explain, male voices approached the clearing. Elena looked around eagerly, recognizing Tarrick's voice, but her face fell at the sight of Henry accompanying him.

"... Aunt Adina took me to the spice market," he said. "I must say, Father, Erindell is absolutely extraordinary."

Elena fought back a scowl. *In meetings with the lords until dinner.*

Tarrick's face lit up at the sight of her, but his smile waned at her black expression.

Henry paused his recounting and took in the group on the bench with an impassive expression. "It would appear this part of the garden is already occupied." He sniffed, walking back along the path that meandered to other groves.

Darius raised his brows in surprise. Rhea glanced nervously between Elena and Tarrick.

The king frowned briefly at Henry's retreating back before mouthing an apology and following him.

"That man might actually be able to charm Princess Malina," Darius muttered.

"You've met her?" Rhea asked, a mixture of awe and jealousy creeping into her voice.

"Once, when I accompanied my father to Skandor." Darius shuddered. "King Halder showed us one of the fishing villages, and she looked at me like I was the bait."

Elena couldn't bring herself to laugh, too hurt by Tarrick's choice to follow Henry.

"Did Henry address His Majesty as *Father*?" Rhea asked. "And Her Highness as *Aunt Adina*?"

"That will certainly get tongues wagging," Darius said, glancing at Elena.

She gave him a bland smile, but on the inside, Elena was seething at the way Henry was manipulating Tarrick and pulling out such calculated moves.

Her own parents had told her stories of people who hadn't realized their children were involved with criminal activities until they had been caught. Of course, Tarrick would believe his own son to be innocent and accept his word over Elena's suspicions. It was a parent's natural instinct to believe the best in their child. Elena would simply have to bide her time until Henry showed his true colors. Until then, she hoped Tarrick wouldn't push her away.

***

Dinner that night was back to its usual noisy affair. Henry spoke animatedly to Aiden and Malik, who leaned in to listen to what he was saying with eager expressions.

Adina and Killian sat next to each other, the prince barely able to keep his eyes off the princess. Her cheeks glowed in the soft torchlight as she gestured wildly as she spoke. From the snatches of conversation that floated down the table, she was recounting stories about her youth. While it brought him immense joy to see Adina back to her usual self, Tarrick's protective brotherly instincts kicked in. At some point, he'd have to have a conversation with Killian about Adina. However, that conversation would have to wait until after they found the scepter.

Leon, Jet, and Mika wore unusually serious expressions on their faces as they spoke among themselves in low voices. The Empaths shot Henry covert looks every now and again. They were still unable to read him the way they could everyone else—including Killian, who Tarrick expected to be wearing a talisman that warded off preternatural powers.

Mika confirmed that the Minotian prince's focus lay on finding the scepter. When Tarrick asked about his intentions toward Adina, Mika gave him an enigmatic smile and said that it was between Adina and Killian. It was her opinion that Tarrick had no reason to interfere in that aspect.

Beside him, Elena sat in her usual spot, but was lost in her own thoughts. She pushed the last morsels of food around her plate absent-mindedly, staring into space. Tarrick forced himself to act the way he always did around her. Henry's comments plagued his mind, and he was torn between the woman he loved and the man who claimed to be his son.

He had sought out Henry that afternoon to learn more about him. Unfortunately, his innocuous comments, sharp observations, and drawing parallels between Elena and Rose had planted the seed of doubt. Tarrick's misgivings and second-guessing were made worse by the fact that Adina and Henry returned from Erindell relaxed and at ease around each other. Adina had requested to speak with Tarrick after dinner. He wondered if Henry had shard any more insights with Adina, but was too afraid to speak with him directly, or if his sister had discovered information about Elena they had overlooked.

At the far end of the table Helene, Mari, Eli, and Rami were discussing something intently. The women were dominating the conversation; every time their husbands interrupted, they were met with flapping hands and shaking heads from Mari and Helene.

Tarrick's interest was piqued when Mari and Helene gave Elena friendly smiles and waves when she entered the room. Elena shook her head when he questioned her about it. The rest of the councilors chatted amicably or ate in quiet contentment. In Tarrick and Elena's absence, everyone had settled into a new sense of normalcy. Still, he would be relieved when his mother returned to advise him on an ideal course of action. He missed her comforting presence and wisdom.

When Adina gave him a pointed look at the end of the meal, he leaned over to Elena.

"I need to speak with Adina and Leon," he murmured. "I'll meet you back in our room."

"I'll try not to fall asleep," Elena said wryly.

The corner of Tarrick's lip quirked up in response.

~ 28 ~

"What's going on?" Leon demanded when they were gathered in Tarrick's office.

"Henry brought some things to our attention this morning," Adina replied.

Tarrick was seated behind his desk, drumming his fingers on the dark mahogany surface. He wore a troubled expression.

Leon cocked his head. "Why isn't Elena here? Shouldn't she be part of this discussion too?"

Adina shifted uncomfortably.

Tarrick sighed. "Henry's perspective on Elena is one we haven't considered before," he said carefully. "Given our ... emotional connection to her."

Leon's brows shot up his forehead.

"He thinks Elena might be playing an elaborate long con on us," Tarrick continued, unable to meet Leon's gaze. He chose to stare at the wall instead, wondering if he had made a terrible mistake in confiding in his brother. After all, Leon and Elena were close.

The prince's face cleared, and he burst out laughing.

Though not unexpected, Tarrick needed his siblings to consider things rationally—he'd already become too invested in both Elena and Henry, and was doubting himself. A level-headed, objective confidant would help him see things clearly.

Adina shook her head.

"You're joking!" Leon's laugh tapered off. "El isn't conning us." He waved a hand impatiently. "Jet would have told us if she was."

"That's what I thought," Adina said, crossing her arms. "But Henry said she was obsessed with magical artifacts. I assumed he was talking about the Scepter of Ilona. She asked Celine for all the books about it in the library this morning."

"She's not obsessed. She's the only one around here doing anything to try to find it." Leon shot back. "And how would Henry know about the scepter since we only found out about it yesterday?"

Adina's cheeks flushed. "He asked me about what Elena could be up to when we went to Erindell. He's a nice man, Leon. More understanding and a better listener than anyone here."

"You told him?" Leon exclaimed. "Adina! You know this is a dangerous object that we need to find quickly and quietly before it sets off an apocalypse, right?"

"You're so dramatic," she muttered.

"Elena wants to find it to prevent King Theo's vision from manifesting," Tarrick confirmed. "What does Henry think she wants it for?"

Adina hesitated before answering. "He thinks she wants to find it and use it."

Leon gaped. "You can't be serious! This man has been here all of two days, and he's interacted with El, what? For a few hours? We've known her for *months*!"

"I knew Rose for four years," Tarrick said reluctantly. "At least, I thought I did. Henry told me more about her when I spent some time with him before dinner. A lot of what he told me does remind me of El," he said hesitantly. "I need you both to give me your honest opinions on both Elena and Henry."

"Tarrick, tell me you've been drinking?" Leon groaned, massaging his temples. "Is *that* the reason you canceled the budget meeting? To hang out with Henry? He *told* us he was a con artist in the human realm. Do you really believe the things he's saying about El?"

"That's the point, Leon," Adina said impatiently. "He's told us from the start about everything. He was honest with us from the start."

"So was Elena," Leon shot back. "She told the entire royal council. Lady Netta believes her. Mother believes her. Are you so blinded by Henry's charm that you're discounting the rest of us?"

"Anyway," Adina said loudly, not giving Tarrick a chance to respond. "We were talking about powerful objects in the realm, and it got me thinking. Maybe Elena has been carrying some kind of amulet that's warded her this entire time. Maybe that's how she's been hiding her plans from us? Something similar to that Minotian necklace Henry brought with him?"

Leon snorted, earning himself a glare from Adina.

"Her mother's badge?" Tarrick rubbed his chin. "That was the only thing she was adamant about being returned when she discovered we had confiscated it."

Adina looked thoughtful. "She wasn't even worried about her phone or passport. Aren't those things more important when traveling? She could have been carrying it with her the entire Peace Summit to prevent the Empaths from reading her at the time."

"Do you hate her so much for surviving Zanthus when Father and Erik didn't that you would accuse her of such horrible things now, Adina?" Leon's voice trembled with anger. His face grew red, and he clenched his fists by his sides. The princess opened her mouth to retort, but Leon swung to his brother. "Elena is the best thing that's happened to you in over a century, and you're doubting her over a con man you barely know?"

"All evidence points to Henry being my son," Tarrick bit out, unwilling to admit that every time he called him "Father", it stirred something in him. That one word held so much power. "Even if he wasn't, his presence here is a reminder of how my mistakes have cost me in the past. I will not risk our family's safety again. Besides, why would he tell us the sordid details of his past unless he intends to start afresh and make an honest life for himself here?"

"I don't know," Leon replied sarcastically. "Jealousy? Insecurity? A reason to gain your favor by painting Elena as a villain?"

"Why Elena?" Tarrick argued. "Why not pit me against you or Adina or one of the councilors? You all play a more important role in this realm than—"

Leon made a sound of outrage as the king cursed himself at the slip of the tongue.

"You did not just say that," the prince said in a hushed voice.

"I didn't mean that." Tarrick's face dropped. "Elena's ... important to me."

"Is she?" Leon didn't bother softening the anger in his voice. "Do you remember what you sacrificed to save her?"

Adina's head swiveled between the brothers. "What are you talking about?"

Leon continued to glare at Tarrick, who looked slightly chagrined as he scratched at a dent in the wood of the table.

When neither of them spoke, Adina let out a huff. "There are other things to consider about Elena too."

Leon raised a brow.

"You haven't been listening to your council." Adina sighed. "You don't know what it's like for them. They're still scared after what happened during the uprising, the Peace Summit, and are worried about the future."

Tarrick saw where she was headed. The claws under his skin itched to break free.

"Instead of accepting Elena, like you thought they would, they fear her." Adina shot Leon an angry look when he snorted in derision. "We need to fix that."

"You're both being ridiculous." Leon shook his head in disbelief. "I don't want to be part of this conversation anymore."

In three long strides, he was at the door, slamming it loudly on his way out.

"Drama queen," Adina cursed, throwing herself into a chair. "Now what?"

"You tell me," Tarrick replied in a low voice. "What happened, Adina? She was your best friend."

The princess exhaled slowly. "I wish Father and Erik survived. It's not fair that Elena gets a second chance when they didn't. The sight of her reminds me of that night."

Tarrick made a sympathetic sound, but Adina brushed it away. "After spending the day with Henry, I'm beginning to see things from his point of view," she admitted. "I didn't know Rose, but from what he told me of her, you're right—the similarities are there."

"Do you really think so?" Tarrick asked, doubt creeping in his voice.

Adina shrugged. "It's hard to ignore the facts. I know you love her. But you love your country more, don't you?"

Tarrick pursed his lips.

She squinted at the file on his table. "Did you find anything else?"

Tarrick gestured toward the document, inviting Adina to read it. She picked it up and sifted through the information within. "Nothing stood out, but I wasn't expecting it to. I went through these reports a hundred times while Elena was recovering from the bullet wound. While we're on the subject, any progress with the hunt for the assassin?"

Adina shook her head. "Nothing," she said gloomily. "Which is also why it validates Henry's suspicions about her. Even if this person was hiding out in Sailon or Skandor, Lin and Halder's guards would have caught them by now. Their security has quadrupled over the summer. It's impossible for anyone to remain hidden for long. Lin's people even found a group of rebels near the quarry."

"Adina," Tarrick addressed his sister in a gentle voice. "Is it possible your grief over Father and Erik is clouding your judgment? If we can't trust Jet and Lin—"

"They trusted Zanthus," Adina fired back. "We *all* trusted Zanthus for centuries, and never suspected what he was planning. Even Mother ..." she trailed off, biting her lower lip. Her eyes welled up, and Tarrick reached over to take his sister's hand. "I can't lose any more people I love, Tarrick."

Adina's words were a knife to the gut as Tarrick thought back to the time he had spent with Zanthus, and, as Adina pointed out, how their uncle had deceived everyone. Including the most powerful Empaths in the realm.

Silence settled over the room as Tarrick pondered the next course of action.

"I'll have a word with Elena tomorrow," he finally said. "We need to get to the bottom of this."

Adina gave him a curt nod. "I'll pick up the hunt for the scepter."

"You might find more than you expect." The corner of Tarrick's lip quirked up.

The princess blushed.

"I'm glad you're smiling again, Adina," he said softly, reaching for her.

She squeezed his hand lightly, smiling. "Don't worry, big brother. I'll be careful."

***

Elena tried her best to stay awake until Tarrick came to their bedroom, but sleep took over while she read one of the books Celine had put aside for her. Her body clock woke her once again right before dawn, and she rolled to the far side of bed, where Tarrick lay on his back. One arm was raised behind his head, and the other rested over the blanket pulled up to his chest. She spent a few seconds staring at his sleeping face before planting a kiss on his bare shoulder and donning her training clothes.

She went through her warm-up quickly and easily before dragging the punching bag out to the ring. Long strips of cotton fabric lay on top of the clean pile of towels and linens in the equipment room, which she wrapped around her hands to protect the skin around her knuckles. Elena punched the bag in a steady rhythm, swapping between jabs, hooks, and uppercuts until a tap on her shoulder had her swinging out a fist.

Her assailant ducked and gave a low laugh. "Your aim still needs work."

Elena dropped her hands and had to stop herself from throwing her arms around Zahra. "What are you doing here?" she exclaimed softly.

"I came to make sure you were okay," her friend admitted, moving the punching bag to the side and holding her hands up, indicating for Elena to keep practicing. "And explain without getting caught."

"Explain what?" Elena lifted her hands to the side of her face and resumed the exercise. She threw all her weight into the punches, knowing Zahra could take the impact of her anger.

"Her Highness was upset when she learned I swapped shifts yesterday when I accompanied you and Prince Killian to town. She implied that if I deviate from the roster again, my job is on the line." Zahra's voice was tinged with anger.

"What?" Elena threw extra force into her next punch.

Zahra didn't even flinch at the impact. "There's something very wrong."

Elena noted the tightness around Zahra's jaw. The open, friendly expression she usually wore was grim.

"I normally trust the princess implicitly, but this situation with Henry still doesn't feel right to me," Zahra confessed.

Elena didn't say a word, but she increased the speed and intensity of her punches. Zahra started moving around, giving her an additional challenge. The exercise was a cathartic release for Elena's growing wrath.

She concentrated on following Zahra around the ring, and soon, the sweat was rolling down her back. Every punch vibrated down her arm on impact as she released her anger in that physical way.

They were so engrossed in their exercise that they didn't notice a shadowy figure sneaking up on them until Zahra shouted, "Watch out!"

Elena swung wildly without thinking.

"What have I told you about using all of your senses?" Leon sighed, stopping Elena's fist with a large hand mere inches from his face. "I wasn't even *trying* to be quiet."

"Good morning, Your Highness," Elena said sarcastically, using the interruption to pause and wipe the sweat off her forehead.

"Your technique is improving," Leon observed, "but Zahra was going easy on you."

Zahra shrugged, not bothering to refute.

"We were just warming up," Elena bit out.

"Is that right?" Leon teased. "Now that I'm here, show me what you got."

He and Zahra moved in unison to attack Elena, but she stood her ground and fought back. Using the footwork techniques she learned during her sword fighting lessons with Zahra, along with Leon's "surprise attack" tactics, helped her avoid the worst of their punches and grabs. She pivoted nimbly on her toes, swinging her arm around to catch Leon in the ribs. He stumbled back, surprised, and gave her a grin. It spurred her on to move onto the offensive, and Elena felt a sense of pride when she managed to dodge Zahra's swing and almost tripped up Leon a few times.

She dropped into a crouch without warning and swung a leg out to trip up Leon, just as he had done with Tarrick when they had been sparring. Unfortunately for Elena, Leon realized what she was attempting and jumped over her leg as she swung around.

They continued practicing until dawn broke. Zahra paused her attack to step back and glanced up at the brightening sky.

"I shouldn't be here," she said quietly when Elena and Leon stopped what they were doing. "I'll let you know if there are any updates from Mother," she told Elena. "Same time, same place tomorrow."

With a quick bow to both Elena and Leon, she jogged back to the barracks.

"What did she mean by that?" The prince frowned at Zahra's retreating figure.

"Adina threatened to fire her if she stepped out of line," Elena told him.

"No!" Leon exclaimed. "Adina wouldn't do that."

"That's what Zahra said." She shrugged.

The prince shook his head in disbelief. "What did Tarrick say to that?"

She shrugged again. Adina wasn't the same person anymore, but Elena didn't want to cause division between the siblings, so she remained silent.

"El, have you two talked about, well, you know?" His eyes dropped to her stomach.

"No." She shook her head sadly. "Not properly. We've been caught up with Henry and Killian and the council."

Leon groaned. "He's supposed to be by your side."

"Yeah, well, Henry is taking up all his time now."

"Mother will be back soon. She'll sort things out," he said hopefully.

"We'll see," Elena hummed.

~ 29 ~

Elena returned to her room and found a note from Tarrick asking her to meet him in his office. After showering and dressing, an inexplicable sense of foreboding settled on her as she walked briskly to his office.

"Enter," the king's deep voice called out when she knocked on the door. "Elena," he acknowledged her when she crossed the room and sat in a chair opposite the desk.

She gave him a nervous smile. Tarrick put down the document he had been reading and leaned back in his chair, assessing her.

Elena's heart hammered in her chest at his indifferent stare. "I missed you last night," she said softly, disarmed by the lack of his usual warmth and affection.

Tarrick opened his mouth to reply, but snapped it back closed.

They stared at each other for several seconds before he spoke. "Elena, we need to talk."

She shifted uncomfortably in her chair.

"Why were you in Sultanahmet Park the night of the attempted assassination on me and Zanthus?" He stumbled slightly on his uncle's name.

Elena reared back at the unexpected question. "You're kidding, right?"

Tarrick sighed after a beat. "You were the only person there that night. It's a bit of a coincidence, don't you think?"

She shook her head in disbelief. "I don't believe this. Why are you questioning me about something I thought we cleared up months ago? What's going on?"

"Well, what about this?" He held up a small, shiny object.

Elena thrust out a hand reflexively. "Give it back, Tarrick," she said quietly.

"Is this really your mother's badge?" His eyes bored into hers. "Or is it something else?"

"It's my mom's badge and you know it," she snapped. "Give it back. *Now!*"

Tarrick shook his head. "I'm holding onto it until we can verify it isn't a dangerous object."

Time stood still as Elena processed his words. "Please," she whispered, blinking back tears. "You know what it means to me. Why are you doing this? Tell me what's going on."

"There have been a number of changes over the past few months," Tarrick said slowly, unmoved by her plea. "I've been remiss in my duty as king of this country. The mistakes of my past mean I have to be extra cautious, extra diligent in the way I approach things. My council wants to know that I have learned from my mistakes."

"What the fuck are you talking about?" Elena shook her head.

When he didn't reply, she dropped her hand. "Is this to do with Henry?" she finally asked.

Tarrick placed the badge in the top drawer of his desk, making a show of locking it before he replied. "There were no anomalies or red flags, aside from what he has already told us about having to change identities and keep moving. Henry has been telling us the truth the entire time he's been in the realm. Everything checks out."

Elena forced herself to keep her hands still in her lap and her voice steady. "Was Mika able to read him?"

"No." Tarrick shook his head. "But there could be a number of reasons for that."

"Such as?"

"We're not sure yet." He shrugged. "I've given her and Jet full access to our libraries to find out why this may be."

Elena frowned, not pleased about the fact that Mika was also unable to read Henry.

Tarrick steepled his fingers. "We cannot treat him as a threat or enemy when he's done nothing wrong. It's not fair to him," he said carefully.

The sinking feeling in the pit of Elena's stomach grew stronger. "I've done nothing wrong either," she argued.

"I'm going to acknowledge him as my son."

Elena was starting to hate his office. Every time she entered it, she received bad news.

"No," she whispered.

"It's going to be a huge adjustment for us all," Tarrick continued as though she hadn't spoken. "And I know everyone will have some concerns about how this will work."

"You can't," she blurted without thinking. "He's dangerous."

Tarrick didn't react. "I've told you, our security teams have looked into him thoroughly."

Tears of anger gathered at the backs of Elena's eyes.

"We need to separate Henry coming into our lives from what's going on between us," he continued. "I need you to understand where I'm coming from and work with me on this, Elena. You and I have a lot of issues to work through."

"And what exactly is going on between us?" she asked, jutting her chin up defiantly. "You still haven't told me why you're interrogating me like a criminal."

Tarrick hesitated. "It's been brought to our attention that there are certain aspects of your story that need to be investigated further," he replied. "I need to be certain of the facts so I can protect you if others accuse you of lying about who you are."

Elena snorted at the pompous way he spoke.

"Brought to your attention by Henry, I assume," she said drily. "It's a bit hard to separate him from us when he's manipulating you into thinking I'm some kind of con artist. It's a bit rich," she added with a derisive sniff.

"Until those facts are cleared up, I don't think it's a good idea for you to be involved in council or palace matters," Tarrick said, ignoring her comment. "Adina will help Killian search for the scepter."

She stared in disbelief.

"Or you could come clean," Tarrick suggested. "Tell us the truth about why you're here, why you took that bullet, who you're working with."

Elena stood to her feet, enraged.

"I am here because you ensured that I was bound to you for as long as you live," she seethed. "After sacrificing a child we would have had in the process." At that, Tarrick looked crestfallen. "I took that bullet because when Zanthus mentioned your mother and father, you had a lot more to live for than I did at the time. And I've only ever worked *with* you and your family for the good of this country."

She spat out the words, her wrath bubbling over at his accusations.

The door flew open, and Adina burst into the room. Her brows were drawn together, lips curled down, and eyes flashed with anger.

"It's impossible to get any work done with all this shouting," she fumed. "What's going on?"

"Tarrick is accusing me of conspiring against you." Elena turned to the princess, searching for support.

Adina crossed her arms over her chest and said, "Well, there are a lot of things about your story that don't add up."

Elena took a step back in shock. "Not you too?" She could hardly believe the princess was the same woman with whom she had gone exploring the palace's secret passageways, snuck out to the Full Moon Festival, and considered her best friend.

"What did you mean by pulling Zahra away from her duties yesterday morning?" Adina deflected.

"Excuse me?" Elena asked incredulously.

"I needed her to go through the roster and reports," she continued chastising. "Except, I found out she had swapped shifts with Ilyas without my approval and went off gallivanting to town with you."

Elena was too shocked to defend herself and continued staring at the princess.

Adina threw her hands up in frustration. "This is how security breaches happen."

"Adina, get a hold of yourself," Tarrick said calmly.

"Zahra works for *me*," the princess argued. "She's head of the royal guard, not Elena's personal bodyguard."

"Tarrick insisted we take a guard with us," she finally spoke, glaring at Adina. "Zahra was walking past, and I asked if she could accompany us. If you had a task for her, you should have told her, and we would have taken someone else."

"Don't tell me how to do my job," Adina snapped back. "I don't report to you. We have certain protocols in place, which you wouldn't know about, since you're not queen. You're not even Leneiran."

"Adina!" Tarrick banged his fist on the table. "That's enough."

The princess glowered at her brother, then stormed out of his office, slamming the door behind her.

"What the hell was that?" Elena said out loud more to herself.

"I'll have a word with her," Tarrick said wearily.

She stared at the door, puzzled. "Why does she hate me all of a sudden?"

"It's complicated," the king sighed, rubbing his temples with his fingers. "And she's tired after working around the clock to investigate Henry."

"She was fine with him," Elena muttered.

"She's making an effort to get to know her nephew. We've all agreed that he's not a threat. He's family, and we will treat him accordingly."

It was as though a bucket of cold water had been thrown over Elena. She sank back into the chair and rubbed her face with her hands. Henry was family by blood—the strongest connection people could have to one another.

"We being ...?" she asked, latching onto the last thing he said.

"Leon, Adina, and I," Tarrick replied coolly.

"What about me? What happened to working as a team and making decisions together?"

Awkward silence settled in the room.

Tarrick finally replied in a low voice. "It didn't feel right leaving Henry waiting on a decision."

"You know what? I'm done with this." Elena shook her head in resignation.

"I think it's clear you wouldn't have agreed to this decision anyway."

"And it's clear you would have gone ahead with it despite my reservations, so I guess I didn't have to be included."

Tarrick's mouth tightened.

Elena shoved to her feet, seeing red. "You know, I always struggled to understand how you all were related to Zanthus. But I was wrong. You definitely share his blood." She stalked out, slamming the door behind her.

***

Pacing didn't help, nor did flinging herself onto her bed and attempting to take a nap—the bed smelled like Tarrick, and Elena hated the way they had left things. She lay on her back, staring at the ceiling, trying to control the thoughts to swirl around her mind. The only conclusion she could reach that explained Tarrick and Adina's flip in attitude toward her was that Henry had done a masterful job of manipulating them. Her intuition was strong, but it meant very little since no one believed her.

Her anxiety spiked at the reminder of everything that had to be done before dealing with Henry. There was no definite count-down to find the Scepter of Ilona before King Theo's horrific vision manifested, adding to the urgency. They also had to convince new nobles to fill the vacated roles, which had, so far, proven far more difficult than they had anticipated.

"I need space," Elena muttered to herself, unable to think clearly and prioritize her next move surrounded by Tarrick's scent.

Jumping off the bed, she strode over to the wardrobe and pulled out her suitcases. It wasn't ideal, but she was too riled up to think clearly.

The smaller case was still filled with the clothes she'd packed for her vacation in Türkiye. She felt a pang when she lifted out the buttery leather jacket she'd been wearing that fateful night in Istanbul. Her well-worn jeans with a red tag on the back pocket peeked out between the soft cotton t-shirts, packed haphazardly. She shoved the jacket back in and zipped up the suitcase, hiding away the memories that threatened to overwhelm her.

Elena opened the bedroom door and stuck her head out into the corridor. A maid rounded the corner with a pile of linens.

"Lady Elena," she greeted her with a curtsy.

Elena smiled at her. "Could you please help me move my things to a guest room?"

The maid frowned in confusion but said, "Of course, my Lady."

The two of them hauled the suitcases to the guest wing, where the maid led her down a corridor, explaining that the larger rooms were now taken up by the nobles and their families.

The first thing Elena noted in her new room was that there was no fireplace. She would be unable to access the secret passages that connected various rooms and wings of the palace. It was simply furnished with a double bed and a small wardrobe in the corner. Sheer curtains flapped in the breeze that drifted in through the window.

"I'll bring the rest of your clothes," the maid said as she dropped the suitcase she was carrying by the bed.

"Thank you," Elena murmured, stepping into the washroom.

It was small and simple with just a shower, toilet, and basin with a mirror hung above. No luxurious bath to indulge in, but the ubiquitous ornate gildings reminded her that she was still in the palace.

The maid returned with Elena's Terralean dresses and tunics piled high in her arms. Elena instructed her to place the clothes on the bed, insisting she didn't need help putting them away. The mindless task of hanging up each item in the wardrobe would give her time to brood.

The thought of anyone else ruling the country made Elena sick. She prioritized the things that needed to be resolved in her mind. Once they had found the scepter and addressed the council issues, she would have a word with Tarrick about the way he'd treated her. Elena understood he was doing his best in an impossible situation, but she also had feelings and opinions that deserved to be heard.

The fading light and darkening room indicated that it was time for dinner. Elena dragged her feet down the hall toward the dining room, where she was the last to enter. Dropping into the empty seat between Leon and Tarrick, she mumbled an apology for being late.

"A maid told me you moved to the guest wing," Tarrick muttered to her as the others conversed amongst themselves.

"I need space," Elena replied in a low voice.

Beside her, Leon frowned but didn't say anything.

After the servers placed the first course dishes in front of everyone, Tarrick cleared his throat.

"I received word that Lady Amaya—Mother—will be arriving tomorrow, in time for the Harvest Feast," he said, smiling at his siblings, who were the happiest at the news. "It will be a good opportunity to formally welcome our guests too."

Mika, Killian, and Henry returned his smile, gratified at the boon.

Elena's heart lifted at the thought of Amaya. Surely, she would be a friend and ally to her.

"I can help with preparations for the feast," Elena offered tentatively.

Tarrick shook his head sharply. "Not necessary. Adina took care of everything this afternoon."

Leon glared at his brother and opened his mouth to say something, but thought the better of it. He shot Elena a sympathetic look instead. For the rest of the meal, she withdrew and ate in silence. Her expression grew unhappier as she observed the way Tarrick chatted with Henry and Killian.

"Tell me more about the Isles of Minos, Your Highness," Henry said to Killian. "I want to learn everything I can about your family and the Seers. I also hear that many of the magical artifacts of the realm were made in your lands."

Killian was only too happy to answer his questions, providing detailed descriptions of his family, how Seer powers worked, and the way the land fueled the magic of the Isles. Henry listened with rapt attention, taking in every word.

Throughout the meal, Killian brushed his fingers against Adina's frequently, and the princess in turn gave him shy smiles. The attraction between the two of them was clear as day to everyone at the table. Ordinarily, Elena would have dragged the princess aside after dinner to debrief and tease her about it until she confessed her feelings. But a civil conversation with Adina would be impossible.

Jet and Mika, on the other hand, cast surreptitious looks at Henry before holding some sort of telepathic conversation between the two of them. Leon was surprisingly quiet, but at ease with the way the conversation flowed around him.

"Father, this is all fascinating. Do we have such objects here?" Henry asked Tarrick.

"There are a few in the armory and around the palace," Tarrick replied.

"Can you show them to me?" Henry asked eagerly.

Elena's eyes narrowed.

"I normally take a walk in the gardens before bed," the king said hesitantly.

"Please?"

Tarrick relented. "Perhaps a quick tour."

After the tea was cleared away, everyone stood, wishing each other good night and making their way out of the room. Elena shuffled out behind Jet and Mika but slipped away before they noticed her and tried to engage in conversation.

She walked into the garden and made her way to the private grove tucked away in a part of the grounds only one person visited. She sat on the stone at the edge of the cliff, hoping but not really expecting that the king would join her. After their heated words in his office and the tense dinner, she desperately needed to speak with Tarrick the man, not Tarrick the king. It was the one place where he was always himself.

The nighttime views of Erindell were spectacular as always, with twinkling lights and the temple of Divine Beings on the hill opposite the palace glowing softly. The sound of the water lapping at the edge of the pool failed to calm Elena. She jumped at every leaf rustling and *lyrabird* swooping behind her, looking around hopefully, shoulders slumping when the person she had hoped to see didn't appear.

The night air grew colder around her, and she shivered in her thin dress, realizing that Tarrick had always warmed the breeze or stopped it altogether when they were there. When she finally decided to return to the palace, she made it halfway down the corridor to her and Tarrick's room before remembering she had moved out.

~ 30 ~

Amaya stepped out of the carriage, beaming at the sight of Tarrick, Adina, Leon, and Elena gathered at the entrance to welcome her. Elena stood away from the siblings, although Leon tried to pull her closer.

"My darling!" Amaya greeted Elena with a warm hug. "You will have to tell me all about Sailon."

Elena merely said, "It's good to have you back, Lady Amaya. We've missed you."

"What's wrong, dear?" she murmured as she tilted Elena's chin up to scan her face.

Tarrick cleared his throat. "Mother, why don't you settle in before meeting us in my office?"

He took his mother's arm and led her up the stairs into the palace. Adina followed without a backward glance. Leon gave Elena a sad smile and followed his family into the palace.

Elena thought for a moment, then walked in the opposite direction through the Royal Quarter. Instead of taking the path into Erindell, she made her way to the steps that led to the Temple of Divine Beings.

Halfway up, she regretted not thinking of borrowing a *pihasi* for this excursion. Despite her training sessions with Leon and Zahra—that they continued to hold defiantly in the small hours of the morning—her legs trembled as she trudged up to the summit.

Elena slowed her steps when she entered the peaceful sanctuary of the temple. Walking past the Sacred Pool, she allowed her intuition to lead her to the wall where Arran's song was engraved.

When she was halfway through reading his song, a soft cough from behind brought her back to the present.

"Great minds think alike," Killian greeted her.

"Your Highness," she murmured. "I trust you're having a good morning?"

"I am," he confirmed.

"Is Adina here with you?" Elena asked, peering behind Killian.

He shook his head. "She's spending the morning with her mother. One of your guards, Samara, accompanied me. I asked her to wait outside."

Elena's shoulders dropped, relieved she wouldn't have to face Adina and deal with any awkwardness or stilted conversation.

"Have you unearthed any clues as to where King Arran might have hidden the scepter?" Killian asked hopefully. He stepped closer to the wall, and his eyes traveled along the lines of text.

"Nothing," Elena sighed, not wanting to admit that Tarrick ordered her off the search. Coming to the temple went directly against his orders, but she was feeling rebellious. She wanted to prove to him—and all her other critics—that she was capable of finding the object that would save the realm. Every time Elena felt misgivings or questioned whether it was a good idea to go against the king's orders, she called up images of Ninaz, Lin, and Zen—her champions who encouraged her and believed she could be queen. "I was hoping his song held the key to solving the mystery, but I haven't found anything yet."

They read the song together in silence. It was a heartfelt piece that depicted Arran equally as a man and ruler. Amaya's words, laced with love and admiration for her late husband, flowed like a river, painting a detailed picture of his life filled with light and shade, vivid colors, and deep shadows. The song was about his love for Terralea, his youth spent traveling the realm, fighting in battles and wars alongside friends, who would go on to become his advisors when he took the crown. She even wrote about his love for music and dancing, and how important his family was to him.

Beyond missing the former king's comforting presence and convivial manner, Elena wished he were alive to ask him outright where the scepter was hidden. She also wanted more time with the Tarrick she fell in love with, who didn't have the responsibility of ruling a country.

When she voiced the thought about asking Arran, Killian reminded her of the oath to secrecy. "It ensured that it wouldn't fall into the wrong hands. The kings and queens who had it in their possession were bound by its magic, so I'm not sure Arran would have been able to tell us even if we asked him outright."

"It's the right thing to do," Elena grumbled, "but why make it so hard to find?"

"Ilona imbued the scepter with the essence and powers of the realm. Whoever wields it holds *all* the power of this land—Elemental, Shifter, Empath, Seer abilities, as well as the ones individuals have been blessed with since the formation of the realm."

Elena's jaw dropped. "You mean, they'd be able to call on lightning and shielding like Tarrick's father and Cassius?"

Killian nodded somberly. "As well as King Halder's ability to control the beasts of the north, Queen Lin's shadow manipulation, Adina's healing abilities, and a whole host of other things."

Elena's head spun at the thought of such power.

"One person cannot wield that much power," she said finally. "They'd explode."

"Exactly." The lines creasing Killian's forehead deepened, making him appear older. "But since the scepter is tied to the land and its magic, it cannot be destroyed without destroying all of Leneira," he explained. "The Divine Beings were furious when they found out what the mystic had done and slayed her." It was his turn to shudder. Kilian screwed up his face as he narrated the legend. "*But they could not destroy the object she had created. They tasked the rulers with sharing the responsibility of hiding the object and keeping it out of the hands of those who would want Leneira destroyed."*

Elena gasped. "They trusted the kings and queens with the responsibility?"

"In a twisted way, it united the rulers," Killian told her. "I'm sure the Divine Beings also reminded them of how much they had to lose if they were to abuse the trust placed in them."

"Why didn't the Divine Beings hold on to it?"

Killian shrugged. "They have their reasons. We don't question them."

She snorted.

"Tarrick mentioned that you met them," Killian said, looking at her curiously. "Would you have argued with them?"

Elena recalled the imposing women with unimaginable powers and shook her head without hesitation. Killian's eyes flicked down to her wrist, where the *lyrabird* tattoo was inked.

"Tarrick *really* downplayed the powers the scepter holds." Elena scowled. "We need to speed up the hunt."

"What are you thinking?"

She regarded the prince with a contemplative expression. "I was reading about rituals that could induce visions. Seers sometimes induced visions at the bidding of a ruler who feared war or received word of threats. Other times, they were induced to confirm what was Seen when the vision came to them in a dream."

Killian stiffened, but Elena didn't notice. "Perhaps we could perform a ritual that would induce your father's vision in you. Jet and Mika could be present to read you when you have the vision and share it with us to locate the scepter? There might be a landmark or location one of us recognizes as a starting point?"

"That won't work," Killian said abruptly.

"The rituals are safe," Elena persisted. "We would make sure you were protected the entire time and stop the moment you feel uncomfortable."

Killian shook his head vigorously. "That won't work, Lady Elena," he repeated, almost angrily.

"We're running out of time, Your Highness," Elena argued.

"Lady Elena, we will not be performing any rituals or inducing visions," Killian said heatedly, all earlier amiability and friendliness evaporating in an instant.

Elena stopped, taken aback by the change in his demeanor.

"If you are unable to help, I'll continue the search on my own." He spun around and stalked down the marble hall. His boot heels clicked loudly against the floor, echoing around the chamber as Elena stared at his retreating figure, hurt and confused.

***

In Tarrick's office, Amaya beamed fondly at her children seated in the leather couches and chairs arranged around the small table in front of the fireplace. A pot of piping hot tea and plates of Amaya's favorite pastries had been sent from the kitchen.

"Tell me everything that's happened, darlings." Her forehead creased. "Why isn't Elena here?"

"She won't be joining us, Mother." Tarrick's gaze dropped to the floor.

Tense silence fell over the room. He could feel Leon's glare. Adina looked away.

"I see," Amaya said slowly. "And why is that?"

Tarrick and Adina took turns to tell her everything that had happened since Henry's arrival.

"What do you think, Leon?" Amaya asked, noticing his dark expression. "You don't agree with your brother and sister?"

"No," he said vehemently. "They're completely wrong about El. She's been nothing but kind, helpful, and generous to *everyone*. She genuinely wants the best for Terralea."

"But what about her obsession with the scepter?" Adina argued. "And all that stuff she said to Henry about winning our people over? She's obsessed with Elemental powers. She's read every single book about our history, and asked Celine for information about how we came to have powers."

"I already told you, she wants to prevent the scepter falling into the wrong hands." Leon scoffed. "And she's already won over the Erindellians with the way she's helped them this summer. I don't believe what Henry says about her."

"Why would he lie?" Adina asked impatiently.

"Darlings," Amaya said loudly, putting an end to the bickering. "Did it occur to you that despite Henry's age, he's still a lonely little boy, desperate for love and attention?"

Adina wore a mutinous expression.

"From what you've told me," Amaya continued thoughtfully, "Henry has never known genuine love or been around positive influences. He only knows how to lie and cheat to get what he wants. That is not something you can switch off or unlearn in a few days after a lifetime of consistently doing so."

Tarrick opened his mouth to defend Henry, but snapped it shut when his mother's words echoed the little voice at the back of his head that knew Elena to be a good person. He had pushed that voice further into the recesses of his mind, but it suddenly came back with a vengeance. *Amaya's assessment of Henry is objective and without judgment*, the voice reminded him.

"Elena, on the other hand, grew up in a loving home with brave parents who raised her to do the right thing." Amaya's face softened. "Again, that's not something you simply stop doing. Even in difficult and dangerous situations," she added pointedly. "And it's natural for her to want to learn about our origins and powers. Did you know she studied history and wrote a thesis about the myths and legends of her world?"

Tarrick did know that. The more Amaya spoke, the worse he felt, but he was too stubborn to admit it out loud. His mother's simple explanation highlighting the difference between Elena and Henry made him realize he had fucked up spectacularly not even a year into his rule. He had believed Henry over Elena out of guilt rather than what he said.

Away from Henry, it was clear that Elena had been telling the truth. She had been completely right when she told him that his desire to be a father skewed his perception of what was really going on. She had already moved out of their room. If he didn't fix it straight away, he'd lose her completely.

He rubbed his chin. "I think I messed up, Mother."

"No shit!" Leon snapped.

"Give him a break, Leon," Adina shot at him. "He's dealing with a lot."

"Leon! Adina!" Amaya admonished them.

"No." Tarrick shook his head. "Leon has every right to be angry with me. I have been unfair to Elena and misjudged everything."

"You've been more than unfair to El," Leon said unhappily. "You kept a life-altering secret from her that's cost her a great deal. Even after the way you told her, she *still* stood by you."

"What are you talking about, dear?" Amaya asked, alarmed. "Tarrick, what does he mean?"

"What I sacrificed to keep her with us," the king mumbled.

Amaya's face hardened. It had been a long time since any of them had seen their mother so angry. She rose from her seat gracefully, her blue eyes flashing at her children. Her lips thinned when her gaze rested on Tarrick.

He flinched when she spoke to him sternly, taking him back to when he was a boy and had been caught doing something he shouldn't have.

"Tarrick, your father and I raised you to act with integrity and kindness. If you cannot show that to the woman you love, what hope do you have of being a good king to your people? I trust you will make this right." She swept out of the room without another word, making him feel small.

Adina exhaled slowly. "I've never seen Mother so angry."

"You haven't seen her when she catches you throwing fireballs at each other." Leon shuddered at the memory. "Remember that, Tarrick?"

The king didn't pay him any attention as he realized with a sinking heart that it might be too late to salvage his relationship with Elena.

"What did you sacrifice to the Divine Beings?" Adina asked.

When Tarrick didn't respond, she turned to Leon.

"You obviously know," she said accusingly.

"It's not for me to tell." Leon shook his head. He looked at her curiously. "What happened between the two of you? You used to be best friends."

Adina bit her lip. "I keep thinking that if Elena hadn't come here, we'd still have Father and Erik."

"If Elena hadn't come here, Zanthus would have killed us all," Leon said coldly. He stood abruptly and muttered under his breath as he marched out of the room.

"I know that." She flushed. "I guess I'm still angry and don't know who to blame."

"Zanthus is to blame," Tarrick said angrily.

~ 31 ~

Elena spent a few more minutes reading Arran's song, memorizing as many details as possible. When she was done, she walked slowly toward the entrance, pausing to read a few more songs on her way out into the sunshine.

The steps going down the hill were just as painful coming up. Elena took her time, knowing from past experience there was no way of getting around the inevitable soreness. At the bottom of the stairs, she placed her hands on her hips and bent over, taking deep breaths to try to get rid of the stitch in her side.

"Lady Elena?"

She groaned inwardly. Of course Henry would find her when she had just huffed and puffed her way down Erindell's most notorious hill.

"Henry," she wheezed in greeting, squinting in the bright sunlight. She felt like the most undignified person in the realm compared to him in his pressed suit. His hair was perfectly styled with not a single strand out of place. Elena's heart ached when she took in the echoes of Tarrick on Henry's handsome face.

"I was just at the Temple of Divine Beings," Henry told her, hitching a thumb behind him. "I spotted you on the way down."

"You were there?" Elena asked, taking in his crisp white shirt and the dark suit jacket he wore. How he managed to hike up and down the hill without breaking a sweat, she'd never know.

"Are you going back to the palace?" Henry asked, ignoring her question.

Elena gave a brusque nod.

"I'll walk with you."

Henry talked incessantly about the market square, where he had spent the majority of the morning before visiting the temple.

"Yes, the florist was interesting enough," he said dismissively. "But being able to manipulate fire! Now *that* would be something else, don't you think?"

Elena opened her mouth to reply, but Henry carried on without pause.

"The people here are exceptionally talented," he told her, "but they're not thinking big enough. When I asked a metal worker about the weapons he forges, he said he only made swords and arrow heads." Henry shook his head in disbelief. "They don't know about guns or cannons or tanks—"

"They don't want those kinds of weapons here," Elena interrupted. "Many Leneirans have already seen the destruction those kinds of weapons cause."

"Nobody *wants* war, Elena," Henry said condescendingly. "But it doesn't hurt to be prepared." He gave her a knowing look.

When he moved on to gushing over how welcoming Tarrick and Adina had been, Elena tuned him out, walking faster even though her legs screamed in protest.

"Absolutely incredible," he continued prattling, keeping up with her easily. "I can understand why you're after the Scepter of Ilona after being surrounded by so much power."

"Who told you about the scepter?" Elena asked, irritated at the insinuation. "And I'm not *after it*. It needs to be passed on to the next ruler."

"El, I'm just joking." He chuckled. "You need to lighten up!"

She scowled at him, feeling hot and bothered by a number of things. Right then, it was the fact that Henry had the gall to fling around suspicions about her intentions, turning Tarrick and Adina against her, then talk to her as though they were friends.

"I mean, look at us." He gestured around the crowded street. "We stumbled upon this amazing realm. Think of the possibilities!"

"Possibilities?"

"How much of this we could share with the humans," he said enthusiastically. "Think of the potential! We could sell package tours of Leneira and make a fortune!"

"Are you serious?"

"Of course!" He grinned at her. "And the technology we could bring here to improve so many lives. At a price, of course. It won't matter that you and I don't have special powers. We could still make a fortune if we brought back—"

"Leneirans don't trust humans," Elena interrupted him.

"That's only because they don't understand how much we've achieved," he said dismissively. "You worked in marketing, right? We just need to spin it in a way that assures the Leneirans that our human brethren mean no harm or ill will."

You don't know shit about me, Elena thought to herself. Out loud, she told him, "Tarrick already tried that and it ended badly. What Rose did put a lot of Terraleans on their guard," she said without thinking.

"What do you mean?" Henry asked abruptly.

Elena paused in confusion. "You know why she was banished, right?"

Henry's eyes narrowed. "She had trouble adjusting and tried to steal a rare artifact."

"Who told you that?" Elena's brows shot up her forehead. She had assumed that Tarrick told Henry the truth about why Rose was forced to leave Terralea.

"Kleptomania was not really understood back then." Henry jutted his chin out defensively. "She didn't mean to, but people judged her harshly. Father has already apologized for it, and I have forgiven him."

Elena snorted in derision.

"And here I thought you were an open-minded, compassionate person," he said coldly.

Henry swept past her and marched up the hill to the palace. Elena followed him, the incline forcing them to slow down, and the narrow path making walking side by side impossible.

She mulled over what Henry had told her and the garbled version of the truth about his mother. What Rose really did was a closely guarded secret known only to Tarrick's family and trusted advisors.

Tarrick's guilt over what had happened combined with Henry's tragic upbringing must have prevented the king from telling him the truth. If he continued to believe that his mother had merely been a kleptomaniac and not a greedy murderer, it wasn't Elena's place to tarnish her memory.

"Henry, I'm sorry. I spoke without thinking and reacted that way," Elena said in an attempt to make amends. "I didn't mean any disrespect."

He didn't get a chance to respond because Tarrick stood at the top of the stairs to the palace, waiting for them.

"Where have you two been?" he demanded. "We've all been worried. I was about to send out a search party."

"I went to the temple." Elena crossed her arms in front of her chest. "Didn't your spies tell you?"

"I was in town, Father," Henry said quietly.

A crease appeared between Tarrick's brows as he stared at Elena. "You know better than to leave the Royal Quarter without guards."

"I didn't want to mess up Adina's roster," she said pointedly.

"Is it true that Leneirans hate humans because of Mama?" Henry interrupted.

Tarrick looked at Elena in horror. "What have you told Henry?"

"I didn't mean to," she pleaded. "It slipped out by accident."

Tarrick clenched his fists by his side and inhaled deeply. His gaze swung between Elena and Henry with a worried expression. Elena tilted her head—a silent challenge to see who he would pick first to console.

"Henry, come with me," Tarrick said wearily. "I'd like you to meet my mother, your grandmother. Elena, I'll be along shortly."

Henry stalked past Elena up the stairs to Tarrick's side, and they walked into the palace together, leaving her alone. She traipsed up to her room, feeling miserable that, once again, Tarrick had chosen Henry over her.

To distract herself, Elena picked up one of the books that Celine had selected for her. She kicked off her shoes and made herself comfortable on the bed, sitting up with a few pillows behind her. The book was one of the more interesting ones about Leneira, and she read well into the afternoon. She was so absorbed in the text that she jumped when there was a loud knock at the door.

"Come in," she called out, wondering who it could be.

Tarrick entered and closed the door behind him. Elena stayed on her bed, knees drawn up to her chest protectively. She arched a brow at him when he stood at the end of the bed with his hands clasped behind his back.

"I'm sorry that took longer than expected," he said, sounding tired. "I didn't want Henry running into Lady Sofia or any of the staff before he got the facts from me."

Elena rolled her eyes and looked back down at the book.

"We need to talk," Tarrick said abruptly.

She bit down on her tongue to stop herself from reacting to his tone. "Okay," she managed to say politely.

"Henry was quite upset after you let it slip that his mother was more than a ... kleptomaniac," he said hesitantly.

"She was," Elena said coolly. "He was going to find out eventually, especially with you welcoming him into the family. How long did you think you could keep the truth from him?"

"I was going to tell him everything," Tarrick said defensively. "I was just waiting for the right moment."

"Remember what happened the last time you tried waiting for *the right moment* to break bad news to someone?" Elena couldn't help saying, injecting as much sarcasm as possible.

"This isn't about us." Tarrick shook his head.

Elena tilted her head to the side, the anger bubbling up inside her once more. "Then what is it about? Why are you here?"

"Henry thinks you're threatened by him, and out to make his life miserable."

"Why would I be threatened by him?" she asked, genuinely confused.

"Because he's my son," Tarrick bit out. "And you're my ..."

Elena shut the book with a loud snap and slid off the bed, keeping her eyes on him.

"Yes, Tarrick?" she asked as she walked around the bed to stand directly in front of him. Elena tilted her chin up. "What exactly am I to you?"

"You know," the king said impatiently. He waved a hand vaguely between the two of them.

Elena shook her head. She was slowly coming to the realization that her presence served no purpose in the palace. It was impossible for her to make positive change with the number of obstacles in her way. "I don't, actually. You've never introduced me as anything other than *Lady Elena*." She raised her hands, forming quote marks around the title she had been bestowed. "It bothered me at first, but not anymore."

"What do you mean?" he growled. His nostrils flared as he clenched his fists by his sides. Frustration filled his amber eyes.

"It means that when I leave, it will be as my own person on my terms. Not your ex-girlfriend, or ex-fiancée, not even the future queen of Terralea, because right now, everyone knows me as Lady Elena who lives in the Terralea royal household as a gesture of goodwill."

"Leave?" he demanded, fury growing. "Where exactly are you planning to go?"

"Back to the human realm," Elena replied in a steady voice. She kept the neutral expression locked on her face despite blurting out what she'd been thinking ever since she found out she couldn't have children. Henry's talk of bringing technology to Leneira reminded her that she had options in the human realm, more possibilities.

Tarrick's anger melted, giving way to shock and fear. "You can't go back," he said quietly. A hint of heartbreak crept into his voice.

"Why not?"

"Because we are going to work through this. And I lo—"

Elena cut him off before he could say the words that would fill her with hope. Before, in her mind, he broke her heart all over again. "Doesn't mean we have to live under the same roof or even the same realm. It just means we both live for as long as the other does." She shrugged.

"And how do you expect to live in the human realm for the next few centuries?" It was Tarrick's turn to speak sarcastically.

"Henry did it for over a hundred years," Elena replied. "Why can't I?"

"You can't be serious." He shook his head.

"I'm not serving anyone by being here. I have no Elemental powers, no standing among your people, no influence," she said as his amber eyes narrowed. "I might as well go somewhere where I can be of service and a productive member of society."

"You're on the Council of Nobles and the Royal Council."

"No. I'm not," she said simply. "You never made it official with any announcements or paperwork. Besides, Henry can take my place. That spot will be easier to fill when your nobles find out

I'm no longer here. In fact, your council problems will probably be solved."

"I don't accept that." Tarrick shook his head. "If you need time and space, that's fine, but you *will* sit on both councils. You *will* be queen. You're forbidden from leaving the realm. Can't you see that I still believe this is possible, that we can do this together? Work with me, El."

"You don't have a say in what I do anymore," Elena said firmly, walking to the side of the bed and scooting back to her reading position. She picked up the book and flipped it open again. "You lost that privilege the moment you kept secrets from me and stopped including me in your decisions."

"You're not leaving," he said roughly.

"Not yet. I made Prince Killian a promise to help him find the Scepter of Ilona," she said, flipping a page, hoping the illusion of apathy would hold until he left. "I always keep my promises," Elena said, leaving out the part where she wouldn't be able to live with herself knowing she left the people of Leneira to their fate when she could have prevented the catastrophe. "Once we find the scepter, I'll leave, once and for all."

"You're bluffing," the king said confidently.

"Tarrick." She sighed. "You believed a con man you've only known for days. You're not being a team player in this relationship. I have my limits."

"What are you saying?" There was a slight crack in his voice.

"This isn't the kind of relationship I want to be in," Elena said, willing herself to remain calm and not break down. "You promised to tell me everything and that we'd be in this together, but you've been lying to me from the start and keeping secrets. Your sister has turned on me. Your so-called son is making an enemy of me. Your council sees me as an obstacle to your continuation as king of Terralea. I have made every effort to get to know your people and adapt to the way of life here, but it isn't enough. I will always be criticized and shunned because of my humanness, and I can't change that." Elena didn't add that the nobles conveniently overlooked that part of Henry's heritage—he was half-Leneiran, which was more than she would ever be.

Tarrick stood stunned into silence.

Elena dropped her gaze, but she didn't take in a word on the page. "You may leave."

Tarrick emitted a low growl before turning and slamming the door behind him as he left the room. Elena winced at the sound and clenched her jaw. She'd already shed too many tears. It was time to take back her power.

As the sun set and the sky grew darker outside, torches flickered to life in her room, thanks to the evening patrol. Just as she wondered if she could send word to the kitchen for a dinner tray to be sent up, there was a knock on the door. A maid stepped in carrying a pile of clothes and shoes in her arms.

"I'm to help you get ready for the feast, Lady Elena," she said.

"Thank you," Elena said to the girl, "but I won't be attending."

The maid stared, uncertain of how to respond. "Her Majes—Lady Amaya instructed me to help you dress."

Elena considered for a moment.

"Very well," she said, and slid off her bed.

~ 32 ~

Tarrick clutched his glass of wine, resisting the urge to snap his head toward the door every time someone entered. He focused on the ballroom, which had been decked out in floral arrangements boasting fiery shades that marked the changing seasons. Guests dressed in varying shades of red, burnt oranges, yellows, and golds, adding to the harvest atmosphere.

Palace servers stood around the edges of the room, using Elemental powers to direct platters of food among the guests. Their eyes never left their assigned trays suspended in the air above everyone's heads. It meant that people could move around and mingle without knocking over glasses and plates.

Leon, who normally kept him company at official events, was deliberately ignoring him from the corner where he stood with Jet and Mika. The Empath siblings stood out in their deep green Sailonese formalwear, as did Killian, dressed in an aqua tunic with gold Minotian embroidery, chatting amicably with Jet. The trio admired the room in between greeting Terraleans from the outer regions who had accepted Tarrick's invitation.

To his surprise, the recent arrivals were unperturbed by the Sailonese representatives present. From the brief conversations he'd had with the influential Terraleans earlier, they showed interest in joining the council. It suggested that they were exactly the open-minded, progressive people Tarrick hoped to have on his council during his reign.

In another corner of the ballroom, Adina stood with Henry, Amaya, and Sofia. Amaya, resplendent in a gold gown, had already soothed Malik and Sofia's concerns over the council being divided. She had spent the better part of the day reassuring them that they needn't fear the changes Tarrick had proposed or his vision for the future of the country. Henry listened politely as Sofia's carrying voice gushed over the decor and other banalities.

Darius stood beside Tarrick, observing the guests. He let out a wistful sigh that had the king peering at his friend in surprise.

"Everything alright, Darius?"

"Yes." The young noble blushed. "Fine."

Tarrick followed Darius's gaze and was taken aback at the sight of Rhea in a beautiful copper-toned gown that warmed her creamy complexion. It set off her auburn hair that cascaded in soft waves to the small of her back. Her emerald eyes, lined with kohl, sparkled from across the room, and her red-stained lips parted in a wide smile at something Mari and Helene were saying. Rhea met Darius's eye and blushed.

"Still interested in becoming Terralea's ambassador to Sailon?" Tarrick teased.

Darius whipped his head around in horror.

The king chuckled. "I'm only joking. Why don't you ask her to dance?"

Before Darius could reply, a hush settled on the room, and heads swiveled toward the entrance. Tarrick stiffened instinctively and took a deep breath before twisting around at the latest arrival.

Elena paused at the threshold and scanned the room. Leon's face brightened, and he pushed past the gaping guests, offering his arm to her when he reached her side. She placed her hand in the crook of his elbow, ignoring the whispers and murmurs from some of the guests.

Tarrick's throat went dry as she swept past him, causing the protective beast slumbering inside him to roar to life at the sight of her on Leon's arm. The low-cut black dress she was poured into hugged her enticing curves while the thigh-high split down the side revealed toned legs that ended in strappy gold heels. Delicate gold chains held the dress up over her shoulders and across her bare back. The diffused kohl lining her warm brown eyes added to the sultry look.

However, it wasn't the way she was dressed that held Tarrick's attention; Elena carried herself with a confidence he had never seen before. Straight back, head held high, meeting everyone's gaze without faltering. A small smile played on her plush lips as though she had a secret. A lump formed in Tarrick's throat at the thought of Elena following through with her threat to leave Terralea.

Surely she wouldn't...

A sharp jab to his ribs had him snapping around.

"Lord Eli and Lord Rami want to say hello," Darius informed him with a knowing grin.

The two nobles bowed respectfully in front of him.

"My Lords." Tarrick smoothed his face into a neutral expression. "Thank you for attending tonight's feast."

The older men beamed at him, more put together and dapper than they normally were. Eli's cloud of fluffy white hair had been slicked back for the event, and Rami's salt-and-pepper beard appeared to be styled in place with copious amounts of wax.

"Your Majesty, we wanted to let you know that we have made a decision regarding our positions on the council," Rami said.

Tarrick held his breath.

"We have prepared official missives to give you tomorrow, but we wanted you to know that we intend to remain on the Council of Nobles," Eli announced.

"If you will still have us," Rami added.

Tarrick stared at them, dumbstruck. The two men who had been the hardest to convince had unanimously decided to stay on before he'd even had a chance to speak with them. It felt too good to be true.

Amaya's laugh cut through the noise and music. Tarrick's gaze shifted to his mother, and understanding dawned on him.

Darius elbowed him in the ribs again. Had they been back at school, Tarrick would have decked his friend for his impudence. Instead, he cleared his throat and smiled at the lords.

"I am pleased to hear that, my Lords," he said graciously. "Thank you for your ongoing counsel and advice. My father trusted you both implicitly, and so do I."

Eli and Rami twisted toward their wives in the crowded room. Mari, Helene, and Rhea had joined Elena and Leon. The four women threw their heads back in laughter—a sight that was also drawing looks from Sofia and Adina.

"I take it my mother convinced you to stay on?" Tarrick asked, tearing his attention away from the group.

Rami shook his head.

"No, Your Majesty," he said, stroking his beard and grimacing at the crusty wax. "We discussed it at length with our wives. They convinced us that it would benefit us greatly to remain on your council."

"And help you navigate what's to come," Rami added hastily. "We want you to succeed and be a great king, like your father. May he rest in peace."

Darius cleared his throat. "I think you'll find Lady Elena played a part in that."

Three sets of eyes landed on him. Darius met their stares with a raised brow.

"What do you mean, Darius?" Tarrick asked, realizing in that moment how unaware he was of Elena's activities in the palace.

"Thanks to Lady Elena, Lady Mari and Lady Helene have also found a greater purpose in Erindell." Darius shrugged as though it was common knowledge. "They have undertaken a project to create more green spaces in Erindell and work at the local schools. I believe they will be teaching the children about gardening and beekeeping."

"Is that what Helene was going on about?" Eli muttered to Rami, who wore a confused expression.

"Your wives have some, er, interesting ideas." Darius smothered a laugh. "It will benefit the community greatly."

"Well, I'm glad Mari and Helene are willing to remain in Erindell," Tarrick said quickly. "It was not my intention for any of you to be separated from your families. They will be good company for my mother too."

Rami assented.

"It will certainly keep them busy!" Eli let out a bark of laughter. "Who would have known my Mari could be so enterprising." He smiled and shook his head.

"I should let Helene know we've told you the news, Your Majesty," Rami said, bowing as he took his leave.

Eli followed his friend to join their wives.

"Elena did that?" Tarrick asked in a dazed voice.

Darius confirmed that she did.

The music that had been subdued and slow until then picked up into a lively folk song. Guests moved to the middle of the room and began to dance, loose-limbed and free of inhibitions after a glass or two of wine or *araki*. Torches and candle flames danced in time to the music. The gold and copper decorations threw spots of bright, warm light around the room, twinkling and sparkling on the walls.

Darius gulped down the last of his wine and gave Tarrick a wink.

Tarrick watched his friend glide across the room to Rhea, who blushed and giggled at his outstretched hand. She passed her glass of champagne to Elena before Darius swept the young woman onto the dance floor.

Elena didn't hold onto the champagne for long. Leon plucked the glass out of her hand and placed it on a tray floating past on a pillow of air. He pulled her onto the dance floor, where the two of them launched into a series of dizzying spins and twirls.

Tarrick tried to tamp down his growing jealousy with little success. Elena allowed the exuberant prince to guide her back and forth, lower her into dips that left her breathless, and spin her until she fell into his chest, dizzy and laughing. They bumped into other couples frequently, but everyone was so jovial and happy that they brushed off Leon's apologies and greeted Elena enthusiastically.

"Good evening, Father." Henry sidled up beside Tarrick, who started at the sound of his voice.

"Henry," Tarrick greeted him.

He wore a burgundy tunic embroidered with gold floral patterns along the edges. It suited him, but he fidgeted with the cuffs of his sleeve and raised his hand every so often to adjust the collar.

"I must say, I've never seen such undignified behavior from royalty." Henry sniffed in disapproval as he watched Leon dip Elena so low she shrieked and clutched onto the laughing prince's shoulder.

Tarrick's lips twitched at the sight. "We do things a little differently here, Henry."

"So it would seem," he said snidely.

"Why don't you like Elena?" Tarrick watched him closely.

Henry shrugged. "I don't trust her. The way she talks, the way she does whatever she wants, the way others"—he glanced at Leon and Jet—"fawn over her without really knowing who she is."

"They know her better than you do," Tarrick told him. "And I trust my brother," he added, ashamed that he hadn't shown that trust to Leon lately.

"Well, Lady Sofia says—" Henry began.

"Henry, that's enough," Tarrick cut him off in irritation. "Palace gossip is not a reliable source of information for the truth. If you really want to know about her, why don't you ask Elena yourself?"

Henry looked at Tarrick with an incredulous expression. "And you trust she'd tell me the truth?"

"She has nothing to hide and no reason to lie to any of us," Tarrick replied firmly—words he should have told Henry from the start. Words he should have believed even when doubt crept in.

Henry turned away, sulking slightly.

Tarrick sighed. "Why don't you join us at the council meeting tomorrow morning, just to observe?" he offered.

Henry perked up at the invitation.

"You can join Sanah and Nadim"—Tarrick pointed out two of the guests standing at the edge of the dance floor, watching with slightly bemused expressions—"and understand how we do things here," he said with a tight smile to soften his chastising.

"Thank you, Father," Henry said diffidently. "That's very generous of you. Of course I'll be there."

The music slowed again. Killian made his way to where Leon and Elena finished their final twirl to a smattering of applause from the audience watching them. The onlookers wore expressions of amusement as the couple gave an exaggerated bow. Elena graciously accepted Killian's hand for the slow dance.

Tarrick shifted his gaze to his sister, who was yet to dance with the Minotian prince. She watched them take to the dance floor with a blank expression as she sipped her champagne. Beside her, Amaya watched the couple with her usual benevolent smile while Sofia tried to catch Mari and Helene's attention across the room.

Elena and Killian swayed to the song, barely moving their feet. They kept an appropriate amount of distance between them, Tarrick noted with satisfaction. From the expression on Elena's face and Killian's clenched jaw, they were having a serious discussion.

Killian shook his head several times while Elena grew increasingly agitated. Her lips moved faster as she spoke in a low voice.

Just as Tarrick thought he should intervene, Killian dropped his arms from Elena's waist and stepped back. His lips were drawn into a thin line, and he gave her a curt bow. The hem of his tunic fluttered in the breeze as he strode off in the direction of the glass doors that led to the terrace adjoining the ballroom.

Out of the corner of his eye, Tarrick saw Adina slip through the crowd and follow Killian outside.

~ 33 ~

Elena watched Killian stride off with a sinking heart. He had come over to apologize for his earlier behavior in the temple. She tried to reason with him again about performing a ritual to induce the vision of the scepter, but the prince had been adamant.

"El?"

She looked up into warm amber eyes shimmering with concern.

"Is everything alright?" Tarrick asked gently.

Elena was all too aware of the people around them who began to whisper. The music continued to play, and couples still swayed to the romantic tune. Tarrick hesitated for a beat, then held out a hand, silently requesting a dance.

He was devastatingly handsome, the way he always was when he dressed up for formal events. Elena realized with a jolt that it could be the last time she would see him like that.

"Everything is fine," she replied, placing her hand in his.

Tarrick pulled her closer and expertly guided them to a quiet corner of the room, still swaying to the song. Her skin heated under his palms, his intoxicating cedar and sandalwood scent taking her back to the first time they ever danced together at the Peace Summit. She resisted the urge to rest her cheek against his chest and listen to his heartbeat.

"I'm sorry about earlier," he murmured. "I shouldn't have said those things. I've been going about this the wrong way, and I want to make things right between us."

Elena remained quiet, not trusting herself to speak.

"Can I start by moving your things back to our room?" he coaxed her. "Or just ... talk. You're right, I shouldn't have trusted Henry just on his word and pushed you to the side. I should have included you in all of our discussions. I shouldn't have let Adina speak to you—"

"Your Majesty," an apologetic voice interrupted.

Jet stood in front of them, twisting his hands. "May Mika and I speak with you?"

Irritation crossed Tarrick's expression, but he smoothed it out and glanced down at Elena. She nodded at his silent request to be excused.

"Shall we go to my office?" Tarrick offered.

The tension lining Jet's face melted. He searched the room for his sister, who was talking to Rhea. When she caught his look, Mika excused herself and weaved through the crowd toward the entrance.

"I won't be long," Tarrick said to Elena with a tentative smile.

She shrugged and stepped back. It was the second time he'd said that to her that day, cementing the fact that, while he was well-meaning, she could no longer trust his words.

Tarrick, Jet, and Mika discreetly made their way out of the ballroom. Elena searched the crowd for Leon, but he, too, had disappeared. She sighed and headed for the terrace, hoping she would find Killian there so she could apologize once again.

The terrace was empty with the faint scent of spiced apples lingering in the air. Some of the guests had enjoyed smoking the customary Terralean water pipes earlier in the evening, but the setup had been cleared away.

Elena held onto the railing, taking in deep lungfuls of the crisp night air, admiring the crescent moon and stars twinkling in the sky. She had been serious about leaving Leneira once she and Killian had located the scepter. But after the strange conversation with him at the temple and the way she had inadvertently angered him, he probably no longer wanted her help.

She started formulating a plan for her return to the human realm, but realized she wouldn't even know where to start. Returning to Chicago was out of the question. Too many people were there who would question her disappearance. The thought of having to move around every few decades and create new identities for herself was as appealing as another encounter with the Divine Beings. The wind blew across the balcony, and she shivered in her thin dress.

A new idea formed in her head. *What if I don't leave Leneira?* She could start a new life elsewhere in the realm. She ruled out the Isles of Minos, even though they sounded idyllic. Her argument with Killian had ensured she'd probably never experience the warm, crystal-blue waters, islands that were plentiful in produce, and large communities of Leneirans without any powers where she could blend in. Sailon was out of the question too; Lin and Zen would find her within days. That left the icy barrens of Skandor.

Even though the harsh land was mostly uninhabitable, Malina had spoken to her about the beauty of the north. The people who lived in small villages and hamlets, pickling vegetables, smoking fish, and curing meat for food and sustenance. No one would think to look for her there. She could live with a few Shifters for added protection.

She was so caught up in fantasies of living a simple, anonymous life up north that she didn't notice Adina striding up to her.

"What did you say to Killian?" the princess demanded.

Elena's hold on the railings tightened, but she reigned in her annoyance.

"Good evening, Your Highness," she greeted the princess coolly.

"I'm serious, Elena," Adina said through gritted teeth. "Why must you upset our guests? Our abilities are not party tricks for your entertainment. You can't ask Killian to See on demand."

"I didn't ask him to See for fun," Elena said with a calmness that surprised even herself. "I'm trying to help him and made a suggestion. If I said something offensive, it was unintentional. I will gladly apologize. In fact, I already did."

"Don't try taking the moral high ground now," Adina snapped. "It's too late. The damage is done."

Elena lifted her shoulders and exaggerated looking around. "What damage?"

Through the glass windows, the guests were still enjoying the revelry in the ballroom. "The only damage is that you and Tarrick have been upset with me for inexplicable reasons, and that's on you."

"You're such a hypocrite," Adina spat. "When you first arrived, you got the best room in the palace, staff who treated you as though you were royalty, the privilege of attending Peace Summit balls and feasts."

Elena stared at Adina in disbelief. She was too shocked to think of a suitable response.

The princess folded her arms across her chest and glared at Elena. "You're jealous that someone else has our attention, and being an only child, you can't bear to share your friends, can you? You were jealous of Erik, and my relationship with Father too."

Elena couldn't believe her ears. Neither could Amaya, who walked up to the pair and caught the last part of what the princess had said.

"Adina!" Amaya was stunned that her daughter would speak to Elena like that. "What on earth has gotten into you?"

"Elena is jealous of Henry, Mother," Adina said swiftly, shooting daggers at Elena.

"I'm sure that's not true." Amaya frowned.

Elena stared at Adina, baffled by how much she had changed in the past few weeks.

"And now she's gone and upset Killian," the princess continued. "She's been messing with my roster, going to town without guards, and being rude to Henry, who's been nothing but pleasant and courteous to us all."

"Adina, get a hold of yourself," Amaya said sternly. "We are hosting an official event. You cannot go around in a temper and shout at your family in public."

"She's not my family," Adina said with venom in her voice. "She never will be. She's not even Leneiran."

"That's enough." Amaya raised her voice. "Go back to our guests. I would like to speak with Elena."

With one last glare at Elena, Adina flounced back into the room.

"My darling, what has happened?" Amaya asked, worried. "You and Adina were the best of friends when I left."

Elena shrugged and tilted her head back to the night sky. "I don't know, Lady Amaya. One minute, Tarrick and I were having a wonderful time in Sailon, the next, we rushed back because Henry arrived." She paused, wondering how much to tell Amaya. She was Tarrick and Adina's mother and would undoubtedly believe their word over hers. "And that's when everything went wrong."

"I must admit, I am puzzled by how much Tarrick and Adina have changed in the few weeks I have been away." Amaya's voice was laced with concern. "Tarrick introduced me to Henry, of course, and he is a charming young man ..."

"Did Tarrick tell you about my situation?" Elena asked, gesturing at her stomach.

"He did, in private. After they all told me about ... recent events." Amaya's voice shook. "I am so sorry, my dear." She reached out to tuck a tendril of Elena's hair behind her ear, then cupped her face. "I cannot believe that was the price he paid, and I'm disappointed he kept it from you. The way he delivered the news to you was callous." She shook her head sadly. "Men will never understand what we go through."

"It's okay. I'm coming to terms with it," Elena said softly. "But I think that's why he's so taken with Henry."

"The son he never thought he'd have." Amaya sighed.

Elena blinked back the tears that had gathered. Amaya stood beside her in silence. Behind them, the music continued to play, laughter and chatter filling the night. The voices in Elena's head quieted for a change.

"I think I'll go to my room," she said. "Before I upset anyone else tonight."

"Darling," Amaya murmured, and covered Elena's hand with her own. "Let me speak to my children."

Elena shook her head. "It's fine. Actually, Leon has been the nicest to me. I'll miss him when I go."

"You're not leaving, my dear," Amaya said with an edge to her voice. "It would break Tarrick's heart."

"It wouldn't." Elena shook her head confidently. "He's made that very clear to me. And I serve no purpose here anymore."

"Elena," Amaya said so sharply Elena startled. Even in the dim torchlight, she could make out the gold flecks in her irises. "Running away from your problems is not the answer, and certainly not how a queen behaves."

"I'm not running away," Elena explained. "Tarrick and I broke up. There's no reason for me to stay here anymore."

"Tell yourself that, if it will help you sleep tonight," Amaya said drily. "But I don't believe it for a second, and nor should you. You are far too intelligent to believe you are not as important and just as capable of being a leader as my son. You're staying right here until we sort this out. As a family."

Elena opened her mouth to argue, but Amaya didn't let her speak. "You are excused for the evening, but I expect you tomorrow at the council meeting. As a member of the royal household, your presence is mandatory."

Elena gaped, too dumbstruck to say anything.

"I'll take that to mean you'll be there." Amaya's face cleared. "Get a good night's sleep, my dear. You and I have work to do tomorrow." Amaya swept away, the train of her dress floating behind her as she stepped back into the ballroom.

A wave of fatigue hit Elena, and she decided to return to her room, taking the long way using the balcony stairs that led to the gardens. At least then she could avoid walking through the room full of people who would be watching her every move and commenting on it. Despite Amaya's assumptions, Elena was resolute in her decision to leave.

She swiftly made her way down the stairs, through the dark gardens toward the back of the palace. At the sight of a guard walking by himself down a path, she stopped short. They were near the kitchen entrance, and he was unaware he had been seen.

The palace guards normally patrolled the gardens in pairs. That night, with the festivities and additional guests, most of the guards were rostered inside the palace, with a unit out the front by the main entrance. There should not have been guards at the back of the palace—least of all, ones wandering around by themselves.

With a sense of foreboding, Elena followed him stealthily, making sure she stayed on the flagstones and didn't accidentally step in the gravel, giving away her position. The guard rounded a corner and Elena hurried forward, keeping to the shadows as much as possible. When she peeked around the corner, she let out a soft gasp.

The guard had vanished into thin air.

~ 34 ~

Elena walked down the path cautiously, all thoughts of sleep and getting comfortable in a warm bed evaporating. She peered around the corners, but it was deserted and showed no signs of someone having walked past in the last few minutes. A thought flashed through her mind when she arrived at the kitchen entrance.

Reaching a hand out, Elena used the brick wall to guide her until she came to the knob that was the entrance to one of the many secret passages within the palace. She hesitated, squinting into the night at the brick wall that hid the door. Without a torch or the ability to conjure a small flame, she was reluctant to go wandering around the passages in the dark by herself. She stepped back and concluded the mysterious guard must have entered the passages. It was the only logical explanation.

The only question that remained now was who. The only guards who knew about the secret entrance were those who had helped her overthrow Zanthus. She decided she would leave the mystery for the night and ask Zahra if any of the guards patrolled the passages the following morning.

The cold night air was refreshing, and Elena was overcome with a sentimental feeling that replaced the adrenaline coursing through her system. If her days in Terralea were numbered, she wanted to make the most of the beautiful night and take a walk through the palace gardens one last time.

The last of the summer jasmine still perfumed the hidden groves that Elena walked past with their heady scent. Water trickled softly in the fountains, and bird baths were scattered around the gardens in secluded nooks. She ran her hands through the soft ferns that lined the torchlit paths. The fond memories flickered through her mind like a movie reel. Her first day in Terralea learning about the realm with Erik and Adina; her conversation with the Skandorian princess, Malina; the numerous strolls with Amaya in the days following Arran's funeral.

The path she inevitably ended up on led to the clearing that overlooked the city of Erindell. Elena forced herself not to call it *Tarrick's garden* and merely referred to it as the lookout. She took a seat on the boulder and gazed out over the views of the city.

A feeling of peace and contentment washed over Elena. She had made the right decision, and her lips curved in a sad smile. While it was the right decision for her, it didn't make it any easier to upend her life and move again.

"You told Mother you were leaving," a voice said behind her.

Elena didn't reply. Her grip on the boulder tightened. The moment she had so desired was finally there—Tarrick, the man she was in love with, had returned to their spot. There were too many conflicting emotions running through her. She remained quiet, letting him lead the conversation, not trusting herself to say what she needed to.

"She said that you agreed to stay and work through everything"—Tarrick hesitated—"but I have a feeling that's not true."

Still, Elena remained silent. The grass crunched beneath the king's feet as he slowly moved closer to her. The breeze carried his scent to her, and she inhaled deeply, savoring the moment.

"I thought you said that because you were angry with me at that moment," Tarrick said sadly.

"I don't say things I don't mean," Elena finally said. Her voice was low and thick with emotion. She took several deep breaths to stop the tears from falling.

Tarrick moved to sit beside her. His expression was filled with sadness and regret when their eyes collided. Elena pursed her lips. She vowed to remain strong and not break down.

"Are Jet and Mika alright?" she asked.

Tarrick hesitated before replying. "They believe Henry's carrying another amulet or talisman that's preventing them from reading him."

"His signet ring," Elena breathed in sudden realization, recalling the gold band permanently wrapped around his index finger.

Tarrick nodded. "Killian pointed it out. It's the one thing he's been wearing this entire time. It's why they were unable to read him even after I took the necklace from him."

"What did Henry tell you about it?"

"I haven't asked him about the ring yet." Tarrick bit his lower lip. "Truth be told, I'm not sure if he even knows what it is. When I asked Killian about it, he thought it was curious that a person would carry two objects to ward them against Empath powers."

"Both objects work against Empath powers?" Elena frowned. "Wouldn't one ward against Elemental or Seer abilities?"

Tarrick shrugged in response. "It's something to investigate properly tomorrow."

They sat in silence, taking in the shimmering lights of the city below them.

"There's nothing I can say to change your mind?" he asked softly.

Elena shook her head.

"I'm sorry, El," he finally said, reaching out for her hand. "I'm so sorry."

Elena stiffened at the contact of his skin, his calloused fingers tracing her own. She bit the inside of her cheek to keep from bursting into tears at the sound of her nickname.

"I wish Father were here to advise me." He sighed, staring out to the Temple of Divine Beings. "You were right. There's no fixing what I did, and I don't know what to do next."

"You'll work it out," Elena said softly. "Your council will help you."

"They can't help me with what I've done to you." He shook his head. "That's all on me."

She didn't disagree. Tarrick continued gazing at the temple. "I haven't visited his tomb since the funeral. He would take us there to pay our respects before we went to the Full Moon Festival in the market square. After we gave thanks to the Divine Beings, he would read us a song from the walls. Leon and I wanted him to tell us stories about the epic battles and wars, but Father read us the songs about the ordinary people of Terralea.

"He wanted us to understand that it's the people of the land that make it a thriving, prosperous country, not its rulers." His intense amber eyes scanned her face. "You've spent more time with my people than I have recently, despite their hesitations and misjudgments. You've done a far better job than me as their leader."

Snippets of conversation, Killian's explanation of the scepter's connection to the realm, memories of Arran's song, Tarrick's stories of Arran at the temple, his belief that it connected him to the past and present of Terralea all flashed through Elena's mind in quick succession. Something clicked into place, and she exhaled slowly. "The scepter is in the temple."

"What?" He stared at her.

"The Scepter of Ilona is hidden somewhere in the temple," she repeated, turning to the structure thoughtfully. "Tell Prince Killian, and go through your father's private diaries. He might have written about it or left a clue."

Elena slipped her hand out of Tarrick's and rose to her feet, relieved that she had managed to keep her word. Somewhat. A deep sense of knowing told her that Tarrick and Killian would find the scepter in the Temple of Divine Beings, and they would pass it onto Halder. All would be well in Leneira. Her countdown until she left was now hours, not days.

Tarrick grabbed her arm, surprising her.

"You once told me you would take however long you could have with me," he said earnestly. "Now I'm asking you to give me this last night with you."

"I need to start packing, Your Majesty," Elena said, trying to tug her arm out of his grasp, but he held firm.

He stood abruptly and moved in front of her, blocking her path. His eyes were filled with fire.

"No," he declared. "When we're here, we're not king and Lady Elena. We're just Tarrick and Elena."

She tried to walk around, but he stepped to the side, blocking her again.

"The first time we had a meaningful conversation as two ordinary people was in this grove," he said fiercely. "I have always been just Tarrick here with you. Tonight doesn't change that, and I want to have these last moments in this space as an ordinary man with the woman he loves."

Emotions rose within her like a tidal wave—love, longing, sadness, and grief.

"Please, El." Tarrick's gaze pierced her soul as he moved closer to her. Every time he looked at her like that, he was showing her the man underneath the layers he had created to protect himself. She forgot about his title, wealth, privilege. Elena had to stop herself from reaching out to stroke his cheek and run her fingers over his lips.

Tarrick, sensing the shift in her emotions, moved even closer until his lips brushed against the shell of her ear.

"We fell in love with each other despite everything. We didn't let Zanthus or the fact that we're from different realms stop us from being together, and I have had no regrets until now," he whispered. Elena shivered at his words and inhaled his cedar and sandalwood scent that always evoked strong feelings in her.

"I will always live with the regret of this past week and that I wasn't honest with you from the start." He lifted his hand and tucked a strand of hair behind her ear. When he didn't move to lower his hand, Elena leaned into the warmth of his palm against her better judgment. He knew exactly what he was doing, and that made it harder for her to walk away. "Please, El, don't let me live with the regret that our last moments were filled with angry words and me driving you away. I know I'm being selfish asking this of you, but I don't want to live the rest of my life knowing you couldn't give me one last night."

"One night isn't going to change anything, Tarrick," Elena murmured. "I'm still leaving."

"I know," he said, slipping a hand around her waist and pressing her to his chest. "But I'm a desperate man with nothing to lose. My pride and stubbornness got in the way of the chance to make a life with you. I'll be damned if I don't get these last few moments."

Tarrick brushed his lips against her cheek as he pulled away. Elena tilted her head, and a sizzle of electricity flashed through her body when their lips met. They kissed softly at first, tenderly, as though it were the first time they were experiencing each other. Tarrick ran his tongue along the seam of Elena's mouth, and she parted her lips slightly, letting him taste her. She bit down gently on his lower lip and ran her hands up his chest. His heart hammered against his chest beneath her palm.

Tarrick tightened his hold on her as he continued to explore her mouth. His cock stirred, and her traitorous hips pressed against him, wanting to feel more. He pulled back roughly, his eyes filled with passion. The unasked question in them had her debating whether it was a good idea.

He was offering her a chance at closure. Of savoring a final night with a man who, even after everything that had happened between them, she loved with every fiber of her being. Very few people had that.

Elena recalled their first night together, when she had made the spontaneous decision to live life without regrets and had a soul-altering night with Tarrick. If she walked away, she would regret it for the rest of her life. The idea of living centuries with this one regret was truly terrifying.

Her pulse quickened at the sight of Tarrick's wolfish grin.

~ 35 ~

Elena followed Tarrick down the path to the *lamora*, where he unlocked the door and held it open for her. It was exactly the same as the last time they had been there, with the silk and satin sheets draped over the bed, plush pillows and cushions, and pillar candles that flickered to life when Tarrick waved a hand, casting a soft, romantic glow in the space.

Instead of the frenzied passion that had them undressed in record time and running their hands all over each other the first time, Tarrick took his time with Elena. She stood in front of the bed while he trailed kisses down her bare back—he knew her body and the sensitive areas that had her begging for more.

Elena's hands hung loosely by her side, letting Tarrick explore her body with his hands and tongue, shuddering when he nipped and bit her neck and shoulders. His hands glided down her body over the smooth fabric of her dress, feeling every dip and curve. She wanted him to rip it off and cool her heated skin, but he took his time, savoring the feel and taste of her.

When he reached the top of the slit of Elena's dress, he slipped his hand under the fabric between her thighs. His fingers found her dripping with desire, and he groaned against her shoulder, muttering, "I want to make this last all night."

Elena faced him and cupped his jaw with a hand, kissing him long and deep, indicating that she wanted to make the night last too. They undressed each other slowly, peeling off each item of clothing, never taking their eyes off each other. When they were fully naked, Tarrick lowered Elena gently onto the bed, kissing his way down her chest, worshiping her breasts, and making her moan as he alternated between gently sucking and stroking her nipples with his thumbs.

He ran his tongue along her hip bone, making her squirm and writhe beneath him. She raked her fingers through his hair and tugged him back up. She pulled him into her so every inch of her was pressed up against his muscular body. Tarrick's cock grew harder between them, and Elena arched her hips, rubbing her wetness all over his length. He moaned into her mouth, and she continued grinding her pussy against his hips, enjoying the friction and pleasure it incited.

She tried to hold back her own sounds of pleasure, not wanting to let Tarrick know how much power he held over her at that moment. Elena had resolved to live life on her terms and according to her will. She was going to take back her power and own every aspect of her life, including her last night with Tarrick.

He made a sound of protest when Elena pushed him back and rolled them over the bed so she was on top of him. His surprise grew when she straddled him and took control, but he relented when she leaned down and kissed him with more fervor, running her hands all over his chiseled chest. She tried to memorize the feel of every crease and indent on his magnificent body, tracing the grooves with light touches, making him shudder and groan when she ran her fingers down the prominent V-shaped muscles of his lower abdomen.

He placed both hands firmly on her hips, but she gently pushed them away. Tarrick was momentarily confused until Elena took hold of his cock and started pumping up and down his shaft. His hands dropped limply by his sides. Tarrick grabbed fistfuls of the silk sheets and jerked his hips when she used both hands to pump his cock. She rubbed her thumb over the bead of moisture that gathered at the tip, spreading it all over the head as he moaned her name, his breathing ragged.

She raised herself on her knees and positioned his cock against her entrance, straddling him.

"El!" Tarrick gasped and jerked his hips again when Elena lowered herself on him, her eyes fluttering shut as he stretched her.

"Tarrick," she moaned his name for the first time when he thrust up into her, sheathing himself entirely inside her. Her eyes flew open when she felt how deep he was in that position.

They stopped moving as Elena adjusted to his size, staring at each other until Tarrick slowly raised his hands to her hips and she moved tentatively against him. She opened her mouth slightly at the feel of him buried so deep inside her. Her walls clenched around his cock, and she cried out when he hit the sensitive bundle of nerves that had bolts of pleasure shooting up her body.

Her cheeks heated under his gaze as her lithe body moved fluidly up and down his cock. Elena increased her pace, wringing as much pleasure from him as she could. When she raised her hands to push the hair back off her face and run them up and down her sensitive body, Tarrick swore loudly.

"Fuck, El!" He jerked up. "I'm going to come just at the sight of you."

She pressed a finger to his lips. "Don't speak," she commanded. "And don't come. Not until I tell you."

Tarrick nodded obediently and slowed down so he wouldn't explode inside her before she gave him permission. Elena rode him long and hard. Beads of sweat gathered on his forehead, and he gritted his teeth at the effort it took not to come. He tightened his hold on her hips, and her breathy moans echoed around the room as she bounced up and down faster, taking him deeper and deeper. "Yes, baby," he growled. "That's it. Take what you need."

Elena saw stars behind her eyes when her orgasm hit. She cried out in pleasure and barely heard Tarrick roaring over the rushing of blood in her ears. His fingers dug into her skin, and he thrust his hips up into her, making her cry out again as he came, unable to wait for her permission.

It could have been her imagination, but Elena's orgasm lasted longer than usual. Tarrick's mouth hung open in surprise. It was as though he, too, felt the waves of pleasure coursing through his body more intensely and for longer than either of them had ever experienced.

They stayed in their positions in the afterglow, too afraid to break the spell and acknowledge that the end of the night was near. When her breathing slowed down and the post-orgasm haze cleared from her head, Elena carefully pulled herself off Tarrick and slid off the bed in the direction of the washroom. She quickly cleaned up, washed away as much of the smeared makeup as possible, and returned to the room. Tarrick was sitting up with a pillow behind him. Just as he had last time, he was arranging the blankets and pillows for Elena, and he looked up at her hopefully when she reentered the room.

Elena hesitated, unsure if she should stay the rest of the night with Tarrick in the *lamora*.

"Just one night, El," he reminded her gently, holding a hand out.

She relented and slid under the blanket he had arranged over the entire bed. She lay back, and Tarrick drew the blanket up to her chin before wrapping an arm around her waist. He nestled closer to her until their bodies were pressed against each other. Elena rolled over so her back was against his chest. He placed a soft kiss on her shoulder before burrowing his face in her hair.

A tear slipped out of the corner of her eye, but Elena didn't bother brushing it away as she listened to Tarrick's steady breathing that eventually lulled her to sleep.

***

The pale light of dawn filtered through the small windows in the *lamora's* roof, waking Elena despite the late night and sex. Her body insisted on keeping to its new routine, but that morning, she was grateful that she could leave without the awkward morning-after conversation.

She raised her head slowly and peeked over her shoulder at Tarrick's peaceful, sleeping face. His arm was still slung around her waist, but he was sleeping too deeply to feel her sliding out from under it. She quickly pulled her dress back on and gathered her shoes, tiptoeing barefoot to the door.

The bolt on the door slid back easily and quietly. The air was still and quiet outside. Not even a breeze rustled through the gardens as Elena padded down the pebbled paths as silently as possible. She reached her room just as dawn was breaking, and heaved a sigh of relief when she flung herself on the bed. Elena waited for the waves of regret to wash over, mentally preparing for the berating she would give herself for acting so impulsively, but she didn't feel a thing.

Elena stared at the ceiling until *lyrabirds* called out to each other at the break of dawn. When she still didn't feel any pangs or surges of emotion, she decided it was time to put the night before in the past and get on with the day.

~ 36 ~

Elena approached the doors to the council chamber apprehensively. She tried to time it so she could enter unnoticed and sit in the corner.

Malik, Eli, and Rami walked slowly from the opposite direction and gave Elena wan smiles. She smothered a grin at their slightly worse-for-wear appearance—they had celebrated with a few too many *araki* and had dragged themselves down for the impromptu council meeting Amaya had called.

Rami pushed the door open, wincing slightly at the bright light streaming through the windows to greet him. He held it open and silently motioned for Elena to enter first. Netta, Leon, Darius, and Aiden were already seated around the large table, talking quietly amongst themselves and arranging various documents in front of them.

Leon tilted his head to the empty seat next to him.

"Where did you disappear to last night?" he asked in a low voice, arranging his own piles of reports and folders in front of him.

"I went to bed," Elena lied smoothly. "I wasn't feeling well."

"You could have told me." Hurt laced his voice. "And you didn't show up for training this morning. You missed seeing me whoop Zahra's ass."

Elena didn't have time to feel bad or apologize because the door opened again and Tarrick, Adina, and Henry walked in. Tarrick and Adina took their seats at the table while Henry made his way to the corner of the room and settled himself in a chair, crossing one leg over the other and sitting back.

Amaya followed moments later with a man and woman, gesturing for them both to take a seat at the table. She scanned the room and raised a brow at the sight of Henry in the corner, but said nothing as she took a seat beside Tarrick.

"We have a few guests this morning," Tarrick announced. There was a flash of emotion when he locked eyes with Elena. "Henry is here to observe."

He didn't elaborate why the man was observing the proceedings of a council meeting. Leon's jaw tightened, and Rami and Malik exchanged nervous glances, but no one said anything.

Tarrick started by thanking everyone for attending. "I'd like to thank Sanah and Nadim for agreeing to join us for this unofficial council meeting. They have expressed an interest in joining the council, and I thought we could take this opportunity to assess the state of affairs, what needs to be done, and invite them to offer their opinions and advice on how to proceed."

A few councilors, including Darius and Aiden, smiled at Sanah and Nadim.

"Some of you have met them already," Tarrick continued. "For those who haven't, Sanah is one of Terralea's finest legal advisors. She's also well-versed in Skandorian and Sailonese legal structures. Nadim has a number of thriving businesses across the country and has advised us as a private consultant on regional economic matters from time to time over the past few centuries."

Elena studied the newcomers with interest—they sounded like perfect additions to the council. Sanah regarded the councilors, her gaze paused on Netta. Nadim tilted his head and assessed everyone. His shiny dark hair was pulled back into a knot at the nape of his neck, and he stroked his lean chin that sported a dark goatee ending in a curl.

Leon and Netta were the only ones who wore expressions of relief. The others gave them weak smiles, although Elena suspected their lack of enthusiasm was largely due to the fact that they were unprepared for the meeting.

The councilors took it in turns to summarize the state of Terralean affairs and issues that needed to be addressed. Sanah and Nadim jotted down notes, listening intently as each person spoke. They asked a few questions but didn't offer any advice. Every so often, they exchanged looks with each other, but for the most part they, too, listened with interest.

Leon scribbled notes as everyone spoke, taking down every word to later summarize in the meeting minutes. Elena squinted at his indecipherable scrawl and missed half of what Netta spoke about as she tried to identify words and make sense of the strange symbols that appeared to be complete sentences. It baffled Elena how Leon could understand his own writing. He caught her staring and gave her a grin as he continued to scribble, adding flourishes to his downward strokes and scrawling nonsensical stick figures in between purely for Elena's entertainment.

Adina, who sat stiffly the entire time, reported on the security and defense measures around the entire country. She also announced that more rebels and Leneirans without preternatural abilities had moved to Sailon since the spring. Word of Zanthus's intentions to use them as scapegoats when executing his plans had spread. They were afraid of being unfairly accused of committing crimes they were not part of.

As the king neared the end of his own summary, the time for Elena to announce her departure was drawing closer. Despite Tarrick's earlier assurances, Sanah and Nadim's expression gave no indication as to whether they were interested in joining the council. Elena trusted his and Amaya's combined powers of persuasion and hoped that her decision would work in Tarrick's favor. Her heart rate increased when he put down his stylus beside his notes.

"That concludes this council meeting," he announced. "Is there anything else anyone would like to raise?"

When no one said anything, he cleared his throat. "Now that we have a clear picture of where we stand on everything, it's time to address the most pressing issue: filling the seats on the Council of Nobles before the end of the season. Lady Amaya has reported that, on her way back to Erindell, she managed to meet with some of the councilors who were unable to travel due to the desert storms.

"Those who have agreed to remain on the council are happy to vote on matters via correspondence until they return to Erindell. However, without a full council, we cannot move forward on the issues that require our attention. Some are more pressing than others. Nevertheless, we owe it to the people of Terralea to ensure their needs are being met and their voices heard."

He spoke calmly without any inflection or emotion, as though the desert storms didn't herald an imminent disaster.

"I have asked Sanah and Nadim to give us their responses tomorrow." He smiled at them with the unspoken assurance that there would be no hard feelings if they declined the invitation.

Amaya spoke up. "I would like to invite Lady Elena to officially sit on the council."

Elena started slightly, as did several others. Henry leaned forward in his chair and clasped his hands together, frowning. Malik and Nadim eyed her warily, but the others showed no emotions as heads swiveled in her direction.

"I'm sure you'll all agree that this is inevitable," Amaya continued. "It makes sense for Lady Elena to join now, while we are navigating the next steps in shaping the future of Terralea."

Elena swallowed and spoke in a clear voice, pleased that she sounded calmer than she felt. "Lady Amaya, thank you for the honor. Before the council deliberates my position, I do have one thing that I would like to raise with the council on behalf of the people of Erindell, and I hope you will vote in favor of their request."

Leon looked at her in surprise. Netta leaned forward with an expression of interest. Darius winked at her. Elena deliberately avoided looking at Tarrick.

Amaya gave her a wide smile. "Please, do state your proposal, Lady Elena."

Elena shuffled her notes but found she didn't need them. She confidently outlined her proposal to introduce a rebate system for Terraleans who volunteered at community spaces. She explained the reason behind setting up the community center in Erindell, the way the locals pitched in without hesitation or question, recognizing that it was something that benefited everyone.

"But this kind of operation takes time and money to maintain in the long run," Elena explained. "The Erindellians who volunteered over the summer still have families to feed, paid employment to prioritize, everyday costs. Having this excise rebate program would incentivize people to contribute time they can spare for the center. It's a sign that the council acknowledges they are contributing more than what is asked of them to keep the country running, community spirit, a safe space for anyone to use."

She paused to take in everyone's reactions. Netta was suitably impressed. Even Rami and Eli had woken from their stupor and took in everything she said.

"How much will this allowance cost the council, Lady Elena?" Nadim asked.

Elena shuffled through her pages and pulled out a piece of parchment on which Rhea had carefully calculated the costs. She leaned over the table to hand it to Nadim, who looked at it with interest. "These are some rough calculations that Lady Rhea has developed for this program."

"My Rhea?" Malik piped up from his seat.

Elena nodded. "She's provided a few scenarios where the volunteers are reimbursed for their time, regardless of whether the council's budget is in surplus or deficit. We were able to work through what we already know, but of course, there's room for adjustments and negotiation."

"Lady Rhea's figures seem quite healthy," Nadim said as he examined the numbers.

Darius, who was sipping on some water at that moment, choked and sputtered at Nadim's words. Leon gave him a few thumps on his back as the lord turned red in the face.

"Who are you and what have you done with Elena?" Leon said.

There were a few chuckles around the table.

Elena's smile waned as she addressed Amaya directly. "I'm glad the council is considering this proposal, however, I must decline your invitation."

Amaya pursed her lips and raised a brow.

Adina maintained her bland expression, and Tarrick pulled up the stony-faced mask he often wore to hide his feelings. Someone sucked in a sharp breath.

"I am unqualified and unsuitable for the role," she continued. "I gave it my best shot in an unofficial capacity."

"El—" Tarrick began to speak.

She continued, raising her voice slightly. "But if the people in this room can't trust or respect my position, how can the people of Terralea?" Elena paused and looked around the room.

A few men shifted uncomfortably in their seats. Someone coughed to fill the silence.

"The role is better suited to someone who has the essence of the realm in their veins," she continued, hiding the tremor in her voice. It took every effort not to break down at that.

Leon opened his mouth to object, but Elena didn't give him the chance.

"I would like to nominate Henry Graham to take my place," she announced.

At that, Leon didn't bother hiding his gasp. Even Adina furrowed her brow at the unexpected development. Elena chanced a look at Amaya—the disappointment was clear on the former queen's face, but she remained silent. She leaned forward and clasped her hands on the table, listening intently to Elena.

"In the few days he has been here, he has made an impression on everyone and shown that he is eager to embrace his heritage," Elena told the councilors. "He has spent time in Erindell getting to know the people and their history. He has expressed ideas to improve life for Terraleans." She paused and turned slightly to Henry, straightening up in his seat. "And it's his birthright as the only son of the current king."

His eyes glittered in triumph at Elena's words.

She stood and addressed Tarrick. "I wish you the best of luck, and I'm sure Terralea will be in good hands."

Everyone waited with bated breath for the king's response.

"Thank you, Lady Elena," he said after a beat. His voice was cool and did not betray the hurt and anger that flashed across his face. "Are there any objections to the nomination?"

Leon and Amaya's hands shot up in the air in unison as they glared at Elena.

"The majority of the council are in agreement," Tarrick said, steadfastly ignoring his mother and brother.

Elena gave him a curt nod and swept over to the door. Before she closed it behind her, Amaya and Leon had exploded.

"Tarrick, you cannot be serious!"

"What the actual *fuck*?" Leon shouted.

***

Elena frowned at the contents in her suitcases—she had only packed enough clothes for a two-week vacation in Türkiye in the springtime. The warmest item of clothing was her leather jacket and one sweater she had worn on the plane, neither of which would keep her remotely warm in the icy barrens of Skandor.

As she threw in her passport and travel documents amongst her clothes, Elena realized that Tarrick still held her mother's badge hostage. She debated whether she should sneak into his office to try to take it back. It had been difficult enough walking away from him in the council chambers, especially after their night together.

Before she fell asleep, Elena felt a flicker of hope that maybe they could work things out. Henry's presence at the council meeting shut down any waning feelings she felt. It was a reminder that he would always be in their lives, and even if she and Tarrick were able to move past the rough patch in their relationship, he still didn't trust her judgment of Henry.

A knock at the door interrupted the internal argument. Zahra entered, shutting it carefully behind her. The guard stopped short at the sight of clothes strewn around Elena, who sat on the floor, folding the items within reach.

"Going somewhere?" Zahra asked sarcastically.

"As a matter of fact, I am," Elena said, not looking at the guard. "I'm leaving." She didn't tell Zahra where she was planning on going. Better for them to assume she was going back to the human realm.

There was a long silence, and she risked looking up at the shocked expression on Zahra's face.

"The princess said you declined Lady Amaya's invitation to join the council," she said finally. "She didn't say anything about you leaving."

Elena shrugged and continued placing her folded clothes in the suitcase. "There's no point in me staying anymore."

"No point?" Zahra exploded. "Didn't Prince Leon pass on my message this morning?"

"Yes." Elena rolled her eyes. "Leon told me he whooped your ass in training."

"No," Zahra said impatiently. "My mother has sent for us. She has information on the scepter." She lowered her voice. "And our new friend."

"I've already told Tarrick to go through his father's diaries. I'm pretty sure the scepter is in the Temple of Divine Beings," Elena said. "And I nominated Henry to take my spot on the council."

"You can't be serious!"

"It's his birthright." Elena shrugged again. "Like it or not, he has royal blood in him."

"That doesn't mean he's entitled to the position," Zahra argued. "Zanthus was a royal, too, and he turned out to be the world's biggest asshole!"

Elena shrugged. "I'm not the one you have to convince. I've tried. Many times. I can't keep second-guessing myself when others tell me I'm wrong. I have to trust myself and do what's right for me now."

She stood, and Zahra frowned at her outfit. When pulling out her suitcase from the wardrobe, Elena couldn't resist trying on her old jeans and favorite cotton t-shirt.

"That's what humans wear?" Zahra wrinkled her nose.

"Yes," Elena said defiantly. "What's wrong with it?"

Zahra made a face before saying, "It's not really refined or elegant, is it?"

"It's comfortable."

That was a lie. The denim was not as soft as Elena remembered. Her cotton shirt was shabby and hung off her frame, limp and shapeless. She had become so used to wearing tunics and pants that fit her like a second skin and moved easily with her. Not to mention the beautiful, hand-embroidered details that elevated even the simplest outfit.

Zahra shook her head. "Well, you can't leave without saying goodbye to my mother. I'd never hear the end of it, and you owe me."

"I do?" Elena asked, bemused.

"I don't like waking up at the crack of dawn to do extra training." Zahra grinned. "Or trekking to the Temple of Divine Beings. Or letting His Highness beat me so he can save face. Or—"

"What?"

"Did you really think he'd beat me that easily?" Zahra scoffed. "I saw his strike coming a mile away, but the other guards had started arriving for training. I let him knock me down."

Elena stared at the smug expression Zahra wore.

"Did you tell him?"

"You believe me?" Zahra asked, surprised.

"You beat up your brother and another guard while you were blindfolded and had only a stick to defend yourself," Elena reminded her.

Zahra smiled fondly at the memory. She shook her head and sighed at the messy room. "We should go now," she told Elena. "Her Highness has given me a few hours off before my evening shift."

"How kind of her." The sarcasm dripped from Elena's voice, and she immediately felt bad. Adina had been a good friend when she had first arrived in Terralea. She was still hurting over Erik and Arran's deaths. But at that moment, Elena was feeling bitter. "Alright." She sighed, shoving the last of her clothes into the large suitcase and leaning on the lid to hold it down while she dragged the zip along the tape. "Let's get this over with." She picked up the smaller suitcase gingerly, testing the weight.

"What are you doing?" Zahra asked.

"I can't carry both suitcases," Elena said reluctantly. "I'll have to leave with whatever I can carry."

"You're leaving *tonight*?" Zahra gaped.

"Yep," Elena popped the *p* with a note of finality. "We can stop by your mother's place before you help me find someone who will take me to the portal."

Zahra stared at her at a loss for words.

Elena jutted her chin out defiantly, daring the guard to stop her.

"You're going to go to Erindell, possibly travel across Terralea, dressed like that?" Zahra finally said, surveying her jeans.

"If Henry can waltz around in a suit, then I can wear my jeans," Elena snapped. She hauled her suitcase in one hand, yanked open the door with the other, and stomped out.

$$\sim 37 \sim$$

The day was warm, but a brisk wind nipped at Elena's exposed skin, raising goosebumps. She wished she had thought to wear her leather jacket before her dramatic exit, but she didn't want to pause and rummage around her suitcase while trying to leave as quickly as possible. They had been lucky enough to avoid bumping into anyone on their way out.

She and Zahra walked into the Royal Quarter, the suitcase bumping Elena's legs as she hurried down the hill. Although it had wheels, she didn't want to draw attention to her departure by dragging it noisily across the flagstones and cobbled streets.

Someone called out when they were halfway down. They turned around and saw Killian jogging after them.

"Lady Elena," he huffed, coming to a halt in front of her. "I'd like to apologize for my behavior last night."

"It's fine." She waved away the apology. "I shouldn't have pushed you."

"No, it's not," the prince said humbly. "Please, hear me out?"

Zahra and Elena exchanged looks.

"Fine," Elena told him. "But we're going to town."

The prince's eyes dipped to the suitcase she clutched in her hands. Elena tightened her grip on the straps, ready to defend herself, but Killian smiled. "Allow me to escort you."

"That's not a good idea," Elena said, afraid that Adina might come after her when she found out, possibly accusing her of kidnapping the prince.

"El, we've got to go." Zahra shifted impatiently.

Killian didn't allow further argument. He swooped down and pried the suitcase from her hand, sweeping Elena's free arm through the crook of his elbow. Before she could protest, he tugged her down the hill toward the path that led to Erindell, carrying her suitcase gallantly.

He looked at her with a nervous expression a few times, and Elena smoothed out the frown she had been wearing since she left the palace.

When they were halfway through the Royal Quarter, Killian scanned the area to make sure they were alone. "The truth is, I've been keeping a secret from everyone." He swallowed hard. His voice was so low that Elena had to lean in. Zahra also moved closer to the pair to hear what Killian had to say. "I don't have Seer ability."

Elena stared at him in confusion. "So?" She shrugged. "I'm not an Elemental. I'm not even Leneiran. And I was led to believe only a few Minotians had Seer abilities?"

"I know." He bit his lip. "And it's true—only a small number of our population can See. That's why I should have trusted you. You're different from everyone else. But my father told us that Terraleans and Skandorians despise those without additional powers, and they believe a Leneiran royal without any extraordinary ability is an abomination ..."

Zahra muttered something that sounded suspiciously like *backwards old fool* under her breath.

"It's one of the reasons he pulled away from mainland politics," Killian explained with a wry smile at the guard that indicated he had heard what she said.

For her part, Zahra didn't look abashed. She continued to trail behind them, ever watchful and alert.

"Father didn't want King Halder or King Arran discovering my secret," Killian continued. "My brothers can See, and those rituals you read about would have worked if they had been here. But since I can't ..." he trailed off sadly.

"I understand," Elena said with an ironic smile. "I've met Halder, so I know where he stands on the issue of non-magical Leneirans. But Arran wouldn't have cared. It's a shame you never got to meet him."

"It's nice being in Terralea." Killian said as they walked further down the path and entered Erindell. Erindellians went about their day, squeezing past each other in the crowded streets. "Father warned me the people here wouldn't tolerate a Leneiran like myself, but that's not true, is it?" He peered down at Elena, who still hung onto his arm. "They have welcomed you and Henry with open arms."

Elena made a non-committal sound, recalling the objections from the nobles about her presence in the country. Even though they had started to warm toward her in the past few days, the judgment and stigma from the initial encounters still stung.

"Lady Elena has worked hard to change the perception of humans," Zahra said loyally. "But there are still many who believe the old tales and superstitions. Your secret is safe with us, Your Highness."

"Thank you." Killian dipped his head gratefully.

"Have you told Adina?" Elena asked sternly.

Killian's tanned complexion turned slightly red.

"Do it sooner rather than later if you intend to court her." She pierced him with her stare. "I speak from experience when I say that your relationship will not last long if you keep secrets from each other."

"I will," he said humbly. "The Terralean royal family has shown that they are more open-minded than I was led to believe. I shall tell them and advise my father to reconsider his stance on relations with your country."

They walked to Ninaz's house without incident. Zahra knocked on the door and entered, announcing herself to her mother and calling out that Elena and Killian were with her.

"Ah!" The old lady beamed and slowly rose to her feet to greet them.

"Ninaz, so nice to see you again," Elena said with false cheeriness.

"And you, my dear." Ninaz looked at her suspiciously. "Your Highness. An honor once more to have you in my humble abode."

"Lady Ninaz, you're as dazzling as always." Killian bent down to kiss the back of her hand.

The old woman cackled with delight and waved to them to make themselves comfortable. Zahra disappeared into the kitchen while Killian dropped Elena's suitcase beside a spindly chair. Ninaz's sharp eyes noted the act, but she didn't comment on it.

"I take it my daughter told you I have information about the scepter?" She raised a brow and sat straight back in her chair.

Zahra reappeared with a tray of tea and coffee for everyone. Killian waited for her to take a seat before asking Ninaz, "You know where it's hidden?"

She lifted her chin. "I do. It's in the Temple of Divine Beings."

Elena silently congratulated herself for reaching the same conclusion. "Did Amaya tell you?"

"Amaya would not have known, and she would have respected Arran's obligation to keep that particular secret," Ninaz said sternly. "She understands there are certain mysteries and magic of the land that we cannot bend to our will. Besides, I don't reveal my sources."

Elena asked doubtfully, "Can we trust your source?"

Ninaz's sharp look said it all. "As for its precise location within the temple," she continued as though Elena had not just insulted her, "that is still a mystery."

"I've told Tarrick to go through his father's diaries in case Arran recorded hiding it anywhere," Elena told the group, sipping her tea.

"Knowing Arran, bless his soul, he probably left a string of clues behind right under his sons' noses." Ninaz chuckled. "He was fond of playing little games like that."

"He used to take Tarrick and Leon to the temple when they were children and read them the songs engraved around the space," Elena said, tapping her chin thoughtfully with a finger. "It would make sense he'd hide it in a safe, sacred space that also holds memories and symbolizes connection to the realm."

Killian stared at her. "You knew the scepter was in the temple?"

"It came to me last night." She shrugged. "You and Tarrick can search for it together."

"Won't you join us?" the prince asked.

Elena shook her head. "This is as far as I can investigate." She carefully set her cup down on the small side table and rose to her feet.

Killian gaped while Zahra's eyes sparkled with unshed tears.

"What about the other matter?" Ninaz demanded.

"What other matter?" Killian asked suspiciously.

"It's no longer relevant," Elena told her. "Thank you for your help, Ninaz."

"Sit down, young lady," Ninaz said sternly. "Tell me what's going on."

Zahra and Killian swung their heads between Ninaz and Elena. The former was glaring at the latter, whose mouth was set in a stubborn line.

"You know I'll find out sooner or later," Ninaz warned. "And I'd rather hear it from you. I knew something was wrong the minute you walked into my house dressed like that." She sniffed at Elena's outfit disdainfully while Zahra tried to smother a smile.

"I'm leaving," Elena said, sitting back down heavily and crossing her arms over her chest. "So whatever you've learned about Henry is of no use to me."

"You're leaving?" Killian gasped, his eyes bouncing to her suitcase before snapping back to her. "When? Where?"

"Why?" Ninaz barked, pointing the end of her cane directly at Elena's face.

She looked apologetically at Killian before returning to Ninaz. "Yes. Tonight, back to the human realm. My work here is done, and my services are no longer required."

Killian inhaled sharply, but Ninaz continued glaring at Elena, who stared back.

"The truth, Elena," Ninaz ordered.

She huffed a sigh. "I have no special powers or useful skills that I can contribute to Leneira, so I'm going back home. And ... Tarrick and I broke up," she mumbled the last part.

"And leave your loved ones just like that?" Ninaz demanded.

"I don't have loved ones here," Elena shot back, feeling her cheeks redden, aware of the fact that Killian was witnessing the spectacular showdown.

"You have more people who respect and admire you here than you do in the realm you call *home*," Ninaz fired.

"Mother," Zahra muttered, shifting uncomfortably. "That's rude."

"That's not rude," Ninaz snapped. "My queen deciding to leave without telling us is rude. Especially when the royal family and this realm needs her the most."

"You're as dramatic as Leon," Elena groused. "The royal family don't need me. They've made that perfectly clear."

"Lady Amaya, Leon, Darius, and all of the guards still need you," Zahra said quietly. "I need you. Kaylee and Chloe need you. What about Bri and Yas? I'm certain Queen Lin and Commander Zen would be upset to find out about your departure."

Elena's expression softened. "I'm sorry, Zahra. I will miss you, really." She turned back to Ninaz. "And I'll miss you, too, Ninaz."

"You would leave the love of your life at the first obstacle you face?" Ninaz demanded.

"He's not …" Elena dropped her eyes. "He doesn't feel the same way about me. I can't give him or Terralea what they need to continue thriving. Henry is here now to learn from his father and continue the line of succession."

"That man is dangerous," Ninaz said sharply. "You cannot abandon Tarrick and his family."

"What do you mean, Mother?" Zahra asked, sitting up straight.

"He's been seen around town with a rebel," Ninaz told her daughter. "They've been meeting at Yas's coffee shop every afternoon since his first visit to Erindell."

Zahra and Elena stared at Ninaz.

"I thought there were no more rebels in Terralea?" Killian frowned. "All of the powerless Leneirans moved to Sailon and our islands after the uprising."

"There are still factions and communities along the borders," Zahra informed him. "But we've got eyes and ears all over them. They haven't been planning anything. They don't have the numbers or resources to cause another riot."

"The troublemakers live in Terralea and Skandor because they know Lin will sniff them out the minute they cross over to her lands." Ninaz snorted.

"And Henry is hanging out with this rebel?" Elena asked in concern. "That doesn't make any sense. How could they have met or know each other? He's only been here a few days."

"Shall I write you a letter detailing everything once the damage is done?" Ninaz's voice dripped with sarcasm. "Or would you like to find out for yourself?"

"You're like a dog with a bone, you know that?" Elena shook her head and sighed. "I'll let Jet and Mika know. They haven't been able to read him since he arrived, but maybe they could make an excuse to have Lin visit, and she'll be able to read him."

"She won't," Killian spoke up. "He's wearing a ring of protection."

He shrank back in his seat when everyone stared at him.

"I thought you knew?" He held his hands up in surrender. "The ring he wears protects the wearer from all Leneiran magic. I thought Tarrick gave it to him."

Elena cursed silently, forgetting about the ring that Tarrick had told her about the previous night. While Henry wore that, it would be impossible for even the most powerful Empath to find out the truth.

"He's had that ring ever since he arrived," Zahra said slowly. "He said the ring was a family heirloom. Humans wear rings, don't they?" she asked Elena.

"Some do," she said thoughtfully.

Ninaz cleared her throat loudly. "I think you're all fixating on an unimportant detail. I believe now is the time Henry meets his mercenary friend at the coffee shop," she said, casually sipping on her tea. "You might catch them there if you leave now. "

"That's convenient," Elena said drily.

Ninaz merely smiled at her over the rim of her cup. "Perhaps along the way you may ponder the *right* questions to ask."

Zahra's eyes narrowed at her mother's cryptic tone.

"Do give my regards to Yasmina, and let me know how you get on," Ninaz said, as though they were going to attempt a complicated recipe.

Elena had a feeling that whatever Henry was plotting, it would be ten times worse if he was working with a Leneiran rebel. It was bad enough that he would plan something treacherous against his own family, but to work with someone who knew the history of the realm and understood the powers imbued in the land could be disastrous.

"Zahra, I can clean up," Ninaz told her daughter.

"Are you sure, Mother?" Zahra asked, piling the empty cups and saucers on the tray.

"You have more pressing matters to attend to," Ninaz said pointedly. "And Lady Elena can leave her suitcase here. You can collect it when you're done dealing with Henry."

$$\sim 38 \sim$$

Tarrick sat at his desk, massaging his temples, trying to block out his mother and Leon talking over the top of him.

"What the hell were you thinking?" Leon yelled.

"I thought you were going to speak with her?" Amaya's voice was filled with anger.

After the uproar Elena had caused with her announcement in the council chamber, the nobles clamored for answers. Tarrick had marched out of the room after assuring them he would get to the bottom of what was happening.

Amaya, Leon, and Adina had followed him to his office without invitation. They alternated between offering solutions, suggesting compromises, and berating him for the mess he had caused.

"Maybe this is for the best." Adina glared at Leon. "We still don't know if she had an ulterior motive, asking all those questions and obsessing over our history."

"Adina, that's enough." Amaya frowned at her daughter. "You and I need to talk about dealing with your grief in a way that doesn't hurt the people who care about you. Perhaps we *should* send you to the human realm for a while so you understand how difficult it can be starting a new life in a realm you know nothing about."

Adina gasped.

"Yeah, you'd want to learn everything you can about that world, too, if you wanted to survive," Leon scorned. "Elena doesn't want our powers. She wants to *understand* them."

"I love you, my darling," Amaya said to Adina, shaking her head. "But you have disappointed me. You are incredibly privileged and lucky to have a loving family and extraordinary powers. I know you're better than this spoiled, petulant person you've become."

Adina went bright red and hung her head in shame.

Tarrick closed his eyes, pinched the bridge of his nose, and inhaled deeply. "I need some time to think—"

"The time for thinking is over," Leon cut in. "You've been thinking wrong this entire time anyway."

"Leon, Tarrick is your king," Amaya said sternly. "You will show him the respect he deserves."

"He didn't listen to me as his royal advisor," Leon shot back. "I'm hoping he'll listen to me as his brother, who has spent more time with Elena this week than anyone else in this room." He paused and glared at Adina, who showed him her middle finger in response. "You've both been driving her away while trying to make Henry a part of this family."

Amaya sighed. "Leon."

"No, Mother," the prince ploughed on relentlessly. "They're both feeling guilty about what happened in the spring with"—he swallowed hard—"Zanthus. And they've lashed out at Elena, who's been nothing but understanding and patient." He thrust a finger at Tarrick. "*You've* been overcompensating"—he swung his hand around to Adina—"and *you're* blaming Elena for something she didn't do."

"None of us are to blame for what happened," Amaya said firmly. She looked at Tarrick with pity. "Darling, I understand why you might want to protect yourself after everything with Rose, but Elena is different. She's proven herself to be trustworthy, and she loves you."

His mother's words made him feel infinitely worse.

Leon flung his arm out, knocking over a small notebook from the pile perched precariously at the edge of his desk. "What's this?" he asked, reaching down to pick it up. He flipped through the pages, pausing at the elegant lines of script.

"Father's diaries," Tarrick replied absent-mindedly. "El thinks the scepter is hidden in the Temple of Divine Beings and suggested I go through Father's diaries in case he wrote down where he hid it."

Leon's eyes welled slightly at the sight of Arran's handwriting. "That was clever," he murmured.

"You need to speak with her, Tarrick," Amaya said sharply. "Go find her. Now."

"What about Henry?" Adina objected.

"I think it's time he and I had a proper conversation," Amaya said coolly.

Tarrick stood, glad to have an excuse to get away from his overbearing family.

Leon started to follow, but Amaya held her hand out to stop him.

"Your brother should talk to her privately," she said in a tone that indicated she would not tolerate any argument.

"Because that's worked well so far," Leon muttered, but he obeyed Amaya.

Tarrick left, striding purposefully down the corridors to the guest wing. Fortunately, he did not encounter anyone along the way, and soon found himself standing outside Elena's room, knocking frantically.

"El," he called out. "We need to talk."

He was met with silence.

"El!" he said impatiently. "Let me in."

Tarrick turned the handle and entered. His heart stopped at the sight of the large suitcase standing upright in the middle of the room. A cursory glance showed that the space was devoid of all her personal items. A quick peek in the washroom and wardrobe confirmed that Elena had packed everything she had brought with her. He opened the drawers to the side tables rapidly before hauling the suitcase onto the neatly-made bed and opening it. It was stuffed with clothes that hadn't been touched in months, but there was no sign of the item he was searching for.

Footsteps thundered down the passage, and Leon burst in, breathless and red-faced.

"Tarrick, you have to read this!" He waved the diary in the air. "It's about—"

"She's gone, Leon," the king choked out.

"What? What do you mean?" the prince's gaze swept the room. "Her suitcase is still here."

"She's left the bigger suitcase behind," Tarrick explained in a rough voice. "Her carry-on is gone. So is her passport."

Leon staggered back until he hit the wall, staring in shock. "She's gone?" he whispered.

Tarrick's eyes swept the room in the hopes he'd find another drawer or nook in which Elena might have hidden the precious document, but the guest room was plainly furnished. Aside from the suitcase, it had been restored to its original state, everything in its place.

A loud knock at the door had them snapping their heads to Sami, who stood at the threshold, slightly breathless. "Your Majesty, Your Highness." She gave a short bow. "We've had a confirmed sighting of the assassin Lady Elena said was working with Lord Zanthus."

Tarrick's stomach lurched at the news.

"Where?" Leon asked.

"In Erindell," Sami replied. "Ali was on patrol this afternoon. He spotted a man who closely resembles the drawings Elena helped us with entering the coffee shop in the market square."

Leon looked at Tarrick in alarm.

"But that's not all," Sami continued, the words tumbling out of her mouth. "He was seen in the company of Henry."

Tarrick swore out loud, causing Sami to pause.

"Anything else?" Leon asked swiftly.

"Ali spoke to Yas, and she confirmed that they have been meeting regularly for the past few days," Sami told him. "She sent word to Princess Adina the first time she spotted them together, but Her Highness hasn't received any correspondence from Erindell for some time now."

Leon's brows knitted together.

"Illyas and I searched the palace and discovered that someone is using the secret passages." Sami's eyes darted between the men. "We've found clothes, cigarettes, a makeshift bed, and the missing letters from Yas."

"Fuck," Leon muttered.

"Do you know who it is?" Tarrick asked.

"Given the latest intelligence, we suspect it's Raz," Sami said slowly. "Illyas, Jai, and Ronan are investigating as we speak, Your Majesty. We wanted to bring you concrete evidence, but as soon as Ali told us that Raz had been sighted, I thought you should know immediately."

"You did the right thing, Sami," Leon assured her. "Go back to the others and collect everything you find in the passages. Bring them to my office."

Sami gave a quick bow and marched down the corridor quickly. As the sound of her footsteps died, Leon looked at Tarrick apprehensively.

The king's gaze dropped to the diary in Leon's hand. "You found something?"

Leon collected himself and handed the diary to Tarrick, holding it open to a page in the middle.

The king took the diary and read the page his brother had indicated. His face crumpled in horror. Leon stared back with a serious expression.

"We need to find Henry," Tarrick whispered.

Leon nodded.

"He's not my son."

"Tarrick," Leon began.

"I need to find Henry *now*," the king cut him off, the earlier fear growing. "We've underestimated him, Leon. He's dangerous."

"And El?" Leon asked hesitantly.

"You search for her. Get her as far away from here as possible. Keep her safe."

$$\sim 39 \sim$$

"We need to make a game plan," Zahra advised as they wove through the crowds in the narrow streets. "We can't go bursting into Yas's shop and scare everyone."

"He might not even be there today." Dread crept over Elena at the thought of Henry conspiring with a rebel against Tarrick and his family.

They reached the end of the alley that spilled out into the market square.

"There he is!" Killian pointed to the door of *Meant To Bean*, where Henry had just emerged. "Who's he with?"

"That's Raz!" Elena gasped when the familiar, sallow-faced man wearing a black cloak walked out with Henry. She felt the ghost of the cold dagger he held to her throat as she watched him melt between the bodies in the crowded market square. "He was the one who knocked me out in Zanthus's office."

"Zanthus?" Kilian asked blankly.

"There's no time to explain." Zahra's eyes darted around the square. "I'll go find out what's going on. You two stay here."

Before they could protest, she slipped through the bodies pressed up against each other during the peak trading hour and entered the coffee shop. Elena watched as Henry and Raz crossed the square and disappeared down the street that led back to the palace. She drummed her fingers against her thighs while they waited for Zahra to return.

They didn't have to wait long, for the guard soon returned, scanning the square with a worried expression.

"Where did they go?" she asked sharply.

"The palace." Elena jerked her head toward the street Henry and Raz had taken.

"Let's go," Zahra commanded, pushing people aside gently to make room for Elena and Killian to follow her strides.

"I don't understand," the prince said breathlessly as he tried to keep up. "What's Henry doing with that man?"

"Mother was right," Zahra said in a low voice. "Yas confirmed they've been meeting at her shop for a few days now. They obviously don't know who she is, or they would have chosen a more discreet location."

"Yas is one of the princess's spies," Elena explained quickly to Killian. "She reports to Adina if she finds out about any rebel activity."

Finally, they broke free of the throng and were able to walk side by side. The street was one of the quieter ones in Erindell, as very few people visited the palace without an invitation.

"Bri spotted them together first, and Yas kept tabs on them," Zahra said without slowing her pace.

"They were pretty friendly," Elena pointed out. "I bet that Raz was the mysterious man who delivered the letter to Henry."

"Why would Raz deliver a letter? Is Henry Raz's son?" Zahra grimaced.

"No." Elena wrinkled her brow as more pieces of the puzzle fell into place. "That can't be right. I wonder if Zanthus was involved," she said slowly. "Zanthus admitted to being in love with Rose before Tarrick came along. It was why he created that toxin in the first place—to prove he could be more powerful if Tarrick didn't have any Elemental powers. While Rose was in Terralea, Leon was stationed at the portal, so he's definitely not Henry's father."

"Also pointing out that Rose isn't exactly the prince's type," Zahra interjected.

"Arran would not have touched Rose." Elena shook her head. "The thought is absurd. The family resemblance points to Tarrick and Zanthus. Who's to say Zanthus and Rose didn't have an affair while she was here? He was, after all, the one who told her about bluestone and that nonsense about killing another Elemental to gain their powers."

"He had so much hatred in him," Zahra said fearfully. "Surely he couldn't love?"

"I think he loved Rose," Elena said somberly. "At least, he was obsessed with her. I don't know if that counts as love. I think *Zanthus* was Henry's biological father. The letter didn't explicitly say it was Tarrick."

"His birth certificate did," Zahra reminded her.

"Rose wouldn't have put Zanthus's name down if it risked exposing her affair with him," Elena said grimly.

"Is that a fact?" Zahra asked in a hushed voice.

"I don't know, but we need to find out."

"I still have no idea who these people are or what you're talking about," Killian said somewhat irately. "But I thought Henry and Raz were going back to the palace?"

The women stopped and whirled around. Killian stood a few feet behind, pointing up the steep stairs that led to the Temple of Divine Beings. "Why are they going up there?"

Elena held a hand to her forehead to shield her eyes against the bright sun. Sure enough, Henry and Raz were halfway up the hill to the temple.

"You don't think they're after the scepter, do you?" Elena pivoted rapidly and started climbing the steps, keeping close behind Zahra.

"This is not what I signed up for," Killian muttered, huffing and puffing as they swiftly made their way up the hill.

"You were going to have to make this trek again at some point," Elena wheezed, clutching the stitch at her side.

"Tarrick would have brought him on a *pihasi*." Zahra smirked, taking the stairs two at a time without breaking a sweat.

Killian gasped. "You have *pihasi*? Why the fuck are we taking the stairs?"

"I wasn't thinking," Elena snapped back weakly. "Besides, it would have taken time to go all the way back to the palace to collect them."

"They must have reached the temple by now." Zahra squinted up at the majestic marble structure that loomed over them.

She quickened her ascent. Elena's thighs and calves screamed at her, but she continued relentlessly. They had to find out what Henry and Raz were up to. When they reached the top of the hill, Zahra checked the area for danger. Elena and Killian paused to catch their breath.

"Let's go," Zahra said after verifying that it was safe to enter the temple. They jogged up the marble stairs but stopped short at the top. Elena caught sight of a body crumpled on the floor between two large pillars.

She hurried over and cried out in dismay at the sight of a priestess breathing shallowly. The young woman clutched a dark red stain growing bigger on her ivory robes.

She gasped, pointing a shaky, bloodied hand toward the temple interior. "They demanded to know where the scepter was hidden. I refused. They attacked and forced me to reveal its location." The priestess hung her head in shame, and a tear trickled down her cheek.

"Fuck!" Elena muttered, peering into the temple. She pressed down on the wound and scanned the area desperately. Zahra rushed to her side, with Killian following closely, horrified at the scene.

"You need to get Adina here as soon as possible," Elena urged the guard.

"He had a weapon." The priestess gasped, growing paler as blood continued to spill out between her and Elena's fingers.

Elena gently moved the priestess's hand away to assess the damage. She sucked in a breath at the sight of a small metal object lodged in the wound. "They have a gun."

Swearing, Zahra jumped to her feet. She squinted down the marble hall.

"Zahra!" Elena whisper-shouted. "Get Adina and Tarrick now."

The guard was torn between leaving them to get help and staying to fight Raz and Henry.

"We'll be fine," Killian told her, rolling up his sleeves with determination. "Elena and I can hold off this Raz and Henry until you return with backup. You'll be faster than either of us."

Zahra finally nodded and sped down the stairs.

"Stay with me," Elena told the priestess. "Adina will be here soon to heal you."

The priestess shook her head, wincing. "You must stop them now!" She tried to sit up, but Elena held her down firmly.

"You have a bullet in you," she said gently. "Don't move or you'll lose more blood."

"The scepter," the young woman whispered. "Those men are shrouded in darkness. They cannot wield the scepter. They know where it is."

"We'll stop them," Elena assured her, trying to calm down the agitated priestess.

"Where is the scepter hidden?" Killian asked urgently, kneeling beside Elena.

Blood still flowed from the wound beneath Elena's palms. The priestess locked eyes with Killian. "The pool," she whispered sadly.

"Go," Killian urged Elena. "I'll take care of the priestess until Adina gets here."

The priestess conveyed the same message through shallow breaths.

"Keep pressure on the wound," Elena ordered Killian, who immediately obeyed and pressed his hands over the bullet wound.

The priestess gasped slightly at the change in pressure.

"I'll be right back," Elena promised, wiping her bloodied hands on her jeans.

The temple was thankfully devoid of people as Elena ran past the pillars toward the Sacred Pool. Despite the cool air in the marble building, sweat beaded on her forehead. She skidded to a halt when she came to the far end of the temple.

Elena's heart stuttered. "Stop!" she cried out at the sight of Henry at the edge of the pool. It was a few feet from where Arran's song was engraved on a wall amongst other Terralean rulers'.

If he heard Elena's order, he ignored her and eyed the pool with a smirk. Without taking off his shoes or jacket, he dipped a foot in the water, causing ripples to shatter the serene, glass-like surface. The wind picked up around them, as though sensing the scepter was about to be discovered. Henry slowly waded into the pool, searching the bottom for his prize.

As she ran through the chamber, Raz stepped out from behind a pillar. He blocked her path with an outstretched arm that held a small metal object. Elena threw herself to the side instinctively and dodged the bullet he fired.

Raz snarled when he recognized her.

He pointed the gun at Elena and fired again. She rolled to the side and hid behind another pillar. She peered around, but Henry was intent on finding the scepter, wherever it was hidden. He ignored Raz and Elena fighting, peering through the agitated water.

The wind howled and grew stronger, nearly picking Elena off the floor. Her hair whipped around her face, blinding her momentarily. She pushed aside locks of dark hair as Henry released a cry of triumph. He had reached the center of the pool, where a golden glow illuminated his face. The water swirled around him, creating a whirlpool as an object came into view, rising gracefully to the surface. He snatched up a long, slender scepter wrapped carefully in a piece of sodden linen as soon as it floated up to the surface of the pool.

The ground beneath them began to tremble, rocks and boulders rolling down the hill, rumbling in the distance. The sky that had been bright blue and sunny a moment before darkened as ominous clouds gathered over the land. Flashes of lightning pierced the sky where the gunmetal clouds swirled in a maelstrom.

"No," Elena breathed. Before she could launch herself at Henry and take hold of the scepter, another shot echoed through the temple. It was followed by an anguished cry.

Elena leapt out from behind the pillar to see Killian writhing on the floor, clutching his leg. Blood flowed between his fingers, and Raz sauntered toward him with a malevolent smile.

Elena pushed herself off the floor and ran to the assassin. She tackled him to the ground, where they both landed with a loud *thud*. Raz swore in his raspy voice as the gun flew out of his hand and skittered along the marble floor until it fell into the Sacred Pool with a soft *plop*. He rolled them over so he covered Elena's body with his own, squeezing her throat with his hands.

Elena gasped for air and clawed at his face. She jerked her knee up, driving it into his crotch. He groaned and dropped to the floor, reaching down to protect his groin from further assault.
Scrambling to her feet, Elena rubbed a hand over her neck.

"You fucking bitch," Raz growled.

"Is that the best you can come up with?" Elena rasped, massaging her neck.

Killian groaned, catching her attention. She sprinted over to the injured prince and heaved a sigh of relief when she saw the bullet had only grazed his leg. She whirled around, searching for

Raz to inflict some permanent damage on him, but he had disappeared.

"I heard banging," Killian managed to say through gritted teeth.

A loud cracking interrupted him, and they both turned to Henry, still standing in the Sacred Pool, unwrapping the scepter. He held the golden rod topped with an enormous raw, clear quartz with his bare hands.

"I gave you the chance to join me, Elena," Henry said in a deep voice that sounded otherworldly. "To work with me. When I overheard you and Killian talking about the scepter, I couldn't pass up the chance to wield ultimate power. To show the world what I'm capable of. Now that I have the scepter, my human blood won't prevent me from becoming Leneira's most powerful ruler."

His eyes glowed a dazzling white as the scepter's power flooded him, threads of electricity dancing up the arm that held the powerful object. Lightning and sparks of blue-white light crackled down the scepter. The power sizzled all over his body, encasing him with all the power of the land.

"Definitely Zanthus's son," Elena said in a shaky voice. A cold, sick feeling crept over her at the sight of him. Horror and dread filled her at the thought of the powers he might wield now. Henry levitated a few feet out of the water and glided over the surface. When he hovered over the marble floor of the temple, he slowly descended back to solid ground.

Killian cursed and struggled to sit up. "He's harnessing the power."

"We need to get the scepter off him," Elena breathed. "He doesn't know how to wield any sort of power. He could kill everyone."

A clap of thunder made them jump. The faint cries of people screaming all the way from Erindell filtered up to the temple.

Elena could only stare in horror as Henry held up the scepter triumphantly.

Through the pillars, bursts of flames rained down from the sky. The screaming grew louder. The ground trembled and shook as an earthquake struck the land. The wind howled, picking up dust and debris that swirled in the form of a tornado.

"Too late." Killian's breath hitched, and true fear struck Elena.

Henry swiveled slowly and stared at Elena and Killian with eerie, milky eyes.

His lips curled upward, and he pointed the scepter in their direction. The crystal quartz at the top glowed and pulsated with power. Elena tried to shield Killian with her body from whatever was headed their way.

Before Henry could blast them with a surge of power, he was thrown off his feet by a snarling beast with sleek, purple-black fur. It was as tall as a horse, with glowing amber eyes, metal claws, and lethal canines.

"Tarrick," Elena whispered in relief, taking in the sight of the king in his jaguar form. He prowled toward Henry, growling with bared teeth.

~ 41 ~

"That's Tarrick?" Killian asked faintly.

"Elena!"

She whipped around to see Leon running toward them.

"Leon!" She scrambled to her feet.

"Thank goodness you're okay," he exclaimed, grasping her shoulders and searching for signs of injury. He paused at the sight of the dried blood on her jeans.

"Where's Adina? Is the priestess okay?" Elena demanded.

"Adina is healing her." Leon jerked his head back to the entrance. He looked down at Killian.

"I'm fine," the prince assured him. "Raz got me."

"He had a gun," Elena explained.

Leon cursed. "Let's get you both out of here," he said, casting a nervous glance at Tarrick, who was still stalking his prey.

Henry's eyes widened with fear at the sight of a jaguar launching itself at him. The golden rod stopped crackling, and the crystal flickered weakly.

"We're not leaving Tarrick," Elena said fiercely.

"He's got it under control." Leon's jaw tightened. "He gave me strict instructions to get you somewhere safe."

"Nowhere is safe as long as Henry has the scepter," Elena argued.

As though emphasizing her point, a loud cracking sound had them all turning to see the scepter spark back to life. Henry spun it around without a second thought, pointing at Tarrick, who leaped to the side. His roar echoed around the temple as the bolt of lightning barely missed him.

Leon swore loudly.

Killian scrambled back, panic-stricken. "The odds are against us. Even with Tarrick and Leon's powers, we are at a disadvantage."

Elena started forward with a determined expression on her face.

"What the *hell* do you think you're doing?" Leon shouted, grabbing her arm.

She shrugged him off and clenched her fists. "I'm taking that imposter down."

"You can't!" Leon cried out. "He can harness *all the power of the land*."

"I. Don't. Care," Elena said through gritted teeth. It was not in her nature to run from a fight, even if that particular one included the added challenge of going up against a man with a lethal artifact. "It doesn't matter where I go," she reminded Leon. "If Henry kills Tarrick, I'll die too. We all have a better chance of surviving if we work together to bring Henry down."

Leon cursed, but Elena's attention was locked on Tarrick and Henry. They circled each other, both baring their teeth and assessing the other with calculating expressions. Not even the Divine Beings would stop her from doing everything she possibly could to protect Tarrick and get the scepter out of Henry's hands.

"El," Leon said desperately, "that means he can harness *Empath* powers. He'll know your every move."

At that, she stopped and studied Leon for a moment.

"Then we fight your way." She grinned and spun around. "Shield your thoughts! I'll follow your lead," she called out to Leon over her shoulder.

Elena ran toward Henry, aiming to tackle him around the waist and knock him to the ground. He was still striking Tarrick with bolts of lightning. Man and beast danced around each other, lunging forward to attack, only to cower back when the other snarled or thrust the rod forward.

At the last second, Henry spun around and aimed the scepter at Elena. She changed course instantly, sending a silent prayer of gratitude in Leon's direction for his training that had made her reflexes stronger than ever. She dodged a rush of flames that shot out of the quartz before Killian cried out in warning.

"That was rude," she remarked when the flames extinguished. Henry was left scowling at the empty space in front of him. The pillar behind her had been blackened with char marks but continued to stand tall.

The broken bond between Elena and Tarrick seemed to have repaired itself as they both attacked at the same time. Although they timed their moves impeccably, Henry disappeared in a ball of shadows the moment Tarrick and Elena both leaped at him.

Tarrick's claws narrowly missed Elena's back as he arched over her. She gasped as the metal talons retracted seconds before his paw brushed her face. Without the lethal points, the touch was affectionate.

Henry reappeared a few feet away the instant the shadows dissipated, holding onto the scepter more firmly. He pointed it once more at Elena, but Leon stepped forward, enraged, and flung out his hands. An inferno sizzled as Henry's flames were extinguished by the thick wall of water Leon had thrown up. Henry emitted a bloodcurdling snarl. Tarrick attacked Henry again, but was thrown back when a gust of icy air with the strength of a tempest took the flames' place.

"Here!" Killian hollered from where he was, still sprawled on the floor, growing increasingly pale as he clutched his bleeding leg with one hand. He slid a small, shiny object across the floor with his other hand, slumping back and breathing heavily.

Elena snatched up the small dagger he had sent her way. She looked up at Tarrick and Leon with a determined expression. A silent signal passed between the three of them before they attacked Henry all at once. Elena swiped at Henry, but he leaped back, narrowly missing the sharp blade she held. Tarrick lunged at Henry while Leon barreled for his knees in a rugby tackle.

Multiple bolts of lightning arched through the air. More marble cracked, and chunks of stone hit the floor, adding to the chaos. The ground beneath them trembled and shook, throwing them off balance. Elena's joints protested as she was forced to slow down abruptly to stay upright.

She desperately used every trick she had learned from Leon, determined to take Henry down: feinting, dropping low, attempting lethal strikes to vital points on his body. She used instinct to attack and react lest he read her mind as she strategized. His attack on Tarrick had made things even more personal; despite the chasm between the two of them since Henry's arrival, Elena would fight anyone who threatened the man she loved. This was a score she needed to settle, and fast. Every time Elena was struck down or caught off guard, Tarrick would snap at Henry, sending him stumbling back before shielding Elena with his body.

"It's no good," Leon grunted. "He knows what we're doing."

"Stop thinking about your moves, then," Elena groaned as she dropped to the floor at Killian's warning. She avoided being crushed by Tarrick flying through the air when a chunk of marble hit him.

The king collided with the wall behind them, but he shook himself off as he rose to his feet, flexing his claws and growling in frustration. He stood protectively in front of his brother and Elena, who picked herself up, dusting the debris off her clothes.

Henry smirked at the trio. "Give up, Your Majesty," he mocked, running his hands down the scepter affectionately. "You're no longer the most powerful ruler in the realm."

"Henry, you don't know what you're doing," Killian pleaded desperately. "That is a destructive artifact that no Leneiran has wielded since Ilona."

Henry merely laughed and eyed the scepter with an insatiable hunger.

"Asshole," Elena muttered.

"Any ideas?" Leon grumbled.

"Get the scepter off him," she suggested.

"You think?" The prince rolled his eyes.

"Why don't you yield now? Perhaps I'll let you live under my rule," Henry called out.

"He definitely gets the take-over-the-world gene from Zanthus," Elena huffed, wincing at the twinge of pain that shot up her back after being thrown around the temple multiple times.

"How did you know he was Zanthus's son?" Leon demanded.

A bolt of lightning interrupted him, and the three of them leaped to the side to avoid being hit.

"We're going to be doing this forever," Elena moaned, raising her body and scanning the temple that was covered with chunks of broken marble, dust, and debris. She was amazed that it was still standing. Henry prowled toward Killian, who was scrambling as far back as he could on his injured leg, looking petrified.

"You and Killian need to get out of here," Leon said, wrapping his hand around Elena's wrist. "Tarrick is getting distracted, trying to protect you."

"I'm not leaving him," Elena said obstinately. "We need to strategize to take Henry down."

"Stubborn woman," Leon muttered, glancing back at his brother.

Tarrick leaped at Henry, opening his jaws to clamp down on the scepter. Leon tensed, then relaxed slightly when a web of white light—whatever power Henry had called up from the scepter—covering Henry and Tarrick's bodies didn't affect his brother.

"Your shielding is useless against him," Elena grumbled in frustration. "All those slick moves you taught us should have knocked him down."

"Don't blame my shielding," Leon retorted.

"You want me to blame your sloppy footwork?" Elena raised a brow and quirked her lip in an attempt to mask her growing fear and desperation.

"You're one to talk, you know that?" Leon gave her a watery smile, recognizing immediately what she was trying to do.

"I definitely believe Zahra now when she said she let you beat her this morning." Elena shook her head.

Leon made a strangled sound. "That's a lie. I disarmed her fair and square."

Elena snorted. "I've seen her take down two grown-ass Elementals. Blindfolded. With just a stick to defend herself."

Across the chamber, Killian called out to Tarrick to watch his back as the fight continued.

"I can't believe you'd bring that up at a time like this," Leon grumbled.

"Now's as good a time as any," Elena snarked back.

Leon narrowed his eyes.

"Would you rather I bring it up at breakfast? Or in the moments Henry grants us before obliterating us with his new toy?"

Leon looked around, formulating a plan. Killian scooted around the edge of the Sacred Pool to avoid Henry. Tarrick had gained some ground by breathing gusts of powerful wind at Henry through the roars he emitted from his deadly maw.

Despite holding onto an object of significant power, panic and fear was evident in Henry's face. Elena noted he chose lightning and fire—the abilities he had overheard her and Killian talking about the day before—over and over again as his main tools to attack. The sparks of electricity and webs of light encircling the golden rod pulsed and glowed incessantly, as though desperate to be unleashed at their full might.

Elena and Leon grinned at each other in unison.

"Calling up the wind power now." Leon stood, wriggling his fingers and flexing his outstretched hands.

Henry let out a howl of rage as he was lifted off his feet and flew back into the pool. At the last minute, he swung the scepter around, and a bolt of lightning hit Leon square in the chest.

Elena stared in horror as the prince crumpled to the floor, falling face down, his arms outstretched. With her heart in her mouth, and her mind screaming the word *no!* over and over again, she rolled him over. Elena shook him hard, crying out his name, pressing her ear to his chest, searching for a heartbeat.

But Leon didn't stir. The ghost of a cheeky grin on his face, even in death, shimmered and blurred as tears gathered in Elena's eyes and fell onto his face.

~ 42 ~

Tarrick emitted a roar that reverberated in Elena's skull. The air stilled, and time was suspended before a loud splash shook her out of the daze that followed Leon's death. The surface of the pool crackled with electricity and bolts of white light. Henry sat up, defying the laws of nature—that he should have died the moment he hit the water that came up to his chest while he sat in the pool. He was still holding onto the damn scepter with a livid expression on his face. His dark hair was plastered to his face, and he shook the water out of his eyes, searching for Tarrick with the intention of ending him once and for all.

Elena rose, shaking with fury. Without thinking, she dove into the pool, not caring about being electrocuted or slammed with any other power that Henry was planning to throw her way. Her only thought was revenge for Leon, and to stop Henry once and for all.

Her skin sizzled, and tiny bubbles effervesced around her the moment she hit the water. Ignoring the burning sensation running throughout her body, Elena reached out and grasped the scepter. The moment she made contact with the rod, a surge of ancient power ran through her veins, filling her deep from within. Her skin no longer burned; it buzzed with untapped energy and potential.

A feeling of invincibility flowed through her, a soft voice humming a tune that was unfamiliar yet comforting. Songs of millenia past became the soundtrack to the battle scenes on land, sea, and even in the air high above Leneira that flickered through her mind's eye. They flashed past too rapidly for her to capture the details, but slow enough for her to understand that she was now connected to Leneira's past.

When the montage of clips faded and her vision cleared, Henry's angry face came into focus beneath the bolts of white lights sparking on his skin. She didn't feel the water around her chest. Henry tugged at the scepter with a snarl. She dimly registered Tarrick's howl of anguish, but she didn't dare lose focus to see if it was over Leon or somebody else.

Elena could have sworn the scepter was fighting to get out of Henry's grip and move closer to her. She focused her energy on willing it to come to her. Henry held on tightly, gritting his teeth and grabbing the scepter with both hands. His efforts were futile; Elena only had to lay a finger on it for it to lean into her touch. It wanted to be in her hands, and her hands only.

While they both fought, white-gold light burst from the quartz and encased them in a dome of dazzling light. The golden wall of light stretched out to the edges of the pool and was thick enough to shield everything on the other side.

She blinked and gasped at the sight of the Divine Beings—Freya, Diana, and Maia—levitating off the surface of the pool. Their purple robes fluttered around their legs, their faces twisted with anger and horror. Elena's stomach dropped. For the first time since entering the temple, the thought that it would be her demise crossed her mind.

"How dare you desecrate a sacred object," Freya hissed at Henry. The lines and creases on the oldest Divine Being's face were barely visible in the dazzling light, but her fury was evident. Her lips curled downward, she bared teeth, and fire flashed in her eyes.

"The scepter is to be revered and respected," Diana said in a harsh voice that raised goosebumps on Elena's skin. Gone was Diana's enchanting aura and seductive smile. Her delicate features were like marble as she stared down coldly at Elena and Henry.

"To wield the scepter is to pay a heavy price," Maia said malevolently, revealing the dimples either side of her pouty pink lips. Elena knew better than to trust the youngest Divine Being, who was innocent and terrifying at the same time.

Elena immediately let go of the scepter at Maia's words, knowing all too well the kind of payment the Divine Beings required. A flash of triumph crossed Henry's face as he wrenched the artifact out of Elena's hands and pointed it at Diana.

"Who are you?"

The hairs on the back of Elena's neck stood up at the coldness in Diana's voice as she said, "You are not worthy of learning my name, Henry Graham, nor are you worthy of wielding such power."

He sneered at them and jabbed the scepter in their direction, but nothing happened.

"Even the scepter knows better than to work against us," Freya said haughtily.

Elena swallowed the bile that threatened to rise. She looked around, desperate for a way out of the dome. All she wanted was to make sure Tarrick was alright.

"The scepter feels an affinity for you, Elena Marie Russo," Diana said, turning to her.

"I don't want it," Elena said hurriedly. "I just wanted to find it so Tarrick could pass it on to King Halder for safekeeping."

"It is clear that the scepter is no longer safe in Leneira, sister," Maia whispered, transfixed by the quartz. "Let *us* guard it."

Henry glared at Maia, inching forward, waving the scepter rapidly, warning her to back off. He was still blinded by his greed, and hadn't learned about the Divine Beings to realize they were infinite power and their word was law.

"Back off," he ordered Maia. "The scepter is mine."

"The scepter belongs to no one," she said unflinchingly, edging closer to him. "But you could be mine," she crooned. Her lips parted, and she looked at Henry imploringly with hypnotic purple eyes.

Freya and Diana made no move to stop their sister and watched with indifference. Maia moved closer to him with a sinister smile and wicked glint. The anger on his face was replaced by fear. Henry scrambled back until he hit the golden wall and started to pound on it.

"Help!" he cried, banging with a fist. Henry even swung the scepter, hitting the dome with a dull *thud*, but it didn't even crack.

He met Elena's horrified gaze with quivering lips and tears tracking down his face. She felt his fear, but stared helplessly as he crumpled and whimpered for mercy.

When Maia stood before him, half-submerged in the water, she reached out and slowly traced her fingers up his chest. She wrapped her thin arms around his neck and pressed herself to him. Henry stilled, the terror on his face growing.

"Do you yield to me?" Maia leaned in and whispered in Henry's ear.

Elena was rooted to the spot. A wave of nausea came over her when he shook his head.

"I shall have you anyway."

Before Henry could shove Maia off him, the Divine Being sank her teeth into his neck, drawing blood and sucking hard. Elena's stomach lurched at Henry's scream, but she was unable to look away. She stared in horror while Freya and Diana continued to watch with blank expressions on their faces. Henry clawed at the air in front of him uselessly, writhing and squirming.

Maia wrapped her legs around his torso, the hem of her robes riding up to reveal the pale, almost translucent skin of her slender legs. She ground her hips against Henry, gyrating against him despite his attempts to shove her off. Elena squeezed her eyes shut, but she could not block out Henry's agonizing cries and whimpers for the torture to end, mingled with wet sucking sounds. Maia moaned in delight, the sound echoing around the dome.

A wave of dizziness overtook Elena. When she thought she would heave from the prolonged cries, the sounds stopped. She opened her eyes to Maia lifting her head from Henry's neck—or what was left of it.

The Divine Being wore a satiated look on her face as she wiped the blood from her lips with the sleeve of her robe. Maia glided back to her sisters and took her position by Diana's side once more.

Henry's limp, lifeless body was drained of blood. All that remained was a husk and an expression of anguish on his withered face. Diana swooped down and pried the scepter from Henry's hands before it could fall into the pool. He sank under the surface and disappeared from view. Elena had a strong suspicion that his body would never be seen again.

"Lady Elena," Diana addressed her, holding the scepter, "I believe you when you say you don't want the scepter."

Elena let out a shaky breath.

"You have saved the realm twice from destruction," Freya intoned, bowing her head. "You are worthy."

"Maia is right," Diana said. "The scepter is no longer safe in the hands of Leneirans. We will take it back and guard it until we are instructed otherwise by the Higher Powers who watch over the realms."

"There are more of you?" Elena asked before she could stop herself.

"We are but servants ourselves," Maia said sweetly. All signs of earlier bloodlust had disappeared, but that dark side of the angelic Divine Being still lurked beneath the innocent veneer. The sounds of her sucking the life out of Henry still echoed in Elena's ears.

"To show our gratitude, we will grant you a favor," Freya croaked reluctantly.

"What's the price?" Elena asked shrewdly.

Freya threw back her head and laughed. "You know us well, Lady Elena."

"There is no price," Diana smiled. "This is not a bargain like the one King Tarrick struck with us to bring you back."

Still, Elena was cautious.

"Is there nothing you wish for?" Maia asked.

There was so much Elena wished for. She thought of her parents, a home to call her own, love, forgiveness, and freedom. But most of all ...

"Leon," Elena whispered.

All three Divine Beings lowered their heads in genuine sadness at the mention of his name.

"Prince Leon has moved on to the Beyond," Diana told Elena. "He did not linger as you did. He made his choice."

A tear rolled down Elena's cheek. Diana saying the words out loud made his death real. Final.

"But he is content." Maia moved forward.

Elena shrank back, alarmed. Before she could defend herself, Maia placed a hand on Elena's forehead.

"Leon!" Arran's anguished voice filled her ears, and Elena had to bite back a sob at his deep voice. "What are you doing here? What happened? Your mother. Tarrick. Adina—"

"All is well, Father." Leon laughed. "The realm is safe, Mother and Adina are fine. They miss you, but they'll be alright. Tarrick is king, and I'm pretty certain he and Elena will be married soon."

"Leon," Arran said sorrowfully. "You shouldn't be here."

"I have served my purpose, Father," Leon spoke in a gentle voice. "And I was told you need my help." The humor in his voice returned.

Arran gave a rueful chuckle. "You're right there. Although, I suspect your mother might be better at this."

"You and I did alright with Adina," Leon scoffed.

***

Adina and Zahra skidded to a halt when they ran down the temple corridor and entered the main chamber. They stared open-mouthed at the scene before them.

Tarrick had shifted back, and was trying to break through the opaque golden dome still encasing the Sacred Pool. He threw spheres of water, jets of flames, and even attempted to create a small tornado to raise the unyielding wall. When nothing worked, he slammed his bare hands against the wall, bellowing in frustration.

Killian had propped himself up against a hunk of broken pillar on the floor, clutching his bloody leg. He winced as he watched Tarrick conjure balls of fire and throw them at the dome. The flames fizzled and died on contact with the golden casing.

"Adina!" Killian called out when he spotted her.

"Killian!" Adina rushed to his side and kneeled down beside him. She gouged out the bullet still lodged in his leg while he bit down a scream of pain.

"It's fine! I'm fine!" he gasped out.

Adina gave him a watery smile. She held her hands over his wound, and he watched in awe as the skin surrounding the edges of the gash stretched and extended to cover the bleeding flesh. In seconds, the new skin had fused, and all that was left behind was a shiny, pale-pink patch.

Killian reached out a hand to gently touch Adina's face. "Thanks," he sighed. The white shirt he wore underneath his long Minotian overcoat, now draped over Tarrick, was drenched in sweat and stuck to his torso.

"Are you wearing Killian's coat?" Adina asked her brother.

Tarrick ignored his sister and continued to attack the pulsating dome.

"What's going on?" Zahra demanded, taking in the mess and chaos. "Where are Elena and Henry?"

Killian pointed a shaking hand at the dome.

"The Divine Beings are having an audience with them," a soft voice said from behind. Everyone turned to stare at the priestess who, other than the stain on her robes, was perfectly fine. A crease formed between her brows as she studied the glowing wall. "They haven't held a private audience in centuries."

"We need to get Elena out of there," Tarrick said, desperately searching for a way in.

"She won't emerge until the Divine Beings let her go." The priestess shook her head. "*If* they let her go."

"She's in there with Henry and the scepter," Tarrick shouted, raking his fingers through his hair in frustration. "Anything could be happening."

"Where's Leon?" Adina asked, swiveling her head around.

Killian reached out to take Adina's hands.

"No!"

He shook his head sadly.

"No," Adina whispered at first before her cries grew louder. "*No! No! No!*"

Killian pulled Adina into his chest while she shuddered and screamed, the sound muffled by his shirt. He locked eyes with Zahra, who looked dismayed at the news, and tilted his head to the corner, where the prince's body lay. The priestess hurried forward and clasped one of Leon's limp hands in both of hers. She murmured incantations and prayers to send him safely to the Beyond.

Adina's sobs were the only sounds in the temple when Tarrick finally gave up trying to penetrate the dome. He fell to his knees on the floor, the knot in his stomach growing tighter with each passing second. Burying his face in the palms of his hands, he made silent bargains and pleas for Elena to return. Tarrick even prayed to the Divine Beings, naming each of them and appealing to their benevolent side, in the hopes they would hear him.

~ 43 ~

Maia lifted her hand from Elena's forehead and stepped back. The tears flowed down Elena's face as her vision came back into focus. "Was that real?" she whispered.

"That is the Beyond," Maia confirmed softly.

"Do you still wish for Leon to be returned, Elena?" Diana asked.

Elena shook her head. "He is at peace and happy. I-I'm glad he's there for Arran."

"If not Leon, then tell us your heart's desire."

Elena thought for a moment, still feeling a maelstrom of emotions going through her body—grief, joy, fear, anger ... She wanted to break free of the eddy and never feel anything again. At the same time, she wanted to savor it, having never experienced such complicated emotions so strongly before.

"I don't want anything," Elena replied, knowing that whatever she asked for would come at a price. There was nothing she was willing to give up in the moment; she had already lost far too much.

Freya studied her.

"Knowing that Tarrick and everyone in Leneira is safe is enough for me," she finally said quietly. "They have all been through so much. All this hatred and anger and greed for power. I have every faith he will maintain the peace that Leneira has known these past few years."

Diana raised a delicate brow.

"I want this realm to know the love and tranquility I just witnessed." Elena's voice cracked. "No more wars or borders or separation. The realm has a chance at true peace under Tarrick's rule."

For a moment, Elena thought she saw her own mother's face in that of Freya's, and she blinked rapidly. Freya moved forward and kneeled in front of her, still hovering inches above the water. She took Elena's hands in her own, and with that same motherly, loving smile, she said, "With him by your side, it is a real possibility, my dear."

The Divine Being pressed her lips to Elena's forehead, stunning her by the gesture. When Freya rose and stepped back in line with her sisters, Diana stepped forward.

She, too, wore a sincere smile on her beautiful face. She raised the scepter and commanded, "Rise, Queen Elena. Go forth and share your message for peace in Leneira with King Tarrick as your consort."

A tingling sensation drew Elena's attention to her right wrist. She watched as a thin black line swirled over her skin and took the shape of a horse rising from cresting waves.

"The *naya*?" Elena whispered.

She looked up for an explanation, but the air shimmered, blurring and obscuring the Divine Beings. The dome pulsated intensely. Webs of white light appeared before exploding into thousands of blinding stars. Rays of golden-white light intensified, forcing Elena to close her eyes.

Scraping and clattering sounds filled the air, but it was impossible to see what was happening. Cries of fear and surprise filled the temple, but as quickly as the light had appeared, it disappeared into thin air.

Elena opened her eyes. She blinked and rubbed them several times to make sure she wasn't dreaming—the temple was intact. The marble walls, carvings, and pillars stood tall as though they hadn't been destroyed moments before. They were unmarked, except for the songs engraved on the surfaces. The shadows of the letters deepened in the soft light of the setting sun.

Her gaze fell on Tarrick, who was on the ground, slowly lowering the arm he had thrown across his face when the blinding light assaulted his vision. A number of emotions crossed his face at the sight of her—disbelief, shock, relief, and then ... love. He stared at Elena as if not really believing she was alive and whole, still sitting in the Sacred Pool.

Elena shifted her attention to Killian, holding onto Adina tightly, his arm wrapped around her protectively. Zahra and the priestess were crouched over Leon's body, their lips moving silently in prayer.

"Elena!"

Her head snapped forward as Tarrick leaped into the pool with a loud splash and waded through the water to her. He gathered her in his arms, and his entire body shuddered against her as he whispered her name over and over again. Tarrick stroked her hair and held her so tight she gasped for air. "I'm sorry. I'm sorry. I'm so sorry."

"Tarrick," Elena said, unable to get any other words out.

"I didn't believe you about Henry. And for driving you away." His voice was muffled by her hair.

"Tarrick," she choked out his name, overcome with relief.

He dragged her out of the pool, and they both stood at the edge, dripping water everywhere, but neither of them cared. His amber eyes moved frantically all over her, checking for signs of injury.

The others gave cries of joy at the sight of Elena, but she didn't hear them. She scanned Tarrick's face and cupped his jaw with her hand. He leaned into her hand and gave a sigh of relief, reassured that she was real and not a hallucination.

"Are you okay?" she asked. "What happened?"

"We're fine." He clasped her face in his hands. "What happened to you in there?" His gaze slid toward the pool. "Where's Henry? Where's the scepter?"

"Henry is …" Bile threatened to rise again when she remembered the way Maia had sucked the life out of him. "He's gone. So is the scepter."

There was a gasp. Killian stared at her, aghast.

"Don't worry, the Divine Beings have taken it," she reassured him. "They said they would take it since Leneirans can't be trusted to protect it any longer."

Her cheeks heated at the awestruck expression on Killian's face. Elena turned to Adina, puffy-eyed and still crying in Killian's arms.

"Adina," she asked with concern. "Are you okay?"

Adina shook her head. "I'm so sorry, El!" she burst out, wrenching herself out of Killian's hold and throwing her arms around Elena's neck, nearly knocking her off balance. "I've been so horrible to you."

Elena stroked Adina's hair and shushed her. "You have nothing to be sorry for," she said lightly.

"She was kind of a bitch," Tarrick muttered. "I heard about what she said to you last night."

Adina raised her head, sniffling. She didn't snap back at her brother or dispute what he said.

"Come here." Elena sighed, pulling Adina in for another hug. "I forgive you. You can wait on me hand and foot for the next month, if that will make you feel better."

"So you're not leaving?" Adina pulled back, searching Elena's face hopefully. "Tarrick told me everything." She lowered her eyes, shifting uncomfortably. "I didn't realize you won't be able to have children," Adina whispered.

"Would that have changed the way you treated me?" Elena asked gently.

The tears started flowing down Adina's cheeks once more. Elena looked across to Leon's body. Zahra glanced up and gave Elena a sad smile before turning back to the prince's handsome face. She held his hand and listened quietly to the priestess's incantations.

"Leon is in the Beyond," Elena said quietly. "Maia showed me a vision of him with Arran and ..." She swallowed hard and looked directly at Tarrick. "And our son."

His lips parted in surprise.

"We would have had a son," she told him, her voice wobbling.

Tarrick stared at her.

"The three of them were in a beautiful garden, like the palace groves." Elena recalled the way her heart swelled to nearly bursting at the sight. It was at that moment Elena thought she would die happy. "Our son was sitting on Arran's lap, and Leon appeared. Your father was shocked, but overjoyed. Leon was so ... happy. And when he met his nephew ..." Elena was lost for words and merely shook her head, smiling through tears that started to roll down her cheeks.

Tarrick covered his face with his hands. His shoulders shook silently as he mourned the loss of his father, brother, and the son he never knew.

"They were happy and at peace, Tarrick," Elena said gently. "I want you to feel that, too, while there's still life to be lived. I would have asked the Divine Beings to bestow that joy and contentment on everyone in Leneira."

Tarrick's head snapped up. "You made a deal with them?" he asked sharply.

Elena shook her head. "At first, I wished for Leon to come back, but he had already moved on." Her gaze drifted to the floor, where the priestess murmured the final words.

The priestess gently placed the prince's hand back on the ground and rose to her feet. Zahra remained where she knelt, stroking Leon's hand.

"They were so happy together, all three of them. I-I couldn't break them up." Elena peeked up at Tarrick through lowered lashes.

He reached down and squeezed Elena's hand in silent agreement.

"I remembered the wishes I made at the Lantern Festival in Sailon," Elena continued wistfully. "Your mother was making her way back to her family, and you are opening your heart again, Adina." The corner of Elena's lip tugged up.

The princess blushed as Killian grinned at her. He brushed Adina's forehead with the tip of his nose, placing a soft kiss on her temple.

"Our history books will have Leon down as the best royal advisor in Terralea," Tarrick said determinedly. "I'll make sure of it."

"That just left my wish for the people of Leneira to continue to enjoy the peace they have known for the past few years," Elena explained. "Freya offered me a favor. Diana promised me there would be no price to pay, but knowing that everyone was safe was all I needed. So I declined their offer."

Zahra emitted a loud gasp that made everyone jump. She stared at the marble wall beside her, slack-jawed and pointing at the words that appeared in the blank space directly below Arran's song. It was as though an invisible hand were writing across the marble in smooth, flowing script. The group watched the words being etched deeply into the hard stone.

"Okay, I am seriously in awe of you right now," Killian blurted out when the words ended above Leon's body.

"*The Naya's Return.*" Elena gulped as she read the title of the song.

Elena silently read the song that had appeared in disbelief. It detailed her arrival in Leneira at the start of the spring, her slaying Zanthus, and the battle with Henry. But it was the final words that had everyone gasping and exclaiming in awe. Tarrick's eyes gleamed in triumph.

"Queen of Leneira." Tarrick pointed to the last line of her song. "It's there in writing. No one can challenge you now."

Adina choked out a half-sob and half-laugh. "You're a badass."

"They called me *Queen Elena*, but I thought it was because I'd stay and we'd eventually rule together." Elena squinted at the words on the wall, searching for a clause or condition. "They called Tarrick my consort."

Adina snorted with laughter through her tears. "That means *you're* the primary ruler."

"So much for declining their offer," Tarrick said with an amused expression on his face.

"Are you okay with this?" Elena asked him fearfully. "It doesn't have to be this way."

"El," he said softly, reaching out and tucking back a strand of her hair. "This is the *right* way forward. The Divine Beings believe in you, and so do I," he said sincerely.

Elena shook her head. "When I said I wanted the people of Leneira to know peace and happiness, I didn't know how the Divine Beings would make that happen. It wasn't something I could put a price on anyway."

"It won't be them who make it happen." Killian shook his head, smiling slightly. "It will be *you*."

Elena looked at him in confusion.

He pointed to the recently etched song on the temple wall and then the tattoo of the *naya* that now decorated her right wrist. "You've been marked with the *naya*—that means the Divine Beings recognized Queen Samara's spirit in you. *You're* the one tasked with uniting the people of the realm, just as she did."

Adina clapped a hand over her mouth. Killian dropped to his knees. Tarrick did the same, but he held onto Elena's hand as he did so, smiling at her. Only love and pride shone on his face. Adina copied them and bowed her head respectfully.

"Queen Elena," Killian said in a serious voice. "I offer you my undying allegiance and vow to serve you for the rest of my days, however long they may be. I promise to help you spread the message of peace amongst the people of the realm."

Adina and Tarrick murmured the same oath, while Elena swayed on her feet. She tightened her grip on Tarrick's hand, and he squeezed back in comfort.

"Please, don't ever do that again," Elena said faintly.

Zahra made her way over to the group. At the sight of Elena's new tattoo, she immediately dropped to the floor. Awe and surprise replaced the curiosity on her face.

Elena blushed hard. "This isn't necessary."

"Your Majesty," the priestess addressed Elena softly, making her jump. She hadn't noticed her glide over to the group. "As one of the priestesses of the Temple of Divine Beings, I am honored to witness your crossing and pledge to protect your song engraved on our hallowed halls."

Elena gaped at the priestess, who smiled back serenely.

"Um, thank you?" she finally said, glancing around at her friends still kneeling before her, feeling as though she were dreaming. She tugged Tarrick, urging him to his feet. "Seriously, stop kneeling! All of you!"

"Can I come with you to tell Halder you're now Queen of Leneira?" Adina's eyes sparkled as she rose gracefully.

Killian chuckled beside her.

"Woah, woah, woah!" Elena held up her hands, shaking her head violently. "I'll start with being Queen of Terralea first."

"I don't think that's how it works. Word will spread the moment people read your song," Killian said, reaching out for her wrist and admiring the tattoo. "Father won't believe it when I tell him. He will want to meet you immediately."

"I'm here to spread peace," Elena told him, "not start wars."

"Mother will have something to say about that," Zahra muttered.

Elena nudged the guard with an elbow. "Let's tell the people of Terralea first. And fix this mess with our own council before unleashing the news on the rest of the realm."

"We should go back to the palace," Tarrick advised.

The glow of the sun dipping lower on the horizon cast a golden glimmer on the temple. The marble shone, and spots of dappled light danced on the surface of the Sacred Pool.

The group nodded and started to slowly make their way to the temple entrance. Elena hung back slightly, admiring the way the temple stood serene and proud once more after the epic battle with Henry. Leon's body was still lying in the corner.

"We will prepare his body for the funeral," the priestess told her, noticing the way Elena's face fell at the thought of leaving him there.

Elena hesitated for a moment before gently letting go of Tarrick's hand and making her way to Leon's body. The others, sensing she needed a moment of privacy, slowly shuffled down the marble hallway toward the entrance.

Elena kneeled beside Leon and took in his handsome, peaceful face. A wave of emotion washed over as she remembered the last few months with the prince.

"Hey, Leon," she whispered to him. "Take care of my boy, okay? Make sure you tell him all the stories about how brave and strong and kind his dad is. Teach him to have fun, play pranks, tease his grandfather, and be as loving and generous and compassionate as you. I can't think of a better uncle and teacher for my son. I love you all so much, and I know you'll be watching over us until we meet again."

Elena kissed her fingers and pressed them to Leon's cold cheek. She sent a silent prayer up to her own parents as well before rising to her feet.

With a final glance at Leon, Elena walked out of the temple just as the first star of the night made its appearance in the lavender sky.

~ 44 ~

"Where are the *pihasi*?" Adina's head swung around, scanning the area.

Zahra cleared her throat awkwardly. "I sent them back."

Adina rounded on the guard in dismay.

"In case we needed reinforcements." Zahra shrugged. "I strapped a note to their necks for Sami and the others to be on standby."

"What were they waiting for?" Elena asked. "It was raining fire."

"The note instructed them to evacuate the Erindellians first," Zahra explained. "Then come and help us if we needed it."

"You did the right thing."

"This is going to hurt going down, isn't it?" Killian sighed.

Adina slipped her hand around his. "I'll help you."

Killian, Adina, and Zahra led the way down the narrow steps back to Erindell in the silence.

"I should have known," Tarrick said hollowly, staring down the hill. He hung his head in shame.

"You couldn't have known," Elena said gently, putting her hands on his shoulders and trying to catch his eye. "Henry didn't even know until Raz told him. I'm assuming Raz told him his father was Zanthus, not you?"

Tarrick nodded. "Leon found an entry in one of Father's diaries where he had written about finding Zanthus and Rose, er, together."

Elena didn't say anything, but wished she had been there to comfort him when Tarrick discovered his father had known about Zanthus and Rose's affair.

"When we searched through Zanthus's diaries," he continued, rubbing his hand over his face, "he had written about Rose being pregnant when she was here. Zanthus must have known it would come out that he was the father, and set up everything that led to her being banished from the realm."

"I'm so sorry you had to find out like that, Tarrick," Elena whispered. "You deserved better."

"I'm angry Father didn't tell me, but I know he was trying to protect me." Tarrick finally lifted his eyes to her. "He gave them a chance to come clean to me about everything."

"He still should have explained." Elena shook her head sadly.

"He probably would have if the uprising hadn't taken place and distracted us all." Tarrick clenched his fists by his side. "By the time the rebels were defeated, Zanthus had wormed his way back into Father's good graces, and we had to focus on rebuilding Terralea."

"I think Arran regretted not telling you the full story," Elena said quietly, threading her fingers through his. "When he danced with me at the Peace Summit, he told me about how he had almost lost you after Rose. That you weren't the same, and how he regretted that you had closed your heart to love."

"Until you came along." Tarrick gave her a wry smile. "And I blew it again."

Elena shrugged. "We went through a rough patch, that's all."

Tarrick snorted. "Adina and I have behaved in an unspeakable way toward you, El. I will have to live with that until my dying day. I promise I will never keep secrets from you ever again. I'll do whatever it takes for you to forgive me for everything."

"You're being a tad dramatic there, Your Majesty." Elena rolled her eyes.

Tarrick frowned. "How can you say that?" he demanded. "How can you behave as though we haven't treated you like shit this past week?"

"Tarrick," Elena said gently, aware that he would be going through a number of emotions after losing his brother, discovering the truth about Henry, his father, and uncle. "This past week is nothing in the grand scheme of things. We still have at least a few centuries ahead of us, right?" she asked casually. Elena started descending the stairs, catching sight of a flicker of hope in his amber eyes as she glanced over her shoulder.

"All relationships have problems. It's part of being in one. Besides, no one is perfect," Elena said, leading them down the hill. "I'm sure if you kept reading, your dad would have written about arguments with your mom."

"So you're not leaving?" he asked hopefully.

"Now that you've come to your senses, I think I'll hang around a little longer"—she gave him another half-smile over her shoulder—"on the condition that you stick to your original promise to do this as a team. I also want to see if a *naya* manifests at some point."

Tarrick squeezed her hand in response, but didn't say anything when two figures panting up the stairs came into sight.

"Bri! Yas!" Elena exclaimed, hurrying down the steps to meet them. "What's happened? Is everyone okay?"

"Everyone's fine," Yas wheezed, doubling over and clutching a stitch in her side.

"Fine may be overstating things a little," Bri said cautiously. "We thought the end of the world was upon us. The ground started shaking, and the skies rained fire. Our powers helped us get to safety, but then ..."

She looked up to the temple that stood at the top of the hill, serene and still once more.

"There was lightning, and the *pihasi* arrived," Bri explained. "Royal guards have been trying to evacuate the town, but with the earthquakes and fire, it was safer to take shelter and remain where we were. It all stopped suddenly, and no one has told us what's going on."

"We're on our way to do exactly that," Tarrick assured the two women.

They stared at him, slightly perturbed.

"Her Highness, Zahra, and the Minotian prince are letting the people know you're alright," Yas said after a pause.

Bri stared at him for a beat and, even in the waning light, turned bright red when she peeked down at the overcoat tied at his waist.

"Thank you, Your Majesty," Bri finally said.

Elena's lips twitched.

Tarrick glanced at Elena. "You know what? As queen of Leneira, this is your moment."

Elena looked at him in alarm. "No! What? Tarrick, I can't—"

"I'll be right by your side," Tarrick soothed her. "But our people will not take me seriously dressed like this"—he gestured to his torso—"and you'll do a *much* better job of reassuring them."

Yas smothered a laugh.

Elena started to protest, but Tarrick had transformed into a jaguar once more. The overcoat slid off his sleek body and he lowered his head, waiting for Elena to continue down the hill.

"Well, no one will be arguing with a giant killer cat by my side," she muttered, descending the stairs once more.

Yas and Bri followed the pair to the bottom of the hill, where hundreds of Erindellians had gathered. Whispers and murmurs rippled through the crowd at the sight of their king in his beast form.

Adina raised a brow in Tarrick's direction. He emitted a low growl, at which the princess nodded.

"People of Erindell, Terralea, and welcome guests," she said loudly, confidently, to the gathered masses.

Elena spotted Jet and Mika standing beside Amaya, and the rest of the palace guests, who were assembled near the front. Sadness clawed at her once more at the thought of telling Jet about his beloved, and Amaya about her son. Already, he wore a look of anguish as he searched for Leon. Amaya lifted a hand to her mouth, and her eyes glistened with tears.

Elena tuned out Adina's speech, assuring everyone the realm was safe. She held herself together by focusing on the hum of insects instead. Torches dotted around the streets of Erindell flickered to life, illuminating the sea of faces turned in her direction. The smell of wild mint from the bushes on the hill wafted down in the cool breeze that lifted the fine hairs off her face. Tarrick's soft head nudged her hand, drawing her attention back to what Adina was saying.

"...not only did she see through his charade, she went out of her way to expose him. Unfortunately, Henry got his hands on a powerful ancient weapon, which is what caused the disturbance this afternoon. My brother"—Adina's voice cracked a little, and she paused to swallow—"Prince Leon and Elena managed to overthrow this impostor."

Hundreds of faces swiveled in her direction. The familiar faces of her new friends shone with awe and admiration.

"Elena saved us all again," Adina continued. "Prince Leon sacrificed his life to save Elena while she fought the man who tried to wield the Scepter of Ilona. She risked her life to stop him from destroying our realm. I know many of you have had your doubts about Elena's intentions"—Adina scanned the sea of faces, pausing briefly on the councilors, who shifted uncomfortably—"and we have done little to address your concerns. Despite her short time in our realm, Elena is as brave, kind, compassionate, and selfless as any ruler I have known. She has put Terraleans before all else to bring our enemies to justice and expose their nefarious plans to destroy all that we hold dear."

Elena's cheeks heated as there were more whispers. She caught sight of Amaya and Rhea smiling at her through their tears. Darius and Killian beamed while Zahra gave her a half-smile, still distraught over Leon's untimely death.

"The Divine Beings have ordained Elena queen of Leneira," Adina announced proudly.

The crowd gasped as one. Elena couldn't help sneaking a glance at Sofia and Malik with a small smirk, gratified that they were suitably awestruck. Rhea and Darius clapped their hands in glee while Aiden's wire-framed glasses slipped off his nose.

"Her song is engraved in the Temple of Divine Beings for all in our realm to read." Adina waved a hand toward the Temple. "The Divine Beings have marked her twice and recognized the spirit of Queen Samara in her. She is worthy of the crown of Terralea and Leneira."

Elena's heart almost exploded as Adina looked at her with pride and love.

"You now bear the mark of our country's *lyrabird* and the legendary *naya*," Adina announced, her voice shaking with emotion. "You are part of the realm and its people. From this day, I bow before you and recognize you as my queen to serve and protect." She bowed low, giving Elena a wink and mischievous grin when the crowd gasped at the latter part.

Adina spoke the words of the oath of undying allegiance for the people of Erindell to repeat as they, too, bowed before Elena. She thought she would faint from the enormity of the moment, and was too overwhelmed to say anything. The crowd stared at her expectantly when they finished their pledge.

"You'll forgive me if I don't get down on my knees, Your Majesty," a voice cackled from the back of the crowd.

Elena could have burst out laughing the moment Ninaz made her way to the front. The old woman used her walking stick to gently shove people aside. Elena caught sight of Zahra shaking her head in embarrassment. Ninaz's wide smile revealed white teeth against her tawny, wrinkled skin.

"You have done a fine job, Elena," she declared. There were a few nudges and murmurs at the familiar way in which Ninaz addressed Elena. "I think now would be a good time to ask your subjects to rise, since the formalities are done."

Tarrick emitted a rumble that Elena interpreted as laughter.

"Please, everyone, rise," she said hastily, using her hands for emphasis.

When the shuffling and groans from older Erindellians subsided, Elena hesitated and spoke carefully. "Thank you for welcoming me to Terralea and giving me the chance to prove myself to you. I vow to always put your needs first, do what's best for the realm, and trust that your loyalty to this land and commitment to peace will ensure that we remain united."

There were murmurs of assent, and the atmosphere lightened considerably.

"Not the most eloquent of speeches, but it will do." Ninaz sniffed. "I think its effect was also somewhat diminished by your wardrobe." She looked in derision at Elena's bloody jeans, ripped at the knees, and the T-shirt hanging limply off her shoulder, also stained with ash and blood.

Elena scowled at her before addressing the crowd. "Please, go home to your family and friends knowing you are protected."

The crowd started to disperse. Zahra ushered Amaya and the others back up the path to the palace. Royal Guards moved amongst the crowd of Erindellians, helping them navigate through the rock and debris from the earlier earthquakes. Those who were able to started clearing the paths with their Elemental powers and restoring the cobbles to their original state.

"At least this time, the recovery will be quicker." Elena sighed. She turned to Yas, Bri, and Ninaz, who remained standing at the bottom of the hill. "It would appear we have more seats to fill on our councils now," she said sadly, thinking of Leon.

Tarrick purred and rubbed his head against Elena's leg in comfort.

"Prince Leon was a fine royal advisor," Ninaz murmured, uncharacteristically forlorn. "My children always spoke highly of him and, on the odd occasion I met him, he always made me laugh with a wisecrack or highly inappropriate comment. And not just to me."

"He was forthright, honest, and not afraid to challenge anyone," Elena said quietly.

Tarrick huffed in agreement.

"Those are rare qualities, and I can think of only one other person who has those abilities in order to fill the role." Elena gave Ninaz a small smile.

The older woman raised a brow.

"Ninaz, I would like to formally invite you to join the Royal Council of Terralea and the Council of Nobles as the royal advisor."

Gasps echoed around them. Tarrick looked up, perplexed.

Ninaz eyed Elena shrewdly. "Are you sure that's what you want, child?"

"It is." Elena held her gaze. "Let's face it, we are a young, inexperienced couple, and need someone who is not afraid to call us out when we have to make difficult decisions. Lady Amaya has already given so much and promised to stay on, but she deserves to spend time with her own family and do the things she loves. I also trust you."

There was silence as Ninaz assessed Elena.

"I shall require a suite at the palace," Ninaz finally said. "I'm not traipsing through the Royal Quarter every day."

"You shall have the very best," Elena promised.

"And I'll need to use the bathhouse once a week for my joints." Ninaz waved her stick in front of her knees.

"Consider it done."

There was a pause.

"Tell Zahra and that Minotian prince to help me pack my things tomorrow," Ninaz ordered. "I shall have to interrogate him about his intentions toward our princess."

Tarrick opened his mouth to growl in protest, but Ninaz lifted her stick and pointed the end at his nose, silencing him. His whiskers twitched in annoyance.

"Consider it my first act as your advisor, Your Majesty," she said sternly. "The princess deserves only the best, and I do not intend for her to settle for anything less."

Tarrick closed his mouth and lowered his head, suitably humbled. Satisfied, Ninaz spun on her heel and hobbled off with a wave in their direction.

"I hope you know what you're doing, El—er, Your Majesty," Yas said, watching Ninaz walk away apprehensively. "She won't hold back."

"I'm counting on it." Elena laughed. "She's the only person who won't be afraid to tell it like it is. Leon got away with it because he was Tarrick's brother and part of the family," she said sadly.

"He also loved this country and its people," Bri said softly. "He wanted what was best for all of us."

Elena agreed. "That too."

Tarrick licked her hand, assuring her that she had done the right thing.

"I'm not quite done." She grinned and turned back to the two women, who were still waiting for their queen to dismiss them. "There are still a few spots left vacant by nobles that resigned. Would either or both of you like to be on the council?"

Bri and Yas's eyes bulged.

"Us?" Yas squeaked.

"We're not nobles." Bri shook her head in disbelief. "And we don't know anything about politics."

"Neither do I." Elena shrugged. "But the others on the council do, and they can teach us. Darius has helped me a lot. And I'm still learning about Terralea and Leneira, so you two are probably more qualified than I am. I'm also thinking of calling it the Council. That way, we can fill the empty seats with ordinary Terraleans. No titles required." Elena grinned.

Yas and Bri stared at her at a loss for words. Tarrick purred in approval.

"The people here trust you both," Elena said earnestly. "You're also enterprising women who have survived uprisings, discrimination, and have succeeded in your businesses."

Yas blushed, and a tear rolled down Bri's cheek at the compliments.

"I'll do it," Bri finally said. "Thank you, Your Majesties."

"I'll join too," Yas said, her voice catching slightly, "if I can still run my coffee shop?"

"Of course." Elena pulled the two women to her in a big group hug. "Thank you. Thank you so much."

EPILOGUE

Six months later

Elena threw down her stylus and rubbed her eyes in relief. She was finally ahead with her reports for the next council meeting to be held after her coronation. In a few short hours, guests would start to descend upon the palace and require her attention. She had spent the morning working alone in her office, enjoying the peace and solitude that was rare for her lately.

It was strange thinking about the fact that in twenty-four hours, she would be officially crowned as queen of Terralea and Leneira. Her stomach lurched when she thought about it. To steady her nerves, she raised her gaze to the portrait that hung on the wall behind her. The three smiling faces brought her unspeakable joy.

The artist in Erindell had done an exceptional job bringing Elena's vision to life—Arran and Leon's faces had been easy enough since the artist had painted them before. Tarrick had accompanied her to the meeting where she described in detail their son's round cheeks and dark hair that ended in little flicks that suggested he inherited Elena's waves. Amber eyes, soft, dark brows shaped like Elena's, but she knew in her heart that, had the boy grown up in Leneira, he would have been the spitting image of his father.

Tarrick had sat in silence the entire time Elena waved her hands, pointing to parts of her own face and his to emphasize the shapes and colors she described. The artist patiently wrote down notes and sketched out a rough image as Elena described everything in vivid detail. Tarrick remained in his seat when the artist invited Elena to sit beside her and review the sketch. They had spent almost two hours finessing it, but it had been worth it.

Amaya and Adina were invited to the unveiling of the final portrait, and both women burst into tears. It was the vision Maia had shown Elena of Arran, Leon, and the baby boy who was unquestionably Elena and Tarrick's son, together in the garden paradise.

Amaya reached out a hand and traced the lines of Arran and Leon's faces in the air. Adina cooed over the smiling baby boy on Arran's lap. She remarked that the expression on Leon's face reminded her of the time he had brought back a whoopee cushion from the human realm and placed it on Tarrick's chair at the dinner table.

Elena bent over, laughing at the thought of Tarrick falling for the prank while Amaya smiled through her tears at the memory. Tarrick scowled at first, but his lips twitched when he, too, remembered his family laughing at the time.

"It had been a long time since Arran laughed so hard," Amaya said in a choked voice.

Tarrick didn't speak or react as he studied the portrait intently with an unreadable expression on his face. He remained staring at it long after the others left for an impromptu tea party that Amaya hosted for all of the palace residents.

***

The following day, Tarrick had arranged for a desk and chair to be placed in Elena's office next to hers. Elena remembered the moment fondly as she was working in her office.

"I hope it's alright?" he asked when Elena walked in and stopped short at the sight of him. "I won't take meetings here."

"Of course," she said, taking her own seat and starting on the pile of paperwork in front of her. She caught Tarrick smiling to himself as he glanced at the painting every so often. They worked in comfortable silence for most of the morning. Elena interrupted him a few times to ask

questions about some requests that had come through or about prominent Terraleans she hadn't met yet.

"I can ask the artist to paint a second portrait for you, if you want?" Elena offered when they paused for a break.

"No," Tarrick replied without hesitation. "There will only be one portrait of them."

"Good." The corners of her lips tugged up. "I kind of like the company."

Tarrick's face broke into a wide smile. His eyes softened and his shoulders relaxed. "I like working with you too. It feels like we're a team again."

A knock at the door shook Elena out of her daydreaming and back to the present. Adina entered and threw herself into the seat in front of Elena's desk. She leaned back with a sigh and stretched out her legs.

"I'm exhausted," she announced. "It's barely lunchtime, and I feel like I've done two days' work this morning."

"Is everything alright?" Elena asked with concern.

"It's fine." Adina waved a hand. "I'm just being dramatic."

Elena grinned. "When are you not?"

Adina made a face in response. Her gaze traveled up to the portrait as it always did when she came to Elena's office. She rubbed a hand unconsciously over her stomach, and Elena noted the gesture with a grin.

She cleared her throat. "How's everything tracking for tomorrow?"

"All under control," Adina said absent-mindedly, still staring at the painting. "Lin and Halder will arrive this evening. Guards have been rostered around the palace and Erindell. Tarrick is in town with Darius and Killian, checking security."

"Good." Elena nodded, satisfied.

They weren't expecting anything to go wrong, but Adina wanted to stay vigilant. She didn't take anything for granted.

"I'm pulling you off event planning. You're no longer in charge of feasts or balls," Elena said abruptly.

Adina sat up, alarmed. "What? Why?"

"Marcel took me through the menu you approved for tomorrow night." Elena placed her elbows on the desk and rested her chin on her hands. She wore an amused expression as she said, "He had some concerns about the dishes you requested."

Confusion lined Adina's face.

"Pickled fish in apricot sauce, Adina? Really?" Elena raised a brow.

Adina wrinkled her nose and muttered, "It sounded good at the time."

"And you said the wines Tarrick and I chose taste like vinegar," Elena continued, shifting her attention to the hand Adina rested on her stomach. "Something you'd like to tell me?"

The princess's eyes widened. "You know?" she asked in a hushed voice.

Elena's wide grin confirmed that she knew Adina's secret.

"Does Killian?" Elena asked, trying to stifle a laugh.

Adina shook her head with a guilty expression. "The royal physician only confirmed it today. I've been sick every morning this week."

"Congratulations," Elena said. Her cheeks hurt from smiling so hard at the image of Adina and Killian's baby. She felt no sadness or resentment toward the princess, who was back to being like a sister once more. Elena pictured them having a girl, but she would love their child as though it were her own no matter what.

"Thank you," Adina said shyly. "It's still early, but I wanted you to be the first to know anyway."

"I won't tell anyone," Elena promised. "It's your news to share."

"You're going to be the best aunt," Adina said.

"Seems only fair since Leon is the best uncle to my boy." Elena smiled.

Adina burst into tears. "I'm sorry." She hiccuped. "I don't know what's happened to me! I've been crying over the smallest things."

"Uh, I believe it's all part of being pregnant," Elena said, whipping out a linen handkerchief from the pocket of her dress and handing it to the sobbing princess.

Adina sputtered out a laugh, blowing her nose loudly and shaking her head. "I thought it was stress." When she pulled herself together, she said, "You know, just because you can't have children doesn't mean you can't be a mother."

Elena gave her a half-smile. "I know. Tarrick and I discussed it, and we've decided that when we're ready, we'll look into adopting."

"That sounds ... perfect," Adina said, tears welling in her eyes again. "And in the meantime, the children at the community center have been asking for you. They miss your stories."

A lump formed in Elena's throat. She wished she had another handkerchief on her.

"I'll visit them after the coronation," she promised. "And schedule story time once a week. Maybe we could host it here in the palace library?"

"Celine would be happy to do that," Adina said eagerly.

"And speaking of children"—Elena cleared her throat—"Before he died, Leon was researching succession laws in Terralea and Leneira."

Adina's brows shot to her hairline.

The corners of Elena's lips curved up. "As it so happens, rulers can name a successor, and the councils vote in favor of or against the nominee."

Adina's lips parted in surprise.

"It's how dynasties have changed. It just so happens your family has ruled Terralea for so long that everyone took it for granted that the oldest child would inherit the crown," Elena explained.

"You mean ...?"

"I was going to ask you if you would be interested in the job should anything happen to Tarrick and me." Elena's smile grew at the sight of Adina raising her hand to cover her mouth. "But perhaps there's another contender to consider in time, if we decide we don't want children. Or if none of our children are interested in the position?" Elena glanced down at the princess's stomach again. "I wouldn't burden anyone with a job they don't want."

Adina's gaze dropped to her stomach.

"El!" she whispered as her eyes welled up with tears again.

"Oh, shit," Elena muttered.

"What have we done to deserve you?" Adina burst into fresh tears.

The door opened, and Tarrick entered. He looked disappointed at the sight of Adina sitting in the room, but rushed forward at the sound of her loud sobs.

"What happened?" He looked frantically between Elena and his sister.

Adina smiled at him with tears still streaming down her face. "Nothing." She sniffled. "El is amazing, you know that?"

Elena desperately wanted to laugh at the confusion on Tarrick's face.

"I'll let you guys talk." Adina hiccoughed, rising from her seat.

Tarrick waited until she left before he spoke. "Should we be concerned?"

"Not at all," she declared. "I think she and Killian need a holiday."

"Good idea." Tarrick's face cleared. "He said she had been feeling a little off lately. Maybe a break will do them some good."

Elena shook her head at how obtuse men were. She felt slightly guilty about not telling Tarrick that his baby sister was pregnant. After all, they had vowed to be open and honest with each other. She told herself the news wasn't hers to share.

"How are you feeling about tomorrow?" he asked softly.

"Nervous," Elena admitted. She rose from her seat and walked around the desk to Tarrick. He opened his arms, and she wrapped her own around his waist. She buried her face in his tunic, inhaling his cedar-sandalwood scent to calm her nerves.

"You have nothing to be nervous about." His voice was filled with warmth and love as he enveloped her and hugged her back tightly. "You were a queen long before you even set foot in our realm."

Elena scoffed. She pressed her ear to the steady beat of Tarrick's heart and reflected on how much her life had changed in a year.

The sky was blue, and a warm breeze blew in the air. The trees were starting to sprout small buds and leaves—the sign that spring was just around the corner. She and Tarrick spent as much time outdoors as possible, walking to and from Erindell to meet with their people, dining at restaurants and cafés, and visiting Mari's rooftop gardens. They had become so popular that she'd been commissioned to landscape the rooftops of nearly all of the taller buildings in Erindell.

Helene's beekeeping business was also thriving with hives set up all over Erindell. Rhea helped her harvest the honey and sell it to the locals. Bri was their biggest customer, creating special teas and infusions that complemented the rich, sweet nectar.

They continued to attend the monthly Full Moon Festivals and enjoyed anonymity on the nights where they blended in with the locals, dancing to the heady music. Adina, Killian, Zahra, Rhea, and Darius were also in regular attendance, preferring to smoke water pipes and drink *araki*.

Aside from the odd disagreement or argument over minor issues, everything was going smoothly. Leneira and Terralea's history was splattered with war and battles, but Elena and Tarrick had promised each other that no matter what came their way, they would face it together. They stood by each other's side and ended each day in their bedroom—or, more often than not, in the *lamora*—as Tarrick and Elena, not king and queen.

"I'm serious," Tarrick continued. "Queen is just a title. You have been kind and compassionate to everyone since the day you arrived. You've handled everything we threw at you with so much grace. You stood your ground and showed your commitment to your people. That is what it means to be queen."

Tarrick's amber eyes were filled with love, respect, and awe for her.

"I've had my moments," she mumbled, recalling the few instances where her temper got the better of her.

Tarrick chuckled. "We all have our moments. It goes to show that even Leneirans have a human side to them."

"I suppose I can keep doing what I'm doing." Elena sighed.

"You'll do more," Tarrick said firmly. "You've already started to unite our people in the regions along the borders. I have every faith that you'll continue to strengthen our ties with Skandor, Sailon, and the Isles of Minos. Just as Queen Samara ruled the realm with kindness and compassion, you will do the same."

"With you by my side," Elena whispered.

Tarrick tightened his arms around her. "Always, Your Majesty."

ACKNOWLEDGMENTS

Thank you—yes, *you*, reading this right now! I've said it before and I'll say it again, without readers, this job wouldn't exist. Your support is everything and thank you for sticking with Tarrick and Elena on their rollercoaster journey until their HEA.

To mum, dad and p for being so supportive and always there for me through the real-life plot twists, and encouraging me to keep pursuing my passions. I love you all so much, and let's keep pretending the spice doesn't exist, okay?

Leneira and its colorful characters wouldn't have come to life without Bree and Bec who read the first draft and encouraged me to keep going. Thank you for the tough love, and late night chats to strengthen Leneira's economy, politics, society, and the plot!

To Lauren M, my ultimate cheerleader and brainstorming powerhouse. I'm so glad I have you to help fix all those holes that creep into my stories. Our catch ups are everything and you are an amazing, talented person and incredible businesswoman who's proven that anything is possible.

Thank you once again to my incredible beta readers and writing buddies—Bri, Lauren G, Chelci, Steph, and Alysha. Your feedback, brutal honesty, thoughtful comments and pep talks strengthened this story beyond anything I could have imagined. All the 'boos' and reactions gave me the confidence to keep going (sorry, not sorry for the trauma?). It's incredible to think we read each others' early scribbles just over a year ago and now we've all written books and call ourselves authors.

Of course, none of this would be possible without Lauren B—I still cannot believe you spent New Years reading an early draft of *The Naya's Crossing* so that I could publish both books this year! What did I do to deserve you? You are an incredible human and I love you so much!

Big, big thank you to Britt, the most incredible editor. Your feedback and attention to detail gave me life, and sorry (but not really) that you had to go through the emotions several times.

Finally, thank you to the amazing author friends who've inspired me to keep going—Hannah Brixton, Genesis Bird, Cherry Keeley, thank you so much for sharing your own words and welcoming me so warmly to the publishing world. Shout out to Hannah and Cherry's street teams where chaos, unhinged madness and daily reminders to charge the vibes reign supreme. You are all truly wonderful humans and my people!

ABOUT THE AUTHOR

Prerna's love for storytelling began after discovering the enchanting worlds of Enid Blyton's *The Magical Adventures of the Faraway Tree.* This early inspiration sparked a lifelong passion for writing. An avid traveler, Prerna finds inspiration in the destinations she explores, weaving the sights, sounds, and cultures of these locations into her stories. When not writing, Prerna can be found experimenting in the kitchen or curled up with a good book. She loves discovering new flavors and getting swept up in different worlds, whether it's through food, travel, or stories. Writing allows her to share a bit of that magic with others.